Kicking The Goat Silly

A novel by Victoria S. Hardy

Written in April of 2009

This is a work of fiction. Names, characters, businesses, places, events and incidents are either the products of the author's imagination or used in a fictitious manner. Any resemblance to actual persons, living or dead, or actual events is purely coincidental.

No animals, fictional or otherwise, were hurt in the writing of this novel.

Behold, I send you forth as sheep in the midst of wolves: be ye therefore wise as serpents, and harmless as doves.

Matthew 10:16

Chapter One

Abbey raked the straw into the dirt yard and kicked the goat as he reared up on his hind legs. He was preparing to butt her with that hard head, yet again. The goat snorted, shook his head, and wandered off into the field to harass one of the does. Abbey sighed, and rested her chin on the end of the rake as she watched the animal stalk cockily through the field. Her daughter, Kelly, had named the goat Silly, but Abbey found absolutely nothing amusing about him, and as a matter of fact, she hated him. Pulling her eyes away from the beast, she finished raking the yard, and scattered fresh straw in the barn.

The barn was actually a chicken house. It was built after her husband, Richard, brought home thirty chickens without a place to house them. Most were dead in the first few hours, as Richard had simply let them loose in the yard making them easy prey for the dogs. She had chased down several chickens in the woods that night as a tornado in the next county sparked the sky with lightning and bent the young pines, while the old hardwoods moaned and creaked over her head. As she chased the frightened birds, the swirling chaos overhead reminded her of every horror movie she had ever seen; and it suddenly dawned on her that she was living in a nightmare.

Over the next few days she managed to find twelve of the thirty chickens, which she deposited in the master bathroom, laying a thick layer of newspaper on the floor and scattering feed in the bathtub. Richard complained that it was verging on mental illness to keep chickens in the house, but Abbey insisted that until they had a safe place to live outdoors they'd stay in the bathroom. The following weekend, Richard built the small structure and she moved the chickens into their new home.

Abbey hadn't minded so much when Richard brought home the ducks, and Kelly had certainly loved them. She remembered her daughter's giggles with a smile as she pitched dirty straw into the wheelbarrow. She had to admit the ducks were cute; their soft fuzz and tiny webbed feet even made her giggle a bit. She jabbed the pitchfork into the pile of straw and lifted the handles of the wheelbarrow, looking over her shoulder to locate Silly. The goat stood about fifteen feet away from the gate and watched her intently with strange, yellow eyes. She had only taken half a dozen steps when he began charging.

The goat's latest pastime was knocking over the wheelbarrow and Abbey had had enough of it. Her hand instinctively went to the pitch folk, but she pulled away fearing that one day she might actually use it on him. She stepped in front of the wheelbarrow and yelled, "Hey!" Silly stopped abruptly and his nose wrinkled as he exposed his teeth. She twisted her hip, ready to throw a kick if he decided to charge, and he reared up on his hind legs in the classic demonic pose.

"Come on, you little shit," Abbey muttered.

The goat landed on all fours, snorted defiantly, and then wandered off to eat some grass growing along the fence line.

Abbey opened the gate and wheeled the straw out of the enclosure, stopping briefly to ensure the latch was secure. She pushed the wheelbarrow across the dirt driveway that encircled the house and glanced over at the ducks that were vocally skimming across the small lake. She smiled. As she stepped into the yard, she scrutinized the grass and made a mental note to throw more seed to fill in the bare spots. She studied the brick foundation of the newly built ranch house, checking for signs of the bulbs that she had planted last fall. She heard a knock on the window and looked up to see Kelly sticking her tongue out.

Abbey grinned and yelled through the glass, "Is the coffee cooking?"

Kelly gave the thumbs up sign and Abbey continued wheeling the mound of straw past the vegetable garden. She pushed the load up a small hill into a five-acre pine forest, a boundary between their home and the state road that connected two small towns. Fifteen miles to the west, the highway ended in the small town of Farmdale; which contained a post office, a feed and seed, a convenience store/gas station, two competing churches, and a large cemetery. Five miles east was the town of Oak Tree, which had a real city hall, large twisted oak trees in the town square, and a grocery store; although the prices were so steep at the local grocery, Abbey elected to drive another twenty miles into Locknee when stocking up.

She dumped the pine straw, now lush with duck and goat droppings, under a tree and carried the pitchfork back toward the house. She stopped at the garden checking the status of their second attempt at corn. The first tender shoots had been eaten by Silly and she only felt nervous when she saw the cool green sprouts making their way out of the dark rich dirt. She lifted her eyes to the barnyard to see Silly standing by the fence watching her, and she pointed the pitchfork at him. "Just try it, asshat."

No, she didn't mind when Richard brought home the ducks, but she sure as hell minded when he had the herd of goats delivered. The goats weren't the small, adorable pygmy goats she'd seen grazing in her neighbor's fields. No, Richard chose to purchase large, intimidating livestock. Silly easily outweighed her by fifty pounds and he seemed to view her as just another doe to be bullied and controlled.

Of course, when Richard had the goats delivered there had been no fence to enclose them and the herd spent their time in the yard, devouring every plant that Abbey had planted right down to the nubs. After numerous arguments, Richard finally had fencing material delivered and they enclosed a two-acre plot of land. The fence was three-sided, with the fourth side left open - the hog wire disappearing into the water allowing easy access for the ducks. And although Silly never got his feet wet, he still managed to escape on a regular basis.

Abbey sat down on the steps outside the back door, and leaned the pitchfork against the porch. She pulled off her boots and gloves, leaving them to deal with later, and stepped inside the house.

"Morning." Kelly smiled, closing the dishwasher.

"Morning, yourself. How'd you sleep?" Abbey kissed her daughter's head, the blond hair still tangled from sleep.

"Good. And you?"

"Not enough," Abbey stated, pouring coffee into the mug Kelly had left in front of the coffee pot.

"Well, get your coffee. I made you an egg sandwich." Kelly extended her arm like a model on *The Price Is Right*.

"Thanks, honey." Abbey sat at the table, admiring the sandwich resting on a paper plate and took a bite. "Hmmm."

"Plenty of mayo, just like you like it."

"You did a fine job," Abbey complimented between bites.

"Mom, do you think we could start school differently today?"

"What do you have in mind?" Abbey asked, wiping mayo off her lips.

"Could we start with reading? I thought about that book all night, it's driving me crazy!" Kelly grinned.

Abbey smiled. "Sure we can."

"Yea!" Kelly clapped her hands and hopped up and down several times.

"It's nice out this morning. Why don't you get on some shoes and we'll start class outside." Abbey rose from the table, threw away the paper plate, and poured herself another cup of coffee. Her eyes fell on the list of chores to be completed, a list created by and decided on by Richard. Today's list included cleaning the bathrooms, mopping the floors, and fixing the leak in the roof of the barn, as well as, various other entries. The lists were a common motivator for their arguments as Abbey insisted, "I'm not a child, and I don't need you to tell me what needs to be done."

"Well, it rarely gets done," Richard would state.

"I also have to teach for five hours a day, that takes time and effort." Not to mention she had to prepare to teach. She couldn't teach what she herself didn't understand.

Richard would shrug, reminding her, yet again, that the decision to home school had been hers and hers alone.

"I'm ready." Kelly stood by the back door waving the book impatiently.

Abbey slid her feet into a pair of slippers and followed her daughter into the sunshine, a cup of coffee in one hand, and a slingshot in the other. They settled into lounge chairs and Kelly opened the book, beginning to read aloud. Abbey listened to the words flowing freely and uttered a silent prayer of thanks that Kelly was healing and growing stronger everyday. Abbey glanced over at the long scars on Kelly's right arm and leg, still red, but not nearly as angry looking as they had been a year ago. The scars on her head were now covered with shoulder length blond hair, although the ridges of scar tissue could still be felt underneath. Kelly stumbled over several words, took a deep, calming breath, and began reading again.

Abbey thought back to the day of the accident and couldn't believe it happened almost two years ago. In some ways, it seemed like a lifetime ago while in others - just yesterday. Abbey had taken the afternoon off from work intending to surprise Kelly with a shopping trip to celebrate her last day of eighth grade. She heard the bus pull up in front of the house, and she stepped to the door in time to see Kelly crossing the street. Suddenly, a sports car came roaring out of nowhere, slamming into Kelly, and sending her spiraling into the air like a little rag doll. A strange calm descended over Abbey as she ran to the phone dialing 911 and pulled a blanket from the linen closet.

The bus driver was just jumping from the bus as Abbey raced by and fell to her knees beside her daughter, who lay in a tangled heap on the concrete. Abbey covered her with the blanket, repeating over and over, "You're going to be okay, baby." At the same time she described what she had seen in detail to the operator. The driver of the car who had hit Kelly was discovered several hours later, dead. The vehicle was wrapped around a tree - a tangled mass of metal - and an investigation showed a high level of alcohol in the teenager's system.

The next few weeks were a blur of hospitals, surgeries, and sheer terror as the doctors threw around terms such as brain injury, amputation, and internal injuries. Kelly somehow survived with her limbs intact and lacking only her spleen. Abbey firmly believed it was a miracle then, and once again now, lying in the warm sunshine listening to her daughter read aloud.

"Mom, Silly's getting out." Kelly sighed, and rested the open book in her lap.

Abbey put her coffee cup on the ground and picked up a small pebble. Leaning forward, she aimed the slingshot carefully, and shot the goat in the butt. He snorted furiously and propelled himself the rest of the way over the fence. "Damn it! I'll get him. Why don't you keep reading?"

"Awww. You'll miss it."

"I'll catch up later, I still have to pull some vocabulary words out of the text."

"Okay." Kelly picked up the book and continued reading aloud.

Abbey stood and went of in pursuit of Silly. He didn't protest being put back in the pen, and in fact it appeared that he enjoyed this daily game. He walked behind her, his head pushing firmly against her rear, as though he was in charge. She opened the gate and pushed the goat through the opening. "Get on in there, brat." He offered no resistance and contentedly trotted off to where the female goats were gathered, scattering them in his usual manner.

*

Silly pushed her, as he always did. He kept trying desperately to steer her away from the predator; he didn't understand why she couldn't smell the scent. She was very stubborn, not like the other does. Of course, she was a human, and not at all like the does. Her kid, the other one, was also stubborn.

The predator was real, but neither the woman nor the kid seemed to be aware of him. Silly kept trying to push her to safety, but she continued to slip away from him. He had tried to steer the other one, too; but the woman grew very angry when he touched the kid, very angry.

*

"Great! Now I smell like goat," Abbey muttered, and

headed back to Kelly.

"The slingshot doesn't seem to be working, Mom." Kelly dropped the closed book in her lap.

"I know. I've been trying to get him to equate the fence with a sting in the butt, but you're right, he just seems to like playing the game. Did you finish the chapter?"

"Yes, ma'am. Can we read one more after we're done with school?"

"If we get everything done in time, yes. Let's throw the ball for a few minutes." Lightly tossing a ball back and forth was part of Kelly's physical therapy and Abbey believed it had worked for both Kelly's mind and body. Kelly alternated tossing the ball first left-handed - then right-handed, over and under, and Abbey had seen great improvement in her dexterity. Abbey smiled as she caught a firm straight throw, Kelly had indeed come a long way.

"What do you want to start with today, History or Science?" Abbey asked, stepping back into the house.

"Science!" Kelly called out, running to her bedroom to gather her books.

"Science, it is," Abbey said, pulling her supplies from the

kitchen counter and settling at the table. For the next hour, they lost themselves in cell division and chromosomes. "Okay, close your book." Abbey carefully removed a worksheet from a perforated book and slid the paper across the table. "While you finish that, I'll take care of the bathrooms."

As Kelly began choosing from the multi-choice answers, Abbey opened the cabinet to retrieve the cleaning supplies from the underneath the sink. She reached for the small bucket containing everything she would need for the bathrooms, but it wasn't there. Instead, she found an odd assortment of empty glass jars and laundry detergent. She sighed.

She grabbed the detergent, bleach, stain-remover, and dryer sheets, carrying them to the laundry room beside the back door. Opening the cabinet above the washing machine, she discovered cookie sheets and bread pans where she usually kept the laundry supplies. She sighed again, resting her head against the open cabinet door for a moment.

She placed the armload of items on top of the washer and pulled the cookware down from the shelf, stacking the pieces on the dryer. She returned the laundry supplies to their rightful place and grabbing the stack of baking pans, she stepped back into the kitchen. She set the pans on the stove and opened the cupboard beside the oven only to discover that it was now filled with cans of dog food.

"What in the hell?" she muttered under her breath, pulling out the cans and replacing the cookware. Squatting on the floor beside the stacked cans, she asked, "Kelly, do you know where the bucket is that I keep the bathroom stuff in?"

Kelly lifted her head from the assignment she was working on. "I think I saw the bucket in the pantry."

"Thanks." Abbey picked up the cans to return to the pantry. She found the blue bucket on the floor beside a 50 lb. bag of dry dog food, but instead of the cleaning supplies, it contained three cans of corn. Abbey picked up the bucket, replaced the dog food and returned the cans of corn to the shelf. She stepped back from the pantry with the empty blue bucket in her hands and felt a growing frustration.

"I'm done." Kelly held out the finished worksheet. Abbey set the bucket on the counter, took the paper from her daughter, and graded the small quiz. "Excellent, a hundred percent."

"Yea, me!" Kelly laughed.

"Honey, why don't you go check the mail while I try to find the bathroom stuff."

"Okay," Kelly said, opening the back door and Abbey began opening and shutting cabinets looking for her supplies. "Mom! Silly's in the garden!"

Abbey jumped up and rushed past Kelly on the porch. "Hey!" she yelled. Silly raised his head, saw her coming, and bent down to eat the small stalk of corn just showing its head above the soil. Abbey furiously kicked him again, but the thin slippers she wore did not faze the goat, and only sent a sharp pain shooting up her leg. "Stupid, stupid, spawn of Satan!" She pushed the goat by his shoulders, watching his hooves crush a tomato plant. "Shit!" She shoved him until they were back on the grass and looked up to see a smile on Kelly's face.

"Go check the mail," Abbey snapped, trying to reign in her frustration.

Kelly held up her hands in mock self-defense. "I'm going."

Again, Silly kept his head pressed against her hip as she dragged him along. She opened the gate and used her foot on his rump to push him inside. He offered no resistance. She shut the gate firmly and taking a deep breath, she went back into the house. She finished looking under the cabinets, noting many items either out of place or rearranged.

She grabbed the phone and dialed, stepping to the picture window in the living room to watch Kelly disappear into the pine trees lining the driveway, and observed that the slight limp was barely noticeable.

"Drs Almond and Brown's office. How may I help you?" the receptionist answered.

"Hey, Candi, this is Abbey. Is Richard available?"

"I think so, hold on."

"Dr. Brown." Richard picked up the phone.

"Richard, where are my cleaning supplies for the bathrooms?" she bit out, trying to withhold her frustration.

"In the bathroom, where they are supposed to be." He sighed.

"No, Richard, I keep them under the sink in the kitchen. That's where they are supposed to be."

"I don't have time for this, Abbey, I have a patient waiting."

"Well, we wouldn't have to do this if you'd leave my stuff

where I put it. I don't come to your office and rearrange your things."

"I have to go." He hung up the phone.

Abbey wanted to scream and throw the phone across the room, but she took a deep breath, then another, and dropped the phone none too gently on its cradle.

Kelly returned to the house and placed the mail on the counter.

"Kelly, where have we always kept the cleaning supplies?" Abbey asked, silently counting to ten.

"Under the kitchen sink." Kelly sat at the table and pulled her History book out from the stack.

"Well, thanks for that, at least I don't feel like I'm crazy. There's nothing quite as frustrating as looking for something and finding it has been moved."

"I don't know why Richard does that. Remember last month when he moved the tampons out of the bathroom and put them on the top shelf of the linen closet? I had to get a stepstool just to reach them. Or the time he put all of my prescriptions in one bottle and threw away the directions on the labels?"

Abbey grimaced, remembering how she felt like an idiot returning to the pharmacy just hours after she had picked up the medications to ask the pharmacist to separate and re-label the pills. When she asked Richard why he had done so, he explained that it was "neater" to place all the pills in one bottle. Abbey sighed - the pharmacist had looked at her like she was crazy. She pushed the memory away, pulled the teacher's manual off the shelf, and sat down to study World War I with her daughter.

As a high-school dropout home schooling Kelly had been more challenging than Abbey had ever imagined, but she loved it. The brain injury was mild and although the doctors cleared Kelly to go back into public school, Abbey knew she would struggle. She decided that Kelly needed time to recover; so despite Richard's objections she joined a home school association and became a teacher.

They finished the day's History assignment and Abbey gave Kelly the worksheet to complete, then grabbed the bucket and went into Kelly's bathroom. She opened the cabinet under the sink and spied the bottle of glass cleaner in the back, nearly hidden behind the towels. She knelt, pulled the spray bottle free, and then felt around checking for any more hidden supplies. Finding nothing, she put the cleaner in the bucket and got to her feet.

She carried the bucket into the master bathroom and opened the cabinet under the sink only to find a folded pile of her jeans and t-shirts. She pulled the stack free, carried them to the dresser, and put them away.

"Mom, I've finished the worksheet and I left it on the table. I'm going to take a shower," Kelly announced from the doorway.

"Okay, honey," Abbey said absently, sliding a drawer closed. Why would Richard put her clothes under the sink?

"Did you find the bathroom stuff yet?" Kelly asked.

"Not yet." Abbey sighed, and went back into the bathroom. She peered under the sink again and saw the bottle of disinfectant she used for the toilet. She pulled it out and placed it in the bucket. A sudden movement through the window caught her attention and she looked up just in time to see Silly land on the ground and wander off toward the vegetable garden. She dashed through the house, slamming the backdoor, and caught him as he nibbled on a rose bush. He ground his head against her butt as she dragged him back to the pen, his musky and unpleasant scent now deeply ingrained in the denim of her jeans.

Abbey returned to the bathroom, again checking under the sink, and found a can of powdered cleanser. She placed it in the bucket and began searching for the toilet brush with a deep, frustrated sigh. "I could have cleaned the bathrooms three times over in the time it has taken to find the damned cleaning supplies!"

Still unable to locate the toilet brush, she carried the bucket back to Kelly's bathroom. Kelly was wrapped in a towel in the steamy bathroom and combing out her wet hair. "Have you seen the toilet brush?"

"I think I saw it in the laundry room, with the mop and broom." Kelly wrinkled her nose. "Mom, you stink."

"I know. Damned goat!"

Kelly laughed and clicked on the hair dryer.

Finally, Abbey found the toilet brush hidden behind the broom in the laundry room. She put the brush in the bucket and stepped back into the kitchen, opening the drawer where she kept sponges and dishtowels. To her frustration, they were gone – replaced by an assortment of tools.

She felt like crying. She slammed the drawer shut and sat

down at the kitchen table, resting her head in goat-scented hands. She heard the hair dryer click off in the distance.

"Mom, are you okay?"

Abbey lifted her head to see Kelly standing in the living room, concern on her face. Abbey stiffened her spine. "I'm fine." She stood up. "Let me wash up and get lunch on the table. Finish getting ready, your ride will be here soon."

"Okay." Kelly turned and headed down the hall to her room.

Abbey washed her hands, arms, and face in cool water and stepped into the laundry room, pulling on a clean t-shirt and a fresh pair of jeans. She threw her clothes, rich with the scent of goat musk, in the washer and returned to the kitchen, pulling leftovers from the refrigerator.

As she worked, she puzzled over the reason why Richard constantly moved her things. He never used the cleaning supplies to clean anything, yet every other week she'd spend most of her day trying to find the things he'd "organized". If she didn't know better, she'd swear he was trying to drive her crazy.

Do you really know better? The unwelcome voice asked and Abbey shook her head violently to push the thought away.

She put lunch on the table as Kelly entered the room wearing a denim skirt, a pink summer top, and a light layer of mascara, which brought out the color of her eyes. "You look pretty today," Abbey commented as Kelly sat at the table.

"Thanks, Mom. I'm sorry you're having a rough day."

"It's bound to happen sometimes." Abbey glanced at the clock. "We should have enough time to get another chapter in before your ride gets here."

"Yea!" Kelly smiled, digging into her food.

They left the dishes on the table and Kelly picked up the book, reading aloud. As she read, Abbey jotted a few words down to be used for spelling and vocabulary. The barking dogs announced that her ride had arrived just as Kelly finished the chapter. "Miss Fay is here!" Kelly jumped up, running to the bathroom to check her appearance in the mirror.

Abbey stepped outside as Fay pulled up to the back porch. "Afternoon, Fay, Brandon. How're y'all doing today?"

"Good," Fay said, as Brandon, her teenage son, waved from the back seat.

"Kelly will be out in a second," Abbey explained.

"The yard is really looking good, Abbey, I can't believe how much y'all have done in such a short time."

"Thanks. Now, if I could just keep that darned goat in his pen. He ate some corn stalks this morning and part of a rose bush."

Fay glanced at the goats in the fenced pen, shaking her head slowly. "I don't know why Richard got such big goats. He looked at ours, and we even offered him a good deal on a few, but he just wasn't interested."

Kelly stepped onto the porch and Brandon watched her as she walked toward the car. She climbed into the backseat beside him, smiling shyly.

"Y'all have fun," Abbey said and smiled, sensing a budding romance between the teens.

"Mom, it's math. No one has fun in math!" Kelly laughed.

"You're driving next week, right?" Fay asked.

"Yes, ma'am." Abbey nodded her head. The home school association had located a retired professor in Locknee to teach the kids math twice a week, and each parent was responsible for a week of car-pooling.

"Okay, we're off to pick up Angela. Seatbelts on?"

"Locked and loaded," Brandon declared, drawing a giggle from Kelly.

Abbey watched the car pull down the driveway, grateful that Kelly was growing stronger everyday. She walked over to the garden shed, opened the door, and stepped inside. To her dismay, she found the cache of dishtowels and sponges that were missing from the kitchen in a large soup pot on the shelf. She stared down into the pot for several moments, asking herself yet again why Richard did these things. Coming to no reasonable conclusion, she set the pot outside of the door. Reaching behind some unused planters on the top shelf and her hand fell on a pack of cigarettes. Sliding the pack and the lighter into the pocket of her jeans, she shut the door of the shed, and carried the pot into the kitchen.

She settled into a lounge chair with a glass of iced tea and lit a cigarette, inhaling deeply. Richard believed she had quit smoking and mostly, she had. She just had a smoke every now and then and today she thought she'd have two. When she thought about her wasted morning searching for the cleaning supplies, she grew so angry she wanted to scream. Unfortunately, she had learned early on that Richard viewed strong emotions suspiciously and she wondered if all psychiatrists held such contempt for feelings.

Chapter Two

Abbey realized her mistake just weeks after she married Richard. His strange quirks and odd behaviors fell to the back of her mind, though, after the car hit Kelly. Totally focused on her daughter she went into survival mode, quitting her job, and living at the hospital. Thankfully her mother was there to lend support, as Richard didn't seem to understand the seriousness of the situation. He was more concerned with the builder's progress in constructing their house, than his stepdaughter's life-threatening injuries.

She glanced into the pen, spotted Silly nosing around the chickens, and felt her anger rise. She felt trapped. Trapped by both the goat and Richard. Why would a man spend his time rearranging a kitchen he never cooked in or moving cleaning supplies he never used? Why would he put her clothes under the sink or the dishtowels and sponges in the shed? Why was he always "organizing" her? And why was his organization always so chaotic?

"Hell, I still don't know where the rest of my cleaning supplies might turn up. I haven't checked the refrigerator, yet." She imagined opening the refrigerator and finding a box of tampons and laughed - the release felt good.

Silly stopped harassing the chickens and turned to look at her. He stared at her for a moment, cocking his head as if trying to understand the sound, and ambled over to the fence. Abbey looked into piercing yellow eyes. "You and me, boy, we're about to have it out."

Silly stared for a moment longer, snorted, and then checking out his underbelly with his nose, he urinated on his face.

"Gross!" Abbey declared with disgust and snubbed out the cigarette. "You are a nasty, nasty animal!"

She threw the cigarette butt away in the trash barrel and returned the pack to the shed. She stepped into house and cleaned up the kitchen. Climbing onto the stepstool in the pantry with the armload of glass jars she'd found under the sink, she noticed something wedged behind the Christmas cookie tins. She replaced the jars, reached behind the tins, and pulled the dustpan free. "Well, I never would've looked there," she muttered, climbing down and returning the dustpan to the laundry room.

She picked up the bucket; now complete with the items she needed to clean the bathroom and glanced through the window to see Silly nibbling on a rose bush. "Shit!" she yelled, dropping the bucket and running into the yard. Silly pushed her back to the pen, his head pressing firmly into her butt. "Crap on a stick, now I smell like goat again!"

Returning to the house, she grabbed the bucket and cleaned the bathrooms. First chore done, she thought with frustration. She glanced at the list, then at the clock, and sighed. She vacuumed the bedrooms and put away the laundry stacked on the dryer. She added a load of clothes into the washing machine and checking the clock again, she decided to have another cigarette.

She stood just outside of the shed door, smoking, and gazing inside at the contents on the shelves. There, amidst the fertilizers and weed killers, she spied a can of oven cleaner and the polish for the hardwood floors. She took another drag, making sure the smoke didn't get into the shed, and continued the visual inspection. Nearly hidden behind a bag of insecticide she saw the bottle of hair conditioner that was missing from the shower and wedged between a bag of potting soil and grass seed, was the mop bucket, filled with empty glass jars. She stepped out into the sunlight, turning her face up to the warmth and finished her cigarette. After disposing of the butt, she returned to the shed and gathered the bucket, cleansers, and dropped the conditioner in the trash barrel.

She mopped the kitchen, bathrooms, and just finished polishing the hardwood in the living room when the barking dogs announced that Kelly was home. Kelly bounced in the back door with pink cheeks and a smile. "How many times did Silly get out while I was gone?"

"Just once, I think. I lose track. How was math?" Abbey leaned against the counter, glancing at the list.

"Good."

"Did he give you homework?"

"A little, but I understand it. It's easy." She opened the refrigerator and peered inside. "Miss Fay invited me over for pizza and a movie on Friday night, do you think I could go?"

Yep, Abbey thought, there's a bit of a romance blooming.

"You're suppose to go to your dad's house this weekend. You'll need to call him and see if he can pick you up Saturday."

"You don't think he'll mind, do you?" she asked, pulling out a container of yogurt and leaning against the counter.

Abbey handed her a spoon. "I don't think so. He knows you're growing up and that you're going to date. I think it'll be fine."

"It's not a date, Mom." Kelly's cheeks reddened.

"Okay, it's not a date this time, but one day it will be, I think your dad is prepared." She winked.

"Well, I don't want to hurt his feelings." Kelly picked up the phone.

"Give him a call and tell him I said it was okay."

Kelly carried the phone and yogurt to her bedroom and Abbey looked over the list again. She had accomplished most of the tasks assigned to her, but there was one chore on the list that she would not do. *There's no way I'm getting on a ladder in the pen with that psycho goat*, she thought, picking up a marker to check the chores she had completed. She glanced at the clock, moved the pot of sponges and towels out of her way, and began preparing dinner.

"Mom, Dad wants to know if he can pick me up Thursday afternoon. They're going to the beach and want me to come. Can I go?" Kelly appeared at her side, muffling the phone against her belly.

Abbey stopped chopping vegetables and thought for a moment. "We'll have to do extra schooling this week and you're probably going to need a new bathing suit."

"Does that mean I can go?" she asked, bouncing on her toes.

"Yeah, okay. It should be fine, we'll work it out."

"Yea!" She jumped in the air and spun in a circle, lifting the phone back to her ear. "I can go, Dad!" She skipped back to her bedroom.

Abbey watched her go with a smile and then her mind went back to the logistics of all she had to accomplish between now and then. She cringed, she would have to ask Richard for the car and she knew how he would react. He would lecture her on planning and claim that it would disrupt his day and his schedule. She sighed. She longed for the freedom of having her own car, but Richard had demanded she sell it after she quit her job. "It makes no sense to have two car payments, when we only have one income," he'd said.

She had conceded, because being at Kelly's side was the most important thing at the time. She hadn't thought about the future, nor had she thought of how it would feel being perpetually stranded at home. She sighed again, finished chopping the vegetables and set them aside.

"Mom. Look." Kelly wore last year's swimsuit, which barely covered her developing body.

"Well, I knew you had filled out this year, but that really tells the tale," Abbey said, sighed, and then laughed. "You definitely need a new suit. Will you throw that in the donation bag?"

"Sure. Mom, am I getting fat?"

"No, you're not fat! You have a beautiful body, breasts and hips like you're supposed to have. You're not a little girl anymore."

Kelly blushed, looking down at cleavage that wasn't there last year. "I guess not." She turned and went back to her room.

Abbey felt a little twinge in her heart; her baby was growing into a beautiful young woman. "Don't forget you need to get a wheelbarrow of straw," she called out, glancing at the clock again.

"I won't."

Just then, she caught sight of Silly heading to the garden. "Damn!" She ran out the door and caught him before he did any damage. Again, he pushed her to the pen and went in without any resistance. How many times has it been today, she wondered. Four? Five? She couldn't remember.

Kelly bounded through the door and stopped when she saw her mother by the gate. "Again?"

"Yes, again." Abbey nodded, drawing a deep breath.

"I hate that goat!" Kelly declared, retrieving the rake from the shed.

"You and me both, honey."

As Kelly made her way into the pines, Abbey returned to the kitchen to continue preparing dinner; and soon the dogs announced that Richard was home from work. He stepped through the door and kissed her on the cheek. "You smell. Did you put on clean clothes today?"

"Of course. Twice," she stated. Good to see you too, she thought.

"Then why do you stink?" he asked, reaching into the

refrigerator for a bottle of wine.

"Because every time I have to put that goat up he rubs all over me!" Abbey snapped.

He poured a glass, looking at her over the rim as he took a sip. "Well, I put up a fence, I don't know what else you expect me to do."

Abbey bit her tongue and reached in the refrigerator for the marinating chicken. She had to ask to borrow the car; she didn't want to start the evening arguing about the goat.

"Abbey, why is there a pot full of sponges and dish towels on the counter?"

"Good question. I found it in the shed."

"Why was it in the shed?"

"I have no idea, I didn't put it there. I figured you did it while you were rearranging the rest of the cleaning supplies." Abbey placed the chicken breasts in the pan warming on the stove.

"Abbey, why on earth would I do that?" He slowly shook his head. "I'm going to change clothes."

Is he suggesting I did it? She thought, retrieving a bag of rice from the pantry. Is he suggesting I'm hiding the cleaning supplies from myself?

Kelly stepped in the kitchen. "The straw is beside the gate."

"Thanks, honey." She lowered her voice. "You didn't put the sponges in that pot and put it in the shed, did you?"

Kelly glanced into the pot, raising her eyebrows. "No, Mom. I wouldn't do that."

"I know, but I had to ask. Could you set the table?"

"Sure thing. When do you think we'll be able to go bathing suit shopping?"

"I don't know. I'll have to ask Richard when I can use the car."

Kelly sighed and set the table.

"Put away your backpack." Abbey looked over the kitchen to make sure it was up to Richard's standards.

Kelly grabbed her pack and carried it to her room. Richard stepped into the kitchen, his suit replaced with jeans and t-shirt. "Dinner ready yet?"

"In just a few minutes." Abbey put the vegetables on to steam.

"I don't know why it's so difficult to have dinner ready on

time. All my life my mother had dinner on the table at 5:30. Why is that so hard for you?"

Because I'm not your mother and I don't have a cook and a maid, Abbey thought. "It's almost done."

"Almost only counts with hand grenades and horse shoes." He laughed, pouring another glass of wine.

"Richard, I need the car this week, Kelly's going to the beach with her dad this weekend and she needs a new swimsuit."

He sighed. "Really? Just seems like another reason to shop, what's wrong with the suit she had last year?"

"It's too small, she can't wear it."

"I've been wearing the same suit for five years. Why do women need a new one every year?"

"I haven't had a new suit in years, but I'm not a teenage girl, she's growing. Last year's suit barely fits her." Abbey pulled the rolls out of the oven.

"I don't believe that, she's the same height as she was last year, she hasn't grown." He sat at the table, moving his water glass and putting the wine glass in its place.

"She hasn't gotten taller, she's filled out. She can't wear the same suit, it'd be indecent." She burned her fingers buttering hot rolls.

"Well, I don't believe that."

"Well, I do. I've seen her in it, it's too small, she can't wear it." She placed the basket of bread on the table.

"Let me see," he said softly, lifting his glass as Kelly joined him at the table.

"See what?" Kelly asked.

"You, in that bathing suit that is supposedly too small."

"No!" Kelly exclaimed, her face turning a deep shade of red.

Abbey felt a strange energy begin in her head and work down her body. "There's no need for you to see it, I've seen it, and it's too small." She placed the rice on the table. Was he serious?

What if he is serious? The unwelcome voice asked.

"I'm really busy this week, it's not a good time," Richard said.

"But I'm leaving Thursday," Kelly whined.

"We can run into town after dinner and see what we can find," Abbey interrupted, cutting her eyes at Kelly.

Richard sighed, a long exaggerated expression. "I suppose

that will be okay."

"Good." Abbey poured the vegetables into a bowl. "Dinner's ready."

"It's about time," Richard said and recited the Lord's Prayer.

*

Abbey cleaned up the kitchen and was mixing up the dog food when Kelly handed her phone. "It's Grandma."

"Hey, Mom. Can you hold on for a second?" She set the phone on the counter and handed Kelly the bowls for the dogs. "Can you feed Tom and Jerry and get the food for the animals ready, but just leave it on the shelf in the shed. We should be ready to go in about twenty minutes."

"Okay," Kelly said, and Abbey held the door for her to step onto the porch.

She picked up the phone, wedging it on her shoulder, and wiped down the counters. "Hey, Mom. What's up?"

"Just calling to chat. How are you?"

"Good, but I don't have time to talk. We're just about to

head into town to go bathing suit shopping for Kelly."

"That's fine. I was planning to come out Friday and spend a few hours, can you squeeze me in?"

"Sure, but Kelly won't be here, she'll be at the beach with Jack and Holly."

"So, it'll be just the two of us?"

"Yes, ma'am, Richard should be at work."

"Sounds good. I'll see you about noon."

"Great. I'll see you then." She hung up the phone, gave the kitchen a quick visual inspection, and went to change clothes.

Richard was sitting on the bed, reviewing the day's list of chores, and preparing the list for the next day. "Why didn't you fix the leak in the barn today?" he asked, as she pulled clean clothes from the dresser.

"Because I'm not getting on a ladder around that goat, he'll knock it over, just like he knocks the wheelbarrow over, and tries to knock me over." She carried the jeans and top into the bathroom and leaving the door open, she stripped down to her bra and panties.

"He's just an animal, I don't know why you take it so personally. I thought you were an animal lover."

"I am," she said, washing off in the sink. "Just not that animal. That animal is a disgusting, foul smelling, jerk." She dried off and reapplied deodorant, adding a dab of cologne.

"You talk about him like he is a human being, he's an animal, Abbey, not a human." He set the papers down on the bed and walked into the bathroom.

"Yes, I know he's an animal." She pulled the shirt over her head. "I also know he ain't stupid," she said, despite knowing that Southern slang aggravated Richard, and slid into her jeans. "I also know he likes to abuse and herd me." She removed the rubber band from the end of her braid and brushed out her hair.

He leaned against the wall and studied her as he often did, as though he was trying to unravel a tightly knotted rope. "People abuse, Abbey, not animals. Abuse requires intent, animals don't have intent. Why do you always speak of the goat as if he is a man?"

Staring into the mirror she braided her hair and thought, I don't have time for this. "Why does it matter how I refer to him? I know he's a goat, I also know he's a brat."

"Mom, are you ready?" Kelly called from the doorway of

the bedroom.

"I'm coming," Abbey answered, relieved to have been saved from a conversation that could go on for hours.

"Wait a minute. We're having a discussion here," Richard said, straightening.

"Richard, I have to go shopping and that could take hours. I have to go." She walked out of the bathroom and he followed. "We've left the feed in the shed, all the animals will come up at dusk, feed them and they'll put themselves to bed. Just make sure to lock up the barn before you let the dogs go." She stopped and faced him. "Okay?"

He sighed. "I think I can handle it."

*

Silly watched the woman and the kid leave and he knew the predator was now in charge. He cocked his head and felt the change of energy he always felt when the woman wasn't around. He herded the does into the corner of the pen and bit one when she grew restless. The does wanted their dinner, but Silly knew there would be no dinner tonight.

Chapter Three

Abbey enjoyed the shopping trip; Kelly was thrilled with the new clothes and excited about spending a few days at the beach with her father. They stopped for ice cream and the mood was light and chatty, but then they pulled onto the dark rural road that led to home.

"Do you think Richard put the animals away?" Kelly asked softly.

"I'm sure he did." I hope he did, Abbey thought.

"He's never done it before. Alone, I mean. Has he?"

"I don't think so, but he's seen us do it enough, I'm sure it will be okay," she said, feeling her stomach tense. She pulled into the driveway and her heart began pounding in her chest.

"Where are the dogs?" Kelly asked.

They drove past the over-sized doghouse, but the animals

were no longer chained and it felt unusually still. By now the dogs should be running along side of the car, happy to see them, their tails wagging. "I don't know."

Abbey pulled up beside the house, the headlights illuminating the barnyard and a dog chewing on a large mound of white feathers.

"Oh, no!" Kelly cried.

Abbey hit the brake and Kelly jumped from her seat, running to the gate, her limp more pronounced. She threw the gate open and yelled at the dog. Abbey left the headlights on and followed, taking in the scene. The barn door was wide open and the barnyard was littered with feathers.

The dog ran as Kelly approached and she fell to her knees. She picked up a broken and bloodied duck, clutching it to her chest. "Mom," she cried, tears streaming down her face, "they killed Max." She buried her face in the feathers, sobbing.

Abbey knelt down and hugged her daughter, the duck between them. "I'm so sorry, honey." She rubbed her daughter's back for a moment, seriously considering strangling Richard, and then heard a chorus of quacks coming from the lake. The moon gave enough light that she could see the ducks on the water and the dogs swimming after them. "Shit! I've got to get the dogs!" She left Kelly rocking the dead duck and ran down to the water, screaming at the dogs. "Tom! Jerry! Here! Now!"

The dogs stopped their pursuit of the ducks and turned back to shore. They arrived in unison, shaking the water from their coats, and approached her, their heads down. She grabbed each one by the collar, dragging them through the field, and passed Kelly, still holding the duck and crying.

Abbey cussed up a storm as she returned the dogs to their house and chained them. She stalked into the house to retrieve the flashlight. "Richard!" she yelled, slamming the back door. "You didn't shut the barn door!" She went into the laundry room, grabbed a large flashlight, and slammed that door also.

"What are you yelling about?" Richard stepped into the kitchen, his hair mussed from sleep.

"You left the barn door open and at least one duck is dead!"

"I forgot." He opened the refrigerator, pulling out a bottle of water.

She turned, ran out the door, and slammed it as hard as she

could. She returned to the pen, panning the high-powered beam through the field. She found the goats, huddled together in the far corner, and the light fell on one dead chicken and then another. "Shit," she muttered. She heard a noise above her head and shined the light up into a tree, spying a chicken perched on a branch. "Hey, baby," she whispered, and then walked over to where Kelly knelt on the ground.

"I'm so sorry, honey. I know how much you loved Max."

Kelly held the duck out and Abbey took it into her arms. "He did it on purpose," she said, standing up and brushing the dirt from her knees.

"Who?" Abbey asked, startled by the anger in her daughter's eyes.

"Richard! We both know he did it on purpose," Kelly snapped, her hands on her hips.

"No, we don't know that. You're mad and hurt and you have every right to be, but we don't know that he did it on purpose."

"You may not know it, but I do." She walked away.

"Where are you going?" Abbey had never seen her daughter so angry.

"I'm getting a shovel to bury Max."

Abbey stood in the barnyard, clutching a flashlight and a dead duck, and felt a wave of exhaustion sweep through her body.

Kelly returned with the wheelbarrow and a shovel. "Where do you want the straw?"

"Just dump it by the barn."

Kelly dumped the straw, took Max out of Abbey's arms and placed him gently in the wheelbarrow, just as Richard stepped out of the house.

"Do you still need the headlights? You're burning down the battery." He stepped to the driver's side door.

"Yes!" Abbey and Kelly yelled in unison.

Kelly placed the shovel next to the duck and picked up the handles of the wheelbarrow.

"I'll help you," Abbey offered.

"No, Mom. I want to do it myself." The tears, slower now, were leaving trails down her face. Kelly pushed the wheelbarrow to the shed, and stepped inside to grab a small flashlight, passing Richard without a word. Abbey watched her disappear into the pine forest, the light growing smaller in the distance.

"Where is she off to?" Richard asked, stepping into the pen.

Abbey turned and picked up one dead chicken and then another. "She's going to bury Max."

"Well, she should be burying the chickens with him. I'll take them to her." He reached for the chickens in her arms.

"No! Leave her alone!" She laid the bodies on the pile of straw.

"It makes no sense to dig a hole for one and not the others." He reached for the chickens again.

"Leave her alone!" she snapped. "She's burying her pet and wants to do it alone."

"It makes no sense, she's just making extra work," he said, shaking his head in confusion.

Abbey sighed, and walked toward the goats, tapping her hand on her thigh. "Come 'ere, Silly."

*

Silly stared at the woman. He could feel the fear and anger rolling off her skin and it made his head itch. The predator stood behind her, but he didn't think the man was a threat to he or the does. He weighed his options. The does were vulnerable left out in the dark; they were skittish creatures and not very smart, and they wouldn't go into the barn without his saying so. Silly rose slowly, looking at her suspiciously, and the does followed his actions. He was careful to keep the predator away from his does as he followed the woman.

*

"Come on, guys," she cooed, clicking her tongue to encourage them to follow her. As the animals followed her back to the barn, she found another dead chicken and picked it up with a sigh. She placed the bird with the others and led the goats into the barn. She shut the door behind them, locking them in, and looked up into the tree where one of the traumatized chickens perched. She panned the light in the treetops and saw another. She walked to the side of the shed, picking up the ladder.

"What are you doing?" Richard asked.

"I'm going to get the chickens out of the trees."

"Why don't you leave them until morning? It's getting late."

"Because our dogs aren't the only predators around here and I don't want more dead animals in the morning. This was bad enough."

"I said I forgot. It's not like I did it intentionally, people make mistakes."

She expelled a breath and placed the ladder against the tree. She climbed up and reached for the terrified chicken, it came to her easily. With a chicken under her arm she climbed down, opened the barn door, and placed it in a nesting box. She locked the door behind her, and carried the ladder to another tree, repeating the process. After returning the second chicken to the barn, she picked up the flashlight and scanned the trees again. She spotted two more birds perched on branches and she pulled them out of the trees, all the while Richard watched her without a word. After putting away the fourth bird, she scanned the trees again and could find no more. Three chickens were dead, four were safe, and five were still missing.

"Can I turn off the headlights now?" he asked.

"I'll do it!" Abbey bit out and stalked to the car, grabbing her keys, purse, and the bags of clothes.

"Well, we've done all we can do here," Richard said, following her.

She turned off the lights and slammed the car door. She stomped into the house, threw her purse and keys on the counter, and set the bag of clothes on Kelly's bed. She stared at the bags for moment, remembering how much fun they'd had shopping and then thought of Kelly's heartbreak. Her anger intensified. "I need a drink," she muttered and turned, running into Richard standing in the doorway.

"I don't know why you're so upset," he said, as she went around him and headed back to the kitchen.

"I'm upset because I have three dead chickens, one dead duck that I know of and my daughter is heartbroken." She opened the fridge, pulled out a bottle of wine and a bottle of water. She placed the wine on the counter and opened the water, draining it.

Kelly stepped in the kitchen, her eyes were red and swollen and smudges of dirt were left on her cheeks where she had wiped away tears. Abbey set the bottle on the counter and hugged her.

Kelly rested her hands on Abbey's waist, not hugging her back, but not pushing her away either. "I'm sorry, honey."

"Yeah, Kelly. I'm sorry, too," Richard said, sitting at the table.

Kelly ignored him. "How many chickens are dead?"

"Three are dead, five are missing."

"How many ducks?"

"I don't know, they're still on the water. I'm going to try to get them in the barn and do a head count."

"Do you need me to help?"

"No honey, I'll take care of it. Why don't you shower and go to bed?"

Kelly nodded, fresh tears running down her face, and turned toward her bedroom. She passed Richard without speaking.

"What? Are you mad at me?" He reached for her arm.

Kelly stepped out of his reach, turning to face him. "Yes, I'm mad at you!"

"Richard, let her go to bed," Abbey said, pulling a wine glass down from the cabinet.

"I made a mistake. Aren't you going to forgive me?" His

mouth curved into a coaxing smile.

"We only asked you to feed the animals and shut the door! That's all we asked you to do and you couldn't even do that!" Kelly yelled. "Not only did you not feed them, you didn't shut the door! And then you let the dogs loose to kill them! No! I won't forgive you!" She ran to her room and slammed the door.

"Are you going to let her talk to me that way?"

"Yes," Abbey said, and poured the wine to the rim of the glass. "She's upset, she lost her favorite pet, and she's right. All we asked you to do was make sure the animals were locked in before you let the dogs go." She drank down half the glass and refilled it, putting the bottle away.

"So what are you going to do? Get drunk?"

"That sounds like a good idea." Abbey took another gulp of wine and wished for a cigarette.

"We're talking about fowl here, I think you're both overreacting."

Abbey sighed, finished the wine, and headed back outside.

"Where are you going?"

"I've got to bury the chickens and see how many of the

ducks survived the massacre."

"Jesus, now it's a massacre? Didn't we have chicken for dinner? I didn't see the two of you crying about that."

"Those chickens weren't our pets!" She snatched the flashlight off the counter and stepped outside. She found the wheelbarrow with the shovel still resting inside and pushed it into the pen. She picked up the dead birds, placed them in the wheelbarrow and rolled it to the far end of the field. Digging the grave, she spoke softly under her breath.

"Okay. I know. I'm in a bad place. Give me a sign, God, tell me what I need to know and I'll fix it. I got swept away, I should have known better." She dropped a shovel full of dirt on the growing mound and stomped the shovel back into the hole, breaking snaking roots. "What's a sophisticated and educated man want with me? Why did he chase me so hard? I didn't see the signs, I didn't listen to Mom, and here I am, in another fix. Give me a sign, God, send me some light." She wiped a tear away. "I did it, I know it. Please forgive me for being an idiot." She placed the chickens in the hole. "I'm sorry, birds." She wiped another tear away. "I really am." As the tears streaked down her cheeks she shoveled the dirt on top of their feathers.

She pressed the dirt down firmly and made a mental note to return to both gravesites in the morning to sprinkle lime and straw to prevent the animals from being dug up by scavengers. She returned to the shed, placed the shovel inside, and noticed the full containers still left on the shelf - the food that Richard hadn't given the animals. She pulled down the pack of cigarettes.

She stared at the darkened house for a moment, a hundred questions racing through her mind, unasked. She picked up the container of duck feed and headed down to the lake to coax the ducks back to the barn.

She sat on the bank, lighting a cigarette, and using the flashlight she spotted the ducks in the middle of the lake in a tight circle. "Hey, babies," she soothed, "come get your dinner." The ducks perked up, lifting their heads. They watched her and moved slowly in her direction. "Come on, it's safe now." She poured some feed on the ground beside her and counted them as they moved closer. "Damn." Two were still missing. She panned the light over the water and onto the banks and couldn't find any more. She shook her head, five missing chickens and two missing ducks.

The ducks slowly stepped out of the water in a line, quacking softly. She stood up and they followed her to the barn. She poured the feed in a bowl and spoke to them quietly as they ate. They finished at the water bowl, slurping down the water as they circled the dish, and she chuckled, the sound startling her. She opened the barn door and Silly raised his head from the back of a doe. He watched as the ducks waddled inside and settled in the straw under the nesting boxes. "Good night, guys, it'll be a better day tomorrow." She shut the door and locked it.

She crept into the silent house and opened Kelly's door a crack, peeking inside. Her daughter slept with a teddy bear clutched to her chest, and her cheeks were still damp. Abbey pulled the door closed, tiptoed through the master bedroom, and locked herself in the bathroom. She walked to the mirror and stared deep in her own eyes. "Give me a sign, God." She pulled off the third set of dirty clothes for the day and stepped into the shower. She turned the water as hot as she could stand, washing away the blood, sweat, and dirt, and then went to bed with wet hair.

She awoke with a start and bit back a scream when she saw Richard standing over her. "What are you doing?" She'd been dreaming of him.

"I'm leaving for work, but I think you were having a nightmare." He sat on the side of the bed.

"I was." She sat up against the pillows.

"Did you take your pill?" His eyebrow rose in question.

"No, I forgot." She shook her head.

"The pill won't work if you don't take it."

"I know." She glanced at the clock. "Why are you leaving so early?"

"I have some paperwork to catch up on." He kissed her cheek.

"Okay. I'll see you tonight."

She thought she should try to get another hour of sleep, but she was wide-awake and didn't want to risk another nightmare. She heard the car pulling down the driveway and stretched, letting her mind drift back to the dream. It seemed more of a vision than a dream and goose pimples broke out on her skin.

It was set in their house and she was like a ghost, present, but unseen. She watched Richard wander through the rooms, and then he stepped into Kelly's bedroom. He opened the drawers of her dresser running his fingers over her things and then moved to the closet, touching the hanging clothes.

He glanced at the clock, it read 7:33, and she followed him as he stepped outside. He glanced into the barnyard as the ducks and chickens gathered, pecking the ground and waiting for dinner. He turned and walked to the dogs chained at the doghouse, their tails wagging in excitement. He reached down and unhooked their chains, encouraging them as he walked toward the gate.

He opened the gate, let the dogs inside the pen, and shut it firmly behind them. Settling down on the back porch, he chuckled softly under his breath as the dogs played tug-of-war with the big white duck. The duck screamed in terror and agony, a noise she had never heard. She covered her ears, but she couldn't muffle the horrible sound. He watched for a few moments and then, amid the squalls and squawks, he walked back into the house and laid down on the couch for a nap.

Chapter Four

"I forgot to take my sleeping pill, it was just a dream," Abbey whispered, as she made up the bed. "It was just a dream," she told her reflection, as she brushed out her hair and braided it. "It was just a dream," she repeated, as she started a pot of coffee and ignored the list of chores on the counter. She glanced through the kitchen window to see the sun just lighting the sky and went to Kelly's room, easing the door open and peering inside. Kelly slept with the teddy bear still clutched to her chest. More like a little girl, than a fifteen-year-old young woman, Abbey thought, and pulled the door shut.

She poured a large mug of coffee, stepped outside, and went to the shed to retrieve her cigarettes. She entered the pen and walked the field, her eyes scanning back and forth making sure there were no more dead birds. She went to the shed for lime and carried it to the two gravesites, sprinkling the material onto the dirt. She raked up the feathers scattered in the barnyard, hiding them under the pile of straw. Returning to the house she poured a second cup of coffee and carried it down to the water, sitting on the bank that was damp with morning dew, and put a flame to her cigarette. "At this rate I'll be back to a pack a day in no time." She laughed harshly, without humor. "It was just a dream," she said again, "that's why I take those damned pills. I hate dreaming."

What if it wasn't just a dream? The unwelcome voice asked.

Abbey shut her eyes and dropped her head onto her knees. Thought ceased and all she was aware of was the sounds of the morning. She heard the birds singing and the waking noises of the animals beginning to stir in the barn. A fish splashed the top of the water, a bee buzzed beside her, and a squirrel crashed through the highest branches in the trees. She lifted her head and opened her eyes just as Kelly sat down beside her.

"Morning." Kelly stared out over the water.

Abbey turned, looking at her daughter's red and swollen

eyes and felt a yawning pain deep inside. Forgetting she still had a cigarette in her hand, she wrapped her arms around the girl and hugged her tightly. "I'm sorry," she whispered before pulling away and wiping a tear off her cheek. "I guess you caught me." She held up the cigarette burning between her fingers.

Kelly smiled, but it didn't reach her eyes. "It's okay. If I smoked, I'd have one too. So what's the count?"

"We're missing two ducks and five chickens." She sighed. "Want to help me let the animals out of the barn?" Abbey snubbed out the cigarette, burying it in the grass. She stood up and reached her hand down to Kelly, silently praying she would take it.

Kelly nodded her head slowly, took a deep breath, and grabbed her mother's hand, allowing Abbey to pull her up. Holding hands they walked to the barn. Abbey opened the barn door and the ducks barreled out noisily, running to the food dish as Kelly poured in feed. The chickens came next, flapping down from the boxes and pecking the feed that the ducks were scattering. Then Silly stood up, signaling the does that it was time to get up and as the small herd stepped out of the barn, the chickens scattered into the field and the ducks fell in line to the lake.

She checked the boxes for eggs, but didn't find any and they went back into the house. "Why don't you read the next chapter to me while I cook breakfast?" Abbey asked, pulling a package of bacon and a carton of eggs out of the fridge.

Kelly picked up the book with none of the fanfare of the previous morning and began reading aloud. She was so excited about the book yesterday, Abbey thought, as she stirred the eggs in a bowl. She flipped the bacon listening to Kelly fumble over the words several times and cringed, remembering how freely the words flowed yesterday.

Abbey placed a plate of food in front of Kelly and sat across the table from her. Kelly set the book aside and they ate in silence. Abbey sighed, pushing away her half eaten food. "If I had a magic wand I could wave and make it all go away, I would. I keep saying I'm sorry and I know it doesn't take away the pain, but for what it's worth, I am sorry."

"I know Mom, I don't mean to be a brat. I'm just so sad and I had nightmares last night. I kept seeing the dogs playing tug-of-war with that sweet duck and I kept waking up crying so I didn't get a lot of sleep." Fresh tears welled in her eyes and she wiped them with the back of her hand. "Besides, it's not your fault, it's Richard's fault." Kelly picked up their plates, carrying them to the sink, and scraped the leftovers into a bowl to be used later in the dogs' dinner. She turned, leaning against the counter and faced Abbey. "I think he did it on purpose."

Abbey let out a deep breath and as the air escaped her lungs, her head suddenly felt like it weighed hundreds of pounds and she had to drop it into her hands before it splintered her neck. She heard the quiet sounds of the forest, cool and soothing in her mind, and longed to be by the water again.

"Mom?" Kelly asked softly, placing her hand on Abbey's shoulder. "Are you okay?"

"Yes, just give me a second." She took a deep breath, released it slowly and then another, the heaviness in her head abating. She lifted her head, now resting her chin on her hands. "Sit down."

Kelly sat and faced her.

Finally, Abbey found the energy to hold her head up without assistance. "It seems I've gotten us into a mess and I'm going to need a little time to figure it out. I don't know whether Richard did it on purpose or if he forgot like he said, but I respect your feelings and I understand how frustrated you are."

"It's not the first time a bunch of animals have died around here because of one of Richard's *mistakes*," Kelly pointed out, making quotation marks in the air.

"I know."

"It's a pattern, Mom," she insisted.

"It may be."

"Are we going to wait for the third time?"

Abbey stared into her daughter's green eyes and smiled. "You're pretty wise for a kid."

"Nearly dying does that sometimes, but you know I'm right."

"I know we're in a mess and I'm asking you to give me a little time to figure it out. I was talking to God last night and I asked for a sign. I guess I'm getting them, I just need a little time, okay?"

Kelly nodded and the phone rang. They looked at each other and laughed. "Man, God's quick," Kelly joked as Abbey picked up the receiver.

"Miss Abbey, it's James Jackson." The gruff voice did not relay the man's advanced age.

"Morning, Mr. Jackson. How are you?" she asked her closest neighbor.

"Good, good. The day's a beauty, it sure is. You a'missin' a couple ducks and sum chickens?"

Abbey laughed. "Thank goodness! Yes I am, do you have them?"

"We found 'em peckin' away in the garden this morning, Miss Annie threw 'em a bit of feed and they's as happy as can be. I don't know where that woman found feed, we ain't kept chickens in twenty years, but she never throws anything away." He chuckled.

"We'll be right there," she said and then remembered she didn't have a car. "Mr. Jackson, I don't have a car today."

"Ain't no problem, y'all get down here and catch 'em, and I'll git you home."

"Thanks, we'll be there in a little bit." She hung up the phone and turned to Kelly, who was staring at her with wide and hopeful eyes. "The chickens and ducks are at the Jackson's house."

"Yea!" Kelly jumped to her feet and hugged her mother.

"Got your walking shoes on?"

"Yep."

"Well, lets go."

They walked to the end of the sandy, pine-lined driveway and turned to the west. Side by side they walked along the old, two lane state road as few cars passed. "You don't have to go to church with Richard tonight if you don't want to."

"I want to go, but only because I want to let Brandon know I won't be in town Friday night."

"You could call him."

"I'm not calling him, he's never called me," Kelly said firmly.

Abbey smiled. "Okay, but you don't have to go."

"I think it will be all right and tomorrow I'm off to the beach." She clapped her hands and skipped a couple steps.

Abbey laughed and ruffled her daughter's hair, pleased to see a little of her natural exuberance returning.

They topped a small hill and the highway unfolded before them revealing forests, fields, and the dirt road leading to the Jackson's house. They turned down the road and the forest loomed closer, crowding the path with low hanging branches.

"How long have the Jacksons lived back here?" Kelly asked softly.

"Best I know Mr. Jackson was born here, back in the early 1900s."

"Wow. He gets around pretty good for being so old, I can't believe he still plants a garden every year."

The road descended, curved, and the Jackson's property came into view. The lush field of thigh high corn stalks ended at a well manicured lawn, a row of stacked rocks separating the yard from the road. The property contained several out buildings and scattered throughout the expanse were rock-lined flowerbeds filled with vibrant colors. The yard gave way to another garden on the far side of the property, which ended at the encroaching woods. The house was small, white, covered in a rusted tin roof, and it sat in sharp contrast against the deep, green forest in the background. As they approached, Abbey could see the old couple sitting in matching rocking chairs on the front porch, their white hair a shock against their dark skin.

They turned into the yard and the old man in overalls stood

up, placing a straw hat over his white hair, and met them in the yard. "Morning," he said with a smile. "I gots your critters 'round back."

Abbey waved at Mrs. Jackson. "Good morning!"

"Morning, Abbey, Kelly." She waved. "After you catch 'em chickens come on in for a piece of pie."

"Thank you," Abbey replied and followed the stooped old man around the house.

The chickens and ducks pecked in the grass, picking up the last bit of feed. "Hey babies!" Kelly dropped to her knees and the ducks waddled over to her, allowing her to stroke their feathers.

"She got a way with animals, don't she? Come help me git this cage down, Miss Abbey."

Abbey followed him to a building and opening the door, he pointed out a wire cage on a shelf. "My arms don't reach thata way no more, think you can git it?"

"Yes, sir." She stood on her tiptoes and latching her fingers in the wire, she pulled it free.

"That should a hold 'em. Now, you just gots to catch 'em." He chuckled.

Kelly easily slid the ducks into the small opening and then

they started chasing chickens. Mr. Jackson sat in a chair in the shade and watched them, letting out a few good-humored guffaws. "Chickens sure is fast!"

After about twenty minutes, they finally caught the last chicken and slid it into the cage. Abbey and Kelly lifted the cage together, setting it in the shade under a tree, and followed Mr. Jackson inside.

"Come on in," Mrs. Jackson said as they stepped into the kitchen. "I poured you sum ice tea. Runnin' down chickens is hard work."

Abbey and Kelly sat at the table and picking up a their glasses, they drained them. Mrs. Jackson re-filled the glasses, chuckling.

"Yes, sir, after seventy it's dang near impossible to catch a chicken, that's why we decided to get rid of 'em, but I sure do miss havin' 'em 'round. It was nice to see 'em in the yard this morning." Mr. Jackson sat down at the table and took a sip of tea. "Of course, all the strays find their way to our house, don't they, Miss Annie?"

"They do, always have. The lost ones always turn up at our door." She placed a strawberry pie on the table.

"Wow. That looks amazing," Kelly said, licking her lips.

Mrs. Jackson returned to the table with a stack of plates and began cutting the pie into generous slices.

"So you've had a lot of strays turn up over the years?" Abbey asked, accepting a plate.

"Yep, after a while you ain't surprised no more," Mr. Jackson said, taking a bite of the pie. "Hmmm, hmmm. Excellent as usual, Miss Annie."

"Thank you, Mr. James." She smiled at him with a twinkle in her eyes.

"How long have y'all been married?" Abbey asked, taking a bite of the pie and closing her eyes to enjoy the explosion of taste on her tongue. "Mrs. Jackson, this is amazing."

"Yes, it is. It's the best thing I've ever tasted," Kelly chimed in.

"Thanks, ladies. Mr. James and I've been together comin' up on 75 years now. Got hitched when we were about your age, Kelly."

Kelly looked at the old lady with wide eyes.

Mrs. Jackson laughed. "Things were a'different back then,

we didn't run off to college like kids these days. We had babies and went to work."

"And you've lived here ever since?" Kelly asked.

"Yep, sure have. We a built this house that first year we was married. Mr. James was a'born in the family house 'cross the road and I was a'born in the house that used to be on the other side of the garden."

"I've never seen any old houses around here," Kelly said, taking another bite.

"Ain't much left of 'em no more."

"I'll point out what's left of 'em when I git you home," Mr. Jackson said, scraping his plate with his fork.

"So do you know who used to live on our property?" Kelly asked, putting her fork across the empty plate.

Mr. and Mrs. Jackson looked at each other for a moment across the table, exchanging some silent communication. Kelly glanced at Abbey and raised her eyebrows. Whatever silent question had been exchanged between the two of them, it was answered when the old lady sat back in her chair and asked her husband to get her cigarettes. The old man stood, pulled down a pack of cigarettes and an ashtray from the top of the refrigerator, placing them on the table in front of her. He picked up the pie, set it on the counter and sat back down, refilling his glass of tea.

"When we was little…" she began, lighting a cigarette. "There was an old foundation of a plantation house back there in 'em woods." She pointed to the rear of the house. "It sets on the other side of the lake from where your house sets now and there was a bunch of rumors. All us kids thought it were a'haunted and we'd dare each other to touch the old chimney or spend sum time in the cemetery."

"There's a cemetery?" Kelly asked.

"Yep," Mr. Jackson chimed in. "Straight 'cross the lake, 'bout a quarter mile, it's a'scary as hell at night, too." He chuckled.

"What kind of rumors?" Abbey asked, stacking the plates and silverware.

"Folks was more superstitious back then. We didn't have no television or 'lectricity, so when the nights were a'long and dark, stories got passed 'round. Sum folks believed there was strange rituals going on back in 'em woods, witchcraft and demon stuff. All our parents forbid us to go back in there, but we was kids and curious, so's we went, daring each other, trying to prove who was tougher, braver." She exhaled a stream of smoke and looked at her husband. He nodded his head.

"Folks 'round here said that sumthin' terrible happened to the family that lived in the big house and they just left one day, left the house and everythin' in it. A couple of their youngens died in sum accident. I don't know what a'happened, but I seen their graves in the old cemetery. A few years after they moved away, the house just up and burned down one night, no one knows why. They said there weren't no storms or lightnin' that night. Anyway, I don't know much about that, that were our great-grandparents time.

"Like I said, when we was kids, despite our parent's warnings, we'd go explorin' the old house and cemetery. One day a bunch of us was out there and my cousin Calvin started a'yellin' for us to come see what he found. He was about two hundred yards south of the cemetery and when we stepped into the openin', he was a'dancing 'round on a large flat rock in the middle of a cleared circle, proud that he had found sumthin' that the rest of us had a'missed. All I knowed is that when I saw him up there, it a'scared me so bad I had to run in the woods and make water. The top of the rock was dark with soot and God knows what else and the grass in the circle was all yellowed and dried, while all 'round the woods was green and shiny.

"Me and a couple other kids was a'scared and admitted it, but the boys tried to act tough, struttin' 'round the circle like roosters. But I could see they was a'scared, too. Finally we left, and boy, was I glad, but on the way back Calvin started a'thinkin'. He started a'talkin' 'bout how them shiny cars with the rich white folks would drive past our houses a'headin' back in 'em woods. It was just us black folk out here back then, so it was mighty strange to see all the white people drivin' past. We a'figured the cars came from Atlanta, cuz no one 'round these parts could afford a car. Calvin decided that that circle was where they was a'headin' and said the next time he seen 'em cars, he was a'headin' back up in there to see what they was a'doin'." She exhaled smoke on a deep sigh and snubbed out her cigarette.

"Calvin was a smart kid, mayhaps too curious, though. So one night, well after dinner, we kids was a'playin' in the yard and it was just gittin' dark when one of them shiny cars a'passed. Calvin said that after his parents went to bed he was a'goin' to sneak out and see what they was up to, we tried to talk him out of it, but he was like a dog with a bone, his mind was made. I watched 'em cars pass that night, men and women, nicely dressed starin' straight ahead and I was a'scared. Well, Calvin snuck out that night and he never came back home. The next morning all the growed ups went a'lookin' for him and found him, a'kilt, on that rock in the circle. He'd been cut up pretty bad, they a'carried him back to the house and sent word to the sheriff. The sheriff came out and we kids told him what we knew, but he decided it was a wild animal that a'kilt Calvin and that was the end of it. Calvin was just a little black boy in his book, not important to the white sheriff." She paused for a moment, looking back and forth between Abbey and Kelly. "I don't mean no disrespect by a'sayin' that, but that just were the way it was back then."

Abbey and Kelly nodded and Mrs. Jackson took sip of tea.

"The cars stopped a'comin' for a while after that, but they started in again a few years later. One night a young white woman came a'bangin' on the door in the middle of the night, she was a'scared and asked us to hide her. She a'begged and a'pleaded for us not to let anybody know where she was and she said they were a'lookin' for her. She was wearin' a long white gown, all torn up from running through the woods and 'er feet was in bad shape, cuz she didn't have no shoes. Daddy took 'er in and we women found 'er sum clothes and shoes and then we a hid 'er in the barn, buryin' 'er under the hay. Daddy sent us back to bed, but he sat up in a chair in the living room with a shotgun on his lap." Mrs. Jackson held up the pack of cigarettes, offering Abbey one, which she took gratefully. The old woman lighted her own and handed the lighter to Abbey.

"It weren't long before two well-dressed white men came a'knockin' on the door and askin' 'bout the girl. Daddy said he ain't seen 'er, but they wanted to look inside the house and Daddy let 'em, cuz that's the way it was back then. They left, went to the other houses and didn't find 'er and when Daddy saw the cars pullin' out early the next mornin' before sun up, he sent me to the barn to get 'er. She had nuthin' and said if she didn't get out of the state, they'd find 'er and kill 'er. We barely had a pot to piss in, but we gave 'er sum money and sent her to our cuzzins, who also gave 'er some money. Our cuzzins took 'er to a white lady in town, who gave 'er sum decent clothes and put 'er on the train headed up north."

"What did the lady say happened in the woods? What was she running from?" Kelly asked, her eyes wide and afraid.

"She said there was witches in 'em woods and they was a'tryin' to kill 'er cuz she had the right blood. It didn't make no sense and she was a'scared, like I said. A couple days later the sheriff come out, the same one that said a wild animal a'kilt Calvin, and he was askin' a lot of questions 'bout 'er. We said we ain't seen nuthin' and that was the last we heard of it." She sighed.

"Then the war come and we didn't see 'em cars for a while, but soon after the war, a new family moved back there on your property. It were a young white family, went by the name Dawson. Mr. Dawson was a nice man and he wanted to start a'farmin'. He built a house and moved his city wife and three youngens out.

"He'd come by often, pickin' Mr. James brain 'bout farmin' and their kids a'played wid ours, right out in the front yard. We didn't see much of Mrs. Dawson, I don't think she took too good to a'livin' in the country. Then one night there was a'poundin' at the door and when we opened it, the Dawson's boy, Allen, was standing there all a'scratched from the woods. He said one word – "help" -

and then he kinda fell in my arms. He wouldn't talk, I nursed his wounds, but he had a lot more blood on his clothes than wounds on his body. We sent word to the sheriff, a different one 'an before and he come out, but the boy still wouldn't talk so the sheriff went up to the house to investigate." She paused and took a long drink of tea.

"When the sheriff got up there he found a mess, but he couldn't a'find the rest of the family. He called in the state police cuz Mr. Dawson was a rich man. They got out here just as the sun come up. They found Mrs. Dawson, a'kilt, in the lake wearing a long white gown. They found Mr. Dawson in the woods, sitting by a tree a'kilt, probably of a heart attack, but they couldn't a find the other youngens. The sheriff tried to take Allen wid 'im, but the youngen just held on to me for dear life and finally the sheriff decided he could stay wid us 'til his family could come git him. He stayed wid us for two days and never said a word. His family come from sumwheres up North and just before he got in the car he a'hugged me and said thank you." She laughed. "About twenty years later he come back and had that house a'burned and a'bulldozed. He stopped by to visit; he didn't talk much then either, and ate a piece of pie. Before he left he handed Mr. James the keys to a brand new truck. Ain't nobody lived up there since then and your chickens and ducks is the first strays we seen in years."

"Do the cars still come by?" Kelly asked.

The old lady looked at her and nodded with a slow, sad smile and said, "Yep, they do."

They were silent for a minute and then Mr. Jackson stood up and said, "Let's git you girls home."

Mrs. Jackson stood up and grabbed the table to steady herself. "I think I wore myself plum out a'talkin'. Thanks for a'listenin' to an old woman, I'm gonna take a nap."

"Thanks for the pie, Mrs. Jackson," Kelly said, remembering her manners, where Abbey had forgotten them.

"Yes, thanks for the pie." Abbey stepped around the table to the old woman and gave her a hug.

"You is always welcome here," the old woman said, pulling away, but still holding Abbey's arms firmly and looking into her eyes. "You is always welcome."

Abbey and Kelly followed Mr. Jackson into the back yard and picked up the cage, sliding it on the bed of the truck. They climbed in the old vehicle that had seen better days in the time before Abbey was born and he backed out of the driveway, heading deeper into the forest.

"Is this the truck the Dawson boy gave you, Mr. Jackson?" Kelly asked.

"Sure is, good ole truck." He drove slowly, passing the garden and stopped in front of the remains of an old rock wall. He pointed into the woods. "If you a'look hard, you can see the old tin roof. That's where Miss Annie was a'born."

Abbey could just make it out underneath a thick stand of black berries briars.

"I see it!" Kelly exclaimed.

He continued and pointed out a crumbling chimney next to a large oak tree on the opposite side of the road. "That's where Calvin and his family a'lived."

He drove a little further and then pointed to another set of remains claimed by the woods. "The reverend and his family a'lived there and 'cross the road." He performed a three-point turn and headed the other direction. "I don't like to go much further 'an the crick, the woods feel strange sumtimes."

He drove back toward the highway and slowed again.

"That's where I was a'born." Abbey gazed into the woods and thought she could make out hints of a foundation. He nodded his head toward the opposite side of the road. "Over there, the Jessups a'lived."

"Where did everyone go?" Kelly asked.

"Times a'change, they moved to the city. All our youngens moved to the city, their youngens stayed in the city, they visit regular, but that's where the money is, in the city." He accelerated up the hill and came to the highway. "When I was a'little this were all farm land, cotton, corn, tobacco for miles and miles. Now it ain't much of nuthin', few cows here and there, but not much else." He turned onto the black top.

They were quiet on the short drive along the hard top. Mr. Jackson turned onto the sandy driveway and stopped short when he saw the goat blocking the way. Kelly sighed and Abbey muttered, "Damned goat."

He moved the truck forward, but Silly stood his ground. He inched the truck even closer, tapping the goat in the side, and finally Silly gave up, kicking up his back legs and running into the woods. "He's a cocky bastard!" The old man laughed and slapped the steering wheel.

"You don't know the half of it," Abbey agreed.

He backed the truck up to the gate and Abbey and Kelly moved the cage into the pen, setting the birds free. When they tried to put the cage back in the truck Mr. Jackson insisted they keep it. "You a'need it more 'an we do."

They said goodbye and Abbey and Kelly watched him drive away and then turned to look at the lake. "What are we going to do, Mom?"

"Get your hiking boots on, we're about to go for a walk." Abbey turned to go in the house.

*

James Jackson pulled the old truck into the driveway and noticed his bride, Annie, sitting on the porch without surprise. He climbed out of the truck, slamming the heavy door, and stepped onto the porch. "I thought you was gonna take a nap, Miss Annie."

"I was." She sighed. "But I a'needed to talk to God."

He settled in the rocking chair beside her. "You did the right thing," he said and rested his hand on hers.

"I a'scared those girls. I ain't so sure that's the right thing."

"You a'told those girls the truth, that's the right thing. Why don't you take a nap?"

"I'm a'thinkin' I'll just set here for a piece."

"Okay." He squeezed her hand gently as they rocked.

"It's a nice day."

"It's a beauty, it sure is."

Chapter Five

"We're going to find the cemetery and that other place," Abbey said, pulling bottles of water from the refrigerator and setting them on the counter.

"Why?"

"Why not? Don't you want to see?" She stepped into the pantry, pulling out some energy bars.

"I don't know. Aren't you scared?"

"Of course, but since we live here I think we need to see it ourselves. Forewarned is forearmed and all that."

Kelly stared at her for a moment and then nodded her head. "Okay. I'm going to change."

"Put on long sleeves so the briars don't scratch you."

"Okay."

Abbey found one of Kelly's old backpacks and loaded the water and food. She pulled on sturdy boots and grabbed a flannel shirt out of the closet. She paused at her jewelry cabinet and reached inside for the elaborate gold compass her mother had given her for Christmas and clipped it onto her belt loop. Her eyes fell on the delicate crucifix Kelly had given her for her last birthday and she clasped it behind her neck, dropping it under her t-shirt. She turned to find Kelly standing in the doorway, now dressed like her mother in flannel, denim, and boots. "Are you ready?"

"I think so," Kelly said, clutching the small crucifix at her neck.

"I put on the one you gave me, too," Abbey said, lifting the necklace from her collar and showing it to her daughter.

Kelly laughed nervously. "Well, at least we're thinking along the same lines."

They stepped into the kitchen and Abbey adjusted the straps, settling the pack on her back. "Will you get the dog leashes?"

"We're taking them? I'm mad at them."

"It wasn't their fault either, Kelly."

Kelly nodded her head with a sigh, retrieved the leashes

from the laundry room, and they stepped outside. "Everything just looks different now, doesn't it? Darker or something."

Abbey agreed and walked to the center of the yard, unhooking the compass. "Mr. Jackson said directly across the lake, right?"

Kelly nodded her head.

"That would be dead east then." She took the leashes from Kelly and walked over to the doghouse. She put one dog, Jerry, on a leash and handed the leather strap to Kelly. Then she attached a leash to Tom and they started across the dam. The dogs, happy to be free, pulled them along and they entered the forest.

"We forgot to put up Silly." Kelly stopped, looking back across the lake at the house.

"I think that's the least of our worries right now. Come on."

"Mom, do you think the stories are true?" she asked softly, falling back into step.

"I think they mostly are, stories change a bit with time, sometimes they get a little distorted, but the Jacksons are pretty sharp for their age. I think the stories are mostly true." They walked quietly for a while, stepping over downed trees and going in wide circles around thick underbrush. They crossed a small creek and stopped for a moment, allowing the dogs to drink.

"I guess this is the creek Mr. Jackson said he didn't like to cross because the woods felt strange sometimes," Kelly said, her eyes wide.

"I think it is, I guess we're getting closer." They climbed a hill and the hardwood trees gave way to pine and briars.

"What do you think killed those kids? What kind of accident?" Kelly asked, keeping close.

"I don't know. Maybe there will be a hint in the cemetery."

Abbey stopped. "Wait a minute," she said, "look at these trees, old oaks in rows. I think we're on an old road or driveway." She turned. "We passed it. Look." She pointed up the small hill they just came down. "The old house is up there."

They walked between the twisted trees, back to the bottom of the small rise. The dogs no longer pulled at their restraints, but stayed close, their ears up and eyes alert. They climbed up the hill and Abbey stared into the untamed growth, attempting to discern some sign of the previous inhabitants. She took a few more steps and then looked down, she was standing on a rock walkway nearly invisible under wild grass. "Kelly," she said, pointing down.

"Holy cow!" Kelly's eyes were bright and excited with discovery.

The walkway disappeared into a thick tangle of briars, brambles, and kudzu. "I guess the remains of the house are under that mess, we'd see it better in winter." Abbey pulled off the backpack, removed a couple bottles of water and handed one to Kelly. She opened her own and drank half of it. She wiped the dampness from her lips with the back of her hand and stared into the thick overgrowth, trying to imagine the family that lived on the land over a hundred years ago.

"I wonder what they were like," Kelly whispered, breaking the silence.

"Yeah, me too. Let's go find the cemetery." Abbey put the bottles in the pack and settled the straps on her shoulders. Turning back they continued down the old road lined in fat oaks as Abbey continued to check the compass to make sure they were still headed in the right direction.

"I wonder when the last time a car could get back in here, the trees in the middle of the road are much smaller than the others."

"Yeah, I noticed, maybe fifteen or twenty years ago, I'd guess."

"Why do you think cars were still coming back here then?"

"Curiosity? A make out spot? I don't know."

"Well, I sure wouldn't want to make out here, it's too creepy."

Abbey laughed and the dogs glanced up at her, wagging their tails slowly. The woods thinned out and opened up into what should have been a meadow, but no flowers grew, just scrub pine, cactus, anthills, and dried, yellow, knee high grass.

"There it is!" Kelly exclaimed in a loud whisper, grabbing Abbey's arm and pointing to a large marble angel, seemingly hovering above the grass about a hundred feet away. Slowly they approached, Kelly still gripping Abbey's arm. "It's so weird to see a cemetery in the middle of the woods."

"It is odd," Abbey agreed, taking in the rusted wrought iron fence around the small line of graves. There were two adult stones topped with angels followed by four child-sized stones adorned with sleeping lambs. "But I guess when folks didn't all live in the city, this is what they did when someone in their family died, just buried them on the land."

The gate to the enclosure was open and the top hinge had broken, allowing the heavy iron to sink into the soil. Abbey dropped the backpack on the ground, knotted Tom's leash on a firm piece of fence and stepped through the opening. Kelly followed, tying up Jerry and then reached inside the front pocket of the pack pulling out a pencil and a pad of paper.

"Good thinking," Abbey said, stepping over to a carved angel, its wings spread out in welcome. The monument was darkened with age, but she could still read the writing. Mary Elizabeth Starnes, born the 12th day of November 1801 – died the 31st day of October 1858, A Good Mother.

"Mom, come here," Kelly said, standing in front of a small headstone. "Look at the dates."

Abbey glanced at each of the small graves, four in row. Daniel Paul Starnes, born on the 5th day of May 1860 – died the 6th day of June 1866, A Good Son. Mary Elizabeth Starnes, born the 11th day of November 1858 – died the 6th day of June 1866, A Good Daughter. Ellen Rose Starnes, born the 4th day of April 1856 – died the 1st day of May 1864, A Good Daughter. William David Starnes, born the 25th day of December 1854 – died the 21st day of March 1863, A Good Son.

"Wow, a child died just about every year," Abbey whispered.

"Mom, these two died on 6-6-66. Number of the beast, anyone?" Kelly asked, scribbling the names and dates on the pad.

Abbey stepped over to other angel-adorned headstone. Abigail Lily Starnes, born the 22nd day of June 1835 – died the 31st day of October 1865, A Loving Wife and Good Mother. A shudder worked down her spine, Abigail Lily was her name.

Kelly stepped beside her and the pencil in her hand stilled. "Mom, that's your name."

"I know. Weird, huh?"

"Well, if I wasn't totally freaked out earlier, I am now." She reached for her mother's hand. "What's going on? I'm beginning to feel like we're in some suspense novel that's about to turn really bad."

"I don't know, Kelly, but that's why we're here, we're figuring it out. I asked for a sign last night, I'd say God has come through, yet again." She laughed softly, squeezing her daughter's hand.

"I'd say. And in a big, creepy way."

"Granted, but we can't freak out. We have to stay calm, forewarned and forearmed and all that. Remember? One step at a time, like therapy."

Kelly nodded. She remembered physical therapy well. She took a deep breath and started writing again.

"Abigail Lily must have been the mother of the kids, they all died in just a few years, one after another." Abbey shook her head, unable to imagine how the rest of the family must have suffered. "I guess the other lady was the grandmother."

"The grandmother and mother died on the same day, Halloween, seven years apart." Kelly's hand stilled again. "It's just women and kids buried here. Where are the men?"

"I don't know, but that's interesting. Mrs. Jackson said the father left after the two kids died, so I guess he's buried somewhere else. Don't know where Grandpa is, though, maybe he died before they moved out here." Abbey walked out of the small cemetery and slid the pack back onto her shoulders. "Let's go find that circle," she said and turned.

"I'm not sure I want to."

"I know I don't want to, but we have to. We have to know how much of a mess we are in." A mess I put us in, she thought, untying the dog. She unclipped the compass, checking the direction. "Mrs. Jackson said south, right?"

"Yes, ma'am," Kelly responded, untying Jerry, and sliding the pad into the backpack.

South led across the field and back into the woods. "Come on," Abbey said, clipping the compass back onto her belt loop. They walked across the field, stepping over low growing mounds of wild cactus and avoiding anthills.

"How do you think those kids died?" Kelly asked softly.

"Well, Mrs. Jackson said the last two died in an accident, the others, I don't know. There were a lot of diseases back then, lots of young kids died. Plus, the civil war was going on back then, it was hard on a lot of Southern families."

"There's a road!" Kelly stopped, pointing off to the right.

"Well, I'll be." The road curved off into the woods, branches hanging so low it looked like a tunnel. "If a car came through there now, it would certainly get scratched," Abbey said, but noticed that only a thin strip of dried grass grew down the center, unlike the other old road full of young trees.

"Yeah, but a car *could* get down here. This must be how all those shiny cars got back here."

Suddenly Abbey felt exposed. "Let's hurry up, see the circle and get out of here."

They crossed the rest of the field quickly. "There's a path," Abbey said, leading them toward the opening. The stepped onto a wide path, lined in a mixture of soft woods and pines.

"Mom, look at the dogs," Kelly whispered. Tom and Jerry held their heads low to the ground, their tails tucked underneath their rumps and the hair along their spine stood on end. "They're scared."

"Yeah, so am I. It's just a little further." The path ended abruptly at yellow knee high grass. Abbey stopped and stared into the perfectly round clearing. She saw the large flat rock, the top dark and discolored, set perfectly in the center of the small field. "I guess this is it."

"It doesn't feel right here," Kelly whispered, as the dogs began growling softly.

Abbey glanced down at the dogs, understanding that they could also sense the wrongness of the area. "You're right, it does feel strange." Her arms erupted into goose pimples. "I'm just going to step into the circle for a second."

"Don't Mom! Don't do it!"

"I have to, Kelly. I'll be quick." She took a deep breath and stepped off the woodsy path onto the crisp dry grass. Her head began tingling and then she felt a little dizzy, as though she had just been spinning in circles. She turned, facing her daughter. "Something is definitely here, some kind of energy. I feel a little dizzy."

"Come back, Mom!" Kelly demanded and the dogs continued growling deep in their throats.

She glanced down at the compass on her belt loop; the needle was spinning in a slow circle. She unhooked it and held it up for Kelly to see. "The magnetic field is screwed up here."

"Like the Bermuda Triangle?" Kelly asked, glancing over her shoulder. "Come on, Mom. Let's go."

Abbey clipped the compass back to her jeans, stepping out of the circle. Her head stopped tingling and the dizziness ceased as soon as she stepped off the dried grass, but her heart began pounding. "Let's go. Quickly."

Kelly turned and jogged down the path, Jerry leading the way. Abbey followed and they burst into the field breathing hard, while the dogs continued to pull them along. As they crossed the old road Kelly stopped, but Jerry continued to tug and coughed when his collar suddenly tightened. "A car's coming. Listen."

Abbey couldn't hear much of anything over her pounding heart, but concentrating the drone of an engine came to her. "Run!"

They ran, the dogs pulling them, and passed the old cemetery. They slid back in the forest and continued, only stopping to catch their breath when they reached the oak lined, unusable road.

"Is your leg okay?" Abbey asked, pulling the backpack off her shoulders and reaching inside.

"Yes, ma'am. It's fine." Kelly accepted a bottle of water. "Who's back here and why?"

Abbey dropped the pack on the ground and drank from her own bottle. "That's what I'm about to find out."

"What are you going to do?"

"I'm going to go look and see who it is."

"No, you're not!"

"I have to, Kelly, you know that. Stay here with the dogs and keep them quiet. I'm just going to the tree line to take a peek."

"What if they see you?"

"They won't. They're not going to expect anyone to be out here, they won't be looking. Just keep the dogs quiet, okay? I'll be right back."

"Okay." Kelly sighed. "Please be careful." Resigned, she sat on the ground and patted her legs for the dogs to join her. They lay down on either side of her and looked up at Abbey.

Abbey bent down and kissed her daughter's head. "I'll be quick." She ran back in the direction they had just come, slowing at the last old oak. She lowered herself, grateful that the flannel shirt she had chosen was green and brown, and crept toward the tree line, as the noise of the vehicle grew louder. She crouched behind the thick tree and peered around it, watching a primer painted gray truck pull into the field.

The engine died and two young white men stepped out of the truck. They met at the back of the bed and the dark-headed one pulled down the tailgate. She studied the young men; they both wore jeans and boots and appeared to be in their late teens or early twenties. The taller one had dark hair and wore a University of Georgia t-shirt, the other, slightly shorter man, was red-headed and wore a black t-shirt with what looked like the logo of a musical group.

They were speaking to each other, but she couldn't make out their words. The dark headed boy pointed back down the road and handed the redhead a small gas-powered chain saw and a fold up extension ladder. The redhead took the chain saw and ladder and walked down the road. The dark-headed boy lifted a small lawn mower off the back of the truck, and pushed it to the opening of the circle, disappearing down the path.

As Abbey turned to head back to her daughter, she heard the chain saw roar to life and a couple yards later, the lawn mower. She found Kelly where she left her, her head in her hands, her hair falling down onto her thighs. When she heard Abbey's footsteps, she jerked up her head. "Thank God!" she said, getting to her feet. "What happened?"

"Two young guys are down there cutting the grass in the circle and clearing the low branches from the road." She picked up the pack and slung it onto her shoulders.

"Oh crap!"

"Exactly. Let's get out of here." She took Tom's leash from Kelly and headed back up the hill, skirting the untamed brush covering the old Starnes house. They retraced their steps quietly, crossing the creek and allowing the dogs to drink for a moment.

"What does it mean, Mom? Another witchy ritual?" Kelly asked, as the dogs finished drinking and they resumed walking.

"I guess so." She sighed. "We have a lot to think about. Richard can't know we came out here or what the Jacksons told us."

"Duh. And have him tell us how crazy we are? I don't think so," Kelly said.

"We'll just tell him we picked up the chickens and ducks, had some pie, got a late start on school work and that's why the chores aren't done." They stepped out of the woods a few yards away from the dam and stopped, gazing across the water at the house.

"It all looks different now, doesn't it?" Kelly asked, leaning her head on her mother's shoulder.

"It does. It's been an odd, strange, sad, and frightening

twenty four hours."

"It sure has been," Kelly agreed.

"Let's hurry up and see what we can get done before Richard gets home."

They hurried across the dam, chaining the dogs, and headed toward the back door. Rounding the corner they found Silly lying in front of the gate. He got to his feet when he saw them, baring his teeth.

"The idiot can get out, but he can't get himself back in," Kelly said, laughing.

"I'll put him up." She handed the backpack and leashes to Kelly. "Go put this stuff away."

Silly went through the gate easily and Abbey turned back to the house, stopping to stare at the water, feeling unnerved by the thick forest on the far shore. She stepped into the house, stripped out of the flannel and boots and put away the compass. She was standing at the counter, staring at the list when Kelly appeared at her side, having changed into her usual attire of sandals and shorts. "I've decided not to go to church tonight."

"What about Brandon?" Abbey asked.

"If he wants to talk to me, he can call me." She stepped over to the refrigerator and opened the door, peering inside. "I'm starving."

"Get a little something now, but since you're not going to church tonight I'll cook us a nice dinner. I'm hungry, too." Usually it was just soup and sandwiches on Wednesday evenings before Richard and Kelly rushed off to church.

Kelly pulled off the top of a container of yogurt and grabbed a spoon from the drawer. "Mom, maybe I shouldn't go to the beach tomorrow."

"Don't be silly, go to the beach. Have some fun. You need it and you deserve it."

"I think if I go I'm going to worry about you," she said, hopping up to sit on the counter.

"Kelly, go to the beach. I'll be fine." Abbey opened the freezer, studying her options. She finally pulled out a package of steaks and set them in the microwave to defrost.

"Mom, don't you think it's strange that a bunch of animals died here last night, you asked for a sign, and today you were shown what could be a sacrificial altar?"

Abbey looked at her daughter and laughed. "Well, when you put it that way, I do."

"It's not funny, Mom," Kelly stated firmly.

"I know it's not funny, but both of us have had a shock in the last twenty-four hours, neither one of us is in the position to make any major decisions right now. We haven't even had time to make sense of what we saw or what the Jacksons told us. We don't know how those children in the cemetery died, it could have been disease striking one after the other, we just don't know. And above all else we don't know that it has anything to do with us, it happened well over a hundred years ago. The circle or the Starnes house isn't even on our land."

"But the Dawsons did live on this land. Mrs. Dawson died right out front in the lake and that was just over 60 years ago."

"We don't know what happened there, Mrs. Jackson said she didn't take to country life, maybe she just killed herself."

"And her husband conveniently had a heart attack and two of their kids simply vanished, all in the same night?"

The buzzer on the microwave sounded and they both jumped. Abbey sighed. "Kelly, what do you want me to do?"

"We could leave," Kelly said softly, looking at the floor.

"We can't just leave, we have a barn yard full of animals and we have responsibilities. Go to the beach, get some sun, eat some seafood, flirt with boys, and go be a kid for just a few days. We'll look at it again when you get home." Abbey grabbed a glass bowl, poured the left over coffee into it, added some balsamic vinegar and then placed the steaks in the liquid. She set the bowl back in the microwave.

Kelly jumped down from the counter. "Okay, I'll go, but I'll be checking in." She threw the yogurt container in the trash and picked up the list.

"Good, check in and when you do, I want to hear that you're having fun and not worrying."

"We'll see." Kelly sat down at the table with a marker and the list. "A lot of this stuff he won't check." She marked a couple items, indicating the chore had been done. "I'll go vacuum."

"Thanks honey. I'll get the laundry started." Abbey watched her daughter walk away, a sad smile on her face. She stepped into the laundry room, started the washer, and began sorting clothes. She pulled out the shirt Kelly had been wearing the night before, the front stained with Max's blood and dirt. She reached for the stain remover, but stopped just short of the cabinet door and looked at the shirt again. She tossed it in the trash, neither one of them needed any reminders of Max's death.

Chapter Six

Dinner was ready and the table was set when the dogs announced that Richard was home. Abbey was just putting the food in serving dishes and setting them on the table when Richard stepped through the door. "It's church night, why did you cook all this food?" he asked, kissing her on the cheek.

"Well, Kelly's off to the beach tomorrow. I thought we'd have a nice dinner, besides she's not going to church tonight." Abbey pulled the rolls from the oven and began buttering them.

"Why not?" He poured a glass of wine.

"She's got to finish her school work and pack for her trip."

"She's had all day to do that." He loosened his tie.

"We got a late start because the missing ducks and chickens turned up in the Jackson's yard. We had to go get them. Why don't you sit down, we'll have dinner."

"Let me go change." He set his wine glass on the table and went to the bedroom.

Abbey put the rolls on the table and then tapped on Kelly's door. "Dinner's ready."

"Okay," Kelly called out.

They met Richard in the kitchen, his suit replaced by khakis and a nice sport shirt. They sat at the table and he recited the Lord's Prayer. "How did you get the birds home from the Jackson's?" he asked, passing a bowl of peas to Kelly.

"Mr. Jackson gave us a cage for them and gave us a ride home," Abbey said, passing a bowl of potatoes.

"You got in a car with that old man? He must be a hundred years old, he could have killed both of you." He looked at his wife and shook his head. "I can't believe he still has a driver's license."

"He drove fine and he gets around pretty good, have you

seen their gardens? He still gets out there and works in them." Abbey took a bite of steak.

"I'm pretty sure that strawberry pie she gave us was worth dying over," Kelly joked.

"So you went in the house and visited with them?" he asked, his eyebrows disappearing under the fall of hair on his forehead.

"Yes. We were pretty thirsty after chasing down the chickens." Abbey chuckled, remembering the way Mr. Jackson had laughed at them.

"Yep!" Kelly giggled. "Chickens sure is fast."

"I don't want you in that house! Do you know how old that house is? It's a lucky thing you didn't fall through the floor," he said firmly, looking back and forth between them.

"Seemed fine to me," Abbey said.

"Yeah, me too. Smelled good in there too, like old wood and strawberries," Kelly added.

"I bet it did, with a dash of mold and God knows what else. You know everybody thinks those old, superstitious coots are crazy. Always telling outrageous stories about the woods."

Abbey kept her eyes on her plate, as Kelly asked, "What

kind of stories?"

"Oh, it seems one of their relatives got killed by a wild animal in the woods about a hundred years ago and ever since they've been passing around rumors of witches and demons in the forest. Craziest stuff I've ever heard. The sheriff came out and told them it was a wild animal, he figured a bear or a bobcat got the kid, but they refused to believe him. They thought it was a racial thing because the sheriff was white. My parents used to talk about them, said they were dangerous in their ignorance."

"Well, they didn't tell us any of those stories, we just talked about gardening and chickens," Abbey said, taking a bite of a roll and choking it down with some water.

"Well, I don't want you two to become all chummy with them, we have a reputation to maintain. I mean, giving them eggs every week is one thing, that's charity, but we're not going to invite them to the house or anything." He pushed back his plate and picked up his glass of wine, changing the subject. "What's this about you not going to church tonight?" he asked Kelly.

"Daddy's coming to get me in the morning, I've got a lot of stuff to do."

"Well, you two are the strangest supposed Christians I've ever met. You," he nodded at Abbey, "never go to church. And this one," he motioned with his wine glass toward Kelly, "comes and goes as she pleases."

"She's got to get ready to go out of town," Abbey said, standing and beginning to clear the table. "Besides, it's kind of funny to have an atheist chastise us about church."

"Church is good for business," he said, laughing. "Once those people figure out there is no invisible man in the sky helping them solve their problems, they come to me."

Kelly rolled her eyes. "Can I be excused?"

"Sure, go finish your school work," Abbey said.

"You should make her help you with this mess," Richard said, rising from the table.

"She usually does, but she has stuff to do."

"Well, I've got to go. I'll see you in a couple hours."

"Okay, be safe," she said absently, putting leftovers in plastic bowls.

He stepped to the back door and opened it. "Abbey, the goat's out."

"What else is new?" she muttered under her breath, following him outside.

As the goat pushed her toward the gate, Richard drove away. She opened the entrance to the enclosure and pushed Silly through with her foot. "I almost went a whole day without smelling like your nasty ass," she said, shutting the gate. Silly looked at her and then investigating his underside, he urinated on his face. She sighed and went to finish cleaning the kitchen.

She fed the Shepherd/retriever mixes and stared at the water while they ate. She could barely wrap her mind around all she had heard that day, but she could imagine Mrs. Dawson floating dead in the lake. She heard the distinctive call of a kingfisher and watched the bird dart across the top of the water, catching small fish. She stood there until the dogs finished their meal and then returned to the house to complete some of the chores left unmarked on the list.

She kept herself busy until she saw the chickens and ducks gathering by the barn and stepped outside to feed them. While they ate, she stared across the lake, trying to put the day's events into order. When they were done, she shooed all of the animals into the barn and locked it. Making sure the gate was latched; she walked over to Tom and Jerry, their tails wagging in unison, and let them off their chains. They ran around the house, sniffing and lifting their legs in various places, and she went back to finish the laundry.

She knocked on Kelly's door with an armload of folded clothes.

"Come in," Kelly answered.

Abbey stepped in to find an open suitcase on the bed and Kelly sitting at her desk staring at a picture on the screen of her laptop. "What on earth is that?" she asked, setting the stack of clothes on the bed.

"It's a picture from about 50 years ago of a satanic ritual," Kelly said, turning the computer so she could get a better look.

"Good God! Why are you looking at that? You're going to give yourself nightmares." Abbey stepped closer to the desk and looked at the picture. It showed a group of people lit by candlelight, wearing dark robes and standing around a wooden altar. She couldn't make out what was on the altar in the grainy black and white photo.

"What was that you said about being forewarned and forearmed? Check this out." Kelly clicked the mouse and a new picture appeared.

The next picture was more modern and in color. It showed a large group of people in dark robes lit by torches and standing along the edge of a lake. On the water was a small boat with a robed figure, while another figure dressed in white was tied in ropes and stretched out across the bow. Long, light colored hair trailed on the water. "Damn," Abbey whispered.

"Yeah, that's what I'm saying. Look." She clicked the mouse again.

The next photo was part of the earlier scene, but shot from the crowd on the edge of the lake. The figure in white, which she assumed to be a woman, was lying on top of what looked to be a rock altar and a group of people in robes stood in a circle surrounding the victim. Some wore black robes, others red, and one was in white, the hoods obscuring their faces. In the background a fire burned at the base of a huge owl. "What the crap?" Abbey whispered.

"I know, you wouldn't think this kind of stuff still happened. It's archaic." Kelly grinned, displaying that she had used a vocabulary word. "Look." She clicked again.

The next shot was a panorama of the crowd while they focused on the victim. Most in the first rows wore similar robes as those under the giant owl, but as Abbey scanned the photo she saw men in the rear wearing suits and women wearing evening gowns. "Weird."

"I know. It could be photoshopped, but on the other hand it could also be real," Kelly said, clicking the mouse again

The next photo was much older, in black and white and very grainy. It showed a group of nude men and women standing around an obviously dead woman on a rock altar. "Jesus, Kelly, stop! That's hideous! Sick!" Her stomach churned and she had to take a couple deep breaths to settle it.

"I know, Mom. And it could be right outside our front door." Kelly closed the browser and turned to face her mother. "There's a lot of info out there, far too much to go through in a night. I don't think whoever goes to that circle are witches, from what I see right now modern day witches are more nature freaks like Grandma than anything evil. I think whoever killed Calvin on that rock was a Satanist or a group of them."

"Can't you just be a kid?" Abbey asked.

"Mom, this is serious."

Abbey sat on the bed. "I know it's serious, but how are you going to sleep after looking at all that? You're going to give yourself nightmares."

"Well, I had nightmares last night, Mom, before seeing this stuff or knowing anything about it. I can't look at a satanic altar in the woods and not think about it and it's not fair of you to expect me to."

"I don't know what to say." Abbey sighed. "It's been a rough day, I'm exhausted and I know you are too. I won't stop you from researching and I don't want you to cut me out of what you're learning. I just," she shook her head, "damn…. you're just a kid, you shouldn't be looking at stuff like that."

"Mom," Kelly said, getting up from the chair and sitting on the bed beside her mother. "I haven't been a kid since I almost died on the side of the road. You can't come out of something like that and still be a kid. Especially when you have a great mom pushing you along." She smiled. "You know I have to do this, just like I knew you had to step into that nasty feeling circle today."

"Okay." Abbey wrapped her arm around Kelly's shoulders

and squeezed her tight. "Just watch some cartoons or something before you go to bed, okay?"

Kelly laughed. "I will, Mom, I promise."

"Why don't I feel better?" Abbey asked.

"Because you're a bright bunny." Kelly winked, returning to the laptop.

Abbey left Kelly at the computer and stood in the living room for a moment, feeling lost. She stepped out onto the front porch and stared at the water, the moonlight reflecting on the surface. "I've got my daughter researching Satanism and my atheist husband is in church," she muttered. "I guess all is well with the universe, huh, God?"

Tom and Jerry ran up onto the porch, damp from the lake, and rubbed against her legs. She sat on the stairs and wrapped her arms around their necks, pulling them close. "You boys need to stay alert," she whispered, imagining how Richard would view her conversation with the animals. "You guys need to stay on your toes, we may need you." Their tails wagged, leaving wet spots on the wood. "By the way, I forgive you for hurting Max." She hugged them again, her t-shirt now beyond repair.

The phone rang and she left the dogs, running to catch it before the answering machine picked up. "Hello?"

"Can I speak to Kelly?" a young male voice asked.

"Sure, hold on." She tapped on Kelly's door and opened it, handing her the phone. "I think it's Brandon," she whispered. "I'm going to take a shower."

Kelly nodded, taking the phone.

Abbey went to the master bath and had just stripped off her clothes when she heard Richard's car. She slipped on a robe and met him at the door.

"Why didn't you tell me Kelly had a date?" he demanded as he stepped into the house.

"What?" she asked, searching her mind.

"Kelly… had a date…. with Brandon," he clarified slowly.

"Oh." She shook her head in an attempt to clear the exhaustion. "Fay invited Kelly over Friday for pizza and a movie. It wasn't a date, it was a family thing, and she's not going, she's going to the beach with her father."

"Why didn't you tell me?" he asked and opened the refrigerator, pulling out a bottle of wine and pouring a glass.

"Because it wasn't a big deal."

"Our daughter dating is a big deal!" he insisted and began pacing.

She took a deep breath and expelled it slowly. "One, it wasn't a date and two, she's not our daughter. She is my and Jack's daughter and when it comes to dating, I will have this conversation with him."

"I just bought four hundred bucks worth of clothes for her." He drank down the glass and poured another.

"No. Her father's child support just bought four hundred dollars worth of clothes." She didn't understand why he was so upset; it was pizza and a movie.

"I don't want her dating that boy," he stressed, pacing.

"Brandon? He's harmless and he's just a kid. He's almost a year younger than her."

"His father is a truck driver."

"So? They're good people." She leaned against the counter, watching him go back and forth.

"A truck driver," he repeated.

"Quit being a snob." She turned and picked up the bottle,

pouring her own glass of wine and thought, will this day ever end?

He turned in his pacing and stared at her. "If I was a snob, I wouldn't have married you."

"Well, there it is, huh?" She sat at the table. "You're not a snob because you married an uneducated, single mother from an unknown family, is that it?"

"What? You want me to encourage her along your path so that she's knocked up and married at seventeen?"

"That wouldn't happen to Kelly, she's too mature and smart. And what if it did? Is she ruined then?"

He ran his hand through his hair, which looked as though it had seen his hand many times in the last hours. "I don't want her dating that boy."

"We are not the ones who will decide who she dates or who she doesn't, she will."

"We're just going to leave decisions like that to a child?" he asked, looking perplexed.

"Of course," Abbey stated, a little perplexed as well. "Did your parents choose who you dated?"

"They made sure I dated within a certain set, an approved

set. It wasn't like I dated the maid's daughter."

"Well, I guess they're turning over in their graves right now, somehow I don't think I would have merited their approval."

"Probably not," he agreed.

"So why did you marry me?" She looked at him as though she could wring the truth from his eyes, like she wrung water from a wet towel.

Kelly stepped out from the hall, slowing when she saw them, and then stepped into the kitchen. "What's going on?" she asked, placing the phone on its base.

"I heard you made a date with Brandon." Richard faced her across the room.

"It wasn't a date," Kelly said, putting her hands on her hips.

"That's not what I heard at church tonight, I heard the two of you had some plans." He made quotation marks in the air.

"What are you saying?" Kelly snapped.

"Yes, Richard, what are you saying?" Abbey got to her feet and stepped between the two of them, facing Richard.

"Kids talk, Kelly," he sneered, looking over Abbey's head at Kelly.

"Yeah, a bunch of backwoods kids in the middle of nowhere Georgia talk because a boy's mother invited me to their house and you believed them? What is it that you do for a living? A psychiatrist?" She laughed harshly. "If you don't know how ridiculous this is, then I'm not going to explain it to you. I'm going to bed. Good night, Mom." She turned toward her room and stopped, turning back. "By the way, I still haven't forgiven you for killing Max." She then went to her room and shut the door softly.

"And as usual, you're going to let her talk to me that way," Richard said, setting his empty wine glass on the counter.

"Just what were you accusing her of and what were these kids saying? And how in the hell do these kids know anything about her or her plans? Who are these kids?" Abbey felt her temper slipping out of control.

"Kids from church," he said, as though he had answered the questions.

"Said…" she prompted.

"Said she was going to do it with Brandon."

She stared at him with wide eyes for a moment, wanting to pinch her skin to see if she was dreaming, but decided it may look odd. Then she laughed … I'm worried about looking odd? Then she laughed harder. And then she laughed so hard that tears began streaming down her cheeks.

Richard grabbed her arm. "You're hysterical," he said and tried to push her down into a chair.

She stopped laughing and snatched her arm out of his grip. "I'm not hysterical!" She took a deep breath, leaning against the counter and wishing for a cigarette. "A bunch of bored kids say that Brandon and Kelly are going to do it and you believe it. You believe it enough to come home and accuse your stepdaughter as though she had already done it. I find that funny and it's a good thing I find it funny, because if I didn't find it funny, you and I would be having a hell of a fight right now."

"Well, how do you know she isn't doing it? That she hasn't done it?" Richard demanded.

"I know because I trust my daughter. She's a good girl with a good head on her shoulders. But guess what? One day she's going to date and one day, she's going to have sex and you and I are not going to be part of the decision making process. Now, I'm not going to discuss this anymore. I'm going to take a shower." She left him standing in the kitchen.

She stood under the shower spray until the water turned cool. She stepped out, dried off, combed out her long hair, and slid into a t-shirt and soft sweat pants. She opened the door, holding her breath and praying that Richard was in bed and asleep; he didn't like it when she had the final say in an argument. Luckily, he was in bed and snoring softly. She tiptoed across the room and stepped out, shutting the door softly behind her. She saw the light still on in Kelly's room and tapped on the door.

"Come in," Kelly called out.

Abbey stepped into the room. "I'm sorry about that."

"He's an idiot," she said, still sitting at the desk.

Abbey sighed and sat on the bed, glancing into the suitcase to see it almost full. "Was that Brandon on the phone?"

"Yes, he called to warn me that Richard heard some kids teasing him about me and that he seemed to be upset. Mom, why would Richard believe a bunch of gossipy kids?"

"I don't know. I just wanted to make sure you were okay."

"I'm fine. Although that was pretty ridiculous, I've got other things on my mind right now." She nodded her head toward the laptop, turning it so Abbey could see what was displayed.

Abbey stood up, kissed her daughter on the top of her head, and looked at the website displayed on the computer screen. She saw the album cover of a popular rock band, a growling demon sneered back at her and at his feet was a bound woman in white. Kelly reached for the mouse and scrolled down the page, each album cover shown had a similar dark theme and each had a terrified woman in white. "Not very original, are they?" Abbey asked.

"No, that's what's weird. Basically it's the same image, changed a little here or there, but every CD is from a different band and there must be thirty of them on just this page. Thirty bands selling satanic rituals and if I found thirty so quickly, there must be hundreds or even thousands of them out there." Kelly clicked on a different tab and more band art was displayed. "These guys had a number one hit back when I was in school, all the kids loved it, and it seemed like I heard it everywhere I went for months. This is the cover of that CD."

The cover art was a photograph of a heavily made-up blonde woman with dark red lipstick. She wore a long white gown, torn in places to reveal her thighs and the underside of one breast. She was bound in chains and had a look of terror on her face. Behind her stood a shirtless, well muscled man wearing leather pants and a fitted demon mask, complete with small horns. He leaned into her suggestively, one hand gripping her hair, while the other held a whip. Abbey recognized the name of the band and vaguely remembered the song. "Who knew this is what they were selling? It's blatantly sexual and demonic."

"I suspect if some of the parents knew their children were singing along to these lyrics they'd be a little upset." Kelly clicked another tab, the website analyzed the lyrics of popular bands. "It's everywhere, Mom, but people just don't seem to see it or they don't care. All I know is the Jacksons aren't crazy."

"I didn't think they were either, honey. It's been a long day, try to get some sleep." Abbey picked up the remote control and turned on the small television on the shelf across the room. She muted the sound and clicked until she found a twenty-four hour cartoon channel. "Watch some cartoons."

Kelly laughed. "I'm almost done. I'll see you in the morning."

Abbey stepped out of the room and went to the backdoor. She slid her bare feet into a pair of brightly colored rubber clogs, a gift from her mother, and slipped out into the night. The nearing full moon high in the sky provided plenty of light as she walked across the yard to the shed. She grabbed the shrinking pack of cigarettes, and pulled one free, lighting it. She wandered over to the porch and sat on the bottom step, suddenly unconcerned that Richard may catch her smoking. The dogs came out of the pine forest, their noses pressed against the ground following a scent. They stopped and raised their heads when they saw her, their ears alert.

"It's just me, boys," she whispered and they ran to her. "Don't get me all stinky." She laughed softly as they brushed up against her. She rubbed one behind the ears and then the other. They lay down at her feet. She finished smoking the cigarette and hid the butt under one of the rocks surrounding her rose garden. "You guys keep your eyes open, okay?"

She crept back into the house and tiptoed across the bedroom, locking herself in the bathroom. She washed the dog scent from her hands, brushed her teeth and opened the medicine cabinet, staring at the bottle of prescription sleeping pills. "To dream or not to dream, that is the question," she whispered and shut the cabinet, leaving the bottle untouched.

Chapter Seven

She was dreaming. In the dream she was aware it was a dream and once again she was an invisible observer watching Richard. He sat up in bed slowly and glanced at her curled up on her side. She thought how odd it was to see herself sleeping in her own dream. He slid out of bed quietly, tiptoed to the door and slipped out. He stood for a moment, listening, and then he moved across the living room and down the hall to Kelly's bedroom door. He placed his hand on the knob and pressed his ear against the wood.

He opened the door a couple inches, saw Kelly asleep in bed

and opened it wider. He glanced around the room, taking in the suitcase sitting closed and upright by the foot of the bed, the laptop closed on the desk, and then he glanced at the muted television as Bugs Bunny danced in a dress. His eyes fell on Kelly and before he shut the door, he watched her for several minutes.

Abbey awoke on a gasp and when she discovered she was alone, her heart began pounding. She noticed the light was on in the bathroom and pretended to sleep. Richard stepped out of the bathroom, but instead of climbing back in the bed he tiptoed to the door and glanced at her. He put his hand on the doorknob and turned it slowly, ensuring that it opened quietly.

"Where are you going?" she asked sleepily.

He jumped. "I'm thirsty, I'm going to get some orange juice."

"Hmmm. That sounds good," she said, throwing back the covers. "I think I'll join you." She followed him into the kitchen and poured two glasses of juice.

"Did you forget your sleeping pill again?" he asked.

"No. I took it," she lied.

"Maybe we need to increase the dosage." He set the half full glass of juice on the counter. "I'm going back to bed."

"I'll be there in a minute."

He disappeared around the corner and she heard the door click shut.

Abbey rinsed the glasses and set them in the dishwasher. She went to Kelly's door and quietly opened it. Kelly lay in the same position as she had in the dream. Abbey glanced around the room, saw the suitcase in the same position at the foot of the bed, the laptop closed on the desk, and she looked up at the muted TV to see Bugs Bunny dancing in a dress.

She closed the door and her eyes fell on the framed photo on the wall, in it the three of them smiled at the camera from a beach in Hawaii. The photo had been taken on their honeymoon. Richard had reserved a suit of rooms, with a huge balcony overlooking the ocean, and Kelly had come along for the trip. It seemed like a lifetime ago, before the accident, before moving out into the middle of rural Georgia, and before she knew people held strange rituals in the woods outside her front door.

She went back to bed, sleeping in increments of fifteen minutes, and having restless dreams of helpless bound women surrounded by dark robed figures with ill intent. She was awake when Richard's alarm beeped. He turned it off and went to the shower. She lay awake, feigning sleep, as he dressed for work and then he kissed her lightly on the cheek before stepping out of the bedroom. She sat up in bed listening for his movements and settled back against the pillows when she heard his car pull out of the driveway, glancing at the clock. Why was he leaving for work so early?

She fell back asleep and slept, dream-free, for a couple more hours and woke feeling better than she had expected. She made the bed, dressed, and stepped outside. She called the dogs several times before they appeared from the woods on the far side of the lake. They ran across the dam and she met them at the doghouse. "See anything interesting out there?" She rubbed their bellies for a moment before attaching the chains.

She went to the barn, let the animals out, gathered the eggs, and returned to the kitchen to find Kelly pushing the button on the coffee pot. "How'd you sleep?" she asked, placing the basket of eggs on the counter to be washed later.

"Weird dreams," she answered, walking to the table with a

limp.

"Yeah, me too. Is your leg hurt?" Abbey pulled a carton of eggs and the butter dish from the fridge.

"It's just sore, running through the woods works different muscles than walking a treadmill, I guess." She sat down.

"What did you dream?" Abbey asked, placing an iron frying pan on the stove eye.

"Well, some were just of those pictures I saw, but we knew that would happen." She laughed. "I know, you warned me. The others, though, were weird. I was being watched and I knew I was being watched, but I couldn't see who was watching me. Weird, huh?"

Abbey placed two pieces of bread in the toaster. I dreamt of her being watched too, she thought, dropping some butter into the warming pan.

"And something about the dogs," Kelly said, as Abbey cracked two eggs on the side of the frying pan and dropped the contents into sizzling butter.

"What about the dogs?" Abbey asked, adding a little salt and pepper.

"I don't know, just something about the dogs. It was really weird because in the dream I reminded myself to remember about the dogs, but I can't remember what I reminded myself. Just something about the dogs." She stretched out her leg, rotating her foot.

"Are you sure your leg is okay?" Abbey asked, buttering the toast.

"Yeah, I'm sure. I'm just feeling muscles in there I haven't felt in a couple years, I think that's a good thing." She patted her leg. "Stuff's waking up."

Abbey slid the eggs into plates and poured some juice. "We should probably get a little school work done this morning." She set the glasses on the table.

"Mom, can we take the day off? I'll make it up next week, I promise, but my head is kind of full right now, digesting or something." She tilted her head and pouted her lips.

Abbey picked up the plates and glanced through the window into the pen. It's been a rough week, she thought, setting the plates on the table. "Okay, lets take it easy."

"Thanks, Mom. And look! Pretty! Sunny side up for a

better day." She grinned and held up her juice glass for a toast.

Abbey lifted her glass, clicking it against Kelly's. "I love you, honey."

"I love you too, Mom."

After breakfast, Abbey cleaned the barn and Kelly showered. When they were together again, they made small talk and didn't discuss the underlying fear they both felt. They talked about previous trips to the beach, laughing over silly memories. They talked about Grandma and her strange eccentricities. They talked about everything they could fill the empty air with except the woods, the altar, and the strange stories the Jacksons had shared with them.

Soon the dogs' barking let them know that Jack had arrived. "You packed everything, right? Toothbrush, underwear?"

Kelly laughed. "Yeah, I got everything."

"Aspirin?" Abbey asked, watching her limp to her bedroom.

"Got it," she called from the hall.

Abbey opened the back door. "Y'all come in, use the bathroom and get a drink."

"Thanks, I could use the bathroom," Holly said, helping a

little girl in dark ponytails out of the car. "Look! It's Aunt Abbey."

"Hey, little bit," Abbey said, walking down the stairs and picking up the chubby toddler.

"All she's been talking about is Kelly, she's so excited she's coming." Holly hugged her.

"I'm glad she's getting away, she needs it," Abbey confided, hugging Holly back with the child squished between their bodies.

"You got some ice tea?" Jack asked.

"Sure do. Come on in," Abbey said, turning and carrying the toddler into the house.

"Come on, Jason," Jack said, pulling his son off the fence.

"I want to see the goats!" Jason yelled and then giggled as Jack threw him over his shoulder, fireman style.

Holly went to the bathroom and Abbey set the toddler, Roseanne, on her feet in the kitchen. "How have you been, little bit?"

"Where's Kelly?" the toddler asked.

"In her room. You remember where, right?"

The toddler nodded, ran across the living room and down the hall.

Jack stepped in the house and set Jason down, mussing his hair. "The yard looks great, Abbey, you've done an incredible job."

"Where's Kelly?" Jason asked.

"In her room. You know where." The little boy ran across the living room, disappearing down the hall.

"Wow. He's getting big," she said. "Glass or to-go cup?" She held up one of each.

"To-go would be great," he said, walking into the living room and looking through the picture window. "It is a great view you have here."

"Yeah, it's nice," she said, putting ice into the large plastic cup and then filling it with tea, as Holly stepped back into the kitchen.

"They say your bladder snaps back into shape after having a baby, I'm still waiting for it to happen." Holly laughed, leaning against the counter.

Abbey smiled and asked, "You want a drink?"

"God, no! We'll never make it to the beach. You said Kelly needed this trip, did something happen?"

"Yeah, her duck, Max, got killed this week," she said,

putting the tea away.

"What happened to him?" Jack asked, picking up the cup and draining half of the tea.

Abbey pulled the pitcher back out of the fridge and handed it too him. "Richard forgot to shut the barn, the dogs got him."

"He forgot? How do you forget something like that?" He refilled the cup and handed back the pitcher.

Abbey sighed and put the pitcher back in the refrigerator. "I don't know, but Kelly was pissed off, I've never seen her so mad." She glanced into the living room to make sure the kids couldn't hear. "She was heartbroken, too. I hated seeing her like that, it's so hard to lose a pet."

"I hope you gave him hell," Jack said, setting his cup on the counter.

Before she could answer Roseanne came running through the living room with Kelly's purse, followed by Jason rolling a red suitcase. Kelly then appeared, masking the limp as best as she could, with her computer bag slung over her shoulder. "I've got everything." She smiled. "Hey Daddy!" She threw her arms around his neck.

"Hey, bunny! I think you grew." He held her tightly for a moment.

"More like I outgrew. Mom had to buy me a couple new bathing suits, last year's were obscene." She laughed.

"Did you hurt your leg?" Jack asked.

"No, it's sore from chasing that idiot goat through the woods," Kelly said, turning to her stepmother and hugging her. "Hey, Holly."

"Sorry about Max," Holly said, patting her back.

"Yeah, me too. Are we ready?" Kelly asked, pulling away, her eyes bright with unshed tears at the mention of Max.

"Yeah, but I want to talk to your mom for a minute." Jack picked up the suitcase and opened the backdoor. "Holly, will you grab my tea?"

"Come on guys, let's go," Holly said, picking up Roseanne and the cup of tea.

Abbey followed Jack as he set Kelly's suitcase in the back of the SUV. "Let's walk."

She fell into pace beside him as he headed toward the lake. "Is everything okay?" he asked.

"Things are fine," she assured him.

"You know you've never been a good liar. Remember, I've known you since you were Kelly's age."

She smiled. "It's a little rough right now, but you know how it goes, highs and lows and all that."

They stopped beside the water and watched the ducks for a moment. "Well, I hope that's all it is, because you don't look so good and Kelly seems nervous and sad."

"Sometimes she's too grown up." She sighed. "Go make her be a kid for a few days."

"Do you need me to kick Richard's ass? Is that it? You know I'd do it, that rich boy was never taken behind the woodshed." He laughed, elbowing her in the side.

"No, but thanks," she said, laughing. "It's just a rough spot, we'll work it out."

"Well, you know we've got your back, Abbey, both me and Holly."

"I know, Jack. Thanks." They turned, heading back to the car. Holly pulled Jason off the fence, as Kelly finished clipping Roseanne into her car seat. Kelly walked over to her parents and

Jack looked at each of them for a moment, trying to discern the secret they were holding. Finally, he gave up, shaking his head and turned to the vehicle. "Okay folks, the countdown is on."

"Bye, Abbey!" Holly waved, finally settling Jason, and walked around to the passenger side.

"Bye, y'all have a good time," Abbey said.

Kelly pulled Abbey over toward the fence. "I want you to be careful Mom. I'm going to be checking in so keep the computer on and check your email, okay?" Her eyes were earnest and worried.

"I will, baby. Don't worry about me and go have some fun, okay?" Abbey reached into the pocket of her jeans, handing Kelly a small roll of twenties. "Go buy yourself something shiny and useless."

"Thanks. Please be careful Mom." Kelly hugged her hard.

Abbey hugged her back just as firmly. "I'll be careful, if you have fun, deal?"

"Deal," Kelly said and Abbey walked her to the waiting SUV. Kelly crawled into the rear seat and gave a big grin.

"We should have her back after lunch on Sunday," Jack said,

leaning out of the window.

Abbey nodded.

"You've got our cell phone number, right?"

"Yeah, I got it. Y'all be safe, okay?"

Jack gave a wave and pulled away, as the children continued waving. Abbey waved back and watched them disappear down the pine-lined driveway, wiping a tear from her cheek. She listened to the motor of the SUV ebb as it got further away and felt lost. She looked into the pen; the goats were on the far side eating off low branches. The ducks were on the lake, the chickens were pecking through the field, and the dogs lay asleep inside their doghouse. She sighed.

I'll just stay busy, she thought, stepping into the house and looking at the list of chores. She completed everything on the list and a few things that weren't and wandered outside. She pulled the tarp off the riding mower and cut the grass. Returning the mower to the shed, she grabbed a pitcher of grass seed and sprinkled it on the bare spots. She turned on the sprinkler system and sat on the stairs of the front porch watching the water while she smoked a cigarette.

Her thoughts were jumbled and she had difficulty separating

her disturbed thoughts concerning the dead chickens and duck, from her fear of the strange altar across the lake - they seemed one in the same. Perhaps it's just because it all happened within a short period of time, she thought, perhaps I just haven't had the time to separate the two things in my mind. She snubbed out the butt, threw it in the barrel and dodging the sprinkler, she ran to the shed and grabbed the string trimmer.

As she headed to the edge of the water she noticed the dogs had come out of their shelter and were staring across the lake. She glanced into the woods across the way and seeing nothing, she cranked the noisy machine. She moved the trimmer back and forth, occasionally popping the water with the string and sending ripples across the surface. Suddenly, she stopped and looked across the lake, she felt someone watching her. She turned and looked at the dogs, their eyes searched the tree line, their ears twitching like small radar dishes.

It's my imagination, she thought and resumed trimming the grass along the edge of the lake. The last two days have been enough to make anyone nervous, she tried to convince herself, but her eyes strayed back to the dogs. "Is it the dogs' imaginations too?" she asked softly under her breath and cut the engine of the machine.

She didn't run, but she walked quickly to the back of the house, left the trimmer on the porch, and stepped inside, locking the door behind her. She grabbed the binoculars off a hook in the laundry room and went to the living room window. She held the binoculars up to her eyes, adjusting the sight and scanned the tree line. She saw nothing out of sorts and scanned it again, slower. Still nothing, she pulled the eyepiece away from her face and looked at the dogs, they were still in an alert mode, on their feet and staring across the lake.

She raised the field glasses again and tried to concentrate on the whole picture, not just the tree line. She scanned the edge of the water and saw half a dozen turtles sunning themselves on a partially submerged log, their feet stretched out behind them, their heads turned up to the sun. Suddenly they scattered, propelling themselves into the water and vanishing under the surface. And then the dogs started barking.

She pulled the glasses down and saw Tom and Jerry facing the same direction as the startled turtles and she lifted the glasses again concentrating on the area behind the submerged log. As she watched, she saw a small sweet gum tree snap back and spring forward as though something large had just passed it, nudging it. Something large and something she couldn't see. "What in the hell?" she muttered. "That wasn't the wind, someone or something is over there." Her heart began pounding hard against her the wall of her chest and the dogs continued to bark, but she could discern no more movement.

She studied the small tree through the eyepiece, bright green in the shadows of larger trees, and then tried to see into the thick vegetation behind it. Seeing nothing, the field glasses range unable to cut into the unruly growth, she scanned the line again, back and forth, and still she saw nothing. The dogs eased their barking and sat down, but still faced the same direction. She lifted the binoculars again, searching the far side of the lake and the dogs quieted, laying down and resting their heads on their paws.

Whatever it was, it's gone, she thought, turning away from the window. Something had been watching me, she insisted, slowly returning to the laundry room and hanging the binoculars back on the hook. Would I feel the eyes of a wild animal on me or was it human? I've heard of bears stalking people, I imagine those people felt watched, I suppose it could have been a bear, she thought. Her heart began to slow its heavy beat and she laughed. "I'm more scared of being stalked by a human than a bear. You are a strange woman, Abigail Brown."

She stepped into the kitchen to see the answering machine light flashing and pressed the button. It was Richard calling to explain that he was having dinner with his partner, Mike Almond, but didn't expect to be very late. Abbey stared at the machine for a moment, glanced at the clock and spoke to the empty house, "I think he's cheating on me." She waited for the pain to hit, for the fear, indignation, and anxiety to set in and was surprised when she felt nothing. "Wow." She sat down at the kitchen table. She glanced at the clock again and picked up the phone, dialing her mother.

Summer answered the phone breathlessly. "Hey, honey! Let me put these bags down, I just walked in the house."

Abbey heard some fumbling as the listened to the myriad of birds tweet in her mother's house. Summer liked birds, she loved to listen to them sing, so she decided the way to hear them year round was to have bird cages, filled with love birds and parakeets, scattered throughout her home.

"How are you?" Summer asked, returning to the line.

"I'm okay. Are you still coming out tomorrow?"

"I sure am, I'm looking forward to it."

"You said noon, but do you think you could come out earlier?"

"Sure I can. I am going out to a fancy charity ball tonight, I pulled the diamonds out of the vault, they're such pretty rocks." Summer sighed in appreciation. "But I imagine I can have one less glass of wine and wake up early, all bright eyed and bushy tailed."

Abbey laughed. Her mother thought of all stones placed in jewelry, no matter how expensive, as rocks, part of the wonder of the earth and part of God.

"You don't sound like yourself, what going on?" Summer asked, concerned.

"A lot. That's why I wanted you to come earlier, I need to talk, and I need my mom's infinite wisdom," she said, chuckling.

"If you're seeking my wisdom, I really am worried," Summer joked. "But seriously, do you need me to come now?"

"No, Mom. The morning is fine. Kelly's on her way to the

beach, Richard's having dinner with his partner, and I'm going to have a quiet evening. Besides, you got the diamonds out, you have to wear them."

"They are pretty," Summer agreed.

"Okay, so I'll see you in the morning. Remember, we rise early out here on the farm." Abbey looked through the kitchen window and saw Silly dodging the water from the sprinkler on his way to the garden.

"I'll bring the coffee," Summer replied.

"Wonderful. Mom, I've got to go, the goat's out again."

"Okay, I love you."

"I love you, too." She hung up and ran into the backyard, turning off the sprinkler. She glanced across the lake as Silly pushed her across the driveway toward the pen. Something had been over there, she insisted, shoving the goat through the gate with her foot. She latched the pen and checked on the dogs, they were both back in the doghouse, asleep.

She went back in the house, heated a plate of leftovers and sat at the table, the weekend stretching out in front of her - long and empty. She tried to remember the last time she had so much alone time on her hands and decided it was last summer when Kelly had gone to an expensive therapeutic resort in Arizona with Summer for two weeks. Being alone was different then, she kept herself busy with Richard's chore list and planting grass, flowering bushes, and building the rock lined rose bed.

She ate as much as she could, scraped the leftovers in a bowl for the dogs and went to the den, booting up the computer. Just as she opened her home page, a ding announced that she had new mail. It was from Kelly. "Hey Mom, did you know restaurants have free WiFi now? I love free WiFi! How are things?"

Abbey wrote back. "Hey, Girlie. Everything's fine, Silly's only escaped once. It's a good day. Grandma will be here in the morning. Have fun!"

The alert dinged again and Abbey opened the second email from Kelly to see a smiley face, the word "okay" and a heart. She smiled; she had raised a good kid.

Abbey left the computer on, went into the kitchen and mixed the dog food. She carried the food to the dogs, they came out of their shelter stretching, and Abbey kept her eyes peeled across the water. She left them eating, returned to the house and feeling restless, she poured a glass of wine and went to the shed for a cigarette. She walked to the front porch, sat on the stairs and stared across the lake. Something had been over there, she thought, something had been watching me.

She finished the cigarette, fed the animals in the barnyard and locked them in for the night. She walked over to the doghouse and unchained the dogs. Immediately, they ran across the dam to the small sweet gum tree at the far corner of the lake and catching a scent, they followed it into the woods, disappearing from sight. It must have been an animal, she thought, returning to the house, turning on the porch light, and locked the door behind her.

She checked her email again and finding nothing, she showered. Stepping out of the bathroom, she became aware of the night pressing against the windows and she went through the house and shut all the curtains and blinds. She couldn't remember ever having done so before; it wasn't like they had any neighbors who could peer into the uncovered windows. She checked her email again and found a note from Kelly announcing they had arrived at the beach. Abbey wrote a short note back, hit send, and heard Richard's car pull into the driveway.

She met Richard at the door. He was tipsy. "Hey, wife."

He kissed her on the cheek.

"Hey, yourself. How was dinner?"

"Good, Mike and I were talking about taking on another partner and other ways to increase the business." He hung his suit jacket on the back of a kitchen chair and pulled a prescription bag out of the pocket, tossing it to her. "I had your dosage increased."

She caught the bag. "You didn't have to do that."

"Well, you don't seem to be sleeping well on the other ones, sometimes that happens. It's normal to build up a resistance."

Abbey set the unopened bag on the counter. "Thanks."

"No problem. Why are all the curtains shut? It's like a tomb in here."

"I don't know." She took a deep breath. "There was something on the other side of the lake today."

"What do you mean *something?*"

"I didn't see what it was or who it was, I just saw some movement on the other side of the lake and the dogs went crazy barking."

"It was probably a deer." He pulled off his tie and picked up his jacket, walking to the bedroom.

"It could have been, but I don't think the dogs would act that way over a deer," she said, following him.

"There's a lot of woods out there. It could have been any number of wild animals, a bear, a bobcat, deer, squirrels." He laughed. "Or it could have been kids or hunters. Lots of woods out there," he repeated and went into the bathroom to brush his teeth.

"It could have been," she said, sitting on the bed.

He stepped out of the bathroom having changed into pajamas. "Are you afraid a deer is going to peek into the window?" He laughed again and pulled the covers down, adjusting his pillow. "I'm going to bed, I've got another long day ahead of me."

She nodded and stood up.

"Are you coming?" He turned out the lamp on the bedside table.

"Not yet, but I'll be here soon."

"Okay, don't forget to take your pill." He crawled into bed.

"I won't," she said, pulling the door closed. She walked into the kitchen, opened the prescription bag and pulled out a bottle of large white capsules with her name on the label. She dropped the bottle back into the bag and took it into the pantry, hiding it behind some can goods. She returned to the computer, responded to an email from Kelly and leaving it on, she went to bed.

She awoke on a gasp, sitting up and glancing over to see that Richard wasn't in bed. She heard the shower turn off and she lay back down. She'd been dreaming again. It was the same as the others, she was an unseen observer, but this time it was set in Richard's office instead of the house.

She saw Richard step into his office, shut the door, and settle down at his desk. He opened a drawer and pulled out a bag from the pharmacy. He carefully removed the staple and shook the bottle free. Unscrewing the child protective top, he spilled half of the pills onto the leather protector covering his desk and reached into the pocket of his suit jacket, pulling out a small, brown envelope.

He unsealed the envelope and poured the contents, a white powder, on his desk. Then he opened each capsule, dumping the material inside into the trashcan. His partner, Mike, walked into the room and they spoke, but she could not hear their words. Richard grabbed a small tool from his top desk drawer and refilled the capsules. When he was done, he replaced the altered capsules back into the bottle and carefully stapled the bag back together. He swept the unused powder back into the envelope and handed it to Mike. They spoke again, their expressions serious, and Richard shoved the bag into his pocket, turned out his desk light, and they left the office, rich with leather and wood, together.

    Richard opened the bathroom door and she pretended to sleep. He kissed her on the cheek and shut the door softly behind him. When she heard his car pull away, she jumped from the bed and retrieved the bag from the pantry. She carried it to the stove and turned on the light in the exhaust hood, looking at the staple. She had torn it the night before when she opened the bag, but she thought she could see two distinct indentations of staples. She pulled the bottle free, studying it for a moment and then poured the pills down the sink. She turned on the water and hit the switch for the garbage disposal. She threw the bag and the bottle into the trash, hiding it deep under the refuse.

Chapter Eight

Abbey opened the curtains, sent a brief note to Kelly, and had just stepped outside to chain the dogs when she heard her mom's old Subaru pull into the driveway. The dogs came running across the dam to meet the car, their tails wagging.

Summer parked the car beside where Abbey was standing on the driveway and threw open the door with a smile. "Hey, boys! I've got something for you." She stepped out of the car, grinning at her daughter and holding her arms wide.

Abbey stepped into the embrace, enjoying the light and familiar scent of her mother. "Hey, Momma. Good to see you."

"You look pale," Summer said, pulling away and reaching into the car to retrieve two large cups of organic, specialty coffee. "One sugar and cream, right?" She handed Abbey a cup.

"Yep, that's it," Abbey said, taking a sip. "Hmmm."

"It's Costa Rican." Summer smiled, reaching into the back seat and pulling out two of the biggest rawhide bones Abbey had ever seen.

"Good God, Mom! What did you do? Hunt down a dinosaur?" Abbey laughed.

"I know!" Summer grinned. "Aren't they funny?" She handed one of the bones to Tom, who attempted to take it, but dropped it on the ground and started licking it.

"Want to walk with me while I do some chores?" Abbey asked.

"Sure do," Summer said, picking up the oversized bone. "Lead the way."

"Come on, boys," Abbey said and headed to the doghouse.

Summer fell into pace beside her, her eyes taking in all the details. "The place looks great, Abbey, I can't believe how much you've done, it's amazing."

"I stay busy," Abbey stated, picking up a chain. "Come on, Jerry." She patted her hand on her thigh and he ran over, receiving a scratch behind the ears after she attached the chain to his collar.

Summer placed a bone at Jerry's feet, rubbing his head. He fell on his butt and leaned against her thighs, his tail beating the ground. Summer laughed, a happy sound, reminiscent of bird song.

Abbey stopped in the process of grabbing Tom's chain, looking at her mom. She'd missed that sound. "I've missed you, Mom."

Summer stopped rubbing the dog. "Tell me what's wrong."

"I will." Abbey patted her thigh. "Come on, Tom." The dog ran up and Abbey latched him to the chain, giving him a good rub on the shoulders.

Summer placed the bone at Tom's feet and scratched his head, wrapping her arm around her daughter's waist.

Abbey reciprocated and led her mom to the edge of the water. "Look over there, Mom. What do you see? What do you feel?"

Summer glanced at her for a moment, concern furrowing her brow and then she turned toward the water, taking in the scene. She closed her eyes for a moment and took a few slow and deep breaths.

Abbey watched her mother's face, studying it for reaction

and felt comfort in the familiar contours. Summer didn't consider herself psychic or even sensitive, but Abbey knew she had a way of discerning hidden truths. As Abbey watched, her mother took another deep breath, beginning to relax in the soft morning breeze, when suddenly one of her eyebrows shot up. She opened her eyes, turning to Abbey. "That's not good."

Abbey nodded sadly, turned her mother and began walking toward the barn. "It's been a weird week, Mom. It's probably been weird longer than that, but I've been focused on Kelly. I haven't seen a lot of stuff and I let a lot of stuff slide, trying to keep the peace." She grabbed a pitcher of feed from the shed and opened the gate. She set the animals free and told her mother about Max, Kelly's reaction, and Richard's assertion that he had forgotten.

"Do you believe he forgot?" Summer asked.

"What's the alternative, Mom? He did it on purpose?" Abbey turned on the hose and rinsed and refilled the water bowls in the yard.

Silly walked over to investigate Summer. "Watch him, Mom, he's an asshole."

"I'm not a big fan of goats," Summer said, stepping away

from him.

Abbey sprayed the goat with the hose. "Go on!" He bucked and chased after a doe in the field, biting her on the rear.

"You know I've never really liked Richard, but I understand he swept you off your feet. He's older, handsome, and offered you a life in the country that you always wanted. It's easy to understand, plus he was so persistent."

"I know, I've been thinking about that lately," she said, pulling eggs from the boxes.

"What are you thinking?" Summer lifted her shirt to make a pocket, placing the eggs gently against the fabric.

"Why?" Abbey said. "Why was he so persistent? There are a lot of women out there that would be better suited for him. Why me?"

"So what have you decided?"

"I don't know." Abbey pulled the last egg free and handed it to her mother. "That's my answer thus far. I don't know is about as far as I've gotten."

They walked back into the house and Summer placed the eggs in the sink, picked up a small brush and started scrubbing them. Abbey grabbed a paper towel and began drying the cleaned eggs, placing them in a recycled carton. "Mom, I think he might be cheating on me."

Summer stopped scrubbing the egg in her hand and looked at Abbey. "How do you feel about that?"

"Funny enough, I don't think I care." Abbey shrugged her shoulders.

Summer went back to scrubbing, rinsed the egg and handed it to Abbey. "You know you could come home."

"Mom, I'm thirty-three, I can't keep running home."

"Why not? It's there, it's your home."

"Maybe its just sex," Abbey said, taking the last egg from her mom and drying it. "And I'm not a big fan of sex, so maybe it's just less pressure on me." She put the carton away, and they walked into the yard with their coffee.

"Mom, you have chicken shit on your shirt," she said.

Summer glanced down and shrugged. "It'll wash out."

Abbey laughed, her mother was a study in contrasts. Diamonds and a charity dinner one night and unconcerned about chicken shit on her designer shirt in the day. They wandered over to the lounge chairs and settled down, watching the sun rise in the sky.

"It is beautiful out here, but there is something un-right in those woods." Summer pulled a pack of expensive clove cigarettes out of the pocket of her jeans, lighting one, and dropped the pack on the ground.

"Yeah, that's another thing I wanted to talk to you about, but there's one other thing I want to talk about."

"What's that?" Summer asked, expelling a stream of fragrant smoke.

"Dad and stuff," Abbey stated and taking a deep breath, she turned to face her mother.

Summer's eyes were wide. "Okay," surprise making her pause, "I'm glad you're ready to talk about it. You never wanted to talk about it before."

"I know, I wasn't ready before, I'm not sure I'm ready now, but I think it's important that I know what happened."

"Where do you want me to start?"

"The beginning."

"The beginning of me and your dad getting together or the beginning of where we met you?"

"When I came into the picture."

Summer took a big sip of coffee, thought back through the years, and said a quick prayer for her daughter. "Your dad was an agent for one of the alphabet agencies, CIA, FBI, NSA, I never really knew and he never really said, but he had been promoted to a special task force investigating ritual child abuse and child sex slaves. It was ugly work, I don't know how he did it, but he had his reasons. The main reason was the fact that his little sister disappeared when he was a child. Martin was always haunted by the loss of her, the way she was there one day, gone the next, and they never knew if she was dead or alive.

"He'd been following this couple across the country, catching up with them and losing them again. This couple had a hoard of kids, but they weren't their kids. In his investigation he learned of what he called birth houses, where women were paid for their babies, no records were ever kept, the women just handed over the child for cash and the baby became part of a traveling hoard of children, essentially sex slaves for the highest bidder. We're not talking small potatoes here, either, we're talking about hundreds of thousands of dollars for just a night with one of the children, even more to buy them outright." She shook her head. "These pedophiles had money, power, and this sex slave business is a multi-billion dollar business."

She paused, taking a drag off her cigarette. "He and his partner, Rex, you know, your Uncle Rex, caught up with them again. They knew they had five children when they pulled behind the secured gates of a very rich and connected family in Colorado. Martin had been following the couple since New Mexico, he knew the faces of those kids, he felt for those kids, and one of those kids was you."

Abbey nodded, staring at the water.

"He'd lost them in Ohio, and he noticed the faces of the children had changed between Ohio and New Mexico, but one, you, and another girl, were the same. He assumed some of the old faces were dead and the new faces were just more throwaway kids. Anyway, when the car came back through the gates he and Rex pulled it over, but there were only two kids left in the car, three were missing. He knew they were in the house and by some miracle, a day later, they were able to get a warrant. It was hush-hush, and never made the news. They searched the house and found none of the children, but they did find some kind of altar in a hidden room in the basement. Martin described it as more of a dungeon than anything else, but they found nothing else and he got a pretty severe dressing down for going after such a rich man, a politician."

Summer snubbed out the cigarette, pulled the leftover tobacco free, sprinkling it on the ground and slid the butt into the front pocket of her jeans. "While they searched the mansion Martin and Rex gave their cards to the staff, asking them to call if they remembered anything. The staff was huge, maids, cooks, gardeners, chauffeurs, nannies, and on and on. The next day one of those children, the other little girl who he had been following across the country, turned up dead in a dumpster sexually assaulted and stabbed to death. A few days later Rex got a call, a relative of one of the maids wanted to talk. They went over there and found this old black woman, Martin said she had to be a hundred years old if she was a day, but she was sharp, he said, sharp as a tack.

"She made them some coffee, sat them at the kitchen table and put out a plate of cookies. Martin said they were the best cookies he had ever tasted in his life. She asked them a lot of questions, feeling them out, and she finally admitted she had one of the missing kids. Her great-granddaughter worked in the kitchen of the mansion and one morning she opened a kitchen cabinet to retrieve a bucket and found you. The granddaughter had heard rumors of the things that happened in that old mansion, as had most of the staff, and she was afraid if she turned you in to the owners of the house or if any of the staff saw you, you would be killed and she would be, too. So she hid you in a closet until her shift was over. She sneaked you out, and took you to her grandmother's house."

Abbey picked up the clove cigarettes and lighting one, she handed the pack to her mother. Summer accepted the pack without comment, lighting her own.

"This old woman said she wouldn't turn over the child unless Rex and Martin could promise to get you out of the state. She didn't want you going into any foster care, she'd heard rumors, and too many of those foster kids ended up dead, she said, so she made them promise. They figured you either came from one of those birth houses or were just thrown away or sold and didn't have a family looking for you, so they agreed to the old woman's terms. I don't know what they thought they would do with you, but the old woman sent them away and told them to return once they figured it out.

"They left, talked it over, pulled some strings, some illegal strings, I'll admit, and had the documents forged. Martin and I had been trying to have kids for years, it just never happened, so he called and asked me if I wanted a terribly abused 7-year-old. I didn't think about how hard it would be, what kind of troubles you may have, I just said yes. You barely talked and you didn't know your name, but you told Martin you liked the name Caroline, so that's who you became. We lived in California then and when he brought you home we just told everyone you were our niece. I told the doctor you had been removed from your family because of sexual abuse, I had to say something to explain the scarring and luckily, they didn't ask so many questions back then." Summer took a sip of coffee and looked at her daughter. "Are you okay?"

Abbey nodded. "Go on."

"The doctors wanted to give you a hysterectomy, if you can believe it, at your age." She shook her head. "They said you were so scarred up there, a young body just isn't equipped for intercourse, that you'd never have children, but I flatly refused. Thank God! You adjusted surprisingly well, but you never wanted to talk about life before you became Caroline. You didn't know how to read or write, so that first year I home schooled and taught you as much as I could to get you ready for school. Once you learned to read, you loved it and I used to find you sitting way up in the pine tree in the back yard, your nose buried in a book. The next year you started third grade, all went well for a few years and your dad continued his work on the task force." She sighed.

"Martin was getting deeper into the investigation, seeing the threads of it running all the way up to the highest positions in this country and others. Martin knew he was in trouble and if he was in trouble, he figured you and I were in trouble. He started making contingency plans for what we would do if something happened to him. Your dad came from money and the only reason he became an agent was because of his sister, he didn't have to work. Martin was also smart, he went into the agency straight out of law school, so he made arrangements to ensure you and I would be safe. He made sure we would have everything we needed, even new identities if it came to it.

"There was an exclusive resort out in the mountains of California, a big place, filled with redwoods in an old forest that had never seen a chain saw. Power brokers from all over the world were coming for a weeklong event, but this meeting wasn't publicized in the papers - this meeting was secret. Rex and Martin's contacts said they were shipping in a bunch of kids, a dozen or more, and they were confident those kids wouldn't live to see the outside of that place. They managed to get an agent in, he sent out word of all kinds of decadence happening inside, bad stuff, very bad stuff, and then they lost contact with him. Martin decided to go in himself, Rex was against the idea, but Martin was determined." She smiled sadly. "Martin was like that, once he set his mind on something he was determined. He went in and never came out.

"Rex was part of Martin's contingency plan and when a certain amount of time had passed, Rex came banging on the door insisting we pack and we left California that night. Rex sent us on a zig zaggy bus, train, taxi, and rental car trip across the country and we arrived in Rex's hometown in Georgia more than two weeks later and I became Summer and you, Abigail Lily. Your dad picked those names and he took care of everything, we had a bank account, a house, and a car."

"I spent the summer learning how to speak in a Southern

drawl." Abbey nodded. "I remember pieces, but not much, I blocked a lot of it out."

"I know. I didn't know if it was best to talk about it or just let it be, I let you decide and you decided not to talk about it again, until now. So why now?"

"Tell me what was happening in that resort and in the mansion I was rescued from."

"Rex says there are satanic cults operating across the world, he says it's been going on for years, maybe centuries. Hell, maybe forever. They use young women and children in the rituals. They use them sexually and they use them as sacrifices. Rex says that they believe that by killing innocents they increase their power and perhaps they do, because according to Rex some of the most powerful people in the world are involved. Maybe they get into it because they're bored. I mean, really, if you can have whatever you want, maybe you begin to want things you're not supposed to have.

"Anyway, they found your dad's body at the base of a cliff, he didn't die in the fall, he was dead when he was thrown over. We couldn't go to the funeral, as we were traveling a crazy circuit across the country, but Rex went, and then he retired not long after with the help of an inheritance Martin left him. About a year later, he moved back to Georgia, he still investigates when he gets a call, more to rescue than to convict, those folks are never going to be convicted. So tell me, why are you asking questions now?"

"Where do these people do this stuff? I guess in the mansion that I was found in, but do they do it in other places?"

"From what Rex has said they tend to like it better outside. He says that there are certain places that are considered more powerful than others, but I guess they can't always do the ritual outside, hence the mansion where you were rescued. But ancient redwoods surround that resort out in California and many cultures believe those trees have some sort of energy, power. So I would have to assume there are other places deemed worthy of their rituals." She snubbed out her cigarette, stripping the butt and pocketing it.

"Mom, we may need to call Uncle Rex." She told her mother what the Jacksons had relayed to them, and then about the altar and the strange circle they found in the woods.

"Well," Summer said, standing up and stretching. "Why don't we get a little bit of brunch, then we'll walk over there and take a look."

"Are you sure?" Abbey asked, picking up the butt and tossing it in the trash.

"Of course, I'm sure. I want an omelet." She smiled.

Abbey laughed.

Summer grew serious. "Yes, I'm sure. We'll check it out and give Rex a call later." She walked to her beat up car and started pulling out bags. "I picked up a few things for you and Kelly."

"You always do, Mom." Abbey helped her unload the car.

"Well, when I'm out shopping I think of my girls."

They carried the bags into the house and Abbey began removing items from the fridge for the omelets. Summer separated the purchases and carried several into Kelly's room, setting them on the bed. "It's not that much really, just some clothes, a couple books, a couple pieces of jewelry, I don't know what else, I forget. Here's your stuff, you can look at it after I leave." She set the bags on the couch in the living room. She walked back into the kitchen with a smaller bag and set it on the table. "What can I chop?" she asked, stepping to the counter.

Abbey put her to work chopping onions and mushrooms and

they made small talk while they finished cooking the meal. They sat down with their plates and began eating.

"Hmmm, this is heaven. When did you become such a good cook, I know you didn't learn it from me."

"Trial and error," Abbey said, taking a bite. "It is pretty good, huh?"

"Better than good. You know I'm going to worry about you now, right?"

Abbey nodded.

"That's why it's a good thing I picked these up." She reached across the table and slid the small bag toward Abbey.

Abbey looked inside. "Cell phones?"

"Yes. One for you and one for Kelly."

"I'm not sure we'll get reception out here," she said, repeating the same thing Richard said every time Kelly mentioned one.

"I made sure the phones have reception out here. Those phones are pretty neat, they'll do just about everything except take out the trash, but for all I know you can program them to do that also." She laughed. "Try it out, they're charged."

Abbey pulled out a phone, turned it on and the bars showed she had full reception. "Well, I'll be. We do have reception out here."

"Good. I want you to keep it on you. You're all over this property, what if you get hurt? This way you'll always be connected."

"Yeah, now Kelly can call me from her bedroom when I'm out cleaning the barn," she joked. "Thanks, Mom. I don't think Richard will like it, but I'm grateful to have them."

"You're welcome. One other thing, and I don't know how you're going to feel about this...." she paused, and took the last bite of omelet, pushing her plate back and asking for water.

Abbey went to the fridge, handing her a bottle.

"I know you've never been real thrilled by money and things, it's really no wonder. God only knows what happened to you in those fancy houses, surrounded by expensive things when you were a child. I told you Martin made plans and you know we've never wanted for anything, right?"

Abbey nodded, her forehead creased, trying to follow her mother's thoughts.

"Well, you know you got a sizable chunk of money when you turned twenty-one, right?"

Abbey nodded again.

Summer laughed. "And it was gone in what? A couple years? You bought that little house for you and Kelly, a car, you gave your ex-husband money to start what turned out to be a lucrative business." Summer shook her head. "You're one in a million, do you know that?"

Abbey smiled.

"Let's see, what else do you do? You put a roof on your neighbor's house; you gave a car to a stranded Mexican family trying to get back to Texas. When I asked you why you just bought and gave them a car, you said, 'because no one else was going to do it'."

Abbey remembered. That money had felt dirty to her, she couldn't explain why, so she gave it away where she saw a need. She did set up a savings account and college fund for Kelly, but only after Uncle Rex gave her a firm lecture about the looking out for the future. She was never one who thought much of the future; she assumed she learned that when she was a child. She didn't have many memories of that time and when the dreams came, she'd just take sleeping pills to make them go away. "People needed things and I figured I had all I needed."

Summer smiled. Abbey was a miracle; there was no doubt about it. She'd been through so much and she still thought of other people, always thinking of others. Summer took a deep breath and said a silent prayer. "Your dad always said one day you would begin to ask questions about what happened to that little girl who never had a name. He said a day would come when you would have to look back before you could move forward and when that day came you were going to need all the help you could get. He set aside a considerable amount for that day. Although people think I'm a bit ditzy, I'm damned good with money," she paused while praying, "and you just became a very wealthy lady." She bit her lip, watching Abbey's reaction.

Abbey leaned back in her chair and thought about the past years of Richard controlling all the money. She had to skim a few dollars here and there just to have cash on hand and he watched the bank statement like a hawk, questioning every purchase. She thought about how she had to beg and maneuver for the car and how much she missed having a car. "How wealthy?"

"Millions," Summer stated, watching the emotions shift across her daughter's face.

"So I'm suddenly a millionaire?" she asked, sitting forward.

"Yes, several times over."

Abbey leaned back again and sighed.

"Is it okay?" Summer asked. Abbey looked like she just had the wind knocked out of her.

"Richard can't know."

Summer nodded.

"I need a car," Abbey said, sitting forward again. "A jeep or something, something big enough for the dogs, maybe with some tinted windows so it won't be so hot inside."

"Okay, I can have one out here by tomorrow."

"Shit!" She stood up and began pacing. "Richard's going to freak out, but I want a car. I'll just tell him you gave it to me, I wouldn't know how else to explain it."

"You'll have to tell him sooner or later, honey, unless you're planning on leaving him. Are you?" Summer asked softly.

"I don't know what I'm doing, Mom. This week…" She

shook her head and dropped back down in her chair. "This week I feel like I've been hit in the head with a sledge hammer - my brain is just stunned. I feel like I've been sleepwalking since Kelly's accident. Just keeping my head down, doing what needs to be done, and simply putting one foot in front of the other - but this week it all changed. I woke up. Kelly's so much better, she doesn't need me like she used to, and now I'm seeing stuff in my marriage I just hadn't seen before." She sighed. "Okay, I probably saw it before, I just didn't want to, if you know what I mean."

"Yes, I know what you mean. It's the lament of millions of women across the world. We'll just take it one step at a time, okay. I'll have a Jeep sent out tomorrow. I'll deliver a nice card with it and call it a late birthday gift or something. Plus, it only makes sense that you need a car, stuck way out here in the middle of nowhere."

"Richard won't like it. Just like he's not going to like the cell phones, but luckily Kelly won't be here to hear the arguing." She sighed again. "I want a car."

"Then you should have a car, and you can certainly afford one. Hell, you can afford a fleet of them."

Abbey stood up. "Let's go email Kelly and check in with her. I don't want her to know yet, Mom, I've got to think about all this for a little bit. She's going to have a lot of questions and I don't think I'm ready to give the answers to her yet."

"Whatever you want, Abbey, one step at a time," Summer said, following her into the den.

Chapter Nine

Abbey changed into boots, flannel, and grabbed the compass from the jewelry box. She retrieved the leashes, some bottles of water, and met her mom at the car. The hatchback was raised and Summer was adjusting a backpack onto her shoulders.

Abbey slid the bottles inside. "You want me to wear that instead?"

"Heck no. This is how I keep my girlish figure." Summer was an avid bird watcher and she kept a pack ready in case the desire arose to disappear into the woods for a few hours. She reached into the wheel well and pulled out a metal box with the name of a gun maker engraved on top. She unlocked it and pulled out a snub nosed .38.

"A gun, Mom?" Abbey gasped. She didn't like guns.

Summer looked at her quizzically. "You never know what you might run into in the woods, you know that." She reached for an elaborately designed leather holster and strapped it around her waist. "Besides it's just loaded with rat shot, it won't kill anything, but it will give them a good sting."

"Even a bear?" Abbey asked.

"I don't know. I've never shot a bear with it." She slid the gun into the pocket and snapped the leather strap over it, securing it.

"You look like a gunslinger." Abbey laughed as her mom pulled a beat up cowboy hat over her long, braided, gray hair.

"I think I was Annie Oakley in a past life. I like the feel of the holster." She patted the leather and shut the back of the car. "Have you seen any bears around here?"

Abbey told her about the previous day, the reaction of the dogs, the way the turtles were startled by something, and how she had felt watched.

"Well, lets go take a look and see if I learned anything in that tracking course I took a few years ago." Summer stared across the lake while Abbey put the leashes on the dogs. And then each taking a leash, they started across the dam.

When they reached the other side, Abbey pointed out the small tree she had seen moving the previous day. Summer handed her the leash. "Stay here."

Summer walked along the edge of the water and when she approached the partially submerged log the turtles on it dove into the water, just as they had done the day before. She walked over to the tree, stepped around it, looking at the ground, and followed a deer trail up into the woods for a little bit. She rejoined Abbey by the dam.

"Something's been through there, but there's a lot of straw and leaves on the ground and I'm not as good at this as Chief Night Wind, so I can't tell if it was a man or an animal that was over there. I can tell you that plenty of deer, raccoons, and birds have been drinking from the lake, but I didn't see any bear or bobcat tracks."

"I guess that's a good thing." Abbey handed her back the leash and they entered the forest.

"Let me go first, I might see something," Summer said.

They followed the same trail Abbey and Kelly had followed earlier, winding around briars and thick undergrowth. As they approached the creek Summer stopped, handed Abbey the leash, and went ahead to investigate the soft soil along the creek bed. "Somebody's been out here," Summer said. "There's a partial boot print, too wide to have been made by either you or Kelly."

Abbey stepped forward and saw the heel print on the edge of the water. She looked up at her mother, her face pale.

"Does Richard ever come out here?" Summer asked.

"Never. He barely goes out into the yard."

"When's the last time it rained?"

"Monday night, a big, booming storm."

"Well, whoever it was, they were here recently."

"This isn't our property, I don't know who owns it, so I guess they can be on their property if they want too," she said, more to herself than to her mother.

"You're right, of course. It could also be hikers or hunters," Summer said, crossing the small brook.

Abbey let the dogs drink as she stared at the print. "Maybe a hiker just wandered over to our land, saw the house, and went back the direction he came."

"That's certainly possible," Summer said, studying the ground on the other side of the creek. "Whoever it was, he went the same way we're headed. And he was here after you and Kelly." She pointed at another print, on top of the ones left by Abbey and

Kelly.

Abbey crossed the creek, looked down, and saw the large boot print marring the smaller ones and felt a twinge of anxiety expand in her stomach.

"One step at a time, honey," Summer soothed, taking Jerry's leash from her hand and turning back to the east.

Abbey followed her up the hill, around more briars, and onto the plateau where the Starnes house used to be. She pointed it out, hidden under creeping vines and sharp thorns. "Can't really see it now, but that's where it was."

"Listen," Summer shushed. "There are no birds. I can hear them off in the distance, but not around here."

"Wow. I didn't notice that the other day." Abbey looked up into the trees.

"That's not good," Summer said.

"I wouldn't think so," Abbey agreed, taking the lead and heading down the incline to the old road.

They stopped at the bottom up the hill, looking up to where the old house used to be. "I bet it was beautiful."

"It's too sad for me to see any beauty," Abbey said, turning back toward the path.

Stepping out into the field, Abbey was more aware of the silence, the lack of animal and insect noises, which she hadn't noticed earlier. She pointed toward cemetery and Summer reached inside the pack for a camera. She took a couple shots as they approached and then stepped into the enclosure, snapping individual pictures of each grave. "Okay," she said. "Let's go look at the circle."

"It's over there." Abbey pointed.

Summer took some pictures as they approached.

"The road comes in over there." Abbey pointed. "It's much wider now."

"We'll look at that after the circle," Summer said, snapping a photo of the now wider opening.

They came to the path leading to the circle. "You go first, Mom, and let me hold the dogs. They don't like it in here." They glanced down at the dogs to see their tails had curved under their rears and their heads had lowered, closer to the ground, while their ears lay flat against their heads.

"No. They certainly don't. The birds and squirrels don't

like it either." Summer started down the path, snapping pictures. "I don't like it either, the hair on the back of my neck is standing up."

"Yeah, me too," Abbey said, her voice dropping to a whisper.

The dogs began to growl deep in their throats and Abbey looked down to see the ridge of hair along their spines standing on end.

"Damn! The batteries just died," Summer said, sliding the camera into her pocket as the path opened up and exposed the circle. "Jesus," she whispered, turning away instinctually. She looked down at the dogs, then glanced at her daughter's pale face, and forced herself to turn back and look at the large discolored rock in the center of the yellow, recently mowed, circular field. "Jesus, this is bad. Please Lord, surrounded us." She longed to take a deep breath, but her body revolted at the thought of breathing the thick, still, and heavy air. Taking a shallow breath, she stepped off the path.

She took one step and felt her head tingle, she took another step and her mind was swamped by a hundred images. Fire and blood, a woman screaming, her eyes wide with terror, and the children… Summer grasped her head to stop the images, and fell to her knees.

"Mom!" Abbey dropped the leashes and ran into the circle. Her head began to tingle as she heard the dogs whimper. She grabbed Summer under the arms as a pain slammed into her head, feeling like a physical blow, and half lifted, half dragged her mother out of the field and into the trees. "Mom! Are you all right?" Abbey pulled her several more steps. "Are you okay?"

"Yeah," Summer exhaled and found the strength to support herself.

Abbey kept her arm around her waist, leading her out of the trees. "Are you sure?"

"Yeah, yeah. I'm okay," she said breathlessly, rubbing her hands on her face. She stopped suddenly and looked around them, twisting her head quickly. "Where are the dogs?"

Abbey ran back toward the circle, and ignoring her mother calling her name, she yelled for the dogs. "Tom! Jerry! Here! Now!" She saw the dogs in the circle, staring at something she couldn't see and backing slowly toward her. Their bodies were low to the ground, the hair on their backs stood on end, and they growled aggressively - their teeth exposed. "Tom! Jerry! Here! Now!" She yelled again and they turned in unison and ran, shooting past her down the path. She felt her head begin to tingle and without looking back, she followed the dogs.

She burst into the field, breathing hard, and found Summer holding the leashes.

"Thank God!" Summer exclaimed and pulled her into a tight hug.

"It's stronger," Abbey said, pulling away. "It wasn't that strong a couple days ago, I felt like someone hit me in the head with a hammer."

"Let's walk," Summer said, taking the dogs and heading toward the road.

Abbey followed her, looking over her shoulder. It's getting stronger, she thought. She caught up with Summer standing beside the road and staring at the ground.

"A couple cars have been back here. See? There're two different tire tracks. The bigger one is probably that truck you saw, the other was a smaller car." She started walking down the road and then, stepping over recently cut limbs, she entered the woods.

Abbey followed her. "What are we doing?"

"I need a minute to catch my breath and I feel exposed out there," she said, pulling off the backpack and sitting down on the ground.

"Yeah, I know what you mean." Abbey sat on the ground, facing her.

Summer opened the pack and pulled out a few waters, handing one to Abbey. She opened her own and lifted it up, draining the contents. She opened the third bottle offering sips to the dogs. They drank carefully and Summer praised them. "Good boys, coming in there to save us. What good little heroes you are."

"They did, didn't they? They went into that nasty place, as scared as they were, to save us." Abbey set down the empty bottle and started rubbing Tom and Jerry, praising their courage.

"I saw what happens in there," Summer stated. "I saw the terrible things that have been done in there and it's awful. I wish I hadn't seen, but I have, and now I really understand what a miracle it is that you survived what you did. I knew it was bad, but I never knew how bad."

"What do you mean? You saw?"

"I saw pictures in my head. Scenes. I saw children. I saw women. I saw blood and torture. I don't want to talk about what I saw, because I don't want to think of it, but it was hideous." She shook her head slowly. "It was awful."

"I'm sorry, Momma," Abbey said, taking her hand.

"It's okay. We'll get in touch with Uncle Rex, see what he knows." She squeezed Abbey's hand. "What are the odds of you escaping such evil only to move right next door to it twenty something years later?"

Abbey looked into her mother's clear blue eyes for a long moment. "That's a good question, Mom."

Summer reached into the backpack and pulled out a package of new batteries. "I hope these still work." She pulled the camera out of her pocket, put in new batteries, and turned it on. "It's working." She stood up, stowing the empty bottles in her pack and settled it onto her shoulders. "I want to see the road now."

They made their way back to the road and Summer started snapping pictures. The recently sawn limbs had been thrown to the sides, forming a small barrier between the road and the woods.

"Someone did a lot of work back here," Summer said.

"Yeah, it's really opened up."

"Where does the road come out?

"Somewhere below the Jackson's house, I believe."

"Well, let's find out." They walked quietly. "I still don't hear any birds," she said.

"Yeah, I noticed," Abbey said, looking into the trees again and seeing no movement, no squirrels jumping branch to branch, no birds flitting through the leaves. "I think they're about to use the altar again."

"I think so too."

"Do you think Uncle Rex will know anything?"

"He might. He keeps up with things."

They followed the road, walking close together, and Abbey reached for her mother's hand.

"One step at a time, Abbey. We'll figure it out."

Abbey nodded. "I know, but it's damn weird that this is at my door again."

"I would say it's a coincidence, but I don't really believe in them, so I'll call it some strange synchronicity." She let go of

Abbey's hand and reached into her back pocket, removing the pack of cigarettes. She pulled two out, lighting both, and handed one to Abbey. "Chief Night Wind said the smoke keeps the evil spirits away."

Abbey took the cigarette and smiled, only her mother would spend a week on the Appalachian Trail camping with an old Indian chief to learn how to track. "Well, if Chief Night Wind said it, it must be true."

The road curved and then descended back into a tunnel. Whoever had been clearing the trail had stopped at the point where they stood. They walked another forty feet and the road dead-ended into another dirt road. "They didn't want anyone passing by to see that the road is cleared," Summer said, peering back the way they had come.

"I guess not. Which way do you want to go? Back the way we came or up by the Jackson's house?"

"I don't really want to go back near that circle, do you?"

Abbey shook her head with a grimace.

"Okay, let's go by the Jackson's."

Abbey turned right and they started walking again. They

had been walking quietly for a few minutes when Summer grabbed her arm. "Listen! You can hear the birds again. Not here, but we're close."

"Thank God," Abbey said, closing her eyes and listening to the birds in the distance. "Mr. Jackson said the woods felt strange sometimes, I think this is what he meant, unnaturally quiet and still." As they crossed a small wooden bridge over a creek, Abbey saw a squirrel dart across the road. "I think I understand why Mr. Jackson doesn't like crossing the creek."

"Smart man," Summer agreed and smiled when she saw a robin land on the side of the road and fly off with a worm.

Abbey showed her mother the old chimneys, rusted tin, and crumbling foundations marking the places where the Jackson's relatives and friends once lived. Summer gasped when she saw the Jackson's gardens. "My God, they're lush!"

"I know. I've got a pretty green thumb, but nothing like this. Makes you want to run in there and just start eating, doesn't it?"

"Yes, it does. I can smell the tomato blooms from here." She inhaled deeply. "Yum."

They passed the Jackson's house, saw that the old truck

gone, and that the doors and windows were shut tight. Abbey sighed. "I wanted you to meet them."

"I'll meet them another time, it's just as well. I've got to get these pictures off to Rex and stop at a Jeep dealership on the way home."

In the jumble of the day, Abbey had forgotten that she was now independently wealthy, and although she still didn't know how she felt about the money, she recognized that it gave her some freedom. Richard was not going to like her having a car and she had trouble understanding how she let it get so bad that she had to fight just to have transportation. She could see the little pieces of independence that she had handed over in the last couple years, it started with small things like the way she folded the towels or how she left her coffee spoon on the edge of the sink. Silly little things, small alterations he asked her to make, and then Kelly had the accident and she quit noticing.

Abbey had always preferred the rural life, away from the city and the hoards of people who may have dark secrets and intentions. When Richard mentioned the property he owned in the country, she had been excited. They broke ground on the land in the first weeks after the honeymoon; she enjoyed picking out a floor plan and deciding how to place the house in the path of the sun. Then Kelly was in the hospital and he was pressuring her to meet with builders, to pick out carpets and drapes. She shut down a part of herself, just focusing on putting one step in front of the other, getting Kelly over one hurdle and then the next. Summer ended up making the most of the decisions about the house, giving her opinion to Abbey, which Abbey relayed to Richard as her own thoughts.

Richard decided they couldn't afford both car payments after they moved on the property, although the payment on her three-year-old Saturn was tiny compared to the lease payment on the Mercedes. Soon she had to beg for the car to get Kelly to doctor appointments, physical therapy, or just to go to the grocery store. Somewhere the constant battle became normal, she had forgotten what it felt like to make her own decisions, to come and go as she saw fit, to buy her daughter clothing without having to explain. She had forgotten what it felt like to be happy.

She would occasionally find the strength to stand up to him as she had when she put the chickens in the bathroom or the battle over the goat fence. And she would always stand up for Kelly, but beyond complaining about the daily lists, she had quit standing up for herself a long time ago. She thought about the house she used to own, a small, two bedroom on several acres on the outskirts of Windslow, an Atlanta suburb. She thought about how calm life was then, how peaceful. She worked in a legal office, making more than enough to cover their expenses, as the house had been bought outright. She longed for the simplicity of those days. That house was gone now; she sold it when she married Richard, rolling the proceeds over into their new home. She sighed as they turned onto the hard top and wondered why she let herself become a prisoner, did it stem from those early years when she was nothing more than a toy for sick people to use as they saw fit? A little girl so unimportant that she wasn't even given a name?

They turned into the driveway and Silly stood in the middle of the path. The dogs slunk back, having experienced the feel of a goat's head ramming into their ribcage one too many times. "I hate that damned goat!" Abbey said and yelled at the goat. "Go, on, you little bitch! Get out of here!"

Silly took a few steps toward the edge of the pines, watching them pass. Abbey glanced over her shoulder in time to see the goat lowering his head and beginning to run toward her. He was building up momentum and coming fast. She dropped the leash, spun around and kicked him squarely in the head. He stopped, took a step back, and shook his head. He exposed his teeth and then ran into the woods.

"I guess those kick boxing classes really paid off," Summer said, picking up the leash.

"I guess so," Abbey agreed.

They chained the dogs, went into the house, and Summer sent the photos to Rex. Abbey responded to Kelly's latest note, and then she was outside saying goodbye to her mother.

"Mom, there's a scar on my hip, do you know how I got it?" she asked, watching Summer lock the gun back in the box.

"Yes. When you came to us, you had a small tattoo of an owl; I guess that's how your keepers identified you. We had it removed shortly after we adopted you. The other little girl, who was found in the dumpster, had a dove on her hip." Summer tossed the holster into the back of the car.

Abbey felt a shiver work down her spine as she remembered

the photos Kelly had shown her of the giant owl looming over the woman on the altar.

"So what color do you want this Jeep?" Summer asked, tossing the backpack inside and shutting the hatch.

"Something light." Abbey pulled her mind back to the argument she knew the vehicle would inspire.

"Okay, something light it is." Summer reached into the car, grabbed her purse, and pulled her wallet free. She opened it and started counting hundred dollar bills. She handed Abbey a thousand dollars.

"What's this for? And why are you carrying so much money?" Abbey asked with surprise.

"I like cash and you might need some until I can handle all the financial arrangements. I'm going to need you to come up to Windslow, sign some papers, go to the bank, and make some decisions."

Abbey sighed; having difficulty seeing beyond a hundred arguments she was going to have with Richard. "Okay, let me know when."

"Honey, money isn't a bad thing, and having money doesn't

make you a bad person. There're lots of good people out there with money who don't hurt children."

"I know. I'm just overwhelmed by everything."

Summer nodded. "There's a lot going on. You'll be hearing from Rex, I gave him the new cell phone numbers, so you girls keep those phones with you, understand?"

"Yes, ma'am." Abbey hugged her tightly. "I'll see you soon."

Abbey watched her mother drive away and stepped into the house. She put the money in her wallet, picked up the bag containing the cell phones and read the instructions. She set the chargers on the counter where Richard would see them when he came in the door and turned to look at the daily list. She picked it up and tore it into little pieces, dropping it in the trash.

Chapter Ten

Abbey was mulling over the grocery list when she heard Richard pull into the driveway, she checked dinner and met him at the door. "How was your day?" she asked nonchalantly, attempting to ignore the knot in her stomach.

"Long." He stepped into the kitchen and came to a stop, his hand poised in the air about to loosen his tie. "What are those?" he asked, staring at the phones charging on the counter.

"Cell phones."

"I know that," he snapped. "Where did they come from?" He pulled off his tie and turned to face her.

"Mom gave them to us."

"Well, we don't need them, you can give them back."

"I'm not giving them back," she stated, watching his eyes widen.

"Excuse me?"

"I'm not giving them back. Every teenage girl in the nation has a cell phone, there's no reason Kelly shouldn't have one."

"We can't afford them." He pulled off his jacket.

"We're not paying for them, Mom is."

"She had no right to do that without talking to us. She's undermining us, our family, but she always has. I said no cell phones."

"No. You said we couldn't get reception out here, but we can."

"We don't need them," he said, throwing his jacket over the back of a chair.

Abbey could tell he was angry, but Richard didn't express anger - not in the normal way. He was always calm, at least on the surface. "Maybe you don't need them, you're in town all day. We, on the other hand, are stuck out here in the middle of nowhere without a car. We could need them and I thought it was nice of Mom to think of us."

"She's always bringing you things, giving Kelly things, spoiling her."

"She doesn't see us often, she misses us. And Kelly is not

spoiled, she's a good kid." The timer on the microwave dinged and she jumped, turning off the burner under the rice. "Dinner's ready, are you going to change before we eat?"

"I already ate, I'm not hungry," he said.

Abbey turned back to the stove and switched off all the burners under the warming food. This was the way Richard expressed his anger and his frustration. She pulled the rolls out and buttered them as Richard stalked into the bedroom to change. Abbey made herself a plate and sat down to eat.

She had only taken a few bites when he stepped back into the kitchen wearing jeans and a t-shirt. "Where's the list?"

She sighed and stood up, scraping what was left on the plate into the dogs' bowl. "I didn't get any of it done today, Mom was visiting."

"So where is it?" he asked again.

"I threw it away." She leaned against the counter.

"You what?" He looked at her incredulously.

"I threw it away," she repeated.

"Why?" he demanded, one eyebrow disappearing under the fall of hair on his forehead.

"Because I've told you before I don't need a list to tell me what to do, I'm an adult, not a child." She crossed her arms over her chest.

"Abbey, we've talked about this," he soothed, irritatingly. "Things don't get done around here without a list. I don't know what it is you do all day, I suspect you lay in bed wasting most of it, but we both know this place would be a mess without the list." He reached in the refrigerator and pulled out a bottle of wine.

"I home school, Richard, that takes time."

He poured some wine in a glass. "Well, that was your decision, Abbey, and not an excuse to let this house fall into ruins."

"The house is hardly in ruins, I missed a day of chores. It's not a big deal." She could feel his frustration from across the room, he was angry, very angry, but she wasn't going to back down this time.

He stared at her, scrutinizing her as though he was a little kid and she was a strange bug he'd just found in the grass. "Are you okay? You're not acting like yourself."

"How am I not acting like myself? You know I've never liked the lists. This is nothing new." She pulled some plastic bowls out from under the counter and starting putting away leftovers, feeling his eyes on her back.

"I know you were abused before you were adopted, sometimes those kids develop a multiple personality disorder, maybe we need to start trying some medications to even you out."

"I don't need evening out, I'm fine. I just don't understand why a cell phone is such a big deal or why I have to do everything on your little lists every day like I am a child, incapable of deciding for myself what chores need to be done."

"Well, what about the way you came screaming into the house the other night, Abbey, that wasn't normal."

"You mean the other night when the dogs were tearing apart Kelly's duck? Is that the night you're talking about?" she asked, feeling her temper slip.

He just stared at her and said nothing.

"No, Richard, I acted normally to an abnormal situation. My daughter was in tears, there were dead animals in the barnyard, and I was upset. I had every right to be upset and frankly, I still am." She took a deep breath and placed the rest of the food in the refrigerator.

"I don't know, I think you overreacted," he stated, taking a sip of wine.

"Well, I do know and I think you under reacted." She looked through the window to see Silly in the garden. "I have to put the goat up." She went outside, for once grateful to see the goat out of his pen, and regained her temper. Silly didn't want to go easily, though, and she ended up shoving him by his shoulders to get him out of the garden. He pressed back, digging his feet into the soft soil and she felt her temper sliding out of control again.

"You stupid son of a bitch! Move!" She shoved harder and he fell back a step. She glanced down to see every corn stalk had been eaten, felt the frustration rise in her system, and shoved him harder, finally getting him onto the grass. He reared up on his hide legs and she jumped out of the way before he could hit her with his hard head. He snorted and ran to the gate. She opened the gate and pushed him through with her foot. "Well, you little dickhead, I smell like goat again." She latched the gate and he ran off to the females standing in a group, scattering them.

She walked into the house, heard the television blaring from the den and washed her hands. The cold shoulder, she thought, mixing the dog food. Now he'll ignore me for a while before round two. She poured a glass of wine, grateful for the reprieve and stacked the bowls, grabbing the glass and heading out the front door. She gave the dogs their food, returned to the porch and sat on the stairs.

Sitting on the stairs was one small piece of herself that Richard hadn't changed. It drove him crazy that although they had patio furniture, she preferred the hard wooden steps and the more he complained, the more she chose the steps. It was a small rebellion, just a way to hold on to a little piece of her.

She took a sip of wine, remembering the night she met Richard. The law office where she worked as a file clerk threw an elaborate Christmas party for the employees and clients at a five star hotel in Atlanta. She caught the enthusiasm of the other ladies in the office, bought a nice dress and had her hair done. The law office supplied limos to pick up and drop off the employees to avoid any potential DUIs and Summer and Kelly made a big deal of it, snapping pictures of her standing in front of the limo all dressed up like she was going to the prom.

She saw him at the bar. He was tall and handsome, with

longish dark hair and clear blue eyes. He watched her for a long time, inspiring teasing from her co-workers and then he finally approached her, almost shyly, and asked her to dance. That night they talked, danced, and drank, and she felt like a princess. He asked for her phone number and she gave it willingly, feeling excitement, probably due to the three glasses of wine she had consumed. The next morning she received a bouquet of daisies.

The next gift was a glass blown hummingbird feeder with an invitation to dinner. The gifts he gave were simple, nothing extravagant that may have scared her away and before she knew it, she was engaged. Three months after they met, they married. She thought back, trying to remember the first thing he attempted to change about her and realized it was smoking. She didn't fight the change at all, she understood smoking was bad for her and she thought he was just concerned about her health. Then it was her choice of cologne, the simple vanilla scent irritated his allergies. Next it was the cat, he didn't like cats, claimed to be allergic, and although she never saw any evidence of the allergies, the cat went to live with Summer.

No, at first the changes were small, but now it seemed she

was constantly under his scrutiny, even something as simple as talking to the dogs caused him to ponder her mental status. If he caught her speaking with the dogs, he would give her his serious psychiatrist gaze and start in on her. "You do realize they can't understand what you are saying, don't you?"

"Yes."

"Then why are you talking to them?"

"Because they like it."

"How do you know they like it? They're are animals, Abbey, not people."

"I know they like it because their tails wag and they smile."

"Dogs can't smile, Abbey."

"Sure they can," she insisted.

"I'm not sure you always recognize the difference between humans and animals, not to hear the way you talk to them, as though you really expect them to answer."

"Oh, I recognize the difference, animals are a lot easier to get along with than humans" she'd state and he would study her a few more minutes and then let the subject drop.

She chuckled out loud, pulling herself from her memories.

She used to think that animals were easier than people, but that was before she met Silly. She saw the ducks stepping out of the water and went to the barnyard.

Silly met her as she opened the gate and reared up on his hind legs. She moved out of his way quickly, not spilling any feed out of the pitchers she carried. "Ha!" She laughed. "You're just pissed off because I kicked your ass today in front of company. Don't worry, you'll get over it, we all get our ass handed to us at times." She poured the feed into two separate bowls.

Silly stepped on a duck, which quacked loudly and ran into the barn, peeking around the doorway.

"You don't always have to be an asshat, Silly, you really don't." She turned on the hose and rinsed out the water bowls, refilling them. "There is no prize at the end of the day for being the biggest dick."

He nudged a chicken, tossing it away from the bowl.

"You're never going to make friends that way." She turned off the hose.

The ducks began circling a water bowl, quacking happily and sending water up into the air. Silly lowered his head, watching them through strangely slashed pupils.

"Don't do it, fucktard." She spoke firmly and stepped in front of him. "I'll kick the shit out of you again. I know it hurt and I'm sorry, but I'll do it again."

He looked up at her and snorted.

"I know. I'm a bitch," she consoled.

He shoved a doe, knocking her away from the food.

"Jeeze, dude, you don't have to be so mean all the time." She stepped between Silly and the doe, pushing him away with her thighs and allowing the female to eat.

He pushed his head into her thighs, slowly propelling her backwards. She rubbed his head roughly, scratching around the small lumps, new horns just beginning to sprout. "I know, I know," she soothed. "That probably hurts. I'm sure it itches." She scratched a little harder and slipped away quickly as he tried to press her against a tree. "I'm nice, Silly, but I'm not stupid."

She shooed the ducks into the barn and the chickens flapped into their boxes. "Go on, girls," she said, lightly tapping the rear of a doe and the females ran into the barn. She turned to face Silly. "Get on in there, boy."

He raised his head, exposing his teeth and clucked.

"I'm not doing this tonight, Silly. Go to bed."

He jumped up on his hind legs and came down aggressively.

"You want to go, do you? Bring it, assclown." She assumed the stance, ready to throw a kick.

He ran at her, his head low and just as he came close, she jumped out of his way and slipped behind him.

"Idiot," she said, pushing him into the barn with her foot and locking the door behind him.

She stepped through the gate, latching it behind her and walked toward the dogs. They were on their feet, tails wagging, and smiling. Dogs do smile, she thought, grinning at them. "How are my heroes tonight?" she whispered, rubbing their heads and letting them go. She walked back into the house.

Richard was still in the den, so she picked up the bags her mother had left for her and went to the shower. She washed the day's sweat, fear, and goat musk off her skin, dried off, put on some underwear, and opened the one of the bags. Inside, she found a couple pairs of designer label jeans and several name brand tops.

She opened the second bag and gasped when she saw a

shimmering green silk sundress. She pulled it out of the bag, enjoying the way the material reflected the light and held it against her body, looking at her reflection. She pulled it over her head, slid it over her hips and turned back to the mirror. It fit perfectly, but as beautiful as the fabric was she couldn't find any enthusiasm, she couldn't envision having a need to wear such a beautiful garment, not when she spent her days battling an arrogant goat. She tugged it over her head, folded it and put it back in the bag with a sigh. She picked up a pair of jeans, checked the size and stepped into them, pulling them over her hips as Richard stepped into the bathroom.

"So your Mom bought you a bunch of clothes, too?" He sat on the closed toilet.

"She always does." Abbey buttoned the jeans and turned to the mirror.

"Those look too small," he said, studying her.

Abbey heard a silent ding in her head, announcing the beginning of round two. "They're not too small, they're slim cut. They're supposed to be snug."

"How much weight do you think you're gained since we got married?" he asked, crossing his ankle over his knee.

"I don't know, my clothes still fit, I haven't thought about it." She pulled off the jeans and self-consciously crawled into her pajamas. She grabbed a small pair of scissors from a drawer and started clipping tags.

Richard watched her, his eyes slightly squinted and moving up and down her body. "I think you've put on a few pounds, you look thicker than you used to be."

"I'm in my thirties now, I hear that happens." She folded the clothes, watching him through the mirror.

He stood up, walked into the closet and returned with a scale, placing it at her feet. "Step on."

"Why?" She picked up the clothes, carried them into the bedroom and started putting them away.

"Because I want to know how much you weigh," he said, standing in the bathroom doorway.

She slammed the dresser drawer, faced him and put her hand on her hip. "How about this? What I weigh is none of your business." She walked out of the room, and he followed her into the kitchen.

"Why are you upset? I just want to know how much you

weigh, you're my wife, I should know."

"Why should you know?" She turned on the dishwasher. "So you can put me on a diet?" She wiped the counters. "So you can control every piece of food I put in my mouth, just like you try to control me with those damned lists. Forget it! It's my body, my business." She looked for something else to do and finding nothing, she straightened the home school supplies.

"See? This is what I've been talking about, these over the top reactions of yours, you may think this is normal, but I can tell you that it's not."

She wanted to scream, she wanted to jump on him and pummel him. She leaned against the counter, thought how badly she wanted a cigarette, and took a deep breath. She looked at him, started to open her mouth and realized it was a waste of time. She gave an exaggerated sigh, shook her head, and went into the den. She threw herself on the couch, picked up the remote and Richard walked in, sitting in a chair.

"Why don't you want to talk about this?" he asked.

"Which this are we talking about, Richard?" She turned on the TV.

He sighed in exasperation. "The way your emotions are all over the place lately."

She flipped channels, settling on a music station and dropped the remote on the couch. "Is that what we were talking about? I thought we were talking about my weight or the cell phones or the list I threw away. I didn't realize we were talking about my emotions. What do you want to know about my emotions?"

"Why do you think you are so upset? Screaming and slamming doors the other night, slamming drawers tonight, throwing away a list that helps us stay focused, why do you think you're doing these things?" He leaned forward, as if expressing compassion.

"I don't know, Richard, you're the expert, why don't you tell me," she said softly, staring at the television.

"It usually goes back to childhood and I don't know much about your childhood. All you ever told me was that you were taken away from an abusive family and adopted. Maybe we should talk about what happened to you when you were a child."

Abbey's heart began pounding in her chest. "No!" She

jumped to her feet, went to the back door and slid on some clogs, stepping out onto the porch. She stared at the sky, asking God for strength, and Richard stepped out on the porch.

She sighed. "Richard, leave me alone."

"Leave you alone? You're obviously upset, I'm not going to leave you alone." He put his arm around her shoulders.

Her eyes went skyward, pleading. "I'm fine, Richard. I just want to be alone."

"What kind of husband would I be if I left my wife alone when she was upset?" he asked, pulling her closer.

The dogs barreled onto the porch, wet from the lake and rich in the scent of skunk. They ran between them, tails wagging and rubbing against their legs. Richard pushed the dogs away, stepped back and the scent hit him, making him gag in his throat. "Jesus!" he shouted. "What is that smell?"

Abbey sent a silent thank you up to the heavens and stifling a laugh, she sniffed deeply. "I'm pretty sure that's skunk."

"Shit!" He ran to the door and slammed it behind him.

"Good boys," she whispered, scratching their noses gently and trying not to get too much of the scent on her skin. "You're still my heroes."

Abbey stepped into the house and heard Richard in the shower. She stripped off her clothes, dropped them into the washing machine and went to the bedroom for her robe. Wrapping the robe around her, she went to the den and pulled up her email. Kelly had sent several emails, worry creeping into the most recent. Abbey answered them all, soothing her worries and went to shower in Kelly's bathroom.

"How long is this scent going to last?" he asked when she opened the door.

"It only got on your clothes, it should be gone. The dogs got the worst of it and probably washed most of it off in the lake." Wrapped in a towel, she carried her robe and underwear to the washing machine. "Where are your clothes? I'll wash them."

He lifted his arm and sniffed. "I can still smell it, I can't go to work tomorrow reeking like a skunk."

"Tomorrow's Saturday," she said, walking back to the master bath to find his clothes.

"I've got group therapies all day tomorrow," he stated, following her.

"When did you start doing group on Saturdays?" She picked up his clothes off the bathroom floor.

"I told you we've been working on ways to build the business, don't you ever listen to me?" he asked, following her back to the laundry room.

"I don't remember you telling me that, Saturday is shopping day, I need to go to the grocery." She dropped his clothes in the washer and turned it on.

"You'll have to go Sunday. What about this smell?"

She leaned into him and sniffed. "You smell fine."

"I can still smell it," he insisted.

"I don't know what to tell you, it'll wear off. I've heard of people who were sprayed taking tomato juice baths, but you weren't sprayed and we don't have any tomato juice."

"Damn it!" he yelled and stomped into the bedroom, slamming the door behind him.

Abbey's eyebrows shot up. "What was that about emotions, Richard?" she asked softly and smiled.

Chapter Eleven

"Abbey." Richard shook her roughly.

She opened her eyes to see him standing over her, dressed for work.

"What do I smell like?" he asked.

"All I smell is cologne," she said, sliding up against the pillows.

"You don't smell skunk?"

"No, Richard, just cologne. Do you smell skunk?" She rubbed her eyes.

"I wouldn't be asking if I didn't. How long does it take to wear off?" he snapped impatiently.

"The last time the dogs got sprayed it took several days, but they got hit with the musk and they have long hair. Other than that I don't know, I don't smell it."

He looked at her suspiciously, as though he didn't believe she couldn't smell the scent, and opened the bedroom door. "I'll see you tonight."

"Bye," she said, stretching.

She listened to him drive away and tried to remember what she had been dreaming when he jerked her awake. She crawled out of the bed and began making it up. Something about the dogs, she thought and stopped, sheets in hand. "What about the dogs?" she muttered, but was unable to recall any details. As she dressed, she attempted to pull up the details again and finally giving up, she went into the kitchen to start the coffee and stepped outside, calling the dogs.

They came running out of the pine forest, tails wagging, and stinking. "I told you the last time those skunks are tougher than you," she said, as they trotted beside her to the doghouse. She chained them, scratching lightly on their heads, not wanting to stink so early in the morning. She dealt with the animals in the barnyard, cleaned the barn, and went into the house for breakfast.

She ate a fried egg sandwich over the sink, checked her email and stepped outside to the shed, pulling the last cigarette out of the pack. She'd just snubbed out the butt when the dogs started barking and she heard a car pull into the driveway. She walked around the house to see a white Jeep Grand Cherokee pulling onto the property, followed by a dark sedan. The Jeep stopped and a young man wearing a mechanic's uniform stepped out. "I guess this is yours," he said, dropping the keys in her hand.

An older man stepped out of the sedan, wearing a suit and carrying a clipboard. "Abigail Brown?" he asked.

"Yes," she said, looking inside the Jeep. She smiled. Summer had done well; tinted windows, manual transmission, cloth seats, and no fancy gadgets.

"I need you to sign some papers," he said, handing her the clipboard and pointing at the Xs.

She signed where he indicated, he gave her copies and then he pulled out a card, handing it to her. "Enjoy." He smiled and both men climbed in the sedan, pulling out of the driveway.

"Wow," she whispered, her hands shaking slightly, and hopped inside. She adjusted the seat, the mirrors, and sat staring out through the windshield with her hands resting on the steering wheel. She looked in the rearview mirror. "Richard is going to be so pissed," she told her reflection.

She read the card from her mom, wishing her a happy late

birthday, and smiled. Summer was one in a million. Stepping into the house, she left the card on the counter, and hid the paperwork in the pantry. She grabbed her bag, tossing the cell phone inside, and picked up the unfinished grocery list.

Pulling onto the road she almost felt like a teenager again, excited to be behind the wheel of her own car. She drove into Locknee, went to the grocery store, stopped at a convenience store and broke one of the hundreds her mother had given her buying some cigarettes. The phone rang as she left the store and she dug in her bag, pulling it free. "Hello."

"Abbey, it's Rex. Are you okay?" the familiar voice asked.

"Hey, Uncle Rex, I'm fine."

"Good, good." He sighed. "I was worried, I just got back in town this morning and saw the photos your mom sent. I'm on my way out to your place now."

"Okay, I'm on my way home too, how long before you get there?"

"I left Windslow fifteen minutes ago, so in about forty-five."

"All right, I'll see you there."

Abbey arrived home, put away the groceries, and hid one

pack of cigarettes in the shed and one in the glove compartment of the Jeep. She put on a fresh pot of strong coffee, just the way Rex liked it, and then the dogs in the yard started barking.

She hadn't seen Rex since Christmas and the rushed and awkward dinner at her mom's house. Richard hadn't wanted to go, they had argued before he finally conceded, but his attitude upon arriving made everyone present uncomfortable. He hurried Kelly as she opened her gifts and then claimed he wasn't hungry when Summer finally managed to get the food on the table.

She stepped on the porch as Rex climbed out of the truck and surprising the both of them, she ran the short distance, throwing herself in his arms. "It's all right, baby girl," he soothed, holding her.

She felt tears spring to her eyes and pulling away, she wiped them with the back of her hand, embarrassed. "Sorry," she said shakily. "It's been a rough week and I've missed you."

"I spoke to your mom this morning, it sounds like you've had a rough week." He put his arm around her shoulders, turning toward the house. "Got some coffee?"

"You know it. Come on in." She led him into the house.

Although Rex was only a few inches taller than Richard, the kitchen seemed smaller with him in it, his presence filling the room. "Have a seat," she said, setting coffee cups, cream, and sugar on the table.

"Where's Richard today?" he asked, settling at the table and stretching out his long legs.

"He seems to be working on Saturdays now," she said, pouring coffee and sitting down.

"Does he know about the altar across the lake?" He stirred sugar in his cup.

"No. He wouldn't believe it even if he saw it, things like that don't exist in his world."

He nodded his head and took a sip of coffee, sighing appreciatively. "You and your mom make the best coffee, I don't know how you do it."

"A touch of cinnamon," she explained.

"Well, that's what you say, but I've tried doing it myself and it never tastes the same. Must be because I don't have that woman's touch."

"Yeah, that must be it." She smiled.

"Your mom said your neighbors had some interesting stories

about the woods over there."

Abbey nodded.

"You think they'll talk to me?"

"I don't see why they wouldn't, they didn't tell me not to tell anyone, they didn't act like it was a secret. According to Richard, they'll tell anyone. He thinks it's all bullshit, though."

"He's not the most astute guy I've ever met, sometimes I wonder how he makes it as a psychiatrist." He paused. "Damn Abbey, I shouldn't have said that." He shook his head.

"No, it's okay. To be honest, I've wondered the same thing." She looked down into her coffee cup.

He reached across the table and put his hand on hers.

She looked up at him and smiled with sad eyes.

Rex felt a sudden desire to find Richard and beat the crap out of him. Any man who put that look in Abbey's eyes, after what she had survived, should have his ass whipped, up one side and down the other. He took a breath and pushed down the emotion. "Summer said you wanted to talk about the past yesterday. I'm glad to hear it. Personally, I think it's too much for anyone to keep bottled up for so long. Do you have any questions for me?"

"What did the tattoos mean? Mom said I had an owl on my hip and that other girl had a dove. Why?"

"Do you remember that other girl, Abbey?"

"I think I do, she was older than me by a couple years, she took care of me like a big sister. I think her name was Caroline or at least that's what I called her."

"Ah. That's why you liked the name Caroline." He nodded.

"I guess so."

"The tattoos designated your role in the organization, what they would have trained you to do when you got older. This thing is complicated, a lot of people are in it for different reasons, but also there is organization at the top. The owl denoted that once your personality was shattered enough by the abuse, they would have taken you into training to work for them in the role of a remote viewer."

"A what?" she asked, confused.

"A remote viewer, it's kind of like a psychic, but it's more focused than that and they use the viewers as spies. The dove tattoo indicates a sex slave, they're pretty disposable, an owl is a little more important to them, but in their mind they're all disposable."

"I would have worked for them? Why me? And why as an owl?"

"Evidently, they see where the children they collect show some potential in one area or another, you must have shown some potential of being a little psychic. So at a certain point they would have brought you in, programmed you, and had you work gathering information against their enemies."

"What do you mean? Programmed?"

"Just like it sounds, brain washing. They would have created little compartments in your head that only they could access, like a computer. You may have lived out your life and never even known that you were working for them. That's one reason they allow the abuse, because seeing and experiencing such trauma as a child makes it a lot easier for them to do their voodoo. That kind of abuse sets up little compartments in the brain, so then all they have to do is take control of them. Another reason is that they make lots of untraceable money off those kids."

"Who's in charge of all this?" she asked.

"Well that's the question, isn't it? Your father and I saw it going all the way to the top, but we never found where. It's a mixed bag and like I said, people are involved for different reasons, we know the pedophiles are there and there's also the Satanists. The Satanists really believe that their dark rituals will make them stronger, more successful. There's also bored folks with too much money and too much time on their hands, just looking for a thrill. And then there is government involvement. One way to control your enemies is to catch them in a compromising situation, like having sex with a child. Somewhere high, high up in government is a black funded program, Martin and I referred to it as the Aviary because of the tattoos, but I have no idea who is at the top."

Abbey stood up, feeling the need to busy herself. "Are you hungry?"

"Always." He laughed.

She began pulling last night's dinner from the fridge and turned on the stove to warm the food. "Tell me how you and Dad started working together."

"We were in law school together. I had gotten a scholarship and I'll never forget stepping on that campus the first day and being one, of probably only ten, black folks in the whole school." He smiled with the memory. "Your dad was in a couple of my classes and he kind of took up with me, over the years we became good friends. After graduation, I was off to change the face of race relations in Atlanta and he went into the agency. Then the Atlanta child murders happened, one of my distant cousins was a victim. Martin told me about the task force, asked me to join him to get the predators off the streets and I did. The rest is history."

The water boiled and she set the colander full of rice inside, covering it. "I know why he named mom Summer, it suits her. Why Abigail Lily for me?"

"That was his grandmother's name, Martin was really close to his grandmother, she was obviously a rock for him after his sister disappeared and she raised him after his parents died. She died while we were in college and I went to the funeral with him. I'd never seen him cry before, he really loved that lady."

Abbey nodded. "You saw the grave of Abigail Lily across the lake?"

"Yeah, I saw it."

"Strange coincidence, isn't it?"

"It's some kind of something," he said.

"It freaked out Kelly when she saw it."

"I imagine it did. Abbey, does she know what happened to you when you were a kid?"

"No more than anyone else, just that I was abused and adopted." She pulled a couple plates out of the cabinet.

"I think you should tell her, you're going to have to tell her sooner or later."

"I know, but she's so freaked out about that altar across the lake, I don't want to tell her now, it'll scare her to death." She filled a plate with food.

"Maybe a little fear will keep her on her toes. I find it too coincidental that you moved into the middle of nowhere and there's a sacrificial altar less than half a mile from your front door. I'm nervous about this, Abbey."

She placed the food in front of him and grabbed some silverware, handing it to him. "It is weird, but we don't know it has anything to do with me."

"We also don't know that it doesn't," he said, as she made her own plate.

She turned. "Do you think it does have something to do with me?"

"I'm not saying that, but it sure as hell doesn't feel right." He took a bite of food. "Good as ever, girl, you've got a way with food, you should give your mom some tips."

Abbey laughed, sitting down with her own plate. "Thanks, Uncle Rex."

"I know we aren't real kin, Abbey, but you know I love you like my own."

Abbey nodded.

"I don't like it, you staying out here so close to that thing. It just doesn't feel right and we both know the terrible things that happen during those rituals. I don't like you or Kelly being anywhere near that stuff."

"I know." She sighed, imagining telling Richard she wanted to move because of a satanic altar in the woods. If he didn't think she was crazy now, he'd certainly think she was if she started talking about rituals in the woods.

"You could go stay with Summer for awhile and let me figure out what's going on out here without having to worry about you."

"I can't leave the animals with Richard and I sure can't take them all out to mom's, she already has a zoo out there."

"Yeah, your mom told me about Kelly's duck. He said he forgot, huh?"

Abbey nodded, chewing slowly.

"Forgot my ass," Rex replied, feeling the urge to beat up Richard rise again.

"I don't know what to think, Kelly thinks he did it on purpose."

"I think Kelly's right, he's got a passive aggressive streak in him like I've never seen. I'll never forget the way he ruined Christmas dinner last year."

"I know, sometimes he can act like a child," Abbey agreed. Rex had never made any bones about the fact he didn't like Richard.

"How do you think he's going to feel about that shiny new Jeep out there?" he asked, biting into a roll.

"Oh, he's not going to like that for a minute. He was pissed about the cell phones, I can't imagine how he's going to react about the car." She picked up his empty plate. "Want any more?"

"No, I'm good. Abbey, he's never hit you, has he?"

"No." She scraped the leftovers in a bowl for the dogs.

"That's not his way."

He almost wished she'd said yes, just so he'd have a good excuse to drive to Locknee and kick his ass. "He better never lay a finger on you."

"He wouldn't, that would be showing strong emotions and Richard doesn't do that." Except last night, she thought, when he thought he smelled like a skunk.

"Do you have a gun?"

"I don't like guns, Uncle Rex."

"Since when? Abbey, how do you live way out here without even a shotgun?" He got up and poured himself another cup of coffee.

"We haven't needed one and Richard doesn't care for them either." She stacked plates in the dishwasher.

"You used to keep a shotgun at the old house and you weren't nearly so isolated then. And you certainly know how to use a gun, I saw to that myself. So when did you suddenly start not liking guns?"

"Weird," she whispered, dropping a handful of silverware into the tray in the dishwasher and turning to face her uncle.

"You're right, I never used to be scared of guns. I even taught Kelly how to shoot." She tried to remember when the fear of the guns began. "That's really odd." She shook her head slowly. "Sometime after we moved out here," she said, trying to remember exactly when she decided she didn't like guns. "Seems I just woke up one day and didn't like guns anymore, strange."

He studied her eyes, fiercely. "Has he been messing around in your head?"

"What do you mean?" she asked, feeling fear at the intensity of his gaze.

"Are you taking any drugs?" he demanded.

"Uncle Rex I haven't taken any drugs since I got pregnant with Kelly, you know that," she defended herself, confused.

"I'm not talking about that stuff, Abbey, I know you don't do that anymore, you just got a little wild in your teens. I'm talking about prescription drugs, pills, anything like that."

"Well, I take sleeping pills. I have since I was young when the dreams get bad, you know that."

"Are they the same ones your doctor from Winslow prescribed?"

"No, I've been taking a new one." She remembered the dream of Richard altering her pills and her eyes widened.

"Let me see them."

He followed her into the master bathroom and she opened the medicine cabinet. "Here." She handed him a bottle of small green capsules.

"Why is Richard prescribing you medicine, Abbey?" he asked, studying the label.

"It was just such a pain in the ass to get the car, I let my old prescription run out and never got a new doctor here, so Richard prescribed them to me."

"Abbey, you should have your own doctor," he chastised.

"I know, I just haven't gotten around to it, I stay pretty busy out here."

"Are you still taking them?"

"No, I haven't been. I don't always sleep as much." She shrugged. "I just haven't wanted them."

"Can I take them with me?"

"Why?"

"I want to have them analyzed, I want to see what's in them.

Abbey, it's not normal to wake up suddenly fearing something that you've never feared before, something that you've always been comfortable around." He closed his hand around the bottle.

"Richard just brought a new pill home a couple days ago, a big white capsule, but I washed them down the garbage disposal. I had an odd dream about them and didn't want to take them."

"Well, I'm glad you didn't take them, but I wished you would have kept them." He slid the prescription bottle in his pocket.

"I don't think Richard is drugging me. Do you?"

"I'm just doing my job, baby girl, checking into all the options. You're standing in an odd place right now and you know it. I'm just doing my job. So I'll check it out, find nothing and feel better knowing you're okay. Are these the only thing you've been taking?"

"Yes, sir," she said nodding, and shut the medicine cabinet.

"Don't take any more pills, not prescribed by Richard. You've got a car now, go to town and find yourself a decent doctor or hell, come up to Windslow and see your old doctor. You always liked him."

"Yes, sir." She smiled, he was more than an uncle, Rex took over the role of daddy after her own father died.

"Now, lets go talk to the Jacksons."

Chapter Twelve

She called the Jacksons to make sure they were up for company and then stepped outside with Rex. "Are you going to look at the circle?" she asked, climbing in the truck beside him.

"Yes, before I leave. I don't want you to go back there, I'll go alone," he said, pulling onto the road.

"I'm not letting you go in there alone! Mom told you what happened to her in that circle, right? How the dogs reacted? I can't let you go alone, Uncle Rex. Whatever that energy is, it's getting stronger." She showed him where to turn. "I don't remember that energy from when I was a kid, I think this is different."

He glanced over at her. "We need to talk about what you do

remember."

"We will, I'm just starting to let myself remember, but we will. Look at the gardens." She pointed out the Jackson's cornfield.

"That is nice! How did he get them so tall so early?"

"I have no idea, but look at the other one, those tomato plants are huge and are already flowering. I don't know how he does it."

She saw the Jacksons sitting on the front porch and waved as Rex pulled into the driveway.

"Afternoon, Miss Abbey. How're y'all doing today?" Mr. Jackson called from the porch as she walked around the truck, joining Rex on the other side.

"Good, good," Abbey called back, walking to the porch with Rex at her side. Abbey introduced them and watched the couple's reaction. Often when she introduced Rex as her uncle to people of her own race, she noticed some type of reaction, usually an uncomfortable pause, but the Jacksons simply smiled as though they had seen it a thousand times.

Rex smiled, shaking their hands. "Nice to meet you folks, Abbey has only nice things to say about you and it's good to know she's got someone out here looking out for her."

"Y'all have a seat and set a spell," Mr. Jackson said, indicating the empty chairs. "How's that goat treating you, Abbey? He's one cocky bastard!" He laughed.

"The same, cocky as ever, but I bet I've added ten pounds of muscle since we've gotten him, I sure wrestle with him enough," Abbey said, laughing.

"Abbey, you best be careful, I've heard of folks gittin' a'kilt by those goats, if they butt you in the wrong way, you's dead," Mrs. Jackson warned.

"Yes, ma'am, I am. I might be thinking of getting rid of them, know anybody that might be interested?" Abbey asked, and Rex looked at her with surprise.

"The Williams, down the road in Farmdale raise goats, they mights be interested. And our grandson's gonna clear that patch of land 'cross the road and put in a trailer. He's a'talking bout gittin' goats, but it'll be a piece 'fore he's ready."

"Your grandson's moving out here? That's wonderful!" She smiled.

"Well, he's our great-gran, he's a'worried 'bout us." Mrs.

Jackson laughed. "He's a good 'un, got a wife and a couple youngens. It'll be nice to have family out in these parts agin."

They sat quietly, Mr. and Mrs. Jackson rocking slowly and in unison. A hawk swooped across the road, silent, quick, and deadly. It landed on the low rock wall separating the road from the yard and sat, looking in their direction. "There he is Mr. James, you see 'im?"

"I sure do, Miss Annie, second time today and he ain't feeding."

"No, sir. He's a'warning," Mrs. Jackson agreed

The old couple continued to rock and Abbey stared at the hawk, no more than thirty feet away. The large bird's head tilted, straightened, and then its yellow eyes seemed to scan their faces slowly. The bird sat for another minute and then took off; so close they could hear the power of his wings.

"He's already done that once today?" Abbey asked.

"Natures got a way," Mrs. Jackson said. "That's what's wrong with the world today, everybody's so busy they don't hear nature no more. That bird is a'warnin' that the bad time is a'comin'. I know it's true, strange cars is a'goin' down the road agin and Mr. James said the woods is quiet down past the bridge. 'Em animals know and when the time comes, they high tail it out, but folks sure don't know."

"Mrs. Jackson, I've told my uncle about Calvin and the Dawson's, could you tell us more about what you mean when you say the bad time."

"My Aunt Tilda used to say, that'd be Calvin's ma, that the earth were a'hungry back in there. Now I admit, Aunt Tilda weren't never the same after Calvin passed, but she'd say that the earth were a'hungry and it was a'gonna eat. She'd say that spot back in 'em woods would sleep for a piece, but it'd wake up all ornery like a bear awakin' up and the only thing that'd ease the ache was blood and death. Now like I said, Aunt Tilda weren't never the same, but I think there's truth to what she said. I know bad things have a'happened back there and that hawk is a'tellin us that whatever it is, it's awakin' agin."

"How many cars have you seen go back there?" Rex asked.

"Two," Mr. Jackson supplied. "A primered old truck with two young white fellas and a old Toyota, dingy blue, with an older, clean-cut, white fella."

"Where does this road end?"

"Oh, it dumps out in the Red Fork, ain't no wheres to go from there less yous is a'swimmin'. Used to be a bridge back there, but that fell in the 1950's, folks was a'movin' away then, so I figured no one saw no need to rebuild it."

"So there's nothing on this road except your place and the road to that old circle?"

"Yep, that's it."

"Have you ever recognized any of the people going back there?" Rex asked, leaning forward in his chair.

"Well, sure. Some locals git back in there to fish the Red Fork, but I ain't recognized no one in them last two cars. I'm a'thinkin' I seen that primered truck in Locknee before."

"Do you remember where?" Rex pressed gently.

"Miss Annie and I was a'tryin' to 'member, we think it was at the Wal-Mart, the big one."

"Are you able to see well enough to get the tag numbers of the cars that pass?"

"I reckon I can see well enough to git 'em."

Rex pulled out a card and handed it to the old man. "Do you

think you can keep a pad out here, record the tags and then give me a call?"

"You a cop?" Mr. Jackson took the card and studied it.

"No, sir. I'm not, but I used to be. I'm familiar with what happens in places like that and I'd like to see if I can stop it before anything bad happens."

"Well, ain't no body ever stopped it 'fore and if Aunt Tilda was right, there ain't no stoppin' it 'fore it gits what it wants," Mrs. Jackson said.

"I plan to try to stop it, I don't like my girls living so close to something like that," Rex said, his brow furrowed.

"I ain't gonna blame you there." Mrs. Jackson nodded understandingly.

"If nothing else, with your help, I might can find out who's involved on the local level. And I agree that I might not be able to stop anything, but I might be able to save some lives."

"Me and Mr. James take the paper and we've been a'watchin' to see if there is any missing women or girls, hadn't seen none yet, but the last times it woke up some folks went a'missin'. I'm a'thinkin' the two things, is one thing."

"When did you start noticing missing people when the circle back there was waking up?"

"Oh, I'm a'thinkin' it was the 1970s, that's when we started takin' a paper. Back 'fore then we got our news at the feed store or the grocery in Oak Tree or just from neighbors stoppin' in to visit and if someone went a'missin' in another town, we weren't always a'hearin' 'bout it. But we started a'noticin' the missin' folk, 'bout the same time them woods went quiet, back in the 1970s," Mrs. Jackson stated and Mr. Jackson nodded his head. "One year, one of those missin' girls turned up a'kilt in the Red Fork, down where the crick goes through Locknee. We was havin' a lot of rain that spring and the crick was a'floodin, plenty power to tote that youngen to town. We figured she gots dumped at the end of the road, after that thing in the circle a'kilt her."

"Does it only wake up in the spring?" Abbey asked, wondering if she would have noticed anything last spring when they'd been in the house just a few months.

"Mostly spring, the year Calvin gots a'kilt it was summer. We had a big ole snow that year in April, so I'm a'guessin it waited for summer."

"Does it wake up every year?" Rex rocked in his chair, appearing to be relaxed, but Abbey could feel the intensity pumping just under the surface.

"Lord, no! Me and Mr. James woulda moved a long time ago," the old woman said and chuckled, patting her husband's hand.

"Long time ago," Mr. Jackson echoed.

"My Aunt Tilda tried to keep up with it. The gas station in town used to give 'way free calendars every year with a fill up and Tilda started keepin' those calendars, marking when that thing started stirrin' and how long it lasted. It didn't have no regular cycle that we could see, sometimes it'd be much as seven years 'tween times, other times, just a couple. Once, it were 'leven years and when it woke that time, me and Mr. James took the youngens up to Farmdale and stayed wid some cuzzins. The youngens was little then and the animals high tailed it from here too, usually the animals just hop over to this side of that little no name crick down there, but that year," she shook her head, "they high tailed it from here, so we did too. I'm a'thinkin' it's 'bout two or four years, best I can reckon, but it's been near three since last time."

"Do the cars always come when it happens?" Abbey asked.

"Yep," Mrs. Jackson said, while Mr. Jackson nodded.

"Let me ask you this," Rex paused, as though working out his thoughts, "have you ever noticed the cars and people coming before you felt it wake up?"

"Matter of fact," Mr. Jackson continued to rock gently, "there were a few times the cars came 'fore the animals high tailed it outta there, the year that girl were found in the Red Fork. What year were that, Miss Annie?"

"It were the 70s."

"Yep, I 'member. The cars went by one night and I 'member a'thinkin' it were strange that I ain't noticed the woods gone quiet. It were 'round dusk when them cars started passin', there were 'bout six of 'em in a row, two or three folks in each car. I wandered back in 'em woods to that little crick and listened, 'em woods weren't quiet. The animals ain't left. Next morning I gots up and wandered back down to the crick and it had done gone quiet. It were like they flipped sum kinda switch. 'Bout three days later the cars came back and the next morning the forest back there were filled up wid animals again. A couple days later they found that girl in the Red Fork, the papers said she were dead a couple days."

"Has the local law ever been out here investigating these stories?"

"I'll tell you, Mr. Andrews, most folks 'roundst here are a'thinkin' me and Mr. James are nuts. The world moves fast out yonder, folks is busy, the world is changed, but me and Mr. James, we's just the same as ever. We ain't got no television, never saw no reason to get one, we sleep when it comes dark, we git up with the sun, we kept the old ways. Out there in the world, folks is forgotten the old ways. The television and radio tells folks what to think these days, when it used to be nature that we paid attention to." She shook her head slowly. "So, no, since the Dawson family died we ain't seen many police out this way."

Rex nodded and stood. "It was nice meeting you folks, you'll probably hear from me again." He shook their hands. "Now, I'm going to go take a look at that place."

"You shouldn't be a'goin back in 'em woods. It's dangerous," Mr. Jackson stated, getting to his feet.

"I'm just going to drive in and check it out."

"You got a gun in that truck?"

"Yes, sir," Rex answered.

"Ain't no bullet going to stop what's in 'em woods," Mrs. Jackson said, also rising from her chair.

"Well, you're not going in there alone," Abbey said to Rex and stood up. "I'm riding with you."

"Miss Abbey, you ain't gots no business back in there," the old man said.

She didn't want to tell them she'd already been back there twice. "Well, I'm not going to let Uncle Rex go back there alone."

She and Rex stared at each other for a moment, a silent debate raged between them and finally he conceded, nodding his head. "But you stay in the truck."

"Yes, sir." She nodded.

"First, I'm going to go to the end of the road, so if you all don't see us back quickly, don't worry," Rex said as they stepped off the porch and climbed back in the truck.

The Jacksons sat back down in the rocking chairs, watching them drive away. "I ain't feelin' good 'bout Abbey a'goin' in 'em woods."

"I ain't either, Miss Annie, I sure ain't." He squeezed her hand.

Driving toward the creek, Abbey pointed out the old homesteads and when they crossed over the small wooden bridge she told Rex to stop the truck.

"Listen," she said.

He leaned his head out of the window.

"Hear how quiet it is?" she asked.

He nodded and drove forward. The road meandered along and Abbey pointed out the road leading to the circle. They continued along for several miles and the birdsong returned after the first mile. The road dipped and stopped abruptly at a fast moving creek, several feet deep and thirty feet wide. Crumbling brick supports remained from the old bridge on both sides of the water, barely visible under blackberry briars. "The old man's right, there's nothing out here but woods and more woods," Rex said, turning the truck around.

As they drove back toward the turn-off Abbey spotted the remains of old homesteads in the woods. "Seems a lot of people used to live out here."

"Seems like. I guess it took a lot of hands to run all those farms," he said and then they crossed an invisible line that only the animals could see and the woods around them grew silent.

Rex turned onto the lane, the trees and bushes scraping against his truck for forty feet and then the path opened up. He slowed, looking at the branches and debris thrown to the side of the road. "Yep, they sure don't want anyone coming up in here."

Abbey showed him where the path to the circle was located and Rex pulled up to it and parked. "Now, I want you to stay here. I'm going to just walk in and have a peek, I'll be right back in less than a minute," he said and touched her shoulder reassuringly.

She nodded and sat back in the seat as he walked around the truck, heading down the path. She counted the seconds under her breath and then a hawk swooped down over the windshield, squealing its distinctive call and startling her. She watched it fly back up over the trees, heading toward the Jackson's house. Her heart began pounding and she could hear Mrs. Jackson's voice in her head. "He's a'warning," she'd said.

Abbey jumped out of the truck and ran down the path. She saw him standing at the opening, staring into the yellow field. "Uncle Rex?" she said and took a step toward him, feeling her head began to tingle. "Uncle Rex, come on." He still didn't move, he was five feet away and she took another step, feeling the pain in her head. "Uncle Rex!" she yelled. She ran up to him and felt a hammer slam into the center of her brain. She grabbed his arm and started pulling. He seemed to wake up then and turned, latching on to her arm as they ran out.

"Shit! Get in the truck!" he yelled, running to the driver's side.

"What happened?" she asked, slamming the door.

He spun around in the field and headed down the road. "That was crazy." He ran his hand across his face, wiping sweat away. "I saw what happened to Calvin, he thought he saw his mother in there, that's why they found him, he thought they were hurting his mother. It wasn't his mother in there, though, it was a white woman on the altar but he saw his mother. Once he was in there he couldn't get out, there were too many of them and he was just a kid." He slowed, pulling through the thickness of the path and the branches slapped his truck.

"All I get in there is a tingle in my head and then a sledge hammer headache, but both you and Mom have seen things, I wonder why."

"I don't know, it's the damnedest thing I ever experienced, it was like watching a movie I couldn't pull away from and I felt hypnotized for a minute. I don't know what would have happened if you hadn't grabbed me and woke me up." He turned onto the road. "Thanks."

"Funny thing is a hawk swooped down over the windshield and I suddenly knew you were in trouble. I wouldn't think a hawk would come in here when all the other animals are gone, but I could hear Mrs. Jackson say, 'it's a warning', in my head."

They passed the Jacksons, still sitting on the front porch, and continued up the hill. "You know when I said I don't remember that energy from when I was a kid?"

He nodded, turning on to the hardtop.

"I don't remember a lot, Uncle Rex, but I'm pretty sure I wouldn't have been able to forget something like that. Do you know what I mean?"

"Yeah, I do." He nodded, and turned in the driveway.

"You want another cup of coffee?"

"I think I need one. A strong one."

She nodded, leading the way into the house. While she put

on a fresh pot of coffee, he went to the bathroom. When he returned he had damp spots on his shirt from splashing his face with water.

"I don't want you to go back there again, understand?" he said, sitting down at the table.

"I won't. I have no desire to. Whatever it is back there, it's getting stronger. The first time all I felt in the circle was a tingle in my head and I got a little dizzy. When I pulled Mom out of there I felt the tingle on the path and got a headache in the circle, today I got the headache five feet away." She refilled the creamer and set it on the table. "The first time I had a compass on me and the needle just started spinning around while I was in there like the magnetic field was thrown off. I guess that could explain the tingle and the headaches."

"I've heard of a place in England like that, a big castle. This was years ago and one of my buddies was investigating the kidnapping of a minister's daughter. They followed the kidnappers to the castle and rescued the girl before anything terrible could happen, but my buddy said that some strange stuff happened that night. When I asked him to describe it to me, he just shook his head and said no one would ever believe him. I'm beginning to understand what he meant."

Abbey set a cup of coffee in front of him and sat down across from him with her own cup. "I know way back in history they used to sacrifice children to the gods in hopes of reaping a good harvest or whatever, maybe it's areas like this that started the traditions."

He stirred some sugar into his coffee. "You know over the years I've been to a lot of these satanic altars, but I never felt that kind of energy. I have to admit, though, I am usually there after the fact so maybe they had already fed it and it had gone back to sleep. And you've experienced them first hand and say you don't remember that energy and I have to agree that it would be hard to forget. Abbey, do you remember anything from that night Caroline died?"

"A little bit." She stared down in her cup. "There were five of us, me and Caroline, two little boys, and another little girl. One of the boys name was Andy or at least that's what he told us. The other little girl hadn't been with us long and never said a word. When we pulled into the gates of the mansion, I was scared. I knew bad things happened in there. We were taken in, given baths and put in these old fashioned clothes like you see little kids wearing in photographs from the 1920s." She took a sip of coffee and stared out the window, not seeing the blue sky, only seeing the past.

"We were taken down into the basement and there were about thirty people, from maybe twenty to sixty years-old, all dressed for a party and wearing masks. There was food, alcohol, and I'm pretty sure they drugged us, time seemed to move funny, jerky and my attention faded in and out. There was a door that didn't look like a door, it looked like a wall, but one of the men touched a button or something and the wall opened. Inside were candles burning and the walls were made of rock and looked old and damp. The people around me started having sex with each other and with Caroline and Andy and then someone carried Caroline into that hidden room. I was scared. She was the only thing I knew to be family, the only one that seemed to care if I was hurt or afraid. They laid her on the altar and about twelve of them were standing around her doing terrible things to her.

"She was crying and I knew they were hurting her. I peered around the door and saw one of the ladies, a blond, hold a dagger in both hands over her head. I could see the candlelight reflecting off the jewels in the handle. When the blade started coming down toward Caroline, I ran. No one saw me and it was a big house, it seems I ran for a long time. I eventually found my way to the kitchen and hid in a cabinet, I was so scared I had wet myself."

She pulled her eyes from the window, wiped a tear away and looked at her uncle, sighing deeply. "Next thing I knew this young black woman pulled me out of the cabinet, made me swear to be quiet and hid me in a closet. Later, we snuck out of the house and ran a long way through the woods to this old, old house. And there this sweet old lady cleaned me up, put me in modern day clothes, and gave me the best cookie I ever tasted in my life."

"I remember those cookies," he smiled and reached across the table taking her hand. "I know it's hard on you, baby girl, but I'm glad you're remembering. Your dad always said that one day you would have to look back just so you could go forward."

She nodded. "Thanks, Uncle Rex, for being here all these years and looking out for us."

"I promised Martin that I would and I would have no matter what, but I never expected you guys to become my family like you have." He squeezed her hand briefly and finished his coffee. "I have to get back to Windslow, I've got to make some calls, and get some folks rounded up." He stood. "Keep that phone on you and if anything happens, you call me, understand?"

"Yes, sir." She nodded and walked around the table, hugging him.

He patted her back. "You're like my own daughter, Abbey, I don't like leaving you here, but I feel better knowing you have a car and a phone. I'm going to feel even better when you step outside and I give you a gun." He felt her stiffen. "Abbey, you aren't afraid of guns, you've got to remember that and fight whatever it is telling you that you are. A gun might just save your ass if anything goes wrong." He wrapped his arm around her shoulders and led her outside.

He reached behind the seat of his truck and pulled out a Glock, handing it to her. "Show me you remember how to pull out and replace the clip."

Although her stomach was tense when he handed her the gun, her hands moved over it as though she had handled them all of her life. She slid out the clip, checked the bullets inside and slid it back in, hearing it click into place.

"Good," he said, handing her a small box of bullets. "Lock it in the Jeep."

She walked over to her new car, unlocked the door and hid the gun and bullets under the passenger seat.

"You taught Kelly to handle one of those, too, didn't you?"

Finding it hard to believe with the fear she felt just holding the gun, she nodded.

"Okay, I'll be in touch, and I want the two of you to stay in touch with me." He hugged her again.

"We will, Uncle Rex." She pulled away, smiling into his handsome face.

She watched him drive away, looked at the Jeep and began to worry how Richard was going to react. She didn't have long to worry, though, because Richard pulled into the driveway.

Chapter Thirteen

Abbey met him at his car with a smile. "Look what Mom gave me!" she feigned excitement.

His head moved quickly, looking at her, the Jeep, and back again. "You can't keep that," he said and walked toward the house.

She knew she had caught him unawares; he was stunned, surprised, and angry. She took a deep breath, shot her eyes skyward in a silent prayer, and followed him into the house. When she stepped in the door, he was reading the card. "Sweet of her, wasn't it?"

"It's not your birthday," he said, tossing the card back on the counter.

"I know, she said late birthday. I think it was really sweet of her. She said the insurance is paid for a year. So I have a car and we don't have the expense." She smiled, wondering when she became such a good liar.

"We can't keep it. It's too much." He pulled off his tie and jacket, folding them over his arm.

"I didn't expect you so early, I haven't started dinner." She began pulling items from the refrigerator.

"We can't keep it, Abbey," he stated again.

"Go get changed, we'll talk about it later," she said, pretending to have trouble choosing between items in the freezer.

"We're not keeping it," he said again and went to the bedroom.

Abbey breathed a sigh of relief; it was going to be a long night. She pulled the previous night's dinner from the fridge and set the rice to re-steam, briefly wondering how many times you could steam rice. She was pulling rolls out of the fridge when Richard stepped back in the room, dressed casually in jeans.

"You can't keep it. I can't even believe that you would consider keeping it. Your mom is living on retirement and you're stealing it right out from under her. Cell phone contracts and a brand new Jeep. Abbey, what are you thinking?"

"She can afford it," Abbey said, placing the rolls on a cookie sheet.

"You told me your Mom's retired, well since I don't think

she was a CEO of some huge company, she can't afford it. She's still young, in her sixties, she could easily live another thirty years and you're taking money from her. I think that's the most selfish thing I've ever heard. You can't take it. You have to return it." He pulled a cooling bottle of wine from of the refrigerator.

She slid the rolls in the oven and then remembered she hadn't pre-heated. She turned the oven on. "I'm not returning it. She can afford it." She stirred the beef and tomato stew.

"If she could afford it, she wouldn't be driving that beat up Subaru. No one would drive that trashcan if they could afford better. Think about it, Abbey, they're trying to tear us apart. I saw Rex leaving here today. What was he doing here?" He unscrewed the cork.

"She has another car, Richard, that's her bird watching car," Abbey defended. "And Rex was in the area and stopped by for a cup of coffee."

"She has a ten-year-old Volvo, I'll say it again, if she could afford better, she would have better. She can't afford it and you're taking it back. We'll do it tomorrow, in the morning, before Kelly gets home. You can return the phones, too." He poured two glasses of wine. "And what business does Rex have in this area? Way out here?"

"He has family in Farmdale, Richard." She picked up the wine and leaned against the counter. "And I'm not giving back the Jeep or the phones. I'm not doing it."

"Honey, don't you see they are trying to tear us apart, giving you things I can't afford, getting in your head, telling you that you need those things. They're making you choose, don't you see?" he cajoled.

"We could easily afford a couple of affordable cars, but you must have that outrageously expensive car, therefore, I have no car. I'm keeping it, Richard. I need it. It's time to teach Kelly to drive and now I can. I'm not returning it." She felt his anger spring across the room. He, of course, didn't display the anger, but Abbey felt it like a punch in the gut.

He looked through the window. "The goat's out," he said.

"Why don't you get him while I finish dinner?" she asked, setting down her glass and checking the rolls.

"I'm not getting him, I just got home from work." His eyes were wide, almost confused.

"Well, I'm tired of getting him," Abbey said, poking a roll in the oven. "I'm tired of wrestling him."

"He's in the vegetable garden," he warned.

"Oh, well." She stirred the stew.

She felt his anger expand again, shooting through the room and reverberating.

"Fine. I still smell like skunk, I guess I'll add some goat to it." He stalked out the backdoor.

She watched through the window. Richard approached the goat in the garden and Silly reared up on his hind legs coming down on a tomato plant. Abbey cringed. Richard took off running toward him, crushing more plants under his feet, Abbey dropped her head in her hands. "Jeeze," she muttered. Silly saw Richard coming at him full steam and ran off into the pines. Richard yelled something she couldn't discern and the goat crossed the driveway, vanishing in the woods by the lake.

When he stepped back into the house, she was checking the rolls. "I swear, Abbey, I've never known anyone to have so much trouble putting the dinner on the table as you and your mother."

She turned off the oven. "I guess we're just a mess." She

pulled down a serving dish and poured in the stew.

"Last Christmas, I was amazed at the disorganization." He picked up his glass and took a sip of wine.

"It was Christmas, it's supposed to be disorganized." She put the rice in a bowl, checking a piece between her fingers.

"It wasn't when I grew up," Richard stated, sitting at the table.

"We don't have staff, Richard. We don't have maids and cooks around to make sure everything goes smoothly." She put the stew and rice on the table.

He spooned through the stew. "And we didn't eat stuff like this either. What is this? Some depression era recipe?"

She pulled out the rolls and began to butter them. "It's stewed tomatoes and steak. I don't think most folks could afford steak during the depression."

"It doesn't look very appetizing." He dropped the spoon.

She rolled her eyes upwards, tossing a roll in the basket.

"Actually, I don't really feel hungry." He sniffed his forearm. "I'm going to take a shower."

She sighed and bit a roll. She made a small plate of food

and didn't bother to sit down to eat it. Then she dumped all the food in the bowl for the dogs. "I guess you guys are eating well tonight," she muttered and began cleaning the kitchen. After she was done, she stepped outside with the glass of wine in her hand and although she wanted a cigarette, she realized Richard was mad enough at her without adding any extra incentive. She walked around the house and sat on the stairs of the front porch. The dogs came out of their house, stretching and then laid down, watching her and waiting for their dinner.

She stared across the lake and wondered about the people who did the things she remembered from her youth. How could they be so soulless that they could hurt a child? She thought about the circle and the reactions of her mom and her uncle and then wondered why she only felt a headache when getting close to the circular yellow grass, while they had visions of the past.

The front door opened and Richard stepped out wearing a clean pair of jeans and t-shirt, his hair damp. "Where are your pills?" he asked, sitting on the patio furniture she shunned.

"I threw them away," she said, turning on the step to face him.

"You what?" he barked, disapproval clear in his voice.

"I threw them away, I don't want to take them anymore." She stood up, and stepped onto the porch, leaning against the rail.

He sighed, squinting his eyes slightly, and assumed the psychiatrist gaze. "Abbey, you can't just quit taking medication. If you want to try something else, we can do that, but you can't just quit."

"I did and I don't want to take the pills anymore." She took a sip of wine.

"What about the new prescription I brought home the other day?"

"I threw those away. I don't want to take them anymore."

"Where?" he asked, standing up. "Where did you throw them away?" His hand was poised on the front door handle.

"I flushed them, Richard. They're gone." She felt his anger ping out again and glancing over her shoulder, she saw that the dogs had risen to their feet.

"Are you crazy? Do you know what can happen when you just quit taking medication?" he snapped.

"I'm fine," she said.

"I think we should go to the hospital, admit you for a few days, even you out."

"I'm not going to the hospital. I'm fine, I don't need evening out," she said, feeling her temper begin to slide.

"I'm your husband, I could make you." He stared at her fiercely.

"I'm not going," she repeated, wishing for a cigarette.

"Abbey, you just aren't thinking clearly. You're taking your mom's retirement money and I know you love your mom, so why are you doing that? You're not thinking clearly and you know it." He sat back in the chair.

"I'm thinking fine. Mom's good with money, she's fine."

He burst out laughing. "That proves you're not thinking clearly. I've been in that dump your mom calls a house, it's pathetic. If she had money, she wouldn't live there. Trust me, I know. Don't you see what's happening? They are giving you things, stopping over, trying to sway you away from me. You need to go to the hospital, get your head straight, and we'll talk about it next week when you come home." He stood up again and put his hand on the doorknob.

"No, Richard, I don't see. What I do see is that you want to keep me isolated out here, no car, no cell phone, and you've taken over the role of my doctor. Plus, you control all the money. I can't even buy a box of tampons without being questioned about it. I see you want to control everything I do and feel threatened when you begin to remember that I do have a family looking out for me." She finished the wine and set the glass on the rail, expelling a deep breath.

"Rex," he sneered, "is not your family, he's a black man, Abbey, and you're white. He's not your family."

"Yes, Richard, he is. We may not share the same blood, but he's been like my dad since my own dad passed. Whether you like it or not, Rex will always be a part of my and Kelly's life." She picked up her glass and went in the house.

She dumped the leftovers in the dog's bowls and added some dried food. She slammed the bowls on the counter and stirred the food just as Richard stepped into the kitchen. "Have you thought of what the neighbors will think if they see Rex over here?"

"What neighbors? The Jacksons? Somehow I don't think they'll care." She picked up the bowls and walked out the backdoor.

He followed her. "What about Fay and Brandon?"

"You mean the truck driver's son you didn't want around Kelly?" she asked and put the bowls in front of the dogs, but they didn't eat, they watched Richard.

"What about your reputation, Abbey? People can't see a black man pulling out of the driveway when I'm not home. They'll have questions."

"So answer their damned questions, Richard, it's not that hard! He's my freaking uncle, how hard it that?" she yelled, realizing suddenly that she had cussed in front of him and that her temper had spiraled out of control.

Silly bounded out of the woods and butted Jerry in the ribs. The dog woofed in pain and ran into the doghouse. Abbey ran toward the goat and the goat ran toward Richard, his head down aggressively. Richard jumped out of his way, his hands raised defensively.

"You little fucktard!" She chased the goat to the gate. Outside of the gate, he reared up on his hind legs. "I'm not in the mood for your shit, Silly." He came down hard on his front legs, pawing the ground. "You want to go, little asshat? Really, you want to go with me now?" she challenged him.

He stepped forward and pressed his head into her thighs. "Okay, pissface." She rubbed his head roughly. She opened the gate and wrangling the goat around, she continued to rub his head as she backed into the pen. She slipped around him and out of the enclosure. "You're not the brightest bunny in the bunch, are you? Dickhead." She shut the gate in his face and he rammed it with his head. "Yeah, that'll work. Stupid."

She turned around and almost ran into Richard.

"Don't you see how out of control you are? Listen to your language," he demanded.

"You sure weren't stepping in to control the little bastard, were you? The damned thing outweighs me by a good fifty pounds and what do you do? Raise your hands in the air like a little girl jumping over a puddle. Jesus!" She stalked in the house. I've got to calm down, she thought, and slammed the back door.

He followed her. "I want you to go to the hospital."

She snatched around. "Fuck the hospital! You go to the damned hospital, ask them why you have such a need to control your woman. Ask them why you are so damned passive aggressive that you refuse to eat dinner when things don't go your way. You're forty-five freaking years old, for God's sake, why do you act like you are six?"

She poured another glass of wine and slammed out the front door. The dogs lay by their full bowls, watching the house.

Richard stepped out onto the porch. "It only takes a couple signatures, Abbey. I think you need to go to the hospital."

She looked at him and she wanted to punch him. She stormed back in the house and pulled her phone from her bag.

"Who are you calling?" Richard demanded, following her.

"Well, if you're going to try to commit me, I'm going to call my lawyer."

"Rex? You're calling Rex?" he yelled, slamming his glass onto the coffee table and spilling wine.

"What else am I supposed to do? Let you lock me away?" she asked.

"Don't you see how irrational you are? Did you not just hear how you talked to the goat? You're talking to a goat, Abbey, think about it!"

"Who put the goat away? You? No! Me! So what if I talk to the little bastard while he's trying to butt me into hell? How does that make me crazy? You're not here! You don't handle it! I do!" She thumped herself in the chest and tried to convince herself to calm down.

He sat down on the couch, shaking his head, and tears filled his eyes. "You just don't see what I see, you just don't see how you are breaking away." He covered his face with his hands and sobbed. "You just don't see." He pulled up the bottom of his shirt and wiped his face, looking at her with red eyes. "Honey, let me take you to the hospital, please. You're just not thinking clearly." He sniffed. "Baby, you're calling me at work to ask where the cleaning supplies are, you're the one who cleans the house and you don't even know where the cleaning supplies are."

"You!" She pointed at him. "You mother fucker," she whispered. "You stupid, pathetic, assclown of a man," she stated a little louder, staring at him across the room and shaking her head slowly. "You!" she yelled, walking across the room until her finger was an inch from his nose. "Stay the fuck away from me," she whispered. "I want you to stay the hell out of my way. You got it?"

He stared back at her, unblinking. His face flushed red and his eyes widened, but he didn't say a word.

She turned, sliding the phone in her back pocket. She stepped out onto the porch, walked around the house to the shed and pulled down the cigarettes. Lighting one and inhaling deeply, she exhaled. "Fuck me!"

Her mind was racing. I hid the damned cleaning supplies? She wanted to scream. She slid the pack into her back pocket, slammed the door of the shed and walked down to the water. She plopped down on the grass and stared across the water. "Okay, God, you've shown me and damn, if you haven't shown me good." She sighed, took a deep drag and exhaled. "Just give me strength. Okay? Just give me strength."

Chapter Fourteen

She put the animals away and was surprised, and a little

disappointed, when Silly went into the barn easily - she could have used the fight to burn off some of the rage flowing through her veins. She locked the barn and walked to the doghouse and noticing the dogs had finally eaten their food, she set them free. She picked the glass of wine up off the front porch rail and carried it into the house. She could hear the television droning from the den and walked into the kitchen. She poured the wine down the sink, grabbed a bottle of water from the fridge, and noticed the phone was off the base.

She walked into the bedroom, wondering who Richard was talking to, and grabbed a t-shirt and pair of sweats from a drawer. Stepping into Kelly's bathroom, and locking the door behind her, she showered. Combing her hair, and leaving it to air dry, she dropped her clothes in the washer. She chose her clothes for the next day, carried them into Kelly's room, and shut the door, locking it, and picking up the remote, she crawled into the bed.

She placed the phone and cigarettes on the bedside table and turned on the television. Flipping channels until she found one that showed only sitcoms from the 50s and 60s, she turned the sound low and dropped the remote on the bed. She dozed and woke startled when a boom of thunder reverberated, shaking the house. The power blinked and Abbey sat up in bed. She had been dreaming, she stared at the television and tried to remember. "Something about the dogs," she muttered and pushed her hair away from her face. Another roll of thunder vibrated the house and she heard the dogs barking.

"The dogs!" she gasped, jumping from the bed. She threw open the door and ran down the hall. "Oh my God! The dogs!" she yelled. She tore through the living room, threw open the front door and ran into the storm.

The rain was coming down hard, fat drops that had her soaked to the skin in the first few steps across the porch. "Tom! Jerry! Here!" She ran down the steps. "Tom! Jerry!" She could hear them barking across the lake and she ran towards the dam. "Tom! Jerry! Here! Now!" She hit the dam, slid in the mud that made up the dirt structure, but regained her balance and continued running toward the sound of the dogs. "Tom! Jerry!" she yelled again and Jerry came running out of the woods, passing her on the dam. "Tom! Here! Now!" She heard him yelp. "Tom!" she screamed and he came out of the woods with a limp. "Come boy!"

she encouraged. When he was met her on the edge of the dam, she grabbed his collar and ran back to the house, calling for Jerry to follow.

"What in the hell's going on?" Richard barked when she ran back into the house soaked to the skin and followed by equally wet dogs. "Get those skunk stinking dogs out of my house!"

"No! Tom's hurt." She called the dogs into the kitchen. Jerry ran to her with his tail wagging, Tom came slower. "Come 'ere, Tom." She patted her leg. He stepped over to her with a limp and she could see blood running down his hip. She dropped to her knees for a closer look.

"What in the hell is wrong with you? Running out into that storm, have you lost your mind?" He threw a towel at her and she used it to clear the blood away and investigate the wound. "That towel was for you, not the damned dog," he said, exasperated. "Do you know it's after one o'clock in the morning? And you're jumping out of bed and running out into a storm. You don't even have shoes on."

"The dog's been hurt. It looks like a bullet hole, I'm taking him to the vet." She stood up. "Stay here, boys." She walked down the hall to the linen closet, pulled out an old blanket and a handful of towels. She wrapped one towel around her shoulders and threw the rest into the living room. The pile landed on the floor at Richard's feet.

"What in the hell are you doing?" he asked, stepping over the mound and following her into Kelly's room.

She pulled off wet clothes, dropping them on the floor. "I'm taking the dog to the vet." She dried off quickly and dragged a clean t-shirt over her head.

"It's the middle of the night!"

"So? The dog's been shot, he needs a doctor." She sat on the bed and yanked on a pair of jeans.

"It can wait until morning," he said, crossing his arms on his chest.

She picked up the phone and cigarettes and slid them in her back pockets. "No. It can't wait until morning." She walked around him and out of the room.

"You're smoking again! Don't deny it! I just saw the pack!" He followed her into the master bedroom.

"I'm not denying it." She sat down on the bed and pulled on

a pair of boots over bare feet. Quickly tying the laces, she returned to the pile in the living room, picking up the blanket and towels and carrying them into the kitchen and taking in the bloody paw prints leading to where Tom lay by the backdoor. She dropped the blanket and towels beside the dog and grabbed a raincoat out of the laundry room.

"Help me get him into the Jeep," she said and turned to Richard, who stood, hair askew, watching her.

"I'm not going to help you. This is ridiculous. Something scratched the dog. Put them out and go to bed." He reached into her bag and grabbed her keys. "There. It's settled. You can't go."

She stalked over to him, and grabbed her purse off the counter, pulling out her wallet and thrusting it into the pocket of her coat. "You're not going to help me?"

"No." He held the keys over her head, teasing her with them and thunder boomed again.

She looked at the keys just out of reach over her head and was reminded of schoolyard bullies. "Give me my keys."

"No, I'm not going to encourage this out of control behavior," he stated with a triumphant smile and jiggled them.

Without much thought, she drew back her arm and punched him in the stomach. With an "oomph" he dropped the keys and she picked them up. "My kid is not coming home to another dead animal!"

Keys in hand she turned back to the dog, wrapped the blanket around him and lifted him as gently as she could, soothing him, "It's all right, buddy, we're going to get you to a doctor."

She heard Jerry growl low in his throat and then bark. She looked over her shoulder to see the dog facing Richard, the ridge of hair on his back standing on end. "Jesus, Abbey, now you have the dogs upset! Why are you doing this? You've been acting like a mad woman all night and now you've punched me."

"I told you to stay away from me, you should have listened." She opened the door, struggling to hold the dog that weighed nearly eighty pounds, and stepped out into the rain. "Come on, Jerry." The dog backed slowly toward her voice, keeping his eyes on Richard, and when his butt was even with the door jam, he turned, following her out into the downpour.

She unlocked the back door of the Jeep and slid Tom onto the seat. "Just lay still, Tom." She rubbed his head, while Jerry jumped in the Jeep and lay down on the floorboard.

Pulling out of the driveway and turning toward Locknee, she noticed a truck parked beside the bridge where the little no name creek flowed. Crossing the bridge, she looked into the rear view mirror to see the truck pull out onto the road and begin following her.

She pulled the phone out of her pocket, dialed Rex, and hit the button for the speakerphone, dropping it into her lap. Rex answered after the second ring, his voice raspy from sleep.

"Uncle Rex, it's Abbey. One of my dogs has been shot, I'm on my way to the emergency vet clinic in Locknee and I think I'm being followed."

"Can you see what's following you, what kind of vehicle?"

"It's a truck, an older one, either white or light gray. It's raining like hell out here, so I couldn't see much. He was parked on the edge of our property and pulled out behind me when I passed. It could be a coincidence, but my dog did just get shot."

"Is he still behind you?"

"Yeah, I'm at the stop sign, about to turn toward Oak Tree. He's stopped twenty feet behind me." She turned to the right; the truck pulled up to the stop sign and then fell in behind her. "He's still behind me, I just turned. I guess he could have business in Locknee in the middle of the night after he just happened to be parked right next to our property, but I think that's stretching the idea of coincidence just a bit."

"Don't second guess yourself, Abbey. Pull that gun out, if you don't already have it."

She reached under the front of the passenger seat and couldn't reach the gun. She simply wasn't long enough. "Damn it, I can't reach it! Hang on." She reached around the back of the seat; the Jeep swerving slightly on wet pavement and her hand fell on cool metal. "I got it!" She put the pistol on the seat beside her, her fear of the gun suddenly outweighed by the fear of the truck behind her.

"Which vet are you going to? I'll call ahead and have them waiting for you."

"It's Locknee Emergency Clinic. There should only be one, I don't know the number, but it's on Cherry Street."

"I found it. Luckily, I left the computer on when I went to bed. Hang on." She heard him speaking into another phone.

"Where's he been shot, Abbey?" he asked, juggling phones.

"Rear, left flank. High up, but not as high as his spine," she said, glancing into the rear view mirror.

Rex relayed the info to the vet. "How long before you get there?"

"Twenty minutes. I'm just making the turn toward Locknee."

Rex passed along her estimated time to the vet and came back on the phone. "The vet's waiting, he's calling in a surgical nurse. Are you still being followed?"

"Yes, sir." The truck was ten feet behind her now, much too close with so much water on the road. "He's closer now. I still can't see well, but the truck is a Ford, looks like it's from the 1970s. Light colored, white or gray."

"Could it be the same one you saw out by the cemetery clearing the road and circle?" he barked in the phone.

"Yeah, I think it could be."

"Hang on." He juggled phones. "Larry, I need you in Locknee now! Meet my niece at the emergency vet clinic on Cherry St. Okay." He came back on the line. "Is he still behind you?"

"Yes, sir! About six feet now and I'm about to go through the marsh." The road between Locknee and Oak Tree was built, levee style, through the center of the marsh. The road was wide, loomed 30 feet above the water, and had no guardrails.

"Can you see who's driving?"

She glanced in the rearview mirror. "No. It's raining too hard." Lightning lit the sky and she could see the trees in the marsh bending with the winds and flying wet flags of Spanish moss.

"How fast are you going?"

She glanced down. "Forty-five and that's almost too fast in this storm."

"Don't go any faster. If you don't run, it's hard to chase you, just get through that swamp."

"He just hit his brights!" The inside of the Jeep was illuminated.

"Duck down low in the seat! Don't let them get a shot at your head!"

She slid down in the seat, barely able to peer over the dashboard and reached up, flipping the rear view mirror away from reflecting the bright light into her eyes. The Jeep shuddered, fishtailing in the water covering the road. "He hit my bumper!" she yelled, righting the vehicle.

"You're going to have to speed up, he's trying to knock you in the swamp. Shit!"

Abbey accelerated, quickly leaving the truck behind her. "I've got some room, but he's coming up fast!"

"Stay as far in front of him as you can! Get out of that swamp!"

Lightning cracked the sky in front of her, blinding her. "Shit!" She blinked rapidly, trying to clear her vision. "He's coming up beside me!" Thunder boomed, vibrating the Jeep. With the sound of metal against metal, the truck slammed into the side of the Jeep. "Shit!" Abbey yelled as the Jeep shuddered and headed toward the sharp embankment. She gained control right before she hit the gutter, overflowing with inches of water. "The asshole hit me!"

"Is he beside you?" Rex yelled.

"Yeah! He's coming in again."

"Slam on the brakes! Now!"

Abbey did as she was told and stood on the brakes. The Jeep jerked hard and spun on the wet pavement, barely missing the rear of the truck as it shot past. The vehicle came to rest in the opposite lane, facing the wrong direction. She looked over her shoulder, the taillights of the truck disappearing in the heavy down pour. She looked in the back seat; Tom was lying on the opposite side of the car. "You okay, boy?" she asked, reaching out to pet him. He raised his head, licked her finger, and dropped his head back down onto his paws.

"He's gone, Uncle Rex," she said, picking up the phone from the floorboard and then turning the Jeep around on the deserted road. "What if he tries to block me up ahead?"

"Ram the back of his truck and move his ass out of the way! Are you okay?" he asked.

"I'm mad as hell is what I am," she said, accelerating down the road as the lighting split the sky again.

He chuckled. "Good."

"He messed up my brand new car."

Rex laughed. "That's my girl. I don't suppose you saw a tag, did you?"

"No, sir." She crossed the Red Fork Bridge and entered Locknee. "I'm in Locknee now."

"Good." He sighed. "Keep your eye out for that truck."

"I am," she said, driving through the dark and deserted town square.

"Once you're in the vet's office, I want you to call the cops and make a report of what happened."

"Yes, sir."

"I'll call you when Larry gets there, he's going to follow you home and keep an eye on things."

"Richard's going to love that." She stopped at a red light, looked both ways, and made a right turn onto Cherry Street.

"Richard won't even know he's there."

She pulled into the parking lot of the veterinarian's office and could see the vet standing under a covered walk way with a dog-sized stretcher. "I'm here, Uncle Rex. I see the vet."

"Put the phone in your pocket and leave the line open until you're inside, behind a locked door."

"Yes, sir," she said, angling the car as close as she could to the overhang. She turned off the car, clicked off the speaker, and dropped the phone in the pocket of her raincoat, jumping out of the Jeep and running around it to help the doctor with Tom. They eased Tom onto the stretcher and Jerry hopped out of the car. Abbey shut and locked the doors, just as another car pulled in the parking lot. She felt fear sweep through her body as she realized she'd left the gun inside the car.

"That's the nurse," the doctor said and wheeled the dog toward the front door of the clinic. A small piece of wood was wedged in between the double doors, keeping one open. Abbey opened the door and the vet wheeled Tom into the building. Abbey stepped in behind him, followed by Jerry. "Keep the door open for the nurse," he said, wheeling the stretcher to an examination room. Abbey shut the door gently against the piece of wood and followed him.

"What happened?" he asked, angling the stretcher next to a metal table. "Give me a hand." He indicated picking up the sheet under the dog. Abbey lifted her side and they slid Tom onto the table.

"I heard them barking in the woods, it sounded funny. I ran out to get them and this one," she nodded her head toward Jerry, "came running out, but Tom yelped and came out with a limp. I didn't notice the blood until I got him in the house. It was raining pretty hard. I think he's been shot."

"Did you hear a gun?" He adjusted the light over the dog.

"No, but it looks like a bullet hole."

He pulled on some gloves and picked up some cotton balls, looking at the wound. "It does look like a gun shot, but we won't know anything until we get inside and have a good look."

The nurse stepped into the room, pulling off her raincoat.

"Get him shaved and prepped," the doctor said and she nodded her head, hanging up her coat.

"Come with me." Abbey followed him into the reception area, Jerry behind her, his nose against the floor. "I hate to talk about money, but this surgery is going to be expensive, easily in the thousands of dollars."

She nodded her head. "That's fine."

He handed her a clipboard and she filled out the paper work.

"Leave your number, we'll call you when we're done."

"I'm staying here until you're done," Abbey stated. "And I need to call the police, someone hit my car as I was driving over here."

He nodded his head and put the phone on the counter. "Dial 9. And when you step outside, make sure to chock the door or it'll lock behind you. There's a soda machine in there." He pointed at a door that had a sign designating employees only. "It might be a couple hours." She nodded and the nurse appeared in the doorway. "Are we ready?" he asked and the young nurse nodded her head, her ponytail bouncing behind her. "All right," he said, leaving the reception desk and heading toward the nurse.

"Take good care of him. He's a good boy," Abbey called after him.

"I'll do my best, I promise." He gave her a slight, reassuring smile and followed the nurse down the hall.

Abbey pulled the phone from her pocket and put it to her ear. "Uncle Rex? You still there?"

"Yeah, I'm here. So the vet thinks it's a gunshot?"

"It seems so."

"You didn't hear a gun?"

"No, sir, just a yelp. Hang with me for a minute, I've got to move the gun out of the seat before I call the police." She opened the door and put down the wooden chock. "Stay, Jerry," she demanded and the dog sat down. She pulled the hood over her head and ran into the rain, opening the door, grabbing the gun, and sliding it under the passenger seat. She ran back in the building and Jerry stood up, wagging his tail. "Done. I need to call the police."

"Use the phone there, I want to keep this line open."

"Okay, hang on." She picked up the phone and dialed the police. The dispatcher promised that officers would arrive soon and she hung up the phone. She put the cell back to her ear. "They're on the way."

"Good, now you hang on." She heard him speaking in another phone. "Larry, I want you to stay back until the police leave. Yeah. Good." He changed phones. "Larry is just about to enter Locknee. He's going to sit back until the police have come and gone."

"Okay," she said and saw a police car pull into the parking lot. "The police are here."

"Drop the phone in your pocket and leave the line open."

"Yes, sir." She dropped the phone in her pocket and went out to meet the officers.

Two young officers stepped out the car wearing plastic covered, wide brim hats and raincoats. She told them what happened, gave them a description of the vehicle that hit her, and they looked at the damage. They came in the office, filled out a report, but said without a tag number the chances of catching the person was low. "There's probably a hundred old trucks like you described in the county," one officer explained, "but we'll keep our eyes open." He handed her a copy of the report and pulled his hat back on. "Looks like the rain is letting up," he said and they stepped outside.

Abbey picked up the phone. "They're leaving."

"Hang on." Rex picked up the other phone. "They're leaving. You see them? Good." He came back on the line. "Larry should be pulling in any minute."

The police pulled out onto the street and turned back toward town. A small, beat-up, red 4x4 truck pulled into the parking lot a few seconds later. "A red truck just pulled in."

"That's him," Rex said.

The truck pulled behind her Jeep and the headlights went out.

"He sees you," Rex said, juggling phones.

Abbey lifted her hand in a slight wave, and the parking lights flashed.

"Okay, Abbey, you're safe. Now get some rest and call me when the surgery is over. I've sent up a prayer for Tom."

"Thank you, Uncle Rex, for everything. I'll call you as soon as I know something."

She hung up the phone, glanced through the glass to look at the red truck and then rubbed Jerry's head. His tail thumped against the floor. "Your brother's gonna be okay," she said and started pacing.

Chapter Fifteen

Larry pushed his seat back, lighting a cigarette, and the phone rang. "Yeah," he answered.

"Do you see her?" Rex asked.

"Yeah, she's in there, pacing. A dog is following her," he chuckled.

"Good. Man, I'm sorry sending you out so quick, I know you just got off a plane a few hours ago, but I need you on this one. I don't know what the hell is going on, but I've got a real bad feeling."

"It's no problem, Rex. Glad to help."

"I've sent you satellite photos of her house, the surrounding land, and the adjacent property where that damned altar is."

Larry reached across the cab of the truck and opened his laptop. "What's the deal with her husband, is he involved in this?"

"I don't know. I don't like him. What kind of man moves a woman so far out in the country and won't let her have a car or a cell phone?"

"One who wants to have control of her," Larry said, opening the sat photos. "Damn. You weren't kidding about her living in the middle of nowhere."

Rex sighed. "Yeah, the bastard wants to control her, that's what I know. I've wanted to kick his ass a few times, I've been looking for a good reason."

Larry laughed. "Maybe we'll find you one." He glanced inside the building to see the woman pull off her raincoat and try to comb her long hair with her fingers. He pulled his eyes back to the computer screen when he realized he was staring at her body appreciatively. "Looks like I can go in by the bridge, I think I can pull the truck far enough in that it won't be seen from the road."

"That's what I was thinking. There probably won't be anything left to find after the storm, but look around out there, the dog was shot right on the other side of the lake."

"We know for sure the dog was shot?"

"The vet thinks so, we'll know more after the surgery."

"How'd she find them in the storm?" He glanced up to see the woman had stretched out on the couch and the dog was lying on the floor beside her.

"She was supposed to be an owl, Larry."

"Oh. Well, that makes sense." Larry pulled up the sat photos of the altar. "That thing is less than half a mile from her house, if this is a coincidence it'll be a world record. I agree with you, this doesn't feel right."

Rex sighed. "I know. Abbey's daughter, Kelly, is coming home today; I want you to keep your eyes on those girls. Her neighbors, the Jacksons, might be of some help. They're old, but sharp, and good people. Keep that in mind."

"I will. I'll be in touch." He hung up the phone and began studying the satellite photos.

*

She was dreaming. Richard sat at a rich mahogany table, sipping a glass of ice water. Her eyes moved around the room, she didn't recognize it. Sheer curtains hung over open teak wood blinds and through the window she could see a beautifully manicured lawn, highlighted by the rising sun. She brought her attention to the other occupants gathered around the large table. Some of the faces she didn't know, but she recognized Richard's partner, Mike, the pastor from the church that Richard and Kelly attended, and Pearl Hollister, the blond, middle-aged, femme fatale who owned the most lucrative real estate business in Locknee.

As she studied the faces, she saw that all eyes were focused on the head of the table. She turned her head and looked at the man holding everyone's attention. He was an older man with white hair and very tan skin. He slammed his hand on the table, angry. Abbey gave up trying to read his lips in the silent exchange and turned her head to see who he was addressing.

It was Richard, looking uncharacteristically discomfited. He squirmed in his seat under the hot gaze of the white-haired man and looked at the table in front of him like a shamed schoolboy. Suddenly, Richard spoke. She glanced around the table to see the white-haired man silent and all eyes on her husband. She turned her head to try to make out his words and she heard her name being called. "Mrs. Brown. Mrs. Brown."

She opened her eyes to see the vet standing over her. "Yes?" She sat up, pushing her hair out of her face.

"I'm done with the surgery."

She jumped to her feet. "How is he?"

"He made it, he's weak. He had been shot and it's lucky you got him here so quickly. If he had made the wrong move, he could have bled to death. I want to keep my eye on him until this evening.

I think he'll be fine; he's young, strong, and healthy. You can pick him up between five and six."

"Can I see him?"

"Yeah." He turned for her to follow him.

"Can his brother come?" she asked with a smile.

The vet turned back, looking at Jerry staring up at him at her side, and smiled. "Yes, his brother can come, too."

She followed him down the hall, Jerry on her heels.

"When did they get skunked?" he asked.

"A couple days ago."

He opened the door to let them pass into the small recovery room. "It'll wear off in a couple days."

She nodded. "Do you still have the bullet?"

"Yes."

"Can I have it?"

"I'll get it for you," he said, one eyebrow rising.

"Thanks," she said, stepping in the room.

Tom lay on a table, drowsy from medication. "Hey, bunny," she whispered, kissing his nose.

His tailed wagged slowly.

Jerry put his front paws on the table and nudged Tom's head with his nose, licking him across the face.

Tom's tail beat a little faster.

"He's going to be fine," the nurse said, wiping the counter. "He did really well in surgery."

"Good to know, thanks." Abbey gently rubbed the dog's head and whispered in his ear, "I'll see you tonight, buddy."

His tail thudded the table.

"That's a good sign. He's a strong boy." The nurse smiled.

Abbey met the vet in the hall and he handed her a small plastic bag with a slug inside. "It was a big gun, he was lucky." She walked back to the couch, grabbed her coat, and dialed Rex.

"Hey. How is he?" he answered on the first ring.

"They think he's going to be fine, and yes, he was shot. I got the bullet from the vet. They're going to watch him today and I need to pick him up this evening."

"Good, good to hear. Now go outside, introduce yourself to Larry and give the bullet to him. He's going to follow you home and keep an eye on you. You're about to get twenty-four hour security, so go home, see Kelly, and try to relax. I'll talk to you soon."

"I love you, Uncle Rex. Thank you."

"I love you too, baby girl. Now, go meet Larry."

She hung up the phone, put on her coat, and stepped outside. The rain had stopped, she looked up to see that the sky had cleared and as she approached the red truck, Larry stepped out. He was in his mid-thirties, blond with brown eyes, and looked like a young Robert Redford. He had a day's growth on his face, a slim build, and was barely half a foot taller than her.

He stuck out his hand. "I'm Larry Sanders."

She shook it. "I'm Abbey Brown."

"How's the dog?" he asked, still holding her hand.

"He's going to make it." She felt her cheeks flush and pulled her hand away. She reached into her pocket and handed him the small plastic bag. "Tom, the dog, was shot. Here's the bullet. Uncle Rex said to give it to you."

He held the bag up to the light. "Lucky dog."

"That's what the vet said." Abbey glanced at Jerry sniffing along the walkway and lifting his leg.

"I'm going to follow you home, I'll drop off at the bridge

below your driveway. I'll be across the lake keeping my eye on things. You won't know I'm there and your husband won't either. I want you to program my number into your phone and I want your number." He reached in his pocket of his flannel shirt, pulled out his phone and they exchanged numbers. "Tell me what you have planned today, who you're expecting, things like that, I'm coming into this pretty fresh."

"My daughter should be home after lunch and her dad drives a blue SUV. I have to pick up the dog tonight between five and six. I don't know what my husband has planned, but he drives a silver Mercedes. Monday and Tuesday I carpool for home school." She searched her mind. "That's all I can think of right now. Can I call you if there are any changes?"

"Please do. I've been studying the layout and the woods and I think I'm pretty familiar with the area now. I'll be right across the lake if you need me. Rex said your daughter had a phone, I want you to give me her number and put mine in her phone."

She scrolled through the numbers her mom had put in the phone and read off Kelly's number to him. "Jeeze, I guess I'm going to have to tell her we have a bodyguard." She sighed and then nodded her head slowly. "I can do this," she whispered under her breath.

"Okay, I guess that's it. Are you ready?"

She nodded her head.

"Anything else I should know?"

"Yes," she smiled, "watch out for the goat." She called Jerry, opened the backdoor of the Jeep and the dog jumped inside. She turned onto the street and called Rex.

"Hey. Is everything okay?" he answered.

"Yeah, I'm on my way home, just gave Larry the bullet. Um, Uncle Rex, isn't Larry kind of small to be a bodyguard?"

"Best I remember Bruce Lee was a rather small man, too," he said with a chuckle.

Abbey remembered Saturday afternoons at Rex's house when she was a teen, where they'd order pizza and watch Bruce Lee or other martial arts movies. "Enough said," she laughed.

"Seriously, Larry may not be a big guy, but I can't think of anyone else I'd like to have at my side when the going was tough or when blows were being thrown. I wouldn't put the most important people in my life in his hands if I didn't think he was capable."

"Okay, Uncle Rex. Thanks again." She felt a little ashamed for underestimating her uncle and the man he trusted.

"It's okay, baby girl, go home and get some rest."

She hung up the phone, tested the lighter in the dash, and pulled the cigarettes out of her pocket.

*

Rex poured a cup of coffee, sat down at his computer, and his phone rang again. "Yeah?"

"It's Larry. I got the bullet and we're on the way back to her place. You didn't tell me she was gorgeous."

Rex laughed. "Of course she gorgeous, she's my niece, she looks just like me. Didn't you see the resemblance?"

Larry laughed, pondering. "What color are her eyes? Yellow or green? Never seen anything like them."

"Both, depends on her mood. Remember, she is a married woman," Rex warned.

"I know. A beautiful and married woman, I'll remember that. Oh yeah, one other thing, she said something about watching out for a goat, what does that mean?"

Rex laughed again; if he wasn't so worried this could be entertaining. "That'd be Silly, the goat. He's a cocky bastard and he likes to butt anything that moves. She gave you good advice."

*

The sun was just beginning to lighten the horizon when she turned onto the rural road that would take her home and she let out a long sigh just as the phone rang. "Abbey, Larry. I'm going to pull off where I said, but I want you to sit at the end of the driveway and wait for my call. Lock your doors and keep the engine idling. It shouldn't take me a couple minutes to get into place. Okay?"

"Is everything all right?"

"Yeah, just feeling a little hinkey."

She smiled. "I'll wait for your call." Welcome to my world, she thought and disconnected the call.

She watched through the rear view mirror as the truck eased off the road into the woods and the lights went out. "And he's invisible," she whispered under her breath and turned on the blinker.

She pulled onto the dirt drive, put it in neutral, and turned off the headlights.

Jerry poked his head over the seat and she scratched behind his ears. "Looks like Kelly was right," she explained to the dog, "seems we have found ourselves in some kind of suspense novel."

He licked her nose.

"Says you," she replied.

She waited, watching the edges of the sky turn pink and jumped when the phone rang again. "Hello."

"Is it always so dark over there?" Larry asked.

"We only have the porch lights as outside lights."

"There aren't any porch lights on. Or any lights in the house. And I don't see a car."

"Well Richard probably didn't leave any lights on because he was mad at me." She glanced at the clock on the dash. "It seems way too early for him to go to church. Are you sure you don't see a car?"

"Where does he usually park?"

"By the back door."

"Nope. No car."

"Then, I don't know."

"Stay where you are and stay on the line, I'm coming over."

The line was quiet for a couple minutes. "Okay, come on down the driveway, I don't see anyone here."

She put the car in gear and pulled down the driveway. She saw him standing on the sandy lane, changed from the flannel shirt into a long sleeved camouflage t-shirt, and stopped beside him. "Give me the key to the house, I'm going to check it out. Same thing, though, stay here with the engine running and keep the line open." She reached down and wrangled the key off the chain, handing it to him.

He moved quickly, stealthily, and in seconds he was across the porch and in the house, the door shut behind him. He gave his eyes a moment to adjust to the dark shadows and then slipped through the house silently, making sure no one was hiding in a closet or under a bed. Satisfied that the place was empty, he opened the back door and lifted the phone to his ear. "It's clear."

Abbey climbed out of the Jeep, stretching, and opened the back door for Jerry.

"Keep the dog with you until I can check out things on the

other side of the lake," he said, his eyes scanning the woods.

She nodded and kept her eye on the dog as he walked behind the garden and did his business. "Come on, Jerry. You're going to be a house dog for awhile." He ran to her, his tail wagging, and followed her into the house.

Larry stepped in behind the dog and shut the door, locking it. "Look around and see if everything is as it should be."

She turned on the kitchen light, saw the bloody paw prints, and followed them into the living room. "I've got a lot of cleaning to do, that's normal."

Larry smiled. "Check out of the rest of the house."

She went from room to room. "Everything seems to be in place," she said, stepping back into the kitchen and heading for the coffee pot. "Do you want some coffee?"

He looked at the coffee pot, thought how little sleep he'd had in the last two days, a few hours on the plane, a few hours before Rex called him. "You know what? I'd really like a cup, but now that it's getting light, I need to go find out what I can before any evidence is gone. Can I get it when I'm done?"

"Sure, I'll go take a shower and make it when I get out."

"Great." He walked toward the picture window in the living room. "Can you me tell what happened last night and point out where?"

"The thunder woke me up." She joined him by the window. "The dogs were barking, it didn't sound right. I heard them over there." She indicated with her finger. "I was just about ten feet from the other side of the lake when Jerry came running out, of course, I was calling them like a mad woman. It's a good thing I don't have neighbors, they'd think I was a crazy lady." She laughed.

I like her, he thought, not a lot of people can keep a sense of humor when their world was as screwed up as hers.

"Jerry ran past and I heard Tom yelp. I was probably right at the end of the dam when he came out of the woods. I just grabbed his collar and ran."

"Where did he come out of the woods?"

"It was raining like hell, but I'd say twenty feet to the right."

"And you didn't hear a gun?" He looked into her eyes, green, as the morning light touched them.

"No," she said, pulling her eyes away. His gaze made her

nervous. "They were barking, Jerry ran out, Tom was barking and then he yelped."

"And you heard his yelp clearly? And it was raining like hell?"

She nodded.

"Okay, I'll be back in a little while. Keep your doors locked."

He slipped out the backdoor and shut it softly. Abbey checked the doors and went to the shower. She dried off, pulled on her usual attire of jeans and t-shirt and combed out her hair. As she stared into the mirror, braiding the long strands, she considered putting on a little mascara. Her hands stilled.

You're not flirting with the bodyguard, are you? The unwelcome voice asked.

She watched her eyes grow wide. "Am I?" She thought about how richly colored his brown eyes were and felt a light tingle work through her body. "Oh shit."

Well, you're not doing that, the voice replied.

Her hands began moving again, quickly, making short work

of the long braid.

Do you hear me? The voice asked, as she stared into her own eyes. *You're not doing that!*

She impatiently tied a rubber band at the end of her hair, gave herself a firm look in the mirror, and left the bathroom. She straightened the bedrooms, put on a pot of coffee, and started cleaning the blood stains off the floor. She was on her hands and knees, her rear facing the backdoor, when Larry tapped lightly on the glass. Embarrassed, she got to her feet and let him in. "The coffee's ready."

"Great, I could use a cup."

She set the cream and sugar on the table, pulled down two coffee cups and filling both, she handed him one.

"Mind if I sit?" he asked.

"No, no. Sit. Seems I'm forgetting my manners."

He sat at the table, added a little cream to his coffee and took a sip. "Nice," he smiled, the skin around his eyes crinkling attractively. "Cinnamon."

"Yeah, just a touch." She sat down across from him and stirred some sugar into her cup. "Did you see anything?"

"Yes. Seems someone was out here trying to poison your dogs. I found chunk of beef still in the woods, probably loaded with poison. I bagged it and put it in a cooler. And about fifty yards south there's a dead coyote. I figure he found the meat after you left for the vet. My guess is your dogs were far more interested in the person, than in the food."

Abbey remembered the over-flowing bowls she gave them the night before after Richard refused, yet again, to eat his dinner and she smiled. "They ate good last night. But why is someone trying to poison my dogs?"

"That's a good question. Do you have any enemies out here?"

"I hardly know anyone, we've just been out here a little over a year, I know some of the locals, but I've never had a problem with any of them. We lived in Locknee for a little while before that, but then Kelly had her accident and I never got around to meeting neighbors or even getting to know any co-workers. I'd only had the job for a couple months when I quit to take care of my daughter. I probably know more people at the hospital than anywhere else."

"Whoever tried to poison them decided it wasn't going to

work, so he tried to just shoot them. And if you didn't hear the gun, but heard the yelp, I'm going to say he had a silencer and he was close. You're damned lucky."

She shook her head slowly. "I just don't know why anyone would want to hurt the dogs. I've never had any complaints about them. They're good boys."

"I noticed that big dog house has chains attached, when do you keep them chained?"

"During the day, when the barn animals are out. I let them go at night to keep predators away and to get exercise. There's a lot of woods around here, lots of predators interested in a duck or chicken dinner."

"It seems the dogs did their job last night. They ran off someone, but I don't think he was interested in a chicken dinner."

Chapter Sixteen

Larry skirted the fence enclosing the barnyard and walked around the opposite side of the lake. He jumped a small spring feeding the two-acre body of water and found a spot that gave him the best view of the house, yard, and driveway. He sat down on the ground, crossed his legs, and resting his wrists on his knees, palms up, he closed his eyes. He took several slow, deep breaths, opened his eyes and watched as Abbey stepped into the yard.

He worked over the puzzle pieces he had, trying to see the whole picture. She was rescued from the Aviary over twenty-five years ago, he didn't know her history, but most of the birds' experiences were similar and terrible. She was married once, as a teenager. The marriage didn't last long, but she remained close to her ex-husband and the father of her daughter. She was single for a long time, living out in the country and raising her daughter. She worked simple, menial jobs, and had no interest in going to college for a better career.

He smiled, listening to her talk sweetly to the ducks and chickens storming out of the barn, and continued running over the facts. She met Richard and by all accounts, he swept her off her feet. She married him a few months after meeting him and moved to a new town. Shortly after the marriage, her daughter was nearly killed in a hit and run accident and then they moved out into the middle of nowhere. Something wasn't right about the husband, he thought. He knew Rex had checked him out, but that just meant he hadn't done time and had good credit, it didn't mean his hands weren't into some ugly things.

"Go on, fucktard!" The breeze carried her words across the water. The goat was on his hind legs, challenging her. He landed on all fours, pawed the ground and then charged. Larry jumped to his feet in one smooth move. The goat moved fast, his head down, but Abbey easily slipped out of his way and popped the animal on the butt with her hand. "You're gonna have to do better than that, dickhead." Larry laughed and sat back down as the goat ran off into the field. So, that was the goat he had heard about.

Once Richard got her away from her family and isolated, he became her doctor, prescribing sleeping pills. Suddenly a woman who had been around guns since she was young, and was comfortable enough with them to teach her own daughter how to use them, became afraid of them. Then their neighbors warn her of a strange circle in the woods, the weird things that have happened over the years, and she goes to look at it. The next day she feels someone watching her from the woods and finds a man's boot print. A couple days later someone tries to poison her dogs and tries to run her off the road and into a swamp.

This was escalating and escalating fast, he thought, pulling his phone from his pocket. "Rex. I don't like this, something hinkey is going on out here. Either they know she saw the circle and they're trying to scare her or they know who she is and they're trying to finish what was started when she was a kid."

"I've been thinking along the same lines," Rex said. "Is Richard back yet?"

"Nope."

"I wonder where the hell he is and how much he knows.

I've been researching the property; it seems the land with the altar on it used to belong to Richard's parents. They bought it in the sixties from the Dawson boy. When they died, Richard inherited just 20 acres of the thousands of acres and the rest of the land went into a trust. The name is BLZ Trust and I can find almost nothing out about it, except that when Richard dies, the land either goes to his child or reverts back into the trust."

"I wonder if Abbey knows she would be homeless if he dropped dead tomorrow. Didn't you say all the proceeds from her old house went into building this new house?"

"Yes, and I doubt she knows. If she does, she never mentioned it."

"Listen, I'm calling a couple more guys out, Kevin and Scott. I'm putting one guy down by that old cemetery to see who's coming and going. And the other one I'm putting on the other side of the house. We're out in the middle of freakin' nowhere here, I can't watch everything," Larry said.

"Sounds good and I'm coming out to see my niece today," Rex replied.

Larry hung up the phone and watched Abbey step out of the

front door with the dog and chain him to the doghouse. She stared at the doghouse for a long time, as though she was unhappy with it, and walked back into the house. He made the call arranging for the additional men, hung up and was watching the ducks chase each other on the lake when his phone rang.

"Yeah."

"It's Abbey, there's a change of plans. My neighbor, Mr. Jackson, is coming up here with a tractor to move the doghouse away from the lake. I want the dogs up behind the house, harder to get a shot at them."

"Okay, thanks for letting me know." He hung up. At least she wasn't a dumb woman, he thought and continued to watch and listen.

*

Abbey checked the roast in the oven and stepped outside to wait for Mr. Jackson. Lighting a cigarette, she sat on the front stairs; she'd feel better once the doghouse was closer to the house. She heard a tractor chugging up the highway, took a couple more drags, and hid the butt under one of the rocks lining a flowerbed. She felt self-conscious and looked across the lake, wondering where Larry was hidden. Her eyes scanned the shore, the short mucky beach and into the tree line. She couldn't see him.

Jerry barked and she turned, watching Mr. Jackson pull down the driveway in his truck, followed by a large tractor with forks on the front. "Hey, Mr. Jackson, I sure do appreciate your help," she said.

He stepped out of the truck, slamming the old heavy door. "Ain't nothin', Miss Abbey. I were glad to see the ole thing start up. So your dog gots shot, did he?"

"Yes, sir." She followed him as he walked down toward the doghouse.

"That's my grandson, Jimmy." He waved his hand toward the tractor, studying the doghouse. "Think we a'told you he were a'movin' in 'cross the road."

The man climbed off the tractor and joined them to stare at the doghouse. Jerry wagged his tail, pleased with the attention, and lay down on his side exposing his belly. "That's a big 'un," Mr. Jackson said.

"Sure is," Jimmy answered.

"It was built there, I know it's heavy. Do you think you can move it?"

"Oh yeah, we'll move it," Jimmy said.

Remembering her manners, Abbey introduced herself to Mr. Jackson's grandson and shook his hand. "Good to know you're moving out here. Nice to have another neighbor."

"Thanks," he said with a smile. "It's a nice doghouse, never seen anything like it."

"Yeah, it is nice. My husband built it." The doghouse was a small building, raised off the ground so the dogs wouldn't get wet in heavy storms as the water washed into the lake. Each dog had its own stall and small slats of wood separated the two, so the dogs could still share body heat inside. The openings of the stalls faced two different directions allowing the dogs a good view of the property and the building was wide enough that they had ample room to move about, but their chains would not become entangled. Richard had built the house in the first weeks after they moved in, before things grew so strange.

"Where'd your dog git shot?" Mr. Jackson asked.

Abbey pointed across the lake to the area and wondered where Larry was hiding.

"Right there?" He squinted his eyes, looking where her finger indicated

"Yes, sir."

"Last night? Durin' that storm?"

"Yes, sir."

"That ain't right, Miss Abbey. He gonna be all right?"

"The vet thinks so. He came through the surgery really well."

"Did you call the sheriff?"

"No, sir."

"Now, I ain't never had to deal wid 'im, but I'm a'thinkin' our sheriff's okay. He's a youngen, a relative of that sheriff we had back when 'em Dawson's lived out here and he weren't a bad man. Jimmy, you took schoolin' wid 'im, right?" Mr. Jackson pulled off his straw hat and wiped his brow.

"Yes, sir, Papa, I did. I think he's okay; he seems to be fair.

I've haven't had to deal with him as sheriff, but those folks I know that have dealt with them, well, I think he treated them fair." Jimmy studied the doghouse. "You think we should use chains?"

"You might should give 'im a call, Miss Abbey. It weren't no hunters out here last night durin' that storm. Yeah, we gonna need to chain 'er, don't want that thing a'movin' once she's up in the air. Show us where you want 'er."

Abbey walked around back and showed them an area between the barnyard and the garden. "I think you can get through here without hitting any flower beds or the shed."

Mr. Jackson and his grandson walked through the area and then stood in the shade, studying it. "You a'thinkin' them dogs 'ill be safer here? You're still a'backin' 'em up to the woods," Mr. Jackson pointed out.

"I know, but they are closer and it's not such a big patch of woods, your road isn't far in that direction, might be harder for someone to come in this way."

"Mayhaps. I'm a'thinkin' you should call the sheriff. It ain't right, Miss Abbey, your dog gittin' shot on your own land."

Abbey nodded her head.

"We can get it through there, plenty of room," Jimmy stated.

"Yep, I'm a'thinkin' so, son," Mr. Jackson agreed.

Abbey detached the chains from the doghouse, attaching Jerry to a tree and out of the way. Jimmy climbed onto the tractor and moved it into position. Abbey joined the old man by the truck, while he shouted out instructions to his grandson. "Lift 'er up, Jimmy. Tilt 'er a hair," Mr. Jackson called and Jimmy complied. "Good job!" he shouted when the house slid gently, settling firmly on the blades. "Wrap a couple 'em chains 'round 'er."

While Jimmy chained the house and Mr. Jackson called out suggestions, Abbey's eyes scanned the far shore, looking for Larry. Jimmy secured the chains, jumped back on the tractor and drove it through the yard as Jerry barked excitedly. Jimmy maneuvered the large structure carefully, making sure not to knock the shed or run over the flowerbeds. He positioned it and called out to her, "Is this where you want it?"

"Yes! That's good!" she yelled over the sound of the engine.

He lowered the forks, climbed on the house, loosening the chains and allowing them drop. Abbey ran up and pulled the chains away, dragging them across the yard to where Mr. Jackson stood. "Miss Abbey, you ain't's gotta do that, Jimmy could of gots 'em."

"It's no problem, Mr. Jackson. I really appreciate y'all giving me a hand."

"That's what neighbors is for," he smiled and watched as Jimmy set the house on the ground. "Gentle, son, treat 'er gentle!"

Jimmy pulled the tractor around the house and came back to pick up the chains.

"Thank you so much," Abbey said.

"No problem, that's what neighbors are for." He carried the chains back to the truck.

"Y'all want to come in for some iced tea?" Abbey asked.

"No, ma'am, not this time, but thanks," Mr. Jackson said, heading for his truck. "I need to gits back, Miss Annie's a'waiting." He stopped and turned. "And she gonna be awful worried 'bout you, Miss Abbey. I sure'd feel better if you called the sheriff."

She nodded. "Hang on, let me get your eggs."

She ran in the house, pulled two-dozen eggs from the fridge and carried them outside. "Here you go. I sure appreciate your help."

"And these eggs is some good eatin', those store bought eggs is never quite as good as yard eggs."

"No, sir," she agreed, "they're not." She waved as he and his grandson pulled out of the driveway.

She moved Jerry to his new location and watched him investigate his surroundings. "You'll be okay, buddy," she assured him, before walking in the house, checking the roast and dialing Larry.

"Yeah?"

"Mr. Jackson said we should call the local sheriff and tell him about Tom, what do you think?"

"I don't know the area or the law enforcement around here, Abbey. Let me talk to your uncle before you do anything."

"Okay, I'll wait to hear. I'm making a roast; can I send you a plate later? Sneak it around the lake all covert-like?" She laughed.

"Maybe, let me find out about this sheriff, I'll be in touch."

"I'd tried to see you over there, I couldn't. Where are you?"

"Well, if you could see me, I wouldn't be hiding very well, would I?" He chuckled softly and the sound of it sent that tingle spiraling down her body.

"I guess not." She hung up and heard the unwelcome voice in her head. *You're not doing that, Abbey*, the voice echoed, but suddenly Abbey wasn't so sure. She dumped some potatoes and carrots in the sink and began peeling them, dropping them into a bowl of cool water. She felt restless and despite knowing she had a hundred things to worry about, her mind kept shifting to Larry's eyes and the way his gentle, soft laugh affected her. The landline phone rang and she jumped, grateful for the distraction. "Hello."

"Hey Mom!" Kelly said with enthusiasm.

"Hey baby, how close are you? I sure have missed you."

"I've missed you, too. Dad says we'll be there in about an hour."

"Are your dad, Holly, and the kids staying for lunch?"

"I don't know, let me ask." Abbey could hear the sound of voices in the background, but couldn't make out the words. "He says, not this time." Her voice changed to a whisper. "The kids are asleep and Holly wants them to stay that way until they get home."

"I understand that, I bet they're exhausted. Did you have a good time?"

"Yes, ma'am, I did. I also did a lot of research, I've got a lot to talk to you about."

Abbey sighed. "Yeah, me too. I forgot to tell you, Grandma got us cell phones, nice ones, with Internet and e-mail on them."

"Really? And they get reception?"

"Yep."

"Woo hoo," Kelly whispered.

"Thought you'd like that. So I'll see you in a little while, I've got a roast on."

"Yum. Love you, Mom."

"Love you, too, honey." Abbey hung up the phone, drained the water from the vegetables and added them to the roast pot.

She was staring through the kitchen window, watching Jerry sniff his new surroundings and the cell phone rang. "Hello."

"Rex is on his way out here, so you can ask him about the sheriff," Larry said.

"Okay, do you know when he'll be here?"

"He said an hour."

"Okay, Kelly should arrive at the same time, I just heard from her."

"Have you heard from your husband?"

"No, not yet," she said, surprised that she had barely thought of him at all since coming home from the vet.

"Should we be worried?" he asked.

"I don't think so, he tends to keep his own hours. I expect he'll be home after church." And won't he be happy to see Rex? she thought, shaking her head.

His voice softened and lowered. "I might ask you to bring that plate out to me later."

Again the tingle, that damned tingle, worked through her body. She felt breathless, excited, and stupid. "Okay," she said and hung up the phone. "I know, I know! I'm not doing it!" she answered the voice in her head.

*

Larry slid the phone in his pocket and shook his head, he wasn't supposed to be flirting with the bird, but damned if he couldn't help himself. Besides the fact that she was gorgeous, had a firm derriere, and changeable green eyes, she was just a likable lady. The way she handled that crazy goat, soothed the chickens, ducks, and dogs, and the respect she showed the elderly Mr. Jackson, he was growing to like her more and more.

He pulled the gently vibrating phone out of his pocket, flipping it open. "Yeah".

"We just pulled in, we're by the cemetery. Where do you want us?"

"Head west in the field and get up in the tree line as far as you can. Use the tarp to camouflage the vehicle. I want you there, watching that road. Stay in the trees, out of that field and don't engage anyone coming in there, this is just observe and report. Send Kevin to me."

"Will do."

Larry shut the phone and slid it into his pocket, he was glad to have the help.

*

Abbey stepped out onto the porch as Jack pulled up to the door. Holly waved, put her finger to her lips and pointed in the backseat, where both kids were sound asleep in their car seats. Abbey nodded, waved back, and walked to the back of the SUV.

"I'm sorry we have to rush," Jack began in a near whisper.

"Who's Jeep is that?" Kelly asked, climbing over the rear seat.

"Mine," Abbey said.

"Really?" Kelly grinned, her eyes wide.

"What happened to it?" Jack asked. "It's all scraped up."

"I had an accident."

"Are you okay?" Kelly and Jack asked in unison.

"Yeah, I'm fine. Insurance will take care of it and I can teach someone I know how to drive."

"Yea!" Kelly whispered, clapping softly and jumping in place.

Jack set Kelly's things on the ground. "I'm sorry just to rush in and out, but we want to get the kids home before they wake up.

You know how it is." He smiled.

"Indeed, I do. Go on and we'll talk soon. Bye, Holly," she whispered.

"Bye," Holly whispered and waved.

Jack shut the back of the vehicle and gave his daughter a hug. "I'm glad you came, bunny, even if you did spend too much time enjoying the Wi-Fi." He smiled at Abbey, and climbed into the vehicle, pulling down the driveway.

Abbey picked up the suitcase and Kelly followed with the rest. "We really have a car now and cell phones? What's going on?"

"Put your things away, Uncle Rex is coming out, we have a lot to talk about."

"Is everything okay?" Kelly asked.

"I think so. A lot's happened since you've been gone. Put your things away, I'll finish lunch and I promise we'll talk about it." She went to the refrigerator to pull out some rolls and the landline rang.

"Abbey, it's Richard. I'm having lunch with the pastor and then I'm going to the office to finish some paper work, I'll be home tonight after the evening service."

"Okay," she said, peeking in the oven.

"Abbey, when I get home, you and I are going to have a long talk," he warned.

"I'll see you then," she said and hung up, suddenly feeling the weight of her worries on her back. She rested her elbows on the sink, supporting her head with her hands and stared out the window. She saw the dog turn his head, his ears rotating as though to focus on a sound and then he began barking.

She stepped outside as Rex's truck pulled down the driveway and was surprised to see her mother sitting in the passenger seat. She walked to the vehicle and opened the door for her mom. "What are you doing here, Mom?"

Summer climbed out of the truck, hugging her daughter. "We need to talk."

Chapter Seventeen

"I haven't had a chance to tell Kelly anything, yet," Abbey said as Rex and Summer followed her into the house. "She just got home a few minutes ago."

Kelly ran out of her room with the new phone in hand. "Wow! It's a family reunion!" She laughed, hugging her uncle and grandmother. "I love the phone, Grandma. I can't believe I finally have one."

"Honey, will you set the table? Lunch is almost ready," Abbey said.

"Set an extra plate, I want to get Larry in on this," Rex said, pulling out his phone.

"Who's Larry?" Kelly asked, reaching into the cabinet for the plates.

"That's something we're going to talk about, your uncle has given us security."

Kelly's eyes went wide. "Really?"

"He's okay, but Tom was shot last night," Abbey spit it out quickly.

Kelly just stared at her.

"It's okay, honey, he's okay, we'll pick him up in a few hours." Abbey rubbed her shoulders. "Set the table, we'll talk, and we'll all be on the same page."

Larry stepped in the kitchen and while Rex introduced him to Kelly and Summer, Abbey placed serving dishes on the table. They all sat down at the table and began eating quietly; Summer was the first to break the silence. "Did you have a good time at the beach, Kelly?"

"Yes, ma'am." Kelly took a bite of a roll, looking curiously at the adults around the table. "What's going on and who shot my dog?"

"It's time to put our cards on the table, we've all been holding back pieces from each other, this is no time for secrets. Abbey, I know you have things to tell Kelly and I know you want to do it your way and in your time, but I think time is growing short," Rex said.

Abbey nodded.

"Mr. Jackson called to tell me a car passed his house heading back up into the woods. I told him it was a couple of our guys looking out for you and Kelly. He seemed pleased, he didn't like that the dog got shot, said his wife was worried."

"So y'all know about the thing in the woods?" Kelly asked, and everyone nodded. "Well good." She let out a breath. "Because, Mom, I was going to insist you call Uncle Rex."

Abbey smiled, but inside her stomach tightened, she didn't know how she was going to tell Kelly about the past. Summer reached over, squeezing her hand reassuringly.

"Abbey, have you heard from Richard?" Rex asked.

"Yes, sir, he called right before you got here. Said he was having lunch with the pastor, then he was going to the office and he'd be home tonight after the evening service."

"As some of you may know, I took Abbey's sleeping pills yesterday and dropped them with a friend at a lab, I wanted to know what was in them and I put a rush on it. I got a call back this morning."

All eyes were on Rex and Abbey's stomach tightened a little

more.

"There was only about half a bottle left and in most of them it was just the prescribed medication, but in a few there was something else," Rex stated.

Abbey felt her body flush hot and then cold. "What was in them?"

"Those capsules contained a blend of anti-psychotic and hypnotic meds that should not have been in them. It was a mild blend and wasn't any standard prescription. The combination of the meds together may have led you to be a little more sedate, suggestible, and confused. Have you been feeling like that, Abbey?"

"Confused?" Abbey burst out laughing and Kelly and Summer joined in. "I'd say confused would fit right in." She grew serious and stood up. "The son of bitch has been doping me?"

"Looks like it. We found some prints on the capsules, I'm pretty sure they are Richard's, but we'll have to get a sample."

"Well, hell!" She began pacing and remembered the dream she had of him altering her medication. She stopped and sat down at the table. "I dreamed he was altering my medication." She quickly told them about the dream.

Rex and Larry glanced at each other. "And those were the pills you put down the garbage disposal?" Rex asked.

"Yes, sir." Abbey stood up again and began pacing. "He's been saying I need to go to the hospital, so they can even me out. We've been arguing a lot lately and last night I punched him in the stomach because he wouldn't give me the keys when I was trying to get the dog to the vet."

Larry laughed, glancing over to see Rex smiling.

"I bet he didn't like that," Summer said, biting back a chuckle.

"No. When he called today he said we were going to have a long talk when he got home. He thinks I've been out of control and maybe I have been, but I like to refer to it as acting normally in an abnormal situation."

Larry watched her pace and admired her spirit; she wasn't broken like most of the birds he had met.

"He pushed me too far last night, he said he could have me committed and pointed out how I couldn't keep up with my own cleaning supplies, like I was hiding them from myself."

"What the hell?" Kelly burst out and then covered her mouth with her hand. "Ooops, didn't mean to cuss, but it's Richard who's hiding stuff. Mom searched for hours the other day trying to find the stuff just to clean the bathrooms. It was scattered all over the place."

Summer stood up and started clearing the table.

"Let me help you, Mom," Abbey said.

"No, no, you do what you're doing. I'm just moving things out of the way. Rex, you want some coffee?"

"You know I do," he said.

"I'll help." Kelly got to her feet.

Abbey sat at the table, facing Rex and Larry. "So he's drugging me, talking about having me committed, and trying to convince me I'm not thinking right, why?"

"That's what we're trying to find out. Hang on." Rex reached in his pocket and pulled free a phone. "Yeah."

As Rex talked, Abbey looked at Larry and feeling her gaze on him, he turned toward her. She didn't pull her eyes away this time and stared into his as though he held an answer she was seeking. She gave him a slow, sad smile, lightly shrugging her shoulders. He smiled, nodding his head as though he understood her unspoken communication.

Rex hung up the phone. "Richard just left the restaurant with a woman, in a car registered to Pearl Hollister. Do you know her?"

"You're having him followed?" Abbey asked, startled.

"Of course," he stated.

"I know who she is," Kelly said, walking around the open dishwasher to see the faces at the table better. "She goes to our church and she is snotty, looks down on everyone."

"I don't know her, but I know who she is, she owns Hollister Real Estate in Locknee. Her picture is everywhere, you can't drive through town without seeing her smiling down at you from billboards."

"Are she and Richard friends?" Rex asked.

"I don't know," Abbey answered.

"Yes," Kelly said, sliding plates into place on the bottom rack. "I see them talking at church, all huddled up. People have been talking about them, wondering if they are having an affair. I didn't say anything, Mom, because there's a lot of gossip in that church."

"It's okay, honey." She smiled at Kelly over her shoulder and turned back to face Rex and Larry. "You know, I had a dream this morning at the vet's office and Pearl Hollister was in it." Abbey relayed the latest dream to them.

"Is that all you remember?" Larry asked.

"Yeah, I thought it strange to see Pearl Hollister, I've never spoken to her before."

"What did the older, angry man look like?" Rex asked.

"I'd guess him to be in his late sixties or early seventies, he had white hair and a very deep tan." They were all quiet for a moment. "Uncle Rex, I don't mean to be nosy, but I thought you just had a small law practice, how do you have all these men, protecting us and following Richard?"

Rex and Summer shared a long look, Summer sighed, nodding her head. "No more secrets."

"I'll tell you, baby girl, but first you need to have a talk with Kelly."

Abbey dropped her head, nodding it slowly. She took a deep breath, expelled it and stood up.

"Tell me what? What's going on?" Kelly demanded.

"Everything's fine, I just need to tell you some stuff. Let's go to your room for a minute." Abbey reached for her hand.

"Yeah, go on, Kelly," Summer said. "I'll finish the dishes and get the coffee on."

"Thanks, Mom," Abbey said, leading Kelly to her bedroom. She shut the door and pulled Kelly down on the bed. "I haven't been completely honest with you about what happened to me as a child…" she began.

Twenty minutes later, the bedroom door opened and Abbey and Kelly walked across the living room with their arms around each other. Both had been crying as evidenced by their swollen and red-rimmed eyes. They sat in adjoining chairs at the table and Kelly held on to her mother's hand.

"Are you all right, Kelly?" Summer asked softly, her brow furrowed with worry.

"Yes, ma'am. It's just so hard to imagine." A tear ran down her cheek. "I've seen those pictures on the Internet, the terrible things, I can't believe Mom lived it and escaped it." Abbey squeezed her hand and passed her some tissues. Kelly wiped her face with a tissue, took a deep breath and sat up straighter as she exhaled. "I'm fine. Tell me the rest."

Larry smiled; Kelly had just as much spirit as her mother.

"Your mother and I have a side business, Abbey," Rex said.

"I just handle the money," Summer said, setting a cup of coffee in front of Abbey.

"What kind of side business?" Abbey asked, dropping a spoonful of sugar into her cup.

"Rescuing kids like you."

Abbey dropped the spoon in the cup and sat back in her chair. "Are you serious?"

"Yes, I am. We get them out. For the younger ones we put them in a decent home, usually out of the country or we reunite them with family, move them and change their identities. For the older ones, sometimes we get the word when there has been a contract placed on them, when the Aviary no longer deems them useful, and we get them out before they can be killed," Rex explained.

"You reunite them with families? I thought we didn't have families." Abbey felt a strange emotion surge through her.

"Well, back in your day most of the kids were orphans, sold black market in birth houses or just throwaways found in foster programs. But it's big business and in the '80s and '90s they began infiltrating day care centers, schools, sporting programs. They'd identify the parent that would give them the least trouble, have the least money, and they'd just take the kid. Do you know how many kids disappear every year?"

Abbey shook her head.

"Thousands. It's an organized network, a mixed bag, but well funded."

"How can you afford to do all that?" Abbey asked. "It must be outrageously expensive."

"We get some private funding, there's good people on the inside who know what's going on, hate it, but feel they can best help by keeping a foot in the door. Larry worked on the same task force as your father, of course, it was years later."

"The task force is still going on?"

Larry nodded. "Yes, it is, and it was damned frustrating work. We rarely got a conviction, seemed like every time we caught some higher up with his hands dirty the evidence disappeared or a judge was bought out and the charges were dropped. The stuff never got media attention and the people in this country would certainly be upset if they knew who was involved. Plus, you never knew which side of the fence your co-workers were actually on - it's enough to disillusion you pretty quick. Finally, about five years ago, I left and came to work with your uncle. We rarely get convictions, but we give people back their lives."

Abbey eyes flicked back and forth between her uncle and her mother. "I can't believe y'all have doing this and I never knew."

"I couldn't exactly tell you, honey, you never talked about the past. I didn't know if you remembered what happened to you or not, so I wasn't going to upset you by talking about it," Summer explained, reaching over to rub her shoulder.

"I know. I'm just stunned. I mean, it's a good thing and I'm glad you're doing it, but damn."

"I know." Summer nodded. "You're in shock, both of you are."

"Rex, I think we should get them out of here. Richard may be involved in this, which means that the target victim could be either one of them," Larry said.

"Yeah, I think you're right," Rex agreed. "You girls should start packing."

"What? I'm not leaving. What about the animals? The dog at the vet? Carpooling tomorrow?"

"Abbey, they may know who you are. It's just too coincidental that you moved out here and it seems like a big, elaborate, set-up to me," Larry stated.

"And what then? Move across the country again? We're running out of coasts. Change our names again?" She looked at Summer. "Spend the rest of my life running? I thought you guys gave people back their lives, running is not a life." She gaze shifted between Rex and Larry. "No. I'm not running again and Kelly's not going to lose contact with her dad, that's not the way this is going to happen."

"What do you suggest?" Rex asked. "They were trying to kill the dogs to make it easier to get to you or Kelly, I believe one or both of you are the target victims for that circle. Larry's right, it's too coincidental."

"I want you to take Kelly back to Windslow with you,"

Abbey stated.

"I'm not gong to leave you out here alone," Kelly burst in.

"I'm not alone, I have security. But I want you safe. You can take your school work and stay with Grandma." She squeezed Kelly's hand.

"Kelly, I think that's a good idea," Summer said.

"And leave Mom out here as bait for Satanists, I don't think that's a good idea," Kelly insisted.

"I'm not going to run the rest of my life from these idiots," Abbey stated. "Uncle Rex, you said yourself that this stuff was a mixed bag, not all connected at the top, not all part of some vast government conspiracy, you said some were in just for thrills. Maybe that's all it is."

"I also said I've never felt the energy that is in that circle and you said you haven't either. This is something I'm not familiar with, which could mean it's even more dangerous than usual." Rex got up and went to the coffee pot, pouring a fresh cup.

"So I just run away and let them win?" Abbey asked, frustrated.

"They only win if they kill you Abbey," Larry stated.

Abbey stared at him. "They've been winning my whole life. My whole life I've felt the target on my back, I've kept my head down, been quiet and polite. I've lived out in the country and tried to be small, invisible, and anonymous. I rarely drew attention to myself because in the back of my mind I knew if I did, they would see me. If I run again, I just grow smaller."

Rex sat and set his cup on the table. "The thing is, we don't know how much time we have, and this thing is escalating."

"We might know, Uncle Rex. Hang on." Kelly jumped up from the table and ran to her bedroom, returning with her laptop. "While I was at the beach I did a lot of research and it seems pagans, whatever they worship, follow dates and celebrations from thousands of years ago, you know, back when they used to sacrifice people." She set the laptop on the table, opened it and turned it on. "Now in the cemetery back there every one of those people died on one of those pagan dates, all except the two youngest kids who died on 6-6-66. Duh. I think we get the meaning there." She sat down and started clicking on the keyboard.

"I've been on some weird websites this weekend, but pagans are a mixed bag." She grinned at Rex, tickled she had used his words. "The next date on their calendar is May Day or Beltane. Like I said, they are a mixed bag, some are just really into nature and believe in God, others believe in a mother God and I guess some believe in gods, but only a few worship Lucifer." She turned the computer, showing him a pagan calendar. "See, April 30th would be the next date."

"That's Tuesday," Larry said.

"Yeah, but it's not tomorrow. So we have some time," Abbey stated.

"This thing isn't normal, Abbey, you felt the energy," Rex said.

"Yeah, I saw stuff about that too." Kelly turned the computer back toward her and started clicking keys.

"One, we don't know that Richard and the circle are connected." Abbey held up her hand to stop the objections. "Yes, we know he was drugging me and yes, I'm going to leave him, but I am not going to run away like a scared kid. We're going to find out what's happening. We're going to find out if Richard is just a random psycho or if he is connected to a ring of satanic psychos."

"How do you propose we do that?" Rex asked with a smile.

"You're following him, right?"

He nodded.

"Let's disrupt his plans," Abbey suggested.

"I'm listening."

"Richard likes to control things and this week as he is losing the ability to control me, he's also losing the ability to control himself. He said tonight we were going to have a long talk, I think he wants me to go to the hospital. If my dreams are correct and I'm beginning to think they are, I don't think he was at a scheduled meeting this morning. If I am the target then maybe he was at that meeting because he's losing control of me, he looked like a chastised and shamed boy in the dream. Maybe if he slips further out of control, he'll have to go to another meeting and you can follow him, find out the names of the other players. He probably has plans to bully me into going to the hospital, but if I have a bully guard." She smiled at Larry. "He's going to be so pissed off his head might explode."

Kelly laughed behind the computer. "No, he won't like you having a bodyguard around."

"Last night after I told him in no uncertain terms to stay

away from me, I noticed the phone was off the base, he called someone. A few hours later our dog gets shot, I rush off to the vet and when I come home he's gone, well before sun up."

"So what are you suggesting?" Rex asked, leaning forward.

"If Richard knows you have given me security and he is involved with what is happening across the lake, I'm pretty sure that would be enough to send him into a panic. And if someone is here, preventing him from manipulating me, and he realizes he can't control me, that's enough to make …" she paused, searching for the right term.

"His head explode," Kelly interjected with a laugh.

"And as much as Richard doesn't like you Rex, if he knows you're involved and helping me, he's gonna bust a seam." She laughed.

"Is this revenge, Abbey?" Rex asked.

"A little, but it's also a fight. I'm tired of running and if Richard is involved in this, I want to know. And if other people around here are involved I want to know who they are. Remember, we're only an hour from Windslow, do we want it spreading there?" Abbey sat back in her seat and watched the faces around the table.

"Larry?" Rex asked.

"If we have a couple days, it might be worth it to let it play out a little, see who's who and what's what. If Richard thinks she has security only because the dog got shot and doesn't realize Abbey knows about the drugging or the altar, he might be careless and he might lead us to the whole group. I don't think he'd be scared enough to run, but he might be angry enough to get reckless."

"So we're just going to poke the boy until he loses it?" Rex chuckled.

"Just gig him a little, Uncle Rex." Kelly laughed, turning the computer that showed a picture of the globe with latitude and longitude lines. "Okay, here's some other stuff, now this is going to be kind of vague because I've only had a few days to look into it and Mom made me promise to have fun at the beach." She grinned at her mother. "Anyway the circle back there is on the 33rd degree latitude, I don't really know what that means, but it's a big deal to some folks on the Internet. Thirty-three is said to be the Christ consciousness, I guess because he was thirty-three when he died, it's also rumored to be the highest level for the Masons and some believe that the 33rd lines of the earth have power." She opened a new window displaying a forum with an ongoing discussion of a thinning veil.

"Mom's compass went all screwy back there in that circle, like there was a disruption of the magnetic field or something. Some folks say that in certain areas the veil between us and whatever is on the other sides - I say sides because it's like a dimension thing - is thinning. Some areas are thin all the time, like the Bermuda Triangle, some areas are thin only on occasion, bear with me now, it has something to do with the sun, solar flares, and the magnetic field. So when the sun releases a flare, it affects the magnetic shield and certain areas on the earth can be affected, it thins the veil and opens doors to let things in or send things out."

"Hang on." Rex answered the phone and everyone turned to listen to his conversation.

After a few short replies, he hung up. "Richard and a blond woman just entered a house owned by Pearl Hollister." He looked at Abbey.

"I've already figured out he's having an affair, Uncle Rex," Abbey said and turned to Kelly. "Go on."

"So according to some freaky websites what you have back in the woods is like a doorway that only opens every now and again. So this is pretty handy dandy to Satanists, because it makes their rituals stronger and if these websites are to be believed, then by spilling blood back there it really will bring over some kind of force from the other side. Apparently the force doesn't last long and once it's fed it goes back to sleep. Now what I wanted to know and never got a real answer, was is it possible for the door to close on its own or will it only close after the force has come through and been fed? I don't know, but the people on the Internet seem to think the door only closes after whatever has been unleashed has been fed.

"These weakened areas appeal to all kinds, not just Satanists, some believe those areas are like star gates or something, where you can jump worlds or realities, others think that if they could figure them out they could learn to travel in time or make space travel much easier. One thing seems real clear to me, though, whatever that circle is it's very dangerous."

"So what we're dealing with here is a run of the mill gateway to hell?" Larry asked with a smile.

Kelly laughed. "Pretty much."

"Well, that can't be good," Summer added.

Jerry started barking.

"Someone's here," Kelly stated.

"I'm not expecting anyone," Abbey said and walked to the front window to see the sheriff's car pull into the driveway. "It's the sheriff," she said and stepped out onto the front porch.

Chapter Eighteen

"Mrs. Brown?" the sandy haired man asked as he stepped out of the car.

"Yes?" Abbey said, meeting him in the yard.

"This is a little unusual, but your neighbor, James Jackson, gave me a call. He's concerned, said someone shot your dog. Is that right?"

"Yes, sir. Last night, happened right over there." She pointed across the lake as the crowd from the house moved onto the porch.

"Mr. Jackson said it happened during the storm, is that correct?" he asked, staring across the lake.

"Yes, sir," Abbey said, as Larry and Rex joined them in the yard.

Rex stuck out his hand. "I'm Abbey's uncle, Rex Andrews."

"Sorry about my manners," the man said, shaking Rex's hand. "I'm Arnold Davis, the sheriff 'round these parts."

"Larry Sanders," Larry said, shaking the man's hand.

"Nice to meet you folks." He looked back across the lake and then turned to Abbey. "Mrs. Brown, why didn't you call us?" he asked.

"I was trying to get the dog to the vet as fast as I could." She glanced at Rex and he nodded. "Plus, I had to call the police in Locknee because someone almost knocked my car in the swamp on my way there."

"They what? Right after your dog got shot?" He pulled off his hat and wiped his brow.

"Yes, sir." She walked toward the Jeep to show the scrape marks along the side.

The sheriff whistled under his breath when he saw the damage. "Do you believe in coincidences, Mrs. Brown?"

"No, sir. Not really," she answered.

"Me either. So why do suppose that someone may be trying to hurt you or your dogs?" he asked.

"Well, Sheriff Davis, that's why we're here, beside being Abbey's uncle, I'm an attorney from Windslow and Larry here is from Songbird Security. I don't know what's going on, but it doesn't feel right to me."

"Andrews, was it?" the sheriff asked, looking at Rex.

"Rex."

"Well, Rex, I agree with you. Do you have any enemies, Mrs. Brown?"

"Abbey," she said. "No, we haven't lived out here long, I home school so I don't get out much and the people I do know I've never had a problem with any of them."

He nodded. "And what does your husband do?"

"He's a psychiatrist. He has an office in Locknee, he and his partner, Mike Almond."

He nodded. "I've seen it." He turned toward his car. "You

filed a report in Locknee about the car, right?"

She walked with him and nodded.

"Let's file one about the dog." He pulled out a metal clipboard.

"Would you like to have a seat on the porch?" she asked.

"Sure."

"How about some ice tea, Sheriff?" Summer asked.

"That'd be nice." He sat at the table and started asking questions, while scribbling on the form.

Summer brought him a glass of tea and he finished the report, having Abbey read and sign it. He handed her a copy, sat back in his chair, and picked up the glass, staring across the water. "You've got a nice view here."

"Yes, it is nice," Abbey agreed.

"Sanders, was it?" Sheriff Davis asked.

"Yes. Larry," Larry said.

"Songbird Security?" he asked.

"Yes." Larry leaned against the railing of the porch.

"Are you out here in an official capacity or just visiting?"

"Official," Larry stated. "I don't believe in coincidences

either."

"Did you find anything in those woods over there?" the sheriff asked, looking across the water again.

"Yeah, I did. I think they tried to poison the dogs, but that didn't work, so they tried to shoot them instead. I found what was left of a hunk of beef and a dead coyote."

"Do you still have the beef?"

"Yeah, it's on ice in my truck."

"Mind if I take it? I'll send it to the lab, see what turns up."

"I'll get it for you," Larry said, stepping into the yard.

"Larry, go ahead and pull your truck up here, I'd feel safer if you were in the house tonight."

Larry nodded and headed for the dam.

"I've lived in these parts all my life and when we were kids there were some crazy rumors about this area. I guess the Jacksons told you about the Dawson family?"

"Yes, sir," Abbey said.

"My grandpa was sheriff back then, he always said that was the craziest case he ever worked. He was young then, his first year in office. That case haunted him. I used to ask him questions about it, but he'd just say there were some things on earth man just wasn't meant to understand." He finished his tea and chuckled. "Whatever happened back then, it sure did give Grandpa an appreciation of that show *The X-files* in his last years."

The sheriff stood up as the beat up 4x4 drove down the driveway. "Mrs. Brown, Abbey, I'm going to put extra patrols out here. I'm not sure how much good it will do since they can't see the house from the road, but police presence may make the person who shot your dog think twice if he has any other plans. One thing I know for sure, it wasn't any hunters out here at that time of night and in that storm. And if anything else happens, call us."

"I will," Abbey said and the sheriff picked up the clipboard, said good-bye to everyone, and met Larry in the yard.

The sheriff held up the meat, inspecting it. "That's a nice cut of beef." He opened the trunk and dropped the bag inside a cooler. "Good to know you're out here," he said to Larry, opening the door to the cruiser. "I sure as hell don't want another Dawson case on my hands." He climbed into the car and drove away with a wave.

Larry stepped on the porch. "So what's the plan?"

"I want Kelly to go stay with Mom," Abbey said. "But I'm going to tell Richard she's with her father, I think he's a little intimidated by Jack."

"What about school and carpooling?" Kelly asked.

"I'll get out of carpooling, you can take your books to Grandma's and call Brandon for your math work. I've got to figure out what to do with the animals, find someone to take them."

"Larry, I guess you need to get cleaned up and official looking to meet Richard." Rex chuckled. "Let's get him good and pissed off and see what he does. And then, Abbey, I want you out of here by tomorrow."

"Yes, sir. I just want to get the animals situated, if I just leave them I know Richard won't take care of them."

"Get the animals taken care of and get out," Rex stated.

"Abbey, I can take care of the animals, let me make a few calls." Summer paused and then asked, "Does that mean you're moving back home?"

"Looks like it, Mom, just until I can find us a place." Abbey looked at Kelly. "Ready to go at it on our own again, kid?"

"More than you know, Mom." Kelly hugged her, looking at

Larry over her mother's shoulder. "You take good care of my mom."

"I will," he said firmly.

"You promise?" Kelly asked, still hugging Abbey.

"Yes," he said.

"Okay." She pulled away. "Guess I'll go pack. How much should I take?"

"Take enough for the week. We'll get out here later, after May Day, and move our stuff out."

While Abbey helped Kelly pack, Larry showered, shaved, and changed into a pair of slacks and a blue sport shirt with Songbird Security embroidered on the pocket. Abbey watched her mom, daughter, and uncle drive away and felt lost; she wiped a tear from her cheek.

"Don't worry they'll have security, too. They'll be okay."

"I need a cigarette," Abbey said and pulled a pack from her pocket. "Mom says that Chief Night Wind said that smoke keeps the evil spirits away. Want one?" She smiled, offering him the pack.

"Well, if Chief Night Wind said it, it must be true." He took a cigarette, pulling a lighter from his pocket.

Abbey put a flame to her own and sat down on the stairs. "You really think they know who I am?"

"I don't know, Abbey, but we have to look all directions, at all possibilities." He sat beside her. "Has Richard ever hit you?"

"No." She shook her head. "I think getting physical is below him. He works out and keeps in shape, but I can't imagine him hitting anyone. He has a strong sense of what is and what is not appropriate. Fisticuffs certainly would be inappropriate in his book. Guess that's why he was so shocked I punched him in the stomach." She chuckled. "I actually surprised myself a bit with that one, but the dog was bleeding and I didn't want Kelly coming home to another dead animal, and he was holding my keys over my head, like a fifth grader taunting a first grader. That's what I mean about the pressure getting to him. He yelled the other night too, first time I've seen that."

"So he's not a yeller or a hitter, how does he vent his frustration?"

"Long circular conversations that leave me wondering if I'm coming or going by the end of them. For a psychiatrist, Richard does not seem to understand emotion, at least not when exhibited by me or Kelly."

"And you've never discussed your past with him?"

"I've never discussed it at all with anyone until this week. It's always been in my head, more conscious on some days than others, but I've never discussed it at all. I've just told those that needed to know that I was taken away from a family because of abuse and that Summer and Martin adopted me. I never go into any details, not that anyone asks." She took a drag. "Funny, Richard was trying to get me to talk about it the other night, said I may have a multiple personality disorder or something."

"Has he ever tried to get you to talk about it before?" Larry asked.

"No, never."

"Do you find it strange that he is suddenly interested?"

"I just figured it was just another passive-aggressive circular argument as he tried to punish me for refusing to return the cell phones. It went from the phones, to my weight, to my past, and a few places in between. He tries to wear me down that way, just going on and on until I want to strangle him."

"What's his issue with your weight?" Larry asked, enjoying the light scent of her skin wafting up to him, teasingly. He dropped the cigarette on the ground, snubbed it out with his foot, and told himself to quit smelling the bird.

"I guess he thinks I've gained weight since we got married, he wanted to weigh me, which really pissed me off. After I refused to get on the scale, he started in about my out of control outbursts and then my past." She dropped her own cigarette and he snubbed it out also.

"You weight looks fine to me," he said. More than fine, he thought and told himself to get his eyes off the bird. "Do you have out of control outbursts?"

"To Richard if you don't do what he says, how he says, and when he says it or if you complain, you're having an outburst." She laughed and leaned back against the stair. "I guess the shoe will be on the other foot tonight, though, I imagine that when he sees you he'll have an outburst."

"Are you using me for a little revenge?" Larry asked softly, turning his head to look into her eyes.

She met his eyes and felt her cheeks flush. "Maybe a little," she admitted. She glanced at his mouth, just inches away, and felt her cheeks get warmer as that tingle worked through her body again.

"You know, Abbey," he said softly, his eyes drifting down to her mouth. "I really want to kiss you." He smiled when her cheeks flushed even redder. "But I really don't think we should," he said and started to turn away.

Abbey closed the distance between them, pressing her mouth against his and felt the tingle turn into a throb. She moaned softly in her throat and moved closer to him. Larry put his hands on her shoulders to push her away, but her mouth opened under his with a sigh and her arms wrapped around his neck. He turned off the voice in his head yelling at him to quit kissing the bird and he kissed her.

He felt something nudge the back of his head and turning, he found himself face to face with a goat. He jumped to his feet, laughing. "Whoa!"

"Saved by the goat." Abbey smiled shakily and stood up.

Silly exposed his teeth and pawed the ground, and then holding his nose up to sniff the air, he turned, walking to the gate.

"Well," she said, "I guess he likes you better than me." She walked over to the gate, rubbing Silly's head roughly, and opened the gate. He went through the opening easily. "Well, look at you. Aren't you being polite today? Not bad for a pissface."

Larry watched her, laughing under his breath as she talked to the goat. He liked her, not only was she attractive, she had spirit, energy, and a sense of humor. He shook his head and picked up the cigarette butts, throwing them in the trash barrel. *I can't get involved with a bird,* he thought and looked skywards. "Keep your hands off the bird," he muttered to himself.

Abbey turned away from the gate, looked at him standing by the porch, and felt totally mortified. Her cheeks turned bright red and she stammered, "I'm going to get my bag so we can pick up the dog." She went to the bathroom and splashed her face with cold water. *What in the hell are you doing, Abbey?* The always-unwelcome voice asked. "I don't know," she muttered, drying her face on a hand towel. "I don't freaking know." *You're not doing that.* The unwelcome voice said and grew silent. Taking a moment to regain her composure, she stepped outside, went to the doghouse, and unchained Jerry. "Come on, boy, let's go get your brother." She opened the back of the Jeep and he jumped in.

Larry climbed in the passenger side and was quiet. Abbey

pulled out onto the road, feeling as though she had put both of them in an awkward situation. "I'm sorry I came on so strong back there, I guess I'm a little starved for affection after the last couple years of being married to Richard," she explained.

"Does he not give you any affection?" Larry asked, wondering if he really wanted to know the answer.

"I get a couple pecks on the cheek a day, that's about it," Abbey said softly.

"Are you saying you don't have sex?" he asked and then wished he hadn't - all he could think of was the way she responded to his kiss.

"Not really. I don't remember the last time, maybe last summer. He doesn't really seem interested in me that way." She turned toward Oak Tree. "When we dated, he wanted to wait until we were married and then when we got married, he wanted to take Kelly on our honeymoon. So even though we had a big suite of rooms, we didn't make love until after we came home. He didn't really seem to care either way, so after a while we just quit. I've never really considered myself a very sexual person, not surprising considering where I came from, but I guess I miss being touched."

She shrugged.

With her words, the idea that the marriage was a set-up grew as a strong possibility in Larry's mind. The man didn't even make love to her, wanted to control her, and kept her drugged. Yeah, he thought, Richard has his hands in something dirtier than the real estate lady.

"You know, all my life I've had these vivid dreams, seemed more like nightmares when I was a kid. Mom finally found a doctor who would prescribe a mild sleeping pill to a kid and I learned I could make the dreams go away. I've always hated them, never understood the scenes I would watch play out. Sometimes they were terrible things, sometimes things I just didn't understand. It was always easier to keep to myself because I would dream about people I knew and see into their lives enough to form an opinion, whether it was right or not." She turned onto the highway that led to Locknee.

"I never gave too much thought if the dreams were really true, it was just something I wanted to push away, like I wanted to push away my past. But these dreams about Richard seem real to me, in the dreams it's like I'm there, but no one can see me. I can see so many details, only I can't hear the words spoken, but now that I just put into words how screwed up my and Richard's sex life is, I think I should tell you my other dreams because Kelly may need more protection." She sighed. "I've dreamt a couple times that he was in Kelly's room, watching her while she slept or he was going through her things, touching her things in a way that just felt creepy. Maybe you should call Uncle Rex."

He was already pulling the phone from his pocket. "I'm on it." He spoke briefly to Rex, filling him in on the latest revelation and hung up the phone. "Rex is calling in a few extra guys to stay at your mom's house."

"Good." She sighed. "I think it's going to be a long night. I'm a little scared, I don't know why he scares me like he does, like I said he's never hit me, of course, I've never really pushed hard."

"I won't let anything happen, Abbey." He reached over, squeezing her hand resting on the gearshift between them and told himself to get his hand off the bird.

"Thanks, Larry." She turned and smiled.

He felt something contract in his chest and pulled his hand away. The phone vibrated in his pocket. "Yeah."

"Larry, Scott. A car just pulled in. Looks like a couple kids parking."

"Get photos, get their faces, the description of the car, and the tag number. We're just pulling into Locknee, I'll be back on the property in less than an hour. Send the photos to me and call if anything interesting happens." He hung up the phone. "Someone's at the circle, the guy watching said it looked liked kids parking."

She nodded her head, pulled into the vet's parking lot, and heard Jerry's tail thumping in the back. "We're going to get your brother, Jerry." She parked the car and opened the door, turning to Larry. "Not exactly the place I'd want to be making out. Unless you were there, of course," she said over her shoulder, sexily, and slid out of the car.

He shook his head. I'm in trouble with this one, he thought, but couldn't stop the smile that crossed his face as he watched her walk into the building. She returned a few minutes later holding a leash attached to a dog with a large white cone around his neck.

"Poor bunny, can you imagine how embarrassed he is?" She laughed, as she helped the dog up in the Jeep. Tom stretched out and Jerry reached over, licking his nose. Tom's tail thumped against the seat.

Abbey climbed in the front and started the car. "Richard has another reason to go off tonight, Tom has to stay indoors and now that I think about, I want Jerry in the house, too." She sighed and put the car in gear, pulling back on the road.

"Sounds like Richard doesn't like animals," he said, reaching back to rub Tom's shoulders.

"Yeah, it's really strange, because he's the one that brought home every one of them. When we got married I just had a cat, turns out he said he was allergic to cats, so ole Snuffy is living with Mom. He brought in the puppies right after Kelly came home from the hospital. It was a lot of work on me, a child in casts recovering from surgeries and then two rambunctious puppies, but I didn't mind too much. Kelly enjoyed them and I figured it was good medicine for her."

"Maybe he was trying to keep you busy and distracted," Larry suggested, seeing nothing positive in Richard.

"Well, he did a fine job of that when he had the damned goats delivered. I was mad as hell about that, we didn't even have a fence. Of course, that doesn't really keep Silly enclosed."

"Has that goat ever butted you? He's bigger than you are."

"Oh yes, he has, but I learned pretty quick. And he's just getting bigger and even more ornery now that his horns are starting to come through his skin."

"So he just dumps an ornery goat on two women as small as you and Kelly?" he asked, shaking his head and remembering how he felt when he saw that goat charging her.

"Yeah, for some reason he wanted a farm, but he rarely even goes out in the yard. He did build the dog house and barn, so he can do stuff like that, but I guess he just chooses not to."

So he drugged her and then gave her far too much to do everyday, he thought, so she'd be docile, malleable, and exhausted. "Abbey, why did you quit taking the sleeping pills?"

"I don't know, sometimes I would forget to take them and Richard would chastise me, so I guess I started forgetting them subconsciously. My head started getting clearer, but then the dreams would come and I would start again. But a few weeks ago I had a dream about Richard and it seemed so real, my gut just insisted I stop taking them."

They were quiet for a long time and Abbey let out a long

sigh. "It's going to be a long, hard night. I'm glad you're here."

The phone vibrated in his pocket. "Yeah."

"Larry, Scott. You know that couple that was here? Well, they went into a wooded area in the south of the field. Sounded like they were having a good time in there, but he came out and left, without the girl."

"Hold your position, I'm going to call the sheriff. Meet him when he gets there, but for now, stay put." He hung up and dialed the sheriff. It took several minutes to get the sheriff on the line. "Sheriff Davis, this is Larry Sanders with Songbird Security. We've got a problem."

Chapter Nineteen

"Oh crap, is it happening already?" Abbey asked.

"I don't know. The sheriff will stop by on the his way out or if not, he'll give us a call later," he said, as she pulled to the stop sign in Oak Tree.

"Are you going down there to meet the sheriff?" she asked, turning toward home.

"Nope, I'm not leaving your side. Scott can handle it and when we get to your house, I'll send Kevin to give him a hand if he needs it."

Just as she approached the turn onto the rural road that she called home, a police car passed, its sirens blaring and lights flashing. The car turned onto the road before her, the tires squealed and she wondered if he would keep it on the road. The officer kept it on the pavement and zoomed up the road, disappearing over a hill. "Well, at least they are responding quickly."

"I think Davis is a good man," Larry said.

She crossed the small bridge below her property just as

another police car passed with lights and sirens. Larry put the phone to his ear as she pulled into the driveway. He spoke briefly and hung up. "Richard and the blond woman just went into the church for evening services. How long do you think it will be before he gets here?"

"A couple hours." She parked and turned to look at Tom. "You're home, boy. Poor little conehead, that's got to suck." She jumped out of the car and walked around to help the dog out. He came out gingerly, a little more alert, and wagged his tail, holding his head up to sniff the air. "You feeling better, buddy?" She reached inside the cone, scratching his head.

Larry called Kevin and sent him down to see if Scott needed help. Hanging up, he asked, "Do you want me to get Jerry?"

"If you could chain him, that'd be great, I don't want him running off to the woods." Abbey was pleased that Tom needed to go to the bathroom and she looked the other way while he tended to his business. "Good boy, Tom. You're gonna to be fine."

They stepped into the house and she made the dog a bed with a couple of old blankets on the floor in the laundry room. She mixed up dog food, sliding a bowl toward Tom and taking Jerry his dinner. She stepped back into the house as Larry hung up the phone. "Are you hungry?"

"Yeah. You might want to make enough for the sheriff, he said he'd be here as soon as the ambulance left."

"They found the girl? Is she all right?" Abbey asked, opening the fridge to pull out the afternoon leftovers.

"Yeah, they found her, she seems to be okay physically, but she's hysterical, saying she saw a demon and that it raped her." Larry sat down at the table, opening his laptop.

"It what? Are you serious?" Abbey froze reaching for the roast.

"Yeah, it seems Kelly may have been more right than wrong about her idea of a gateway into hell back there. Come here and look at these pictures. Do you recognize these kids?"

Abbey stepped over to the table, looking at the photographs that showed a dark-haired girl and a redheaded boy kissing in front of an old Toyota.

"The boy who cleared the road down there was a redhead," Abbey said.

Larry clicked on another photo, a close up of the boy's face.

"Is this him?"

"It looks like him, I wasn't close when I saw him, though, so I can't say positively, but it looks like him."

He clicked on another photo, a close up of the dark-headed girl. "How about her? Does she look familiar?"

Abbey shook her head. "No."

She returned to the fridge, pulling out the roast. "Sandwiches okay?"

He nodded his head with the phone at his ear. He spoke briefly and slid the phone back into his pocket. "Looks like the car is registered to David Hollister. Could that be Pearl's son?"

"Could be, she's old enough to have a son his age. Kelly should know if you want to call her." She sliced meat, dropping it onto a plate.

He nodded, dialing Kelly. "Kelly, it's Larry. She's good, slicing roast beef right now. Do you know if Pearl Hollister has a son?"

"Okay, thanks. Your mom will call you later." He hung up. "Yep, that's Pearl's son. As your daughter said, he's a snotty redhead, she says he has tried to talk to her a couple times at church, but she finds him creepy."

"The plot thickens," Abbey said. "Richard's having a fling with Pearl and her son is clearing the road that leads to the altar."

"Things are definitely coming together." He dialed Rex.

While he talked, Abbey set the table, put out a loaf of bread, and a small collection of condiments. Jerry started barking and she set the plate of meat on the table, walking to the front door to see the sheriff come up the drive. He parked and stepped out of the car. "You hungry, Sheriff?" she asked.

"Matter of fact, I am," he said, walking up the stairs.

"Come on in." She opened the door and he followed her inside, pulling his hat from his head. "Have a seat. Iced tea?"

"Yeah, that'd be nice." He sat down at the table, across from Larry, and set his hat in the chair next to him.

Larry turned the computer to show him the photos.

"Yeah, your guys by the cemetery showed me those. You got hard copies?"

"I can get them. Abbey, do you have a printer?"

"Yeah, back in the den," she said, setting out glasses of tea.

Larry inserted a zip drive, pushed a few buttons, pulled it out and stood up. "I'll be right back."

"It's not much," she said, putting a bowl of potato chips on the table.

"I appreciate it. It's going to be a long night and I've got to get to the hospital and check on the girl."

"I hope she's okay." Abbey sat at the table as Larry stepped into the room.

"They're printing," he said.

"Thanks."

"Y'all help yourself," Abbey said and the men began constructing towering sandwiches.

After she finished making her own sandwich, Abbey heard clicking on the floor and Tom sat down beside her, begging for treats. "I guess you are feeling better, huh boy?" She dropped a small piece of meat in his mouth.

The sheriff swallowed a bite of food. "I forgot to ask, did you get the bullet from the vet?"

"I did. I gave it to Larry," Abbey said, biting into her own sandwich.

Larry pulled the small, plastic bag out of his pocket and slid it across the table to Sheriff Davis. The sheriff held it up, inspecting it under the light and glanced down at the dog gently taking a piece of meat from Abbey's fingers. "That's one lucky dog."

"I think he used a silencer. Abbey heard the dog yelp, but didn't hear the gun fire," Larry said.

"Mind if I hold on to this?" the sheriff asked, taking another bite of the well-stuffed sandwich.

"You're the sheriff," Larry said.

"Do y'all have any idea of what is going on back there by the cemetery? Somebody cleared the road, cut the grass."

"We believe that somebody would be David Hollister and another young man we haven't identified yet," Larry said and popped the last of his sandwich into his mouth. "I figure they are getting ready for a gathering back there."

"A gathering of what?" the sheriff asked, sitting back in his chair and sliding a chip in his mouth.

"Well, that's a sticky question, isn't it?" Larry drained his glass of tea. "Sheriff, you've been here all your life you said, your grandpa worked the Dawson case, and you're familiar with the rumors. What do you think is going on?"

"When I was a teenager a bunch of us guys used to go fishing down at the Red Fork and we went back in there a couple times. I've been in that weird circle a few times when I was a kid and I know the rumors, but I never really believed them until today." He shook his head. "Your guy met the first responding officer and they went into the circle and found the girl on that rock in there. At first they thought she was dead, she wasn't moving, but when they touched her she started screaming about demons. My guy drew his gun. He said it felt like they were being watched. Your guy, Scott?"

Larry nodded.

"Well, he said he felt dizzy and nauseous in there, said his hair was standing on end. And my guy was shook up, said there was something in there that he couldn't see, but could sure feel. When they pulled the girl out of the circle she was hysterical and screaming about things touching her. Her clothes were disheveled as though she had had sex and Scott said that she and the boy were going at it pretty hot and heavy down there and the pictures show that. They'll do a rape kit at the hospital, but it looks consensual between the two of them." He picked up his glass. "Like I said,

I've been in there a few times and it always felt a little creepy, but nothing like it felt today. Just walking down the path the hairs on my arms and the back of my neck were standing on end. And stepping into that damned thing, wow." He took a sip of tea.

"When I stepped into it, it felt like I had been hit in the head with a hammer," Abbey encouraged him to continue.

"Let's just say I didn't stay long." He sighed. "Are you saying that the rumors are true? The stuff about demons, witches, and rituals?"

"I don't know about the demon and witch part, but I'm pretty sure the stuff about rituals is true. And I think it's about to happen again," Larry said.

"Have any idea when?"

"We're thinking this week."

"Is that why you have a man down there?"

"One reason. The other reason is to prevent someone from there, coming through the woods to here. We've found some tracks back there and believe that someone has been hanging out on the other side of the lake."

He nodded. "It private property, some kind of trust. I can't put my men on the land, but I'm not going to say that you can't, as far as I'm concerned I never saw them." He stood up and picked up his hat. "I've got to get to the hospital, the guys in Locknee are looking to have a talk with Mr. Hollister."

"Let me get you those photos," Larry said, rising and heading to the den.

"Thanks. And, Abbey, thanks for the food, it hit the spot. And don't hesitate to call if you need anything."

She nodded and Larry stepped into the room, handing him a small stack of papers.

"I'll let myself out." He put on his hat and went out the front door.

Abbey looked at Larry, sighed and stood up. "Richard will be here soon." She started cleaning up the kitchen.

"Are you okay?" he asked, watching her briskly put condiments away and load the dishwasher.

She shut the dishwasher and pressed the power button. The machine roared to life and Abbey leaned against it. "I'm scared to death," she said, holding her hand up to show the tremble.

He put his hand on her shoulder. "I'm here, I won't let

anything bad happen." Get your hand off the bird, he told himself and pulled his hand away.

"Want to join me for the evening chores?" she asked, feeling awkward.

"Sure," he said with a smile and the skin around his eyes wrinkled, making him even more attractive.

She felt the tingle and turned quickly toward the laundry room. "Would you mind holding Tom's leash while I take care of the other animals?" she asked, pulling the leash off a hook and attaching it to the dog. "He might need to go again."

"Not at all," he said, following her outside.

She made short work of putting the animals away and was just shutting the gate when Larry informed her that Richard was on his way home. She sighed and pulled out the cigarettes out of her pocket, lighting one. She took a few drags, snubbed it out on the ground and left it. "Oh yeah, he's also pissed off because I'm smoking again. I think I forgot to mention that one." She walked over to Jerry, unchained him and grabbed his collar. "No running off in the woods for you tonight, little man." She led him into the house and opened the laundry room door.

Larry brought in Tom and he joined his brother happily. They licked each other's faces and as Abbey shut the door Jerry was gently investigating the wound on his brother's hip. She stepped back into the kitchen, leaned against the counter and looked at her bodyguard. "Are you ready for this?"

"Yep. Piece of cake," he smiled.

Abbey paced nervously, glancing at the clock over and again.

"You're going to wear yourself out, sit down, try to relax."

Abbey jumped when the dogs barked. "He's here," she said, quieting the dogs and stepping to the backdoor to meet him.

"Whose truck is that?" Richard asked.

Larry stood up, stepping into view. "Mr. Brown," he said, approaching him. "I'm Larry Sanders with Songbird Security." He held out his hand. "Rex Andrews hired me to keep an eye on Abbey."

Richard looked at Larry, glanced down at his hand and then turned to Abbey. "What the hell is going on here and who is this man?"

"Rex sent him out." She laughed nervously. "I have a

bodyguard."

"Well, send him away, you don't need a bodyguard."

"Mr. Brown," Larry began.

"Doctor," Richard interrupted.

"Dr. Brown," Larry began again. "Your dog was shot last night, a truck almost ran your wife into the swamp between here and Locknee while she was trying to get the dog to the vet, and I found some poisoned meat in the woods. Someone meant to kill both of your dogs. It is my opinion that she does need security."

"Well, this is my house and I don't want you here," Richard stated.

"It's also my house and I do want him here." Abbey leaned against the counter, crossing her arms.

"This is ridiculous, a hunter's stray bullet hit the dog and you're making a federal case out of it." He pulled off his tie.

Larry laughed. "Hunters? In the middle of a storm that spawned tornados in three counties? I don't think so and hunters don't use pistols with silencers, Dr. Brown."

Richard's anger filled the room, Abbey felt it wash over her and a dog scratched at the door.

"What are those skunk stinking dogs doing in the house?" he demanded.

"I'm not putting a dog that just had surgery outside and I'm not leaving Jerry outside to be shot."

"I appreciate you coming out Mr. Sanders, but you can leave now, we don't need your services," Richard said, standing taller in an attempt to make Larry look small.

"You didn't hire me, Dr. Brown. Rex did and I'm not leaving until he feels his niece is safe."

"If you don't go, I'm calling the sheriff," Richard threatened.

"I'm sure he wouldn't mind stopping out here again, he's already been here twice," Larry said.

Richard's face reddened and he turned to Abbey. "Why was the sheriff out here, Abbey?"

"Our dog was shot, Richard, and that's illegal, especially since it happened on our property. I filed a report. And something happened to a girl back there in the woods. We heard all kinds of sirens and then the sheriff stopped by again, he had dinner with us."

Richard looked back and forth between them. Abbey could

feel his anger, his frustration building, and her stomach tightened. "I'm going to change," he said and pulled off his suit jacket. "This discussion isn't over." He walked to the bedroom and shut the door firmly.

"Ding. End of round one," she whispered. "He's mad."

Larry nodded.

"I need a drink." She pulled out a bottle of wine and grabbed a corkscrew from the drawer. She unscrewed the cork, poured a glass and leaving the bottle on the counter, she sat down at the table. She took a sip, glancing at Larry. He leaned against the counter, casually, his feet crossed at the ankle. Abbey laughed, she couldn't help herself - the situation suddenly seemed beyond absurd. Larry raised his eyebrows and then winked. "This is so ridiculous," she whispered, smiling. "It's really funny."

Her humor vanished when she heard the bedroom door open; she stood up, leaned against the counter and watched Richard walk across the living room and down the hall. He returned a few seconds later. "Where's Kelly?"

Abbey heard the silent ding in her head, announcing the next round. "Considering all that has happened, I sent her to her dad's house."

"What about school?" he demanded.

"I sent her assignments with her, she's ahead anyway, it'll be fine," Abbey assured.

His eyes snapped between them, finally settling on Abbey. "Have you lost your mind? You send our daughter away and bring in some man in our house that you don't even know, are you insane? I knew you hadn't been thinking straight, but this proves it. You've become so paranoid that you send our daughter away because a stray bullet hits the dog. You're behaving irrationally."

"I believe she is behaving perfectly rational," Larry said. "Did you not hear me when I said someone tried to run her off the road last night?"

"I'm not talking to you," Richard snapped.

"First of all, she's not our daughter. She is my and Jack's daughter and she is with her father, in the town where she grew up, I'd hardly call that sending her away. Second of all, Mr. Sanders comes highly recommended by Uncle Rex and that's all I need to know."

"Uncle Rex," he sneered. "That man is not your uncle. I

knew he was trying to break us apart, I told you that. Oh…." he paused, "I got it now." He turned to Larry. "Are you fucking my wife?"

Abbey's eyes widened, she had never heard Richard use that word and then her cheeks flushed, remembering the way she behaved with Larry on the porch stairs.

"No, Dr. Brown, I'm not fucking your wife," Larry responded, feet still crossed at the ankles. "I am protecting your wife."

"Protecting her from what?" Richard demanded, taking a step toward Larry.

Larry didn't move or alter his position. "From whatever I deem as a threat."

"I'm not playing any macho games with you," Richard said, taking a step back and turning toward Abbey. "I want to talk to you in the bedroom, alone." He turned, expecting her to follow.

"No," Larry said. "She stays in my sight."

"Are you serious?" Richard turned quickly, facing Larry.

"Yes, Dr. Brown, I am. It's clear that you are upset. Mrs. Brown stays in my sight," Larry said calmly.

Abbey held her breath and wondered if this was the point where Richard's head would explode.

Chapter Twenty

Richard's face turned redder than Abbey had ever seen it and his hands trembled slightly as he shoved them into his pockets. "How about the living room? Can I speak to my own wife, in my own house, in my own living room?" Richard barked.

"You can speak to your wife wherever you'd like as long as I can see her," Larry said, still leaning, cool as could be, against the counter.

"Abbey, I'd like to speak to you in the living room," he bit out, his anger washing over her in waves, each one stronger than the last.

Abbey glanced at Larry and he nodded. "Okay," she said and followed him into the living room. She sat on the couch and placed her glass on the coffee table.

He sat next to her, speaking softly, soothingly, but she felt the rage pulsing just under the surface. "Honey, what is going on? Why did you send Kelly away? Why do we have a strange man in our house telling me I can't talk to you?"

"I've been trying to tell you what's going on, but you don't seem to want to hear me. Richard, someone tried to push my Jeep into the marsh last night, someone shot our dog, and I don't feel safe," she said.

"Well, it's hard to hear you, honey, when you've been so out of control. Listen, I'll take the day off tomorrow, I'll stay here until you feel safe. We'll go get Kelly and I won't even complain about the dogs," he smiled and rubbed her shoulder reassuringly.

His touch sent a shiver of revulsion down her spine and she had to reign in her own temper, she wanted to punch him again - harder this time, and in the face.

He mistook the shiver as one of passion. "Maybe we can make love tonight," he whispered. "We'll get Kelly tomorrow, spend the day together and get back to normal. Send Sanders away, I'll take care of you. After all, I am your husband." He chuckled softly.

"No." She stood up, feeling the need to get away from his touch and his lies. "Mr. Sanders stays and Kelly stays where she is until I decide otherwise." She picked up her glass, moving to a chair.

"You are my wife," he said, still whispering, but louder now. "I have rights, I have a say so in my own home."

"Richard, I also have rights and I am afraid for my and Kelly's safety, so until I feel otherwise she will stay with her father."

"Damn it!" he yelled, jumping to his feet. "This has gone too far!" He stalked into the kitchen, passing Larry and picking up the phone. He stomped back to the den and the TV came on, blaring to mask the conversation he was having.

Abbey sighed and stood up, walking back into the kitchen. "Ding," she whispered. "End of round two."

"Are you okay?"

"Besides the fact I want to punch him and throw up? Yeah,

I'm fine." She finished the wine, poured another glass, and sliding the cork back in the bottle, she returned it to the fridge.

"Is that the only phone in the house?" Larry asked.

"Yes. I'd like to know who he's calling. Are you ready for round three?" she asked.

"Yeah, I'm ready, how about you? Seems you're getting the worst of it."

She nodded as Richard returned to the room, stepping between them to hang up the phone. "I've called the hospital, they're waiting for you. I've put this off long enough, you can't just quit taking medication, Abbey, you need to go in, have a blood test and speak to a doctor. If you can't see how out of control this situation is that's just more evidence to show how detached you are from reality."

"I'm not going to the hospital, Richard, I'm fine." She took a sip of wine and set the glass on the counter.

"Yes, Abbey, you are going to the hospital. I'm tired of this insanity and if I wasn't tired of it before, I sure as hell am tired of it now." He turned to Larry. "I want you to leave. You're not welcome or needed here. The only thing Abbey has to be scared of is the delusions in her own mind. She was an abused child, sometimes the problems that that creates don't turn up until later in life, you don't understand what you are involved with, there are no bad guys, just a damaged mind struggling to accept reality." He turned back to Abbey. "Get your purse."

"No," Abbey stated firmly.

"Did you know she got physical with me last night?" Richard asked, as though she had not spoken. "I could have called the sheriff and pressed charges, but I didn't, sometimes I'm too nice." He laughed, but Abbey could feel his rage pulsing through the house. "I'm sure you're a nice guy, Larry, a nice guy doing his job, but you don't understand what you've stepped into here. She attacked me last night, she hit me." He shook his head slowly.

"Would that have been when you were holding her keys over her head, taunting her as she was trying to get her bleeding and injured pet to the vet?" Larry asked. "Because I have to tell you, Richard, I understand why she would do such a thing. And I'm pretty sure Sheriff Davis would understand as well."

"That's it!" Richard exploded. "You're going to the hospital." He grabbed Abbey's arm, but his grip slipped away quickly, leaving her unharmed. She didn't see Larry move, but the next thing she knew Richard was laying on the floor five feet away in front of the laundry room and Larry stood protectively in front of her. The dogs barked and one scratched at the door, growling aggressively.

"You son of a bitch!" Richard jumped to his feet. "Buddy, I don't know who you are, but you're going to jail."

"I don't know what you're talking about, Dr. Brown, you must have tripped," Larry said calmly.

"You fucking kicked me in the chest! Abbey! You saw him! He kicked me in the chest!"

"I didn't see anything, Richard," she said honestly. "All I know is you grabbed me and you fell down."

"You bitch!" he yelled and went for her again. Larry moved quickly and Richard landed on the floor again.

"It's not going to happen, Dr. Brown." Larry stood over him and reached down a hand to help pull him up. "She's not going to the hospital and if she needs a doctor, I'll take her to her doctor in Windslow."

Richard's head didn't actually explode, Abbey observed, but

something inside of him cracked. He slapped Larry's hand away and Larry stepped back, allowing him to get to his feet. "You stupid bitch!" he raged. "You stupid, uncouth, foul smelling bitch!"

Larry stepped in front of Abbey, his demeanor calm but lethal.

"You think I actually wanted to marry a backwoods, uneducated, country bumpkin?" he laughed harshly. "Have you ever given any thought why I would want to attach myself to something as pathetic as you? Probably not. I don't think thinking is something you excel at - a damned high school drop out!" he sneered. "You'll find out soon enough, stupid bitch, and you will rue the day you ever disrespected me." He slammed out the back door and the Mercedes roared to life, spraying sand as the car screamed down the dirt driveway.

Larry was already on the phone. "He's moving," he said and slid the phone into his pocket.

Abbey drained her glass and looked at Larry "I guess that worked," she said, setting the glass on the counter.

He put his hand on her shoulder. "Are you okay? That was rough."

She nodded her head. "I want more protection on Kelly. He's too interested in Kelly."

"I agree." He pulled the phone out and hit a button. "Rex," he said. "I think Kelly may be the target."

While Larry talked to Rex, Abbey calmed the dogs, put on their leashes and stepped outside. She walked them along the tree line, allowing them to lift their legs, and then sat on the porch stair, wrapping both leashes around one wrist and lighting a cigarette.

Larry sat beside her and rubbed the dogs' heads. "Rex is calling in two additional men. Kelly's going to be fine, with Rex and four good men watching her, she's safe. Richard is heading toward Locknee. We've slipped a GPS tracker on both his and Pearl's cars. I've added an additional man to follow him, we'll know every move he makes." He watched her as she stared off into the pen and smoked a cigarette. "Abbey, are you okay?"

She expelled a long stream of smoke. "Well, one thing we know for sure is that I'm an idiot. How did I believe he loved me? How did I believe enough to give up my house and move my daughter out into the middle of nowhere, where we knew no one? What in the hell was I thinking?"

"It happens, Abbey, you made a mistake. You are anything but an idiot. It happens everyday, to women everywhere. You made a mistake."

"Pretty big mistake, huh?" she asked, still staring at the barn. "I put my only child in harms way and after everything I survived, I moved her into what I escaped." She shook her head, took a drag off her cigarette and dropped it to the ground. "I'm going to call Kelly." She stood up, cooing to the dogs and they got to their feet, following her inside.

Larry stood up, expelling a breath and remembering how tired he was. He walked to his truck, pulling out a pack and lighting his own cigarette. He hated seeing her so disheartened, so lifeless, staring into space and hating herself. He leaned against the truck, pulled out the phone and made sure that the guys relieving Scott and Kevin were in place. Satisfied that all was well, he headed back to the house and sat on the step, finishing his smoke.

Abbey went to the bedroom, dialed the phone and Kelly answered quickly. "Hey, Mom."

She sounds happy, Abbey thought. "Hey, honey."

"How'd it go? Did his head explode?"

"Pretty close. It was bad and I owe you an apology."

"For what?" Kelly asked slowly. "Are you okay?"

"I'm fine, just a hard dose of reality. Baby, I'm sorry for getting you in this mess. I don't know what I was thinking then or what I've been thinking this last year while we've been out here stranded and isolated."

"Mom, you got caught up. You fell for the wrong guy, you're not the first and you won't be the last, you know that. Don't blame yourself." Abbey heard some noise in the background. "Uncle Rex just brought in a load of guns." She laughed. "I'm going to be fine. You're a great mom, you've trained me well, remember the shooting lessons and karate classes? I can take care of myself, that's how you raised me and you did a good job," Kelly soothed.

Abbey felt some optimism and strength returning to her system. "You're right, Kelly, but I want you to know that I am sorry and I want to admit that I made a mistake."

"I hear what you're saying, Mom, and I forgive you. I can't wait to get our new house; I'm excited about that. I was thinking I'm ready to go back to school. What do you think?"

"I agree, I think you're ready and you're getting too smart for me." Abbey sighed and then remembered Richard's words; she was just a high-school drop out.

"How's Tom?" Kelly asked.

"He's good, he's eaten and gone to the bathroom, all good signs. He's got a cone on his head, I imagine he's terribly embarrassed, but he's making due."

"Oh, that's funny, I've seen those cones on TV, poor baby." Kelly laughed.

"I'm bringing them out tomorrow, I still don't know what I'm doing about the rest of the animals."

"Grandma was talking to Miss Sylvia, do you remember her?" Kelly asked.

"Very eccentric lady, smokes a pipe?"

"Yes, ma'am, that's the one. She may want to take the ducks; she even has one of those duck houses on the water, pretty cool. They're still negotiating, but you know Grandma."

"That is excellent news, tell Grandma thanks." Abbey paused and for the first time let herself think of Caroline. She remembered Caroline's words, her last words, and she spoke them to her daughter. "Honey, if anything bad happens, you run. And if they catch you, fight like a dog and pray to the God, cuz there's nothing God loves more than an underdog." Abbey wiped a tear off her cheek. How had she forgotten the little girl with such sage advice?

"That's cool, Mom, I'll remember that. Here, Grandma wants to talk to you. I love you and I'll see you tomorrow, right?"

"I'll see you in the morning, honey. I love you, too."

"Abbey?" Summer asked.

"Yes, ma'am."

"I've got a place for the ducks. Sylvia will take them with very few stipulations. And a petting zoo is coming to pick up the goats and chickens tomorrow." She paused. "How'd it go? Are you all right?"

"It worked, he's off doing whatever and I feel beat. That's great news about the animals, Mom, that's a load off my mind. You've got good security there, right?" Abbey asked.

"You wouldn't believe." Summer laughed softly. "We, here over in Fort Raines, are safe as can be. It sounds like you also have strong security, too. Get some rest. I know how ridiculous it sounds to say, considering, but at least try to. I'll see you in the morning and don't forget the ducks."

Abbey hung up the phone smiling, she looked around the room and was surprised that she felt no pain knowing that she was leaving the house, the husband, and the dreams she once held. She walked into the kitchen and found Larry sitting at the table with two phones and his laptop open. She set her phone on the charger and grabbed a bottle of water out of the fridge.

"Are you feeling better? Did you talk to Kelly?" Larry asked, turning in the chair.

"Yes. Do we have time in the high intrigue for a lady to take a bath?" she asked, stepping beside him to look at the map on his computer screen.

"I think a bath and a few hours sleep is on the agenda. Richard is at the Hollister house and I don't believe he'll be leaving anytime soon, but when he does I'll get a call. So go take a bath, it's been a rough day."

She nodded her head and turned toward the living room.

"Abbey, you did good."

She smiled. "I'll see you once I've washed the goat off of

me and clear my head a bit."

She grabbed her robe and went to the master bath, turning on the water in the over sized tub. She knotted her braid on top of her head and poured some vanilla bath beads in the water. Sinking down into the warmth she pushed all thought away, closed her eyes and envisioned a beautiful meadow, while she focused on her breathing. One step at a time, she thought, one step at a time.

As her body began relaxing, her mind shifted to Larry. She remembered the way she had reacted to his touch and the sudden wave of passion.

You're not doing that! The unwelcome voice spoke sharply, startling her and causing water to splash over the side of the tub.

"I know, I know," she muttered, relaxing back into the warm water. Her thoughts drifting to Larry again and the way he showed no arrogance when he dealt with Richard. He didn't flaunt his power or mock or sneer, he was strong and respectful and he didn't play any games. She remembered the attractive wrinkles around his eyes and the tingle worked down her spine.

You're not doing that, Abbey! The unwelcome voice demanded.

"I know, I don't even like sex," she muttered, thinking about sex. Despite an early interest leading to an unplanned pregnancy and marriage when she was a teen, she never really cared about or was motivated by sex. She'd wanted Richard when they married, months of petting had warmed her up, but when they had sex it was disappointing, clinical and quiet. Her mind shifted back to Larry and the kiss on the porch. She pulled the plug, rinsing the film from her skin, and stood up. She grabbed a towel, dried off, and stepped in front of the mirror, looking at her naked body. She brushed out her hair, pulled on a t-shirt and sweats and found Larry in the living room.

"I'd figured we'd get some sleep, where do you want me to bed down?" he asked.

"You can sleep in Kelly's room," she said, leading the way. She opened the door, stepping inside and switching on the bedside lamp; it cast a dim glow in the room.

"Thanks," he said, setting his phone on the bedside table. "Do you feel better?

She lifted her head and looked him in the eyes. "I feel a lot of things."

"It's normal, you've been through a lot. A good night's sleep will make things look better," he said and sat on the edge of the bed, pulling off his boots.

"I was just laying in the tub thinking about things and it occurred to me that I have never felt the way I did today when you were kissing me. What do you think that's about?" she asked, biting her lower lip.

"Sometimes excitement, life and death stuff, affects people that way," he said, looking at the spot where her teeth touched her lips.

"Do you think that's all it is? Just excitement?" she asked.

"It's been an exciting day."

"I was thinking about coming in here and trying to seduce you, but that's probably a bad idea."

He let out a breath, relieved. He hated to admit to himself that she wouldn't have to try very hard to seduce him. "Yes, that wouldn't be a good idea. Not to mention I've only had a few hours of sleep in the last couple days, I'd probably go to sleep on you anyway." He smiled.

"I was wondering, though, do you think I could sleep in here with you? Maybe you could just hold onto me for a little while…" she asked and felt her cheek bloom with heat.

He looked at her reddened cheeks and wondered if he had ever seen a bird blush before, most were used completely up by the time they reached their teens. She was different. "Yeah, I think that would be all right," he said softly and stretched out on the bed, patting the pillow beside his head. She lay beside him, reaching over and turning out the lamp. He wrapped his arm around her waist and pulled her back firmly against his chest, his nose buried in her hair. "Get some rest," he said, drifting off to the scent of sunshine and vanilla.

Chapter Twenty-One

She was dreaming. She was seven-years-old again and in the mansion where Caroline died. Caroline was crying as she lay on the altar and Abbey's eyes fell on the blond woman poised over the girl with a dagger in her hand. Abbey didn't want to watch and turned her head away, only to see herself, small and terrified, peering around the corner. The blond woman raised the dagger, the smaller version of Abbey ran away and the observer Abbey had become turned her head in time to see the dagger come down into Caroline. The blond woman laughed and pushed the hair from her face, dislodging the mask. It was a younger version of Pearl Hollister. With blood on her face, she turned and passionately kissed the man beside her, an older gentleman with salt and pepper hair and a deep tan.

The dream shifted and she stood over Pearl and Richard asleep in bed. The alarm sounded and Pearl sat up, looking down at Richard lying beside her with disgust on her face. He opened his eyes and her expression changed immediately, she smiled down at him, kissing him lightly on the lips. They rose from bed and began dressing. In the hidden moments when Pearl knew Richard couldn't see her, her disdain for him was obvious. Dressed, the two walked hand and hand down an elaborate staircase and stepped outside. Abbey awoke with a gasp, as the phone on the bedside table began vibrating.

Larry reached over her and picked up the phone. "Yeah," he said, listening. "Stick with them." He hung up the phone and yawned. "They're on the move."

"Yeah, I know. I was just dreaming about them." She glanced at the window, noticing it was still dark outside.

"What were you dreaming?" He sat up on the side of the bed and started pulling on his boots.

"Pearl doesn't like Richard, when he can't see her face, her dislike is obvious, she's using him. I also saw a much younger version of Pearl kill Caroline in that mansion in Colorado. There was a man with her, he was older with salt and pepper hair and they were kissing over Caroline."

"Pearl was in Colorado?" Larry asked.

"If my dreams can be believed, she was. I remember the woman who killed Caroline, but she wore a mask. In the dream I saw myself run away and then the woman dislodged her mask, exposing her face and it was Pearl. What are the odds of the same woman killing the closest thing I've ever had to a sister and also having an affair with my husband 26 years later?"

"About slim to none," he said, standing up and stretching.

"I'm going to get started. Why don't you try to sleep a little more?"

"Yeah, I think I will." She rolled over into the warm spot he left, but could not reclaim sleep. Her mind was too full of questions and replaying scenes from the last few days. She climbed out of bed, showered quickly, and dressed in a t-shirt and jeans. She pulled down a small suitcase and tossed articles of clothing inside. Gathering enough for several days, she closed the case, zipped it secure and left it on the bed. She stepped into the kitchen without turning on the lights and was pouring water into the coffee machine when movement outside the window caught her attention. The sun was just rising in front of the house, leaving the backyard in slowly dying shadows, and as her eyes adjusted to the light she realized the movement was Larry.

He was in the middle of the sandy drive, moving gracefully and smoothly, sliding from one karate form to another. She was captivated, the movements weren't aggressive or violent, and it almost looked like a dance, a slow and focused dance. Suddenly, the movement stopped, his eyes were closed and his hands were poised under his chin as though in prayer. He opened his eyes, with a hint of a smile curling his lips, and bowed in four directions. He slapped his hands on his thighs and walked over to his truck. "He is beautiful," she whispered, as she hit the button to start the coffee brewing.

He stepped in the back door; his hair damp with sweat and in his hands was a change of clothes. He smiled when he saw her, the skin around his eyes wrinkling and sending that tingle through her again. "Didn't get back to sleep?"

"No. My mind is spinning."

"Let me get a shower and we'll figure out our day."

She nodded, watching him walk across the living room and disappear down the hall. She sighed and shot her eyes skyward. "Sometimes I'm pretty sure you have an odd sense of humor, God," she whispered and went to the laundry room to check on Tom and Jerry. She took the dogs out, walking them along the tree line to tend to their morning business and when they were finished, she put them back in the house.

She tended to the chores in the barnyard and pulled the eggs from the boxes. Thankfully, Silly was more interested in pestering chickens, than he was in her and she escaped the barnyard with only a little chicken shit on her t-shirt. When she stepped into the house

Larry was staring at a map on his computer screen and talking on the phone. She set the eggs into the sink and stepped in the bedroom to pull on a clean shirt. She returned to the kitchen just as Larry hung up the phone. "It appears Pearl and Richard are heading to Atlanta." She nodded her head and started cleaning the eggs.

He stood and stepped to the counter, watching her work. "The police talked to David Hollister, he said it was a prank and he planned to go back and get her, but that he just wanted to scare her a little. The girl has been admitted to the Locknee Hospital's psyche ward, she's still clinging to the story that a demon raped her. She admitted she had consensual sex with David, but claims after he left her there something appeared and raped her. David said the girl was into horror movies and haunted houses and he'd heard of the place from some locals. He said he just wanted to give her a good scare, and claims he'd never been there before yesterday."

"Well, I guess it worked, he scared her crazy. What if she really was raped by something that stepped through a gateway? The psychiatric community would never believe it." She set the eggs in a carton and slid them in the fridge.

"No," he agreed. "Most people would never believe it. And

for something else unbelievable, guess where Pearl Hollister first went to real estate school?"

"Colorado?" she asked, sliding bread into the toaster.

"My, you are one smart cookie. She was there in 1983, the year you were rescued. After that, she went to California."

She pulled out a carton of orange juice and set it on the counter. "What does that mean?"

"The coincidences continue to mount. She was in Colorado when you were, she was in California when you were, and she moved to Georgia the same year Rex did, settling in a town just over an hour away and starting a very successful real estate business."

She reached in the fridge, pulling out a chilled carton of eggs. "How do you like your eggs?"

"However you fix them. It's becoming clear that she knows who you are. So if she knows who you are, has followed you across the country and is now having an affair with your husband, a man, according to your dream, that she does not like, the question is why? If she wanted you dead she's had ample time to kill you, so what's her angle?"

The toast popped up and Abbey buttered the pieces, placing them onto plates. She dropped some butter in a pan and as it began sizzling, she cracked a few eggs, plopping the contents into the pan. "Who is she and where does she come from?"

"I don't know, Rex is trying to find out, the earliest record we can find on her is Colorado, before then, nothing. She's never been married, she has only one child, whom she had in her thirties, and no father is listed on the birth certificate. She came into town with money and in the first year in business she won Business Woman of the Year. She has attended Locknee Baptist Church since she moved to the area, she's on all the right committees and rubs elbows with all the right people."

"So I guess that means you have no record of her joining Satanists Are Us, huh?" she joked.

"No, that we don't have." He laughed. "When did Richard start going to the church?" he asked.

"He was a member when we got married, the pastor performed the service." She slid the eggs onto the plates and poured some orange juice, setting everything on the table.

"So, let's suppose that she and Richard were lovers before

he met you, lets suppose the marriage was a set up, a way to get you under control, doped up, and ineffective. If she knows who you are, then she knows that you showed potential as an owl and therefore a special blend of sleeping, anti-psychotic, and hypnotic meds would be required to dull your senses, your ability to see. I don't know how Kelly's accident plays into this, if it was really an accident or part of a greater plan." He took a bite of food, picking up his phone. "Rex. What do we know about the kid who hit Kelly?" He listened for a moment. "Okay, let me know."

"You think it wasn't an accident?" Her mind reeled. Not an accident? Could the accident have been avoided if she had stayed away from Richard?

"I don't know, Abbey, but it would work toward getting you more isolated. It could have been an accident, and if it was, it worked in their favor by getting you away from people. Either way, it added to you isolating yourself. Rex is looking into it, we'll know soon enough."

She shook her head and picked up her plate. "If I was responsible for that, I don't know how I could ever forgive myself." She carried the plate to the sink, dumping what she had yet to eat down the garbage disposal.

"Abbey, you are a strong woman and you raised an equally strong young woman. Sometimes in life we are born under a cloud, but you have an amazing ability to free yourself. You don't see what I see." She was a bird that somehow managed to survive unbroken; in his experience she was a miracle. He stood from the table and crossed the short distance to where she stood, placing his hands on her shoulders. "I don't want you to beat yourself up, it's just speculation and I could be wrong."

She took a deep breath. "I'm okay. That just kind of took my breath away. I'll deal with it." She shook her head in an attempt to clear it. "I wasn't expecting that."

"Are you packed?" he asked, stepping away from her.

She nodded her head.

"I hear we have to load of a gaggle of ducks."

"I think that would be a gaggle of geese." She smiled. "But we do have a cage of ducks waiting to be loaded."

*

They picked up the cage of ducks together. "This will fit into the bed of my truck," Larry said.

"I'd feel better if we could ride together, can one of the guys get your truck?" Abbey asked.

"You're going to put ducks in your brand new Jeep?"

"It's for transportation, they need transporting. I've got a tarp."

"Yeah, I can have someone pick up my truck."

Abbey spread out the tarp in the back and they hoisted the birds into the Jeep. "Your car is going to smell like duck shit," Larry said.

"There's worse things," she responded, cooing to the ducks. "Let's get our stuff." Abbey walked into the house and stood silently, searching for any emotion about leaving her home and finding nothing, she moved quickly. She grabbed the photo albums off a shelf, stepped into Kelly's room and picked up a few knickknacks, and then went to her bedroom, lifting her suitcase off the bed. She sighed deeply and carried everything to the Jeep.

"Got everything?" Larry asked, as she finished loading the dogs.

"I think so. I guess we're ready."

"Looks like it," he said.

She felt a strange sense of nothingness as she pulled onto the road. She sighed, looking over her shoulder to see the property disappearing in the distance, and felt a small weight lift off her shoulders. She drove through Oak Tree, pointing out the town square to Larry as they passed. The courthouse sat in the middle of a large grass and oak tree setting, owls statues stood on the top of all four corners of the building observing the town. "Weird, huh?" she asked as the scene disappeared in her rear view mirror.

She turned onto a two lane state road that curved around the Interstate and supplied far better scenery. "Tell me about the Aviary," she said, pulling sunglasses out of her purse. "Tell me about the birds."

He sighed. "What do you want to know?"

"All of it and none of it." She laughed softly. "Uncle Rex said y'all rescue people, tell me about that."

"It can be ugly work, Abbey."

"Then why do you do it?"

"Because sometimes when you are able to see a bird set free

you'll give up a chunk of yourself to ensure that it happens. Most of them are so broken, perhaps beyond repair, but you give it your best hoping that God will have His way and there will be a miracle."

"Tell me, how does it happen? Mom said I had an owl tattoo on me. Uncle Rex said owls are remote viewers. Mom said Caroline had a dove tattooed on her, Uncle Rex said doves are sex slaves. Are there more birds?" Abbey asked, taking a detour on a gravel road with a view of foothills and water.

"Yes, there are more. Hawks, they are assassins, mostly sleepers. They are triggered when some politician, or a bill going through the house, needs a media distraction. They're tricky, their programming intense and booby trapped, typically when they break down they take others with them. Hawks usually do those mass shootings that have become so popular in the last decades and they certainly get the attention of the people off whatever else is going on. Then there are the mocking birds - we don't handle those anymore – there's no saving them. They were a massive screw up, somebody got greedy, wanted all birds blended into one and those kids cracked. Mostly they self destruct or are put down, they're psychotic."

"What do you mean, all the birds blended into one?" Abbey asked, pulling out a cigarette and rolling down a window.

"Someone decided to train one person for all the roles of the birds, the psychic, remote viewing part, added with the willing sex slave, and then they threw in a little twist of assassin. I guess one was better than three, more cost efficient, but the brain can only take so much, there are only so many compartments, there are only so many doors to hide things behind, those kids are a mess. You're lucky you escaped as early as you did, before the training and the programming became worse." Larry rolled down his own window, pulling out a smoke.

"So what would have happened had I not escaped? And if I wasn't killed in some psychosexual ritual?"

"The way young birds are treated is pretty typical among all birds. The psychosexual thing breaks them down, creates escape routes in the brain. Not to mention it brings in hoards of cash, more than you can imagine. Around nine or ten, they round them up and bring them into the program. The program educates them and instills the behavior that is desired, but it also masks it. It takes a hold of those escape routes the children have already created and controls them."

"Yes, but how does it work in the real world? How are these birds useful?" she asked, turning on a back road that skirted a lake.

"Okay, from what I understand, it's like this. The child is used when young, then brought into the program and trained. With the training, the child's earlier experiences are erased from memory. Then they place the child in a home. Sometimes the memory is instilled in the child that the family they are with has always been their family. Other times, the children understand they are in foster care or have been adopted. The cases vary and are pretty individualized. The kid goes to school, college, gets a job or is placed in a job where it is easy to watch them." He pulled open the inboard ashtray and snubbed out his cigarette. "So just imagine you're at work and get an assignment or have to go to a seminar or a meeting or something, but instead of that a handler meets you, you go do your assignment, be it murder, sex or remotely spying on an enemy. You go back to work with a memory of a seminar and never suspect a thing."

"That sounds like science fiction," she said, snubbing out her cigarette.

"Of course it does. That's another layer of protection the bird keepers have, but some birds are smart. Some have a way of keeping up with their time, so they begin to notice missing time. It's set up inside of them that when they start questioning they are sent on a wild goose chase. Sometimes they think it's aliens or sometimes they think those who raised them perpetrated the abuse they are remembering. The psychiatric experts seem to lead them in this direction of family abuse. I don't know if this is deliberate, but I've seen a lot of cases and the next thing you know they're on all kinds of pills, undergoing hypnosis, only strengthening the delusions. Like I said, it's an ugly business."

"Then why do you do it?"

"Tell me, why do you take care of Silly? Why do you rub his head where his horns are sprouting and itching? Even though you know he may turn on you any minute and try to ram you into hell?"

She laughed. "Because if I didn't do it, who would?"

"So you do understand," he stated softly.

"I guess I do." She smiled. "Yep, I think I get it."

Chapter Twenty-Two

Abbey pulled into her mother's driveway and found the gate shut tight. A man appeared out of the flowering bushes inside the yard and giving Larry a wave, he opened the gate. "I guess it really has become Fort Raines," she said, pulling down the driveway.

The driveway was long, the house set several hundred feet from the street and as she followed the curve, the house came into view. The two-story, roomy bungalow was chosen by her father for them to have a safe place to recuperate after his death. The entire property was fenced, one of the first things Summer handled after they took up residence. She parked the car, cut the engine, and turned to look at Larry. "I guess I'm home. Are you going to run off to protect some other bird?"

"No. I'm with you until this is done," he said, stepping out of the car. He met her at the back of the Jeep and helped lift the cage of ducks, placing them in the shade of a dogwood tree. He opened the back door and let the dogs free. Jerry ran carelessly and Tom followed a little more carefully, his cone getting in the way as he tried to sniff under a bush.

"Mom!" Kelly ran from the house and threw her arms around her mother. "I know it's only been one night, but I missed you!"

"I missed you too, honey. I got some things out of your room." She pointed to them in the back seat. "I didn't know when or if we'd be back."

"Thanks. I don't care if we ever go back," Kelly said, pulling out the items and carrying them into the house.

The sound of birds greeted them as they stepped into the bungalow. "Wow. It's like a pet store in here. I guess Summer likes birds?" Larry asked.

"You think?" Abbey passed him in the small foyer. "Mom!"

Summer stepped out of the kitchen, wearing an apron Abbey made for her in Home Economics in the 9th grade. "Hey, baby! Larry, good to see you."

They followed her into the kitchen to see the large oak table had been turned into communications central. Rex finished his conversation with a man who was busily connecting wires and clicking buttons on several open computers and turned to Abbey. "Hey, baby girl," he said and took her in his arms. "I hear you had a rough night."

She nodded, her head against his chest.

"Well, we're getting close to done now, just a couple more days. We all need to sit down, talk strategy, and catch up."

Abbey pulled away. "Where are we going to sit down?" she joked.

"That's what I'm saying," Kelly agreed.

"Summer has a dining room." Rex chuckled.

"Who sits in the dining room? We're kitchen folk," Kelly said, peering into a pot on the stove.

"Larry, the dining room." Rex pointed and they followed him into the room where the family rarely spent time, except to dust.

"We've got to separate them and disappear. Richard's gone underground," Larry said, sitting at the table and opening his laptop.

"I know, I know," Rex said. "I'm working on places." The doorbell rang. "I'll get it," Rex said, standing up from the table and leaving the room.

"Seems Snuffy likes you," Abbey said as the fat black and white cat jumped into Larry's lap, purring contentedly and kneading his thighs.

"Looks like it," he said, stroking the animal, and turning his attention to the computer screen.

Rex returned a few seconds later with Jack in tow.

"Hey, Jack," Abbey said. "What are you doing here?"

"Hey Daddy!" Kelly ran to him and hugged his neck.

"Hey. Seems I've been summoned by the great and powerful Rex." He smiled at Abbey and kissed Kelly on the head.

Rex introduced him to Larry and asked him to sit down. "What's going on? It's a fortress in here."

"I'm liking the name Fort Raines." Summer laughed. "Hey, Jack. Have a seat. Would you like some tea?"

"I guess so," he said, sitting down at the table.

"Jack, remember years ago when you came to me and told me that Abbey was pregnant and you were going to marry her? Do you remember that day?" Rex sat down, facing him across the table.

"Yeah, I remember, we drove up to the lake, walked around.

Yeah," he said, confusion thick in his voice.

"Do you remember what I said that day?"

"Yeah, Abbey's special, she's not your average girl. A relationship with her will be hard, stuff like that." He accepted the glass of tea from Summer and set it in front of him.

"Is that all I said, Jack?"

Jack sighed. "What do you want, Rex? I'm confused here, this is ancient history."

"You made me a promise that day, Jack. Do you remember?" Rex pressed.

Jack's eyes widened. "You said one day I may have to take Abbey and disappear, it might be for a week or it might be for a lifetime. Yeah, I remember."

"It's that time, but instead of Abbey, you have to take Kelly and disappear. Today, in the next couple of hours."

"What? I can't do that! I have a freaking family, Rex! Are you crazy?" Jack stood up.

"You made a promise, Jack," Rex said.

"I was a teenage boy, Rex! Out in the middle of nowhere with the not-so-jolly-black-giant, of course I promised! I was scared to death! I'd just knocked up a girl. Come on, man, this is crazy."

Rex stood up. "You want to talk about crazy? Okay, let's talk crazy. I used to be a cop on a special task force to break up child sex abuse and ritual child abuse cases. I ran into a hoard of Satanists, stole a little girl, forged her adoption papers, changed her name, and rescued her from a life of hell. You married her and fathered her child. The Satanists have found her and want both of them. The government will do nothing about it because many of them are in on it. We have to separate and go underground for a while, today, or one of these women might die. Now, how's that for crazy?" Rex asked, sitting back down with a coaxing smile.

Jack sat down hard. "I can't afford to just pack up and run, I have bills, a mortgage, employees. Jesus, I have a life!" He ran his hand through his hair.

"Jack, you have to take her and go. Who else am I going to send her off with? Who else will protect her like you will? Pick a place, take Holly on vacation, the kids will have a blast and they're not in school yet." Abbey put her hand on Jack's arm and turned her head to address Summer. "Mom, can I afford a private jet and a wonderful vacation spot for them?"

"Yes, honey," Summer said, handing a glass of tea to Larry.

"Their mortgage and all that stuff?"

"Yes." Summer nodded and sat across the table, beside Rex.

"I'll take care of it, Jack, all of it. Just pack up the kids, Holly, and get Kelly as far away as possible."

He shook his head. "How can you afford to do all that?"

"I've come into some money. Money my father put away for me for this day." She glanced at Summer. "I guess Dad always knew this would happen, huh?"

"It would appear so," Summer agreed.

Kelly sat down in the chair with her mother and Abbey slid over to make room for her. "You're sending me away?"

"Just for a little while, until we get things settled here." Abbey pulled her close, kissing her on the forehead.

"But I just unpacked," Kelly complained.

"I know, it's just for a little while," Abbey assured her.

Kelly sighed and nodded her head, looking at her father. "Are you going to take me?"

Jack sighed and stood up. "Let me call Holly," he said and

left the room.

"What did you mean about Richard going underground?" Abbey asked.

"I don't know how much of this you know, Abbey, I can't remember if we've talked about it, but the property your house is on was left to Richard by his parents."

Abbey nodded.

"Well, Richard's parents used to own all of that land, including the land with the cemetery and the circle. It's thousands of acres. When they died, they left Richard only 20 acres and the rest of the land rolled over into BLZ trust. This morning Richard and Pearl went to the offices of the attorneys that handle the trust. Pearl just left, alone and in a cab, Richard's car is still in the parking garage. Maybe they caught sight of the tail, but they're splitting up so I'm guessing he's going on the offensive and underground."

Jack walked back into the room. "Holly wants to go to Yellowstone National Park."

"Yea!" Kelly jumped to her feet and clapped her hands. "I've always wanted to go there!" She ran across the room and threw her arms around Jack's neck. "Thanks, Daddy."

"I'd rather it was further away, but it'll do," Rex said, smiling at Kelly's excitement. "I'm sending two of my guys with you, Jack."

"Great," he said with little enthusiasm.

"I'll have a private plane meet you at the airport. You're going to go in the back way avoiding the concourse and you're going to need my guys to do that, they have the clearance."

"Who in the hell are you people? I feel like I just walked into a spy movie."

Kelly kissed his cheek. "It's okay, Daddy. I prefer to think of it as a suspense novel. I'm going to get packed." She bounded up the stairs.

"Now we need to take care of Abbey and Summer," Rex said, looking at Larry.

"I'm staying here," Summer said.

"This is the first place they're going to look, Summer, you can't stay here," Rex said.

"I've got tons of security and I'll put on my holster, you know I'm a good shot, Rex. I'm not leaving my house, I'm not leaving my birds, and that's the way that's going to be." She crossed her arms over her chest.

Rex sighed. "Fine. We're set up here, anyway."

"I'll be back in an hour to get Kelly," Jack said, turning to the door.

"Don't tell anyone where you're going," Rex warned.

"Yeah, okay." Jack let himself out.

"So that leaves Abbey. What's the plan Larry?"

"First, did you find out anything about the kid who hit Kelly?" Larry asked.

"Yeah, I did. Not much on the kid, he was an average student, from an average family and his friends were surprised he'd been drinking - they never knew him to drink. Turns out he graduated in the same class as David Hollister. They were friends, played on the same basketball team in high school. It's a small town, so it could be yet another coincidence, but I think its suspect."

"So it wasn't an accident?" Abbey asked, feeling a punch in her stomach.

"It's not looking like it, Abbey," Rex said softly, watching her for reaction.

"I think Abbey and I are going on a little tour of all the

tourist traps along the Appalachian Trail and keep moving. A moving target is always the hardest to hit. And by the route Abbey took to get us here, I'd say she's comfortable on the back roads." He laughed, trying to lighten the mood.

"Ahhh. You took him along the scenic route," Summer smiled.

"My old stomping grounds." Abbey smiled sadly. "Mom, since you are staying here, can I leave the dogs? Tom needs to get some rest."

"That's what I was thinking. I picked up dog food yesterday. I've never had security at the grocery store before, but it was convenient." She laughed. "I had extra hands to push extra buggies. I bought enough stuff that we could stay here for a month."

"Uncle Rex, did you find anything more on Pearl?"

He shook his head. "Nothing except that she didn't exist before 1983, no school records, nothing. The real estate school she attended closed years ago, I'm looking for people who may have gone to the school with her, but nothing yet. I've also sent her picture and put out some feelers in the agency to a few of my contacts. I'm waiting to hear back." Rex stood up and stepped into the kitchen, returning with a piece of paper. "Do you recognize this man, Abbey?"

He placed a picture of a white haired man in front of her and looking down at it, she gasped, "That's the man from my dream, the one who was so angry at Richard."

"That's Winston Chambers, he's the attorney in charge of the trust. He keeps a low profile. There were no pictures of him on the Internet, so one of our guys snapped this one. Funny thing is I can't find any information about him before 1987, the year Martin died. There's something vaguely familiar about him and I've been racking my brain trying to place him. He appeared in California, a sudden partner in a large law office in '87. In '89 he moved to Atlanta, opening his own office and one of the first things he did was create BLZ Trust. The website for the trust says they sponsor educational programs for the enlightenment of the masses. They offer things like channeling classes, seminars on ESP, and other programs with vague names like Spiritual Awaking and Freedom from Dogma. There was some protest last year when the local college screened a porn movie in a sociology class on campus. The trust actually made the movie and sent it out to colleges, evidently the trust uses it in one of its own classes to help people overcome their inhibitions."

"Jesus," Abbey whispered. "Porn in college classes? There's something wrong with students and teachers watching porn together in a classroom, right?" She looked around the table to see heads nodding in agreement.

"There was speculation that some of the actors in the movie were underage, but nothing was ever proven and the protest just faded away," Rex said. "I've sent Chambers' picture in also, let's see if anyone knows anything else."

The radio on Rex's belt crackled. "There's a big woman here who said she's supposed to pick up some ducks. She's smoking a pipe."

Summer laughed and stood up. "That's Sylvia. You want to help me, Abbey?"

Rex pulled the radio off his belt. "Send her in."

Abbey followed her mother outside and watched Sylvia's old truck pull down the driveway. The woman parked and stepped out of the truck. "What the hell's going on here, Summer?" she asked, chewing on the end of a corncob pipe.

"You wouldn't believe me if I told you," Summer said and got down to business. "I've set up your account at the feed and seed, pick up whatever you need. We sure appreciate you taking the ducks."

Sylvia stepped over to the cage, inspecting the birds. "They look good, healthy. Good job, Abbey."

Kelly ran out of the house, kneeled at the cage, and stuck her fingers between the wires to pet the ducks. "I'm going to miss you, guys, but I'll see you again."

"They probably won't be as tame in a few weeks, Kelly," Sylvia said, tapping out the tobacco from her pipe on the bottom of her shoe.

"That's okay, I know they're going to a good place." She stood up.

"All right, let's load them up, I don't have all day," Sylvia said, sliding the pipe into the front pocket of her overalls.

They moved the cage into the back of the truck, Sylvia securing it so that it wouldn't slide. "I'm gonna be real upset, Summer, if I get a bill from the feed and seed." She jumped down from the bed of the truck.

"Your bills now come to me, Sylvia, I told you that when we made the deal," Summer explained.

Sylvia studied her for a moment, leaning against the bed of the truck, and repacking her pipe from a small bag of tobacco she pulled from her back pocket. "We'll see," she said, her eyes squinting suspiciously under the brim of her Braves baseball cap.

"Trust me." Summer smiled.

"Trust me, trust me," Sylvia grunted and spit. "Famous last words." She lit her pipe and walked to the door of her truck. "Y'all have a good day." She stepped into the truck, slammed the door, and left a cloud of smoke as she pulled away.

Summer laughed. "She's something."

"She's kind of scary," Kelly said.

"Like a rabid dog," Abbey added.

"Now, girls! Sylvia is okay. She's a little rough around the edges, but she's going to give a good home to those ducks and you both know it."

Shamed, Kelly spoke, "I'm sorry, Grandma, I didn't mean anything. I'm glad they're going to her. Cuz I know if anything comes near those ducks, she'll blow them to kingdom come." She giggled.

Abbey laughed. "Yeah, Mom, I appreciate it, too. We were just kidding. Sylvia's cool in my book." She grinned at Kelly and winked. "A little scary, but cool."

The humor, masking fear, slipped away and they stood quietly for a moment. Summer sighed, taking each of their hands and pulling her girls close. "It's hard to know what to say, all the roads that have brought us here." She looked each of them in the eye, smiling. "But we're tough women, we come from good stock, and I'm not talking about genetics, I'm talking about God. We're staring into the abyss and God is the only thing that prevents it from staring back into us. We're ready for this; each of us in our own way has been prepared for this. Trust what you know, trust your instincts, and trust the signs. We are women who exist because of miracles and we have to trust in what God has in store."

They hugged, shared a few tears, and with arms wrapped tightly around each other they walked back into the house, accepting whatever came next.

Chapter Twenty-Three

Stepping into the house, Abbey touched Kelly's arm and pointed to the stairs. Abbey followed her daughter into her old bedroom, looking around at the old artifacts and Kelly's recent additions.

"I liked sleeping in here last night, I felt close to you," Kelly said, sitting on the bed.

Abbey looked over the titles of books she loved as a child and turned to face her pretty, bouncy daughter. "Did you know that I found out I was pregnant with you in that room over there?" She pointed at the bathroom door. "I wasn't much older than you are now. I was scared. I knew Mom and Rex would be disappointed in me, but I was laying in bed one night, just a few days after finding out about you, and the strangest thing happened."

Kelly looked at her and laughed, tapping her hands on her

thighs impatiently, as though she was calling a puppy. "Well? Enough of the dramatic pause, what happened?"

Abbey smiled. "I don't know what happened, but it was like this spirit, this energy, this wonderful thing descended on me and I knew whatever I had to do, I was having my baby. I knew that no matter what it took I would face the biggest monsters in the world to keep you. I remember telling Uncle Rex, little five foot nothing me, telling six foot forever Rex that I was pregnant and I was getting married. I wasn't scared he would hurt me, but you know the look he has when he's not pleased."

Kelly nodded. "I know the look."

"He didn't get the look that night, it was odd, it's like he felt the energy, too. He just nodded his head and said okay." She laughed. "Of course, then he said your dad had to come talk to him. Poor Jack, he was scared, but he was determined. Your father is a good man. It wasn't his fault the marriage broke up, maybe now that you know a little bit more about my history, you understand why it didn't work."

Kelly nodded.

"Okay, let's do this thing. Are you ready? Did you pack

everything?" Abbey asked, fighting back tears.

"Yes, ma'am. I even have my school work, which I could have conveniently forgotten." Kelly stood up, smiled and held her arms open. "Mom, we're going to be fine, it's just a rough spot." They hugged.

She helped Kelly get her things downstairs and Rex called a meeting. They gathered around the table, just the family and Larry. "Okay guys, this is it. You girls have your phones, right?"

Abbey and Kelly nodded.

"Your mother and I will be here, we'll keep in touch." He sighed. "I have no great speech to give, all I can say is be strong and if the worst happens, fight like hell. How's that for a speech?" He laughed.

"Pretty good, Uncle Rex." Kelly clapped in appreciation.

The radio crackled, announcing that Jack had arrived. Abbey walked Kelly out and while Jack loaded her things into the back of the SUV, she stepped over to the passenger window and tapped lightly.

Holly rolled down the window. "I've always wanted to go to Yellowstone, thanks." She smiled, but her eyes were swollen from crying.

"I'm sorry," Abbey said.

"I lost my job, I just took days off last week, and I'm new there." She sniffed. "They fired me."

"I'm sorry, I'll make it up to you." Abbey promised.

"I'm going to see a geyser and buffalo," Jason announced from the back seat.

"Will you catch me a buffalo and bring it home?" Abbey asked, attempting to lighten the mood.

"I'll try, I'm pretty sure I can catch one," he assured. "But I don't think Momma will let me bring it home."

Holly laughed. "It's okay, we'll talk after this is over. And we'll take care of Kelly, you know that."

Abbey nodded. "I do."

Abbey gave Kelly another hug, watched her climb into the vehicle and waved.

"Okay Jack, your contact is on the street there, parked at the curb. You follow them to the airport - they'll take care of getting you in. Just leave your car on the strip, put the keys on the visor and someone will take care of it." Rex pulled out a large sum of cash and handed it to him. "You're working on cash. A rental car will be waiting when you land in Wyoming, drive straight through the park and go into Montana." He handed him a map. "There's a fishing lodge, marked in red on the map, rent enough rooms for you and the body guards. Use cash and a fake name, they won't ask for ID." He smiled. "And then go enjoy the park, but remember, use cash. You should have more than enough, if you need more, call me."

Jack took the money, shoved it in the pocket of his cargo shorts and shook Rex's hand. "I woke up in a freaking spy movie this morning," he muttered and climbed into the truck, shaking his head.

Abbey watched them drive away, feeling like she lost part of herself, and Rex put his arm around her. "She's going to be fine, baby girl."

"I screwed up bad, Uncle Rex." She sighed.

"It happens, Abbey." He hugged her and then they walked into the house together.

"The petting zoo people just called, they picked up the chickens and three female goats, they couldn't find a fourth one,"

Summer said.

"Silly must have taken off into the woods. Damned brat. He'll be fine for a couple days, there's certainly enough food and water out there for him."

"What about predators?" Summer asked.

"I feel sorry for anything that tangles with that goat, he's not helpless and he's got enough asshole in him to survive. I'll go find him after all this is over."

Larry stepped into the room with his briefcase in his hand. "We've got to go now! Two black SUVs just pulled onto your property, kicked in the doors and they're searching the house and out buildings. They'll probably be here soon."

They quickly loaded a case of water and a couple bags of food in the Jeep. Abbey hugged her mother and uncle and wiping a tear off her face, she jumped in the car. As they pulled out of the driveway and onto the street, Larry asked, "Do you know any more of those back roads that will take us north and into the mountains?"

"I do." Abbey said, turning onto a two lane state road. "Up here about a mile is a dirt road and if I can remember correctly, I can get us all the way to the Chattahoochee National Forest without hardly touching any pavement."

"Good. Do that." He pulled out a map. "How do you know all these roads?"

"That's what rednecks call date night." She laughed and turned onto a gravel road that soon turned to dirt. "I haven't been up this way in a few years, there's a lot of turns, let's hope I remember."

He opened his computer and pulled up satellite imagery of the area. "This isn't real time," he said, "but it should help us if we get lost."

"I think a satellite map is an insult to my redneck heritage," she joked, rolling down the window and lighting a cigarette.

"Why did you get married so young?" he asked suddenly. "I mean, I understand why you had Kelly, but people don't just get married anymore because a baby's on the way."

"I wanted to do the right thing. I wanted Kelly to know her father. Of course, the marriage was doomed to fail, we were so young, but I'm glad we did it." Abbey turned onto a smaller road, slowed to go around potholes and as the road bottomed out, splashed through a low creek. "I guess the rain the other night washed through here pretty good."

"You were still teenagers when you divorced?" he asked.

"Yep. I moved back home with Mom and got my GED, but I really didn't want to go to college. I was never a big fan of school, too many people and rules. I found a job that was tolerable and Kelly and I moved into a little trailer a couple miles away from Mom's house. Life was pretty good." Abbey topped the hill and turned off the rutted road onto a maintained one.

"Well, you must have done okay for yourself, Rex said you sold a house when you married Richard." Larry consulted the satellite image. "Looks like a highway is coming up."

"Yeah, we'll just cross over it." She stopped at the two-lane highway and pulled across, entering another dirt road. "My dad left me some money, I got it when I was twenty-one, and I blew through it fast. I gave a lot of it away, but I did buy a house outright, and set up a couple saving accounts for Kelly."

"You gave it away?" He laughed.

"Yeah. I guess I'm a reverse snob. The money scared me, it felt dirty or something, I felt better when it was gone. Of course, I hear I have to get over that since I just inherited some more money, but now I see it as a way to be free, which I didn't see when I was younger. Living with Richard and having no money or having to ask for money certainly taught me that lesson." She took the right side of a fork in the road. "It's pretty up here," she said, pointing out a colorful scene of pastures, meadows, grazing cows, and a white farmhouse, complete with a bright red barn. "So what about you? Where are you from? What's your family like?" She snubbed the cigarette out in the ashtray.

"Not much to tell, I grew up in Boston, an only child to a working class family. My dad was a cop and he was killed in the line of duty when I was ten. It was rough, suddenly Mom had to take care of everything, she worked two jobs and wasn't around much. I spent a lot of time on the streets after school and probably would have ended up on the wrong side of the law, but one day a karate school opened in town. I passed it on my walk to school and I'd stand on the street, watching the classes inside. I was intrigued, I wanted to take the class, I wanted to be one of those people, but we couldn't afford it."

Abbey crossed a shaky, wooden bridge hovering over a wide and rocky creek. "I wonder how much longer this thing will last," she muttered and let out a sigh of relief when she arrived on the other side. "Go on."

"I got a newspaper route in the mornings, but still couldn't come up with enough money, so one day, gathering my courage I stepped in and talked to the owner. His name was Jeff McGuire, a 30ish, soft-spoken, white guy. I approached him with my proposal, told him how much I could give and what chores I would do to be able to take his classes. He accepted my deal and over the years he assumed the role of father figure to me." He chuckled. "And I certainly needed it. He wouldn't take my money, but I had to do chores around the place and I found a way to spend my free time without getting into trouble. My mom's retired now, lives in Florida with her sister."

"So how did you end up doing what you do now?"

"Part of the deal my karate teacher and I worked out was that I had to keep my grades up and he wanted to see my report cards. It was enough motivation for me to excel in school and I managed to get a scholarship to Harvard. I worked as a security guard for extra cash and found I enjoyed that more than hitting the books, so I quit school and joined the police force. I moved up the ranks quickly and became a detective. Then one day I caught the eye of someone and got a call inviting me to join the task force. I jumped at the chance. I saw it as a way to do good work and help kids, kind of like the way McGuire helped me. Unfortunately, it turned out to be nothing like that, I just saw a lot of bad things, dead kids, and rarely, if ever, did we get a conviction. I'd heard about Rex from some old timers in the agency, so after a particularly brutal case I gave him a call."

"What is this agency? Is it CIA, FBI, NSA?" Abbey asked, turning onto a narrow, rutted road.

"All of that and none of that, my badge simply read Federal Officer. It's a convoluted mess, good guys and bad guys working together always unsure of where the other stands. I got tired of having to watch my back, watch my words, and step carefully."

Abbey inched along the road as branches slapped the windshield. "So does Songbird Security just take cases like mine?"

"We take any job where someone needs security, our specialty in bird rescue is on the down low, it's not something we advertise."

"Then how do the people know how to find you?" she asked,

turning onto a well-maintained road.

"Word of mouth. The word gets around. Yeah," he said, putting the phone to his ear and listening. "Okay. Let me know." He hung up. "Two SUVs just pulled up to Jack's house, four guys kicked in the doors and searched the place. Rex expects them at Summer's any minute."

"How do these guys just go around kicking in doors? Where are the cops?" she asked angrily.

"It appears Jack's neighbors called the police, but they arrived after the bad guys were gone. Rex is ready for them and I hear Summer is wearing her holster. The good news is that Kelly's plane took off without incident."

"Good." She sighed. "Seems like we got away just in time. Has anyone spotted Richard?"

"No, his car is still in the parking garage and Pearl is back in Locknee. I've got one guy watching the exits for Richard and one guy following Pearl. Not much going on, she's showing a house."

The road transitioned into hardtop and Abbey turned off, bumping across a field. "It gets a little tricky here, I hope the farmer hasn't fixed his fence." Tall grass slapped underneath the

Jeep as they passed through the unused pasture. She pulled up beside an old barn, turned onto a dirt road, followed it until it became gravel topped, and then turned again onto another dirt road that skirted a large dairy farm.

Larry laughed. "I'm impressed, you sure know your way around here."

She smiled. "Just good old redneck knowledge, a bunch of us teens used to come this way to spend the day in Helen."

He looked at the map. "I've heard of it, but I've never been there. I haven't had a lot of time in the last few years for recreation."

"It's a cute little touristy town, they call it the Alpine Village. We used to come up here during Octoberfest and watch the hot air balloons or we'd come up in the summer and tube down the river." She pulled out onto a hard topped road, traveled down it for about a mile and turned onto another dirt road.

Larry pulled out his phone again. "Yeah."

The last time she had come this way it had been Kelly's birthday and she'd borrowed her mom's Subaru, she recalled. They spent the weekend hiking, tubing, and exploring the shops in town.

That was the summer before I met Richard, she thought, the summer before I drove our lives into hell, literally.

Larry slid the phone back in his pocket. "The thugs cruised by your mom's house, saw the shut gate, the security, scoped out the place, and drove away. Rex feels certain that they will be back. On a lighter note, Summer brought the dogs in, the cat freaked out and managed to knock over a birdcage. Two birds got away and are now sitting on top of a bookcase in your old bedroom. Rex said it was five minutes of total chaos." He laughed.

"That's a normal day at Mom's even when not being chased by Satanists." She smiled.

He continued with the news. "Richard's car still hasn't moved, I've pulled the guy out of Atlanta and sent him to keep his eye on Richard's office. We're tracking the car - we'll know when it moves. Pearl is showing another house and nothing has happened since the break in at your house."

She turned onto a small path and pulled down about fifteen feet into heavy, purple vinery and parked. "I need the ladies room," she said, hopping out of the Jeep.

"Good idea." Larry opened his own door and stepped into

the encroaching forest.

Returning to the car, Abbey lifted her head and breathed deeply. She loved this little spot in the spring, the wisteria hung thickly, heavy with bees, fluttering butterflies, and the sweetest scent she had ever smelled. Inhaling deeply one more time, she climbed back in the Jeep and reached around the seat to grab a bottle of water.

"Wow," Larry said, leaning in the open door. "It smells amazing out here."

"Ain't it something?" She laughed. "Do you want a water?"

"Thanks." He drew in another breath, smiled up at the heavy, purple canopy, and climbed back in the Jeep.

"It's wisteria. I think it's in the top ten of the best smells in nature." She handed him a bottle of water.

"You keep a list of the best smells?" he asked, laughing.

"Well, not really." She chuckled. "It's not like I keep a written list of them or anything, but sometimes the way nature smells just reminds you of something better." She backed out of the purple cathedral. "It reminds you, I guess at a basic cell level, of goodness. You may not have ever experienced this goodness in your entire lifetime, but that scent, for just a second, lets you know it exists." She continued along the trail.

"I've got a great smell," he said. "Up in Boston, when the snow would start to melt, and the little patches of ground would begin to appear, you could smell the dirt. Hmmm. It smelled so good and it just made you excited to know summer was coming."

"So, I'm not such a freak after all?" she asked.

"You're a lot of things, Abbey, but a freak isn't one of them." He smiled at her and winked.

Abbey turned her attention back to the road, feeling a little blush spread across her cheeks. The twists and turns returned to her as though it had been days, instead of years, since she had last passed and finally, she wound down a sharply graded hill, crossed a shallow, rocky creek and dead-ended into black top. "Here we are. One way takes us into the town of Helen and the other takes us deeper into the mountains. Which way am I going?"

"Head into town and let's see what's going on."

She turned and wound into town, smiling at the crystal clear river running along the side of the road. "We used to tube in there."

"Looks nice, kind of low though."

"Oh, yeah, if you're not careful you can go home with rock bruises on your butt." She laughed. The town opened up in front of her and reminded her of happy times. "There's a lot of tourists here for a Monday in April. Of course, they're pretty smart, August can cook your shoes sometimes."

"Tourists are good, makes it easy to get lost in the crowds. I think we should get a room, get some food, a shower, check in with everyone, and get a good night's sleep. We're doing more driving tomorrow and I know you must be tired."

"We could have gotten here a lot quicker on the main roads, but the scenery's not nearly as good. So where do we stay?" She drove through town while he inspected the hotels and turned around when the road turned rural again, driving back through the village.

He pointed out a small motel, set on the water, and she pulled into the wooded parking lot. "Go down to the end and back in, I'll get us a room." He stepped out and went into the small office.

She pulled to the far end of the lot, parking between a truck and a stand of trees. Just as she turned the key, her phone chirped announcing a text message. She read it and smiled. Kelly had landed in Wyoming and was amazed by the size of the Rocky Mountains. She sent a note back and Larry opened the door. "Okay, we have a room." He grabbed his brief case and backpack.

Abbey gathered her suitcase and purse and followed him into the room. It contained a sofa, a queen-sized bed, a small table with chairs, and a glass door leading to a balcony that overlooked the Chattahoochee River. Abbey dropped her bag on the bed and suddenly felt like crawling under the covers and sleeping for a week.

"Do you want to shower before we get something to eat or after?" he asked, pulling out his computer.

"I think I will now. I might not be able to stay awake after eating," she said and carried her suitcase into the bathroom.

She dropped her clothes on the floor and stepped under the spray, the hot water reviving some of the energy she had lost on the intensive and bumpy trip. She reached for a pair of jeans in the suitcase and saw a flash of green in the things she had packed. She pulled out the dress her mother had given her days earlier, and held it against herself looking into the mirror. *It's too pretty to never be* worn, she decided and pulled it over her head. She slid into a pair of sandals and added a light layer of mascara on her lashes. Leaving her hair down, she looked in the mirror and decided she looked like a tourist.

She stepped out of the bathroom and Larry hung up the phone, his eyes running over her.

Abbey blushed. "It's kind of touristy, right?"

"Yes," he said, cautioning himself not to look at the way the green silk hugged her body. "It looks touristy and that's what we're pretending to be, just tourists. Let go get dinner," he said, opening the door. Larry locked the door, pocketing the key, and took her hand. They walked into town holding hands and looking like just another couple on vacation. He chose a small restaurant and they had dinner on the deck, amid the trees, listening to the water on the rocks below. The conversation was light as they discussed their teenage years, first dates, first cars, and after winding through the years, the conversation came back to the present.

"Are you worried about the goat out in the woods?" he asked, leaning back in his chair and pushing the plate away.

"No. I really think he'll be fine, the barn door should be

open so he can still get in there for shelter. Plus, he's psychotic, that should keep the predators away." She laughed.

"Would you do it again? The chickens, ducks, and goats?"

"Yeah, I think I would. Well, I don't know about the goats." She smiled. "But I enjoy animals, I like taking care of them, but next time I'll be prepared when I get them. There's nothing like having chickens in your bathroom." She briefly told him the story of how the chickens came to her. "They were kind of cute, though, perched on the side of the tub."

He laughed and pulled the phone from his pocket. After a few brief words, he hung up. "We need to get back to the motel, Rex is sending some pictures, and he wants you to take a look at them."

Chapter Twenty-Four

Abbey stared at the photo on the computer screen while Rex spoke to her over a speakerphone. "Does he look familiar to you, Abbey?"

"It looks like the man that was there, kissing Pearl, right after she killed Caroline," she said.

Rex sighed. "This is Stan Boyer, he worked with us on the task force from '85 to '87. He was the agent your father went in to save the night he died. We always assumed Stan died that night, although we never turned up his body. He didn't have much family, just a daughter who I spoke with on the phone a couple times. Go to the next image, Larry."

Larry clicked and a new image appeared on screen. The

photo showed a shot of Stan and his family before his hair turned salt and pepper. Abbey's eyes went over the faces of the woman and a teenage girl. "That's Pearl!" Abbey exploded. "What in the hell?"

"I know. Will wonders ever cease?" Rex asked. "Now it gets interesting. Pearl wasn't Pearl back then, she was Melissa Boyer and her mother died when she was fifteen. Coincidentally, the date of her death is listed as May 1st. Mrs. Boyer was found in the woods in Virginia and even though the police on the scene felt that the death was occult related, that aspect was never investigated. The murder, of course, is still unsolved."

Abbey looked at Larry, and shook her head, whispering, "What does it mean?"

"There's more," Rex stated. "At the time Stan worked as an attorney in a prestigious office in DC, but after his wife's funeral he quit his job, sold his house and he and his daughter disappeared. This part is a little iffy, the contact who remembers this is a little long in the tooth, but she seems to remember seeing Melissa/Pearl in a birth house in Chicago, around Christmas, selling a baby. A little girl. If it's true, that means she was already pregnant when her mother died. Stan must have had a solid resume when he joined the task force, but now I can't find any information about him from the time his wife died until he began working with Martin and me and all the employment records in the agency have disappeared. Only your dream places them together in 1983. Go to the next image, Larry."

A side-by-side comparison appeared on the screen, Stan Boyer on the left, Winston Chambers on the right. "Well, damn, they look like they could be brothers," she gasped.

"They're not brothers, they are the same man, after a little plastic surgery," Rex pointed out. "Now when Chambers appeared in Atlanta, he also started rubbing elbows with all the right people, including Richard's parents. He started the trust and they just handed over thousands of acres of land. I don't know what that's all about, but it damn sure is interesting."

"So let me get this straight. Pearl and Chambers are father and daughter? And Chambers is Boyer, the agent who got my father killed? And Pearl is having an affair with my husband, while attending meetings with Chambers? Jesus," she sighed, "what a mess. So why are Chambers and Pearl so interested in me and

Kelly?"

"That's a good question," he replied. "I imagine to finish what didn't get finished back in that mansion in Colorado."

"Well, it seems they've known who I was and where I was since shortly after we moved to Georgia, so why now?"

"I don't know, Abbey, maybe it has something to do with the circle and whatever door gets opened in there. And as much as I hate to say it, it may have something to do with Kelly hitting sexual maturity and being innocent, I understand that makes a sacrifice even more powerful." He sighed. "Tomorrow's the 30th, so as long as you and Kelly are away until sun up on May 1st, you should be safe."

"Any sign of Richard?" she asked.

"Nothing yet, his car hasn't moved and he hasn't turned up at his office, but an interesting collection of people has turned up at Pearl's house, including the Locknee chief of police and Richard's partner, Mike Almond. They all appear to be tense and worried, I guess they're sitting down to regroup and figure their next steps."

"The chief of police is at Pearl's house? Shit, Rex, that's not good," Larry said.

"I know, but you were with the agency, you know they're a lot of double agents in there working for one side on the surface and another underneath. I don't know which side of the fence this chief is on, we'll have to wait and see. Abbey, I guess you know Kelly has landed and is safely on her way to Montana?"

"Yes, sir. She sent me a text."

"Good, then all I can say is get some rest and hit the road early, you're still too close for my liking."

"Will do." Larry shut the phone, cutting the line, and they sat quietly for a moment.

"I don't understand what all this means, why us, why me? My mind is working on it, has been working on it and I think underneath way down deep, it's making connections, but up here on the surface ... I just don't get it." Abbey shook her head and her phone chirped. She picked it up, read the text from Kelly and laughed.

He looked at her quizzically, his eyebrows rising slightly.

"Jason saw a buffalo and he's crying. He wants to bring it to me and his mother probably wants to ring my neck. It's a long story," she laughed again, harder and snorted. She covered her mouth, embarrassed, and then giggled. "I may be a bad influence."

He watched her for a moment, amazed that she could still smile. That thought reminded him of what they were facing and he grew serious. "I'm going to get a shower, I want us out of here early, well before sun up." He grabbed his backpack and stepped into the bathroom.

Abbey stood up, wiped away the tears from the giggling fit and stepped out onto the balcony, staring down at the water moving briskly across the rocks and reflecting the lights of the small town. She remembered so many good times and a few hard times spent beside the river. The first time she had set foot in the cold water it had been just weeks after her father died and she had just taken the new name of Abbey. She remembered how cold and clarifying the water felt at the time, how it cut through her with both pain and peace, the awakenings of a new life.

"This is where you tend to send me when my life is about to change, God. Kelly was conceived here, Mom brought me here in the first weeks after we escaped damnation and became new people, and here I am again." Her attention was drawn up river, as a couple slid their feet into the cool water and laughed loudly. She glanced upwards, but the heavy tree cover blocked the sky so she looked back into the water. "Things are getting pretty squirrelly down here, God, but I trust you. And I trust that you won't give me more I can handle, and I think we both know there are things I can't handle."

Larry stepped out of the bathroom, barefooted and shirtless, drying his hair with a towel as she stepped back in the room. There was an awkward silence as though both of them had been caught in a moment of introspection. Larry was the first one to break the strange hold that held them. He tossed the towel onto the back of a chair and stepped across the room, placing his hands on her shoulders. "How are you doing?" he asked softly.

"I'm all right," she said, exploring his eyes. "I don't know what I'm doing here," she admitted. "But I think you're the prettiest man I've ever seen." She smiled and ran her fingers across his lips. His eyes crinkled in the way that sent the damned tingle spiraling through her body and she grew serious. "I don't know if you've noticed, but I'm kind of a mess. I don't know what I doing with you, I've never experienced anything like this so I don't know what's around the corner, but what I do know is this…" she paused, "God tends to bring me to this river when my life is about to undergo a change and he put you with me in all this chaos and that's good enough for me," she smiled shyly. "And I'd really like you to make love with me."

Larry stared into her eyes, green, like the leaves when they first opened in the spring, and he realized he didn't know what he was doing either. Professionally, he was beyond wrong, and as a man, he was nearly bewitched by her gentle, honest, and natural way. He started to speak, but couldn't find any words, and pulled her into his arms.

*

Pearl stepped into the parlor. The men had gathered; they were expecting her. She dressed in a form fitting black dress; deep in cleavage and ending in expensively designed tatters. Her blond hair was down, hanging nearly to her waist and she had a glass of wine in her hand. She entered the room and paused for effect, aware that the backlighting emphasized her figure through the fine material covering her hips and legs.

The men were angry, upset, and it was her job to soothe them, to appease them, and to strengthen their desire to please her. They stood as she stepped among them, offering her a seat, and maintaining their southern gentility. She sat carefully, ensuring that the delicately sewn tatters fell away, exposing her bare thigh and the garter holding up her hose. "We've got a problem, boys," she said with a slight southern drawl.

"You better know we have a problem, they're both gone," Randy Thomson, the chief of police, barked.

The other men looked at him, made uncomfortable by his frank words, and a maid stepped into the room. She wore a short skirt, a white blouse, and little else, and she carried an open bottle of wine. She poured them each a glass ensuring that they got a good view of her cleavage and the lack of panties under her skirt. Pearl nodded at her and the maid quickly disappeared.

"Sit down, everyone, enjoy your wine," Pearl said, having a sip of her own glass.

The men sat and Pearl smiled. "This is nothing we can't handle," she soothed.

"We need a new girl," Randy said, taking a sip of wine and

turning up his nose, he was more of a beer man.

"I think he's right," Pastor Munis agreed, swallowing a mouthful of the dark liquid, and thought of how the thin white blouse barely covered the maid's cleavage and nearly exposed her nipples.

"No. We need this girl and we're going to get her, if we don't all convince ourselves that we can't. We have to see her, we have to focus on her, and then, boys," she uncrossed her legs and then provocatively, crossed them again, "we will have her."

"We have to get serious, the girl is gone. They both disappeared and Pearl, where is Richard? I know he went off to Atlanta with you this morning and no one has heard from him since, where is he?" Mike Almond took a sip of wine and closed his eyes appreciatively. In his mind he saw the maid's short skirt and he sighed.

"Richard is out of the picture," Pearl stated. "All he had to do, Mike, was keep Abbey distracted and get the girl. He had one job, but he screwed it up. The local sheriff got involved and some security company came to protect them. He screwed up, he had a simple task and he couldn't even follow through." She shook her head. "It's a shame, but it is what it is."

"So what are we going to do?" Mark Reese, principal of Locknee High School, asked, his eyes fixed on her garter.

"We're going to find her," Pearl purred and stood up. "We're going to find her. Get your glasses, boys, and follow me."

The men did as they were told and followed Pearl down a long hall, appreciating the view as the light slid through her skirts showing a fine figure. She opened a door, stepped down two steps and turned. "Come on in and shut the door behind you." The room was filled with flickering candles and placed in the middle was an altar. On the altar were more candles and a crystal bowl full of water.

"We'll find her, this is destiny," she said and kneeled, praying a prayer that should never be uttered in a church. She gazed into the water and the room seemed to vibrate with energy. The men glanced at each other, uncomfortable, but returned their attention to the beautiful woman in the center of the room.

Pearl stared into the water, pulling energy from the air and waited for an image to become clear. The vibration in the room showed itself in small ripples across the top of the water and Pearl began to see images. A buffalo, a snow capped mountain and a sign. The sign read, Traders Fishing Lodge.

She stood up, turned with her hands on her hips and faced the men. "Traders Fishing Lodge, out west, around Yellowstone I would guess. We'll get her and have her here in time for the ceremony. You don't want to miss this, boys, everything before this was just practice. Tomorrow night will blow your minds." She smiled at each of them, slowly and suggestively, reminding each of them the time they had shared with her. "I need to make some calls and I'll talk to y'all soon. So if you can find your way out…" She waved with her hand, dismissing them, and then turned back to the altar, kneeling.

*

Abbey was dreaming and once again watching Richard. He was in a large office with a view overlooking the Atlanta skyline. Pearl was at his side and he faced the white-haired man across a desk. The white-haired man was shaking his head and Richard pleaded. The man slammed his fist on the desk and turned toward Pearl, pointing at the door. Pearl stood and Richard grabbed her wrist. She shook him off with a laugh, blew a kiss to the man behind the desk and let herself out. The white haired man picked up the phone, spoke briefly and hung up. Another door opened in the office and two large men, wearing black security uniforms, stepped into the room.

    The men grabbed Richard's arms, lifting him from his seat, and he began to cry. The white-haired man waved them away and as the men forced Richard through the door, the old man's attention drifted to the paperwork on his desk.

    They half carried, half dragged Richard down a deserted hall and into a service elevator. The doors of the elevator opened, revealing the back end of a white, paneled van. One man opened the back doors, while the other shoved Richard inside and climbed in behind him. The other man went to the driver's side and pulled the van onto a busy street. The dream shifted and she had a bird's eye view of the white van traveling down a highway and then it parked in a wooded area. The driver opened the back doors, pulling Richard out and the two security men walked him through the woods with a gun pressed against his spine.

The path ended at a rocky ledge overlooking a large lake. Richard pleaded for his life, but one man fired two shots through the back of his head and pushed him into the water below. As Richard's body hit the water, Abbey screamed, waking herself from the dream.

Larry pulled her into his arms, holding her. "It must have been a bad one," he said softly, plumping the pillow behind his head.

"Richard's dead," she said, calming her breathing, while resting her head on his chest. "Chambers had him killed. They shot him in the head and threw him in a lake."

"Well, damn," Larry said, checking the time and reaching for his phone. "Since we're up, we might as well hit the road."

She nodded, kissing him lightly on the cheek and crawling out of bed. She picked up the green dress off the floor, carried it into the bathroom and folded it, setting it back in the suitcase. She looked in the mirror while she piled her hair on top of her head. "I guess you're a widow now," she told her reflection. "A widow who committed adultery. I guess I screwed up pretty good there, huh,

God? I brought my daughter into a dark and demented world and I committed adultery. I'm not batting a thousand, am I? I know you move in mysterious ways and all that and I know I'm supposed to accept whatever comes my way trusting you know more than I do, but I sure would appreciate it if I could get out of this with as much family as I came in with," she whispered, paused, and tilted her head as though listening. "Okay, I'll let you think about it awhile." She stared into her eyes for another moment, found she had nothing to say to herself and stepped under the hot spray. She dried off and dressed in her usual attire of jeans, boots, and a t-shirt, pulling her hair back into a long braid.

"I've got a bad feeling this morning," Larry said, as she stepped out of the bathroom. "It's too quiet, the calm before the storm." He went into the bathroom as Abbey gathered her things.

"Who's driving today?" he asked as they stepped out of the motel room.

"I'll drive, it keeps my mind busy," she said and they tossed their things in the Jeep. She stopped at a gas station and Larry filled up the tank. She reached in the back seat to see what was in the bags her mother had sent along and pulled out a package of fat, bakery fresh cinnamon rolls. "Yea, Mom," she whispered, pulling the package into the front seat as Larry climbed in with coffee.

"Those look good," he said, setting the coffees in the cup holders and pulling the seatbelt across his lap.

"Mom never misses a beat," she said, tearing open the package and pulling out a roll. Taking a bite and setting it on a napkin in her lap, she started the vehicle. "North, right?"

"Yep," he said, biting into a roll.

She pulled onto the road and entered the Chattahoochee National Forest. She wound through the mountains entering North Carolina just after sunrise and Larry pulled out a map. "Let's head toward Gatlinburg," he said and she nodded.

They drove quietly, each lost in their own thoughts and the air was thick. "You're right, today just feels off." Abbey expelled a breath. "Even the air feels heavy." She rolled down the window.

"Yeah, we need to be on our toes, it's too quiet." He rolled down his own window, reached into his backpack and pulled out a pack of cigarettes, lighting one and blowing the smoke out of the window. "Something just isn't right."

They continued winding through the mountains, entering the

Great Smokey Mountains National Park, and although the scenery was beautiful neither commented on it. They were nervous and waiting for the unknown to occur to break the spell.

Abbey had just pulled into Gatlinburg and was looking for a fast food restaurant when Larry put the phone to his ear. "Yeah?" He listened. "Shit! Okay, okay." He listened some more and as Abbey parked at a burger joint, he said, "Yeah, we're headed back." He hung up and took a deep breath, turning to face her.

"What?" she asked. "You're scaring me."

"They got Kelly." He spit it out and watched her eyes grow wide. "They, Jack and Kelly and the family, were just coming out of the motel room to go into Yellowstone when a SUV came up and four guys with guns jumped out. They grabbed her. Jack was shot."

"Oh God." She dropped her head on the steering wheel, feeling her whole world shift.

"Jack's going to make it and his wife and kids are okay. One of our guys is dead and the other is injured." There, he said it and it might have been the hardest thing he'd ever done.

Abbey didn't move. She felt paralyzed. Kelly? Jack?

"No!" she yelled and began punching the steering wheel.

Larry grabbed her hands and held them, preventing her from doing any more damage. "We're going to get her! Abbey, we're going to get her!" He pulled her into his arms, whispering in her ear, "Anger is good, but don't let it take you over, we're going to get her." He pulled back, lifted her chin and looked into her eyes; they were yellow and full of pain as quiet tears slid down her cheeks. "We've got to get back to Georgia. Let's go in, go to the bathroom, get some food and get out of here." She nodded her head, wiped her cheeks and climbed out of the Jeep. Larry came around the car and put his arm around her, guiding her inside.

Returning to the car with food, Larry held out his hand for the keys. "Let me drive. You look at the map and find the most direct route."

Chapter Twenty-Five

"I don't want you and Rex to play any macho games with me," Abbey said.

"Abbey we need to get to your mom's and make a plan, we can't just rush in, it's going to be dangerous. We've already got two dead and two injured, we have to be prepared and careful," Larry said, wondering how he was going to keep her safe in Windslow instead of in harms way down in Oak Tree.

"I'm going," she stated firmly.

"Uh oh," he said as a Locknee city police cruiser passed him heading the opposite direction. He looked into the rearview mirror to see the car turn around and fall in behind them. He pulled out his phone. "Rex, I'm about 20 miles out of Windslow on route 17 and there is a Locknee city police cruiser on my tail." He paused. "I know they're out of their jurisdiction. Shit, here come two more!"

Abbey looked through the windshield to see two police cars coming in their direction, lights flashing. The car behind them turned on its lights and siren and the two cars swerved across the road, blocking their way.

"We're getting pulled," Larry said into the phone and leaving the line open, he dropped it into his pocket. "Don't resist," he said, stopping on the shoulder. "Rex knows what's going on, he's got someone on the way. Just don't resist or this could end up a lot harder to get out of, especially if we're dead."

Abbey nodded and a voice on a loud speaker spoke to them. "Driver, step out of vehicle with your hands in the air. Passenger, stay in the car."

"Just do what they tell you, don't talk and wait for your lawyer, and be calm and look for a way out." He leaned across the seat and kissed her. He struggled with the words he wanted to say and settled on "be safe" and then opened the door, raising his arms above his head.

"Now, face me and step backwards toward the officers behind you. When you reach the hood of the car, place your hands on the hood and let the officers check you for weapons."

Larry did as he was told and three large men in uniforms approached him. Two stood on either side of him, while one frisked him for weapons tossing the items from his pockets onto the hood of the Jeep.

"Now, we're going to put the handcuffs on until we figure out what's going on here. This is for our protection," the man on the loud speaker announced.

As soon as the cuffs clicked an officer pulled his stun gun and shot Larry, sending electricity through his body. He convulsed and then fell out of view. Abbey screamed. The passenger door was yanked open and Abbey was dragged from the car by one of the men. He carried her, almost as though she weighed no more than a football and threw her in the back seat of one of the cruisers. He calmly slid into the front seat and pulled away. Abbey looked back to see Larry convulsing on the road while the Jeep reversed and drove around him, scattering the items left on the hood onto the road. Just before they topped a hill and the scene disappeared from her view, she saw Larry being jerked to his feet and dragged toward a cruiser.

*

"Damn it," Rex muttered softly, closing the phone and looking around the room, his eyes settling on Summer. "They just got them."

Summer's face paled, and she took a breath, nodding her head. "Well, we're just going to have to get them back," she said firmly and stood. "Who's hungry?"

"Food sounds good, Summer," Rex said, his eyes scanning the faces of the men in the room and falling on Danny Downs. Danny came to work for Songbird straight from his days on the LAPD SWAT team; he was in his thirties, experienced and solid. "Okay, Danny, I want you to lead this one. I want you to take five men out, in full gear, and surround that circle, lay low and wait to hear from me." He stepped over to a map tacked to the wall. "Go in by this bridge, there's enough room up in there to get the cars off the road. Hang on." He held up a hand and pulled a phone out of his pocket. "Yeah."

"Mr. Andrews? It's James Jackson."

"Yes, Mr. Jackson. How are you?" he asked, staring at the map.

"It's a fine day, Mr. Andrews, but that ain't why I called ya.

I just seen four big, black and shiny SUVs head down the road. I ain't for sure, but it looked like a bunch of men was in 'em. They gots their windows so dark I can't say how many. I sent my grandson down the road to take a gander at what they's doing and he said they gots the road blocked right past that little crick. He said there's soldiers down there. Soldiers with guns."

"Thanks for calling, Mr. Jackson and let me know if you see anything else." Rex hung up the phone and sighed, looking at the map again. "Make it eight, Danny, I don't know what we're going to be up against down there. Mr. Jackson said there are armed guards placed at the bridge, here." He pointed at the map.

Danny stood up, pointed to several men in the room and pulled out his phone. "Will do, Rex, we'll be in place in about an hour and a half."

Rex nodded. "Be careful, Danny. Try not to engage them, but if you run into them take them out as quietly as possible."

Danny nodded and the men he picked followed him out of the house.

Rex sat at the table and Summer placed a cup of coffee in front of him. He took her hand, looking into her eyes. "I'm going to get the girls, Summer."

She nodded her head, patting his hand, and smiling sadly. "I know you will, Rex."

He let go of her hand, dialed a number he hadn't called in years and put the phone to his ear. "Senator Atkins office," a female voice answered.

"Put Neal on the phone, this is Rex Andrews," he barked.

"Hold, please," the voice soothed.

"Rex! How in the hell are you doing? It's been years."

"I need to call in that favor, Neal," Rex stated without preamble.

The man laughed. "Well hell, Rex, I had hoped you had forgotten about that."

"I bet you had."

*

"Where in the hell are you taking me?" Abbey demanded, her fingers biting into the metal screen that separated her from the officer driving the car.

He said nothing, nor did he show any indication that he heard her speak.

"Answer me, asshat!" She slapped the screen. "You can't just drag people off the road like that!"

Again, the man showed no response to her questions and she threw herself back into the seat with a huff. "Dickhead," she muttered under her breath. "Pissface. Freaking son of a satanic whore," she muttered, slapping the screen half-heartedly. I've got to be calm, she thought, they've got Kelly, they have me, and they have Larry. We're screwed, she thought and sighed.

We all know how this is supposed to play out, the unwelcome voice said. *Stay calm, keep alert and relax, it's going to be a long night – conserve your energy.*

Abbey leaned back against the seat and practiced deep breathing. The police car entered Locknee on a road she was not familiar and passed the police station without stopping. He turned into a low-income area, passing poorly maintained and empty houses, and then onto a single lane road; the pavement shattered in spots and drove through a tunnel of trees. The small road opened into the broken concrete parking lot of an old motel on the banks of the Red Fork Creek.

The motel had seen its boom years after World War II and then, in the 70s, it had been converted into low-income housing. Later, the creek flooded, washing through the bottom floor and the building had been condemned. The officer parked beside other cars in the lot and turned, speaking to her through the wire mesh that separated them. "Are you going to walk? Or do I have to carry you again?" he asked.

"I'll walk," she said.

He opened the door and wrapped his large hand around her upper arm. "This way," he said, leading her up an old metal staircase to the second floor of the building.

A smiling Mike Almond opened the door after a brief tap on the warped wood by the officer and the room behind him was filled with candles. "I'm glad you could make it, Abbey, now we can get this party on the road." He laughed and she thought he seemed a little tipsy. "Bring her in."

The officer pulled Abbey into the room and placed her in a chair. "Where's Kelly?" she demanded, taking in the squalor around her. The windows were covered with dirty sheets and debris and broken furniture had been pushed into the corners of the room. The peeling paint and wallpaper exposed mold and filth.

Mike reached into the pocket of his jacket and removed a small pouch. He opened the leather container and pulled free a syringe. "She's here, taking a little nap before the festivities begin." He pushed the plunger, sending a small spray of liquid into the air. "Now, we can do this the hard way or the easy way, Abbey. This is just going to relax you so we can get you dressed and ready for the ceremony. Officer," he said and the large man held her down in the chair while Mike slid the needle into her arm. "There, now that wasn't so hard, was it?"

"You know they killed Richard," she said and then felt warmth invade her body. Her limbs suddenly felt as heavy as lead, nearly impossible to lift without help, and her mind grew hazy and slow.

"Richard had a simple task," he said, replacing the syringe in the pouch and sliding it back into his pocket. "He failed. He knew what would happen if he didn't deliver, that's what happens when you play ball with the big boys."

"And you have no problem with the fact that he was

murdered?" she slurred slowly, struggling to hold onto consciousness.

"He knew what would happen, he had a simple task," he repeated.

"Wonderful!" A female voice spoke and then Pearl stepped into the light wearing a form-fitting black dress. "Everyone's here." She smiled and pulled Mike aside, whispering softly in his ear.

Abbey dozed and was awakened when she heard Pearl speaking directly in front of her. "Help me get her undressed and in the tub." Abbey tried to fight as the officer pulled her shirt over her head and unsnapped her bra, but her limbs and mind just wouldn't work together. Mike kneeled down to untie her boots and she ordered her foot to kick him in the face, but her foot only moved an inch and the attempt made exhaustion sweep through her body, sending her back into unconsciousness.

"No need to fight, Abbey, you're about to be pampered, I thought all women enjoyed that," Pearl soothed, pulling off Abbey's jeans and panties as the man in the uniform lifted her out of the chair, the assault dragging her back into awareness. He set her back in the chair, naked, and Pearl stepped behind her, winding the long braid onto her head and clipping it.

The large man picked her up like a rag doll and carried her into the bathroom, placing her gently down into cool, fragrant water. The small room had no windows and candlelight showed the obvious decay.

"Not the ideal surroundings," Pearl said, stepping in the room. "It would've been nicer for you had you not caused so much trouble. You have only yourself to blame." She kneeled beside the tub, sprinkling dark powder into the water and speaking in Latin.

"Where's Kelly?" Abbey slurred, the cool water clearing her head a bit.

Pearl picked up a cloth and started bathing Abbey like a child. "She's here, taking a nap."

"Why are you doing this?" Abbey asked, her voice sounded as though her mouth was full of rocks.

"Because we have to do things the right way, an offering must be clean and it must be cleaned in the proper fashion." She sprinkled more powder in the tub while chanting a phrase in Latin.

Abbey tried to shake her head, but she still couldn't find the coordination between mind and body. "No. All of this."

"Because I can," Pearl laughed, picking up a small glass jar filled with pink liquid and dabbed a bit of the liquid on Abbey's brow, chest, and then sprinkled a few drops into the water. "Besides, I had you, therefore I own you, it's not so difficult to figure out."

"What do you mean you had me?" Abbey slurred, spitting out water, as Pearl poured the scented water over her face and body.

"You're mine, I hatched you. You were conceived on an altar and tonight you will go back to the altar, finally completing the circle." Pearl picked up one of Abbey's feet and started scrubbing. "Back in the day before we had much money I had to sell a couple babies, they were both girls. The money was good and we certainly needed it. But later, I wanted to find those girls, especially after my life changed. They were like weights hanging behind me and holding me back." She picked up a brush, loaded it with soap and went to work on Abbey's toenails. "It took us a while to find those girls and quite a lot of money." Her hand stilled. "But finally we found them!" She smiled. "I was to get rid of both of them that night, but one little bitch ran away. Do you know who that was?" she asked, dropping one foot unceremoniously and picking up the other.

"Me," Abbey said softly, wondering how long the medication would hold her captive. "And who is we?"

"Yes, it was you and we tore up the house that night looking for you, you sure ruined the party. I should bill you." She laughed. "If you knew how much we paid to be there that night." She shook her head and took the brush to Abbey's other foot. "Hundreds of thousands of dollars to take care of my own litter and then you ran off. We searched and searched." Her hand stilled again. "I don't know where in the hell you hid, but the party was over after that and all that money washed down the drain." She dropped Abbey's foot and stood up. "Ted, I need some help in here."

The officer returned, lifted Abbey from the water and held her upright while Pearl dried her and pushed a white, silk negligee over her head. "Make up!" Pearl declared and the officer carried Abbey into the main room, setting her in a chair in front of warped built-in dresser and a cloudy and cracked mirror.

Pearl approached her with blood-red lipstick and applied it to Abbey's lips. "Who is we?" Abbey slurred again, staring into the mirror as the flickering candle light made the splintered images dance.

"Me and Daddy," Pearl said, applying a heavy coat of eye shadow. "Oh, I guess you don't know," she said, standing back and scrutinizing her work. "Your dad is also your grandfather, if you weren't stepping over tonight I guess you could write a famous country song." She stepped to the dresser and picked up a small container of blush. "I don't think it's your color," she said, applying the red powder onto Abbey's cheeks. She pulled the clip from Abbey's hair, unleashing the long braid. "I never understood why you did this to your hair, you're such a pretty woman, why ruin it with this ridiculous braid." She leaned down, looking at Abbey in the ruined mirror, their reflections separated by the cracked glass. "Of course, you are beautiful, though. You look just like your momma."

*

Rex pulled into the parking lot of the Locknee Police Station followed by four state police vehicles. He stepped out of the car and was met by Captain Mark Wellington. "Leave it to me, Mr. Andrews." The captain smiled, took off his hat and stuck out his hand. "Rex, it's nice to meet you, I've heard good things."

"Thanks, Mark." Rex shook his hand. "Let's get this done."

"Yes, sir." The young officer shoved his hat back on his head. "This way, men," he said, throwing open the doors of the small building. He walked inside and his men, totaling seven plus Rex, followed him. "I need to see Chief Thomson," he stated to the middle-aged, wide-eyed, overweight blond sitting in a caged alcove, a headset tangled in her hair.

"Chief Thomson isn't here right now," she said nervously, looking at all the men in the small foyer. "I could have him call you when he returns."

Chief Wellington took off his hat, wiped his brow and leaned forward, his face just inches from the metal divider. "How about this, um…" he looked at her nametag, "Ms. Simon, you tell Chief Thomson that either he is in this office in ten minutes or I am issuing a warrant for his arrest. How's that sound?" He leaned back, replacing his hat.

"I'll call him," she said, pushing some buttons on the

switchboard.

"You do that." He rested his hip against the counter.

*

Abbey struggled to accept the truth; she was the product of incest? "You said two girls, who was the other one?" she asked, noticing that her words were less garbled.

Pearl worked her fingers through the long locks, untangling the strands. "Your sister, the other one that was there that night. Do you know how long we chased you? I mean, we knew what we were doing when we sold you, the money was too damned good not to, but after years we finally got the two of you together." She sighed, picked up a brush and ran it through Abbey's hair. "But then you ran off and ruined it all, it could have all been done that night. In another sense, though, by your running away, you gave us a foot inside. We had proof of a rogue cop and it gave us the key to get our feet inside the door."

*

"He's on his way in," the overweight woman said to the man who was young enough to be her son.

"That's a good thing, Ms. Simon, because I'd really hate to arrest all of y'all." Captain Wellington tipped his hat to her and stepped outside, followed by his men.

*

"She really was my sister?" Abbey asked, gazing into the distorted mirror as emotions raced through her body. "Caroline really was my sister?"

"Her name wasn't Caroline!" Pearl barked, brushing harder. "You girls were never supposed to have names. Who knew you could get so much for a baby? Pretty, white, blond haired, light-eyed babies are worth so much more and I was a little baby machine back then." She stopped brushing for a moment and stared off into the corner. "The truth, though, is that you were mine no matter how much money they gave me for you, you were still mine. In the end, though, it paid off. We found a rogue agent, an agent who could become a serious problem to the program. And that was all we needed to start a new life." Pearl threw Abbey's hair over her shoulders and stepped in front of the mirror to take a look. "Good enough," she said.

"You've known who I was for years, why now?" Abbey asked, her voice growing clearer and stronger.

"Timing is everything, daughter. We were going to take you when you were sixteen, but you were already pregnant. That intrigued Daddy and me, you should have never been able to become pregnant, grown men were having sex you when you were a toddler. The fact that you did become pregnant was almost like a miracle, so I mean really..." she laughed, shaking her head at the irony, "we're not really miracle people. A miracle must be sacrificed, but a miracle sacrificed, innocent, ripe and blooming is so much better than a newborn miracle, so much stronger, the blood so much more healing. So we waited, it's not like there aren't plenty of other young women people won't miss. Have you watched the news lately? Young women disappear every damned day, but we knew Kelly would be special, she's an aberration, a freak!" She laughed. "Her blood is very, very powerful. Her blood is our blood."

*

"What in the hell is going on here?" Randy Thomson demanded as he stepped out of his cruiser, the setting sun on the horizon illuminating his face under the wide brim of his hat.

"What's going on is you're in deep shit, Randy." Captain Mark Wellington met him at the car and looked into the back seat. "Who's that?"

"Disorderly conduct, resisting arrest, no big deal. What in the hell is going on?"

Mark looked at Rex and Rex nodded his head. Mark opened the back door, pulling the prisoner out. "Unlock his cuffs," the captain demanded.

"What in the hell are you doing? That man assaulted an officer!" the chief snapped.

"Unlock his cuffs," Captain Wellington stated again.

"Damned state police coming in here thinking they have a

clue about what is going on. That guy assaulted an officer!"

"Unlock his damned cuffs and quit fucking with me, Randy." The captain's free hand reached for the gun at his waist.

"Fine, fine. You'll find out after he punches one of your guys in the jaw," he said and unlocked the cuffs.

"Now, Randy, where is Abbey Brown?" Mark asked, as Larry walked over to Rex.

"I don't know who you're talking about," Chief Thomson said, sliding the cuffs onto his belt and leaning against his cruiser.

"The woman who was with him when you picked him up, outside of your jurisdiction I might add. Where is she?"

"I don't know what you're talking about, I only picked up one perp." He crossed his arms on his chest.

"You're not very bright, are you, Chief Thomson? We know you picked them both up! His freaking phone was on, we have a damned recording, idiot, we heard everything! Now where is she?" Captain Wellington leaned forward menacingly

"I said I don't know, I only picked up the one guy." Randy slid away from the car and began heading toward the building.

"Tasering an unarmed man in cuffs and kidnapping a

woman?" Mark shook his head slowly and followed. "You're really screwing up here, Randy. What do you think this is? The Wild West? And you don't have to answer to anyone?"

"I tased him until we were able to get the cuffs on him, Mark, he was resisting. Just what is it you accusing me of?" Randy turned, pulled off his hat, and wiped his brow, shoving the hat back into place.

"I'm accusing you of being a red necked asshole, but that don't mean shit! What does mean shit, though, is that you have eyes all the way from Washington DC on down looking at you right now!" He laughed. "And it's about freaking time as far as I'm concerned." Mark walked over to Rex, spoke to him quietly for a moment and called his guys back to their cruisers. He turned back to Randy and spoke softly, "And it would be the best thing for you that I don't run into you again tonight. Do you know what I mean, Randy?"

"I have no idea what you're talking about, Mark." Randy turned and stepped up on the single step leading to the front door of the police department.

"You or any of your men! I better not run into hide nor hair of you or your men tonight, Randy, because if I do it's all gonna come down on your head," Captain Wellington called out and climbed into his car.

*

Silly stood in the yard and stared up at the house. It was dinnertime and he wondered where the woman was. He spent the night in the woods sure she would come looking for him, but she never did. He'd slept up under some briars, missing the warmth of his does and the soft snoring sounds the ducks made in their sleep.

He clucked softly as he ambled into the pen and passed the opened gate. He thought about the woman. She never left the gate open and the sight of it, hanging there unattended, made him feel lost and alone. He liked the woman, he liked the way she talked to him, and how she scratched his head. He pulled some hay from the mesh bag hanging on the side of the barn, chewing thoughtfully, and stared at the house.

He looked into the barn expecting to see his does and found nothing. The ache inside of him grew. He wandered into the yard and nibbled on the rose bushes, sure that the woman would come running from the house. She didn't. He walked up onto the porch, the clunk of his hooves disturbing the uncomfortable silence.

He stepped to the door and paused, the scent here was wrong. He could still smell the woman and the other one, the kid, but there was another scent over top of it, a wrong scent, a scent that shouldn't be. He pushed open the door with his snout and stepped inside, the smell was stronger here, and it was the odor of predators, male predators. Had they taken the woman?

He nibbled on a piece of paper he found on the floor, remembering the same aroma from earlier in the day. He'd seen them in the woods, smelled them as he attempted to eat the yellow grass that looked appealing but tasted dead. He didn't like that area in the woods, it made his head itch worse and his teeth hurt, but he was sure he would find the woman there.

Chapter Twenty-Six

"How are you feeling?" Rex asked, pulling onto the street behind the line of cruisers.

"Like I've been cooked from the inside out," Larry said, rubbing his face with his hands and then slapping his cheeks briskly.

"How many times did you get hit with the taser?" Rex asked, handing over a small bag with a wallet and keys inside. "One of our guys found this on the road, the phone was smashed, but I have a new one for you." He passed over the new phone.

"Thanks. I think I was hit twice." He sighed. "Not pleasant. Do we have any idea where Abbey and Kelly are?"

"No, I've got Danny down there with a crew watching the circle, we'll see them when they bring them in. There's also some kind of private security force that has the road below the Jackson's blocked off, they're not letting anyone come in that way. I don't know who the guys are, but according to Danny, they are armed and seem serious."

Larry nodded. "Danny's a good choice to lead it. So what's the plan now?"

"We're going to go have a talk with Sheriff Davis," Rex said, crossing over the Red Fork Creek and entering the marsh.

*

"So Richard was a set up from the beginning?" Abbey asked, moving her fingers lightly on the arm of the chair.

"Of course. I really didn't expect you to fall for it, but you did. I trained him well, but he had his own motivations. You didn't know he liked his girls a little young, did you? And if he believed that at the end of this he got Kelly, what was the harm in letting him believe that? For such an educated man, he wasn't the sharpest knife in the drawer." Pearl stepped closer, adjusting the hair flowing over Abbey's chest.

Abbey moved her toes lightly under the long flowing garment; she could feel the control of her body coming back to her.

"I know you killed him," she said.

"I didn't kill him and why do you care? He knew and was completely willing to participate in your death, with the goal of screwing your daughter, I would think you'd be happy he's gone. Such a stupid, arrogant man." She shook her head.

Abbey laughed harshly. "But you plan to kill both of us tonight, so which one of you is worse?"

Pearl placed her hands on her hips, her eyes narrowing. "You know, it's an honor to give yourself to the Master. Even in your Christian bible you worship a man who was crucified, you praise him for his sacrifice, but don't want to give your own. You're a hypocrite. Why do you celebrate the day of his death if you don't appreciate a good sacrifice?"

"It's a little different, don't you think?" Her fists curled on the arms of the chair.

"How is it different? You Christians sacrificed a man to your God and it's all about light and joy, we sacrifice someone to our God and it's sick and twisted. The only difference is a hypocritical attitude. Of course, then we have the Crusades and the Inquisitions, all motivated by your belief system and perfectly acceptable to you people who have a religion based in love." She laughed.

"That was a long time ago, things have changed," she said, twisting her feet gently so not to disturb the folds of the gown.

"Nothing's changed, it's just hidden better these days. How many Christians support this war in Iraq when their book says not to kill? You're still reaping the benefits of spilled blood, but now you just call it patriotism. Your television shows are full of murder and blood, but now it's just entertainment. The old ways still exist, spilling blood onto the earth gives us power, and now you fools will pay just to watch and still call yourselves Christians."

"Ma'am?" the officer spoke from the shadows. "I've been called back to the station."

"You can't go, I need you," Pearl snapped. "And where the hell is Randy?"

"I don't know, ma'am, but I've been called back." He walked to the door and let himself out.

"Well, damn." Pearl walked over to the connecting door and opened it. "Mike, have you heard from Randy?"

"No, I haven't heard from him." Mike spoke from the other

room. "Are we ready?" He stepped into view and whispered, "People are getting anxious."

"Almost," she said. "Start waking up the girl." She shut the door and stepped over to the built in dresser, picking up a phone. Turning her back to Abbey, she dialed. "Hey Daddy, where are you?"

Abbey twisted her feet at the ankles, pleased to see the gown bouncing out at the hemline. She tried to lift her arms and found she could pull them from the wooden arm of the chair, but they felt weak and shaky.

"What do you mean you're not coming? We've been planning this for years, everything's ready, everybody's here." Pearl walked toward the bathroom, her voice low.

Abbey worked on lifting her legs off the chair, one at a time, keeping her eyes focused on Pearl's back.

"Jesus, Daddy, he's just a small town sheriff, I don't know why you're so worried, besides it's private land and it's guarded. They are not going to be expecting us to come up through the creek, by the time they figure it out, it'll be too late." She paused, listening and then stomped her foot, the acoustics of the small room echoing the sound. "I'm not calling it off, you know it has to be tonight." She paused again. "I'm going anyway, I have faith and I believe that with such a generous offer I will be protected." Pearl hung up the phone and when she stepped back into the candlelight, Abbey could see tears in her eyes.

"I have a question," Abbey said. "If you intended to use Kelly as an offering, why'd you have her run over like a dog?"

Pearl wiped the tears away. "Oh, I didn't do that, my idiot son did." She grabbed a tissue off the ruined dresser and bent into the shattered mirror, dabbing her eyes. "Evidently I create smarter girl children than I do boy children. He'd heard his grandfather and I talking about her, he was jealous, thought she was going to steal his inheritance or something. He's an idiot, but don't worry, he was punished."

"Did you ground him?" Abbey asked sarcastically and found the ability to roll her eyes.

"That and more." She picked up a canvas bag and set the makeup basket inside. She looked around the room, gathering a few things and dropping them into the bag. "Are we done with confession time?"

"So you're just going to take me and Kelly out into the woods and kill us?" she stalled.

"You don't understand how powerful what you are undertaking is, Abbey. There are other worlds out there, you're just stepping over into a new reality, it's really not scary."

"Then why don't you take my place?" Abbey suggested.

"Funny, funny girl." Satisfied she had gathered everything, she walked to the door connecting the rooms and opened it. "Mike, come give me a hand."

"What do you need?" he asked, stepping into the room.

"I need help getting her robe on. Is the girl awake?"

"Yes, she's groggy, but awake," he said, stepping behind Abbey's chair.

"Good, we're almost ready." She pushed a dark garment over Abbey's head and slid her arms into the sleeves. "Now lift her up."

Mike put hands under Abbey's arms, lifting her and Pearl drew the garment to the floor. "Okay, put her back down." Pearl adjusted the dark robe and pulled the hood up to cover Abbey's head. "Bring the girl in here and we'll finish getting her dressed."

Mike left the room and returned with Kelly in his arms. She was dressed in a similar white gown, but her face was scrubbed clean. Mike placed her in a chair beside Abbey; her body was limp and her head rolled onto the back of the chair.

"I thought you said she was awake," Pearl said, another dark garment in her hands.

"I said she's waking up, she'll be awake by the time we get there." He helped Pearl push the robe over Kelly's head, sliding her arms into the over-sized sleeves and then lifted her, while Pearl tugged the garment down to her feet.

"Okay, have everyone put on their robes, we'll be leaving in five minutes," Pearl said, carrying a bag into the bathroom.

Mike left the room and Abbey could hear him talking through the connecting door. "All right everyone, get your robes on, we're almost ready."

"Kelly?" Abbey whispered, reaching over and touching her daughter's arm. "Kelly?" She shook her gently.

Kelly groaned, lifting her head a bit and opening her eyes. "Mom?"

"I'm right here, honey, you need to wake up," she

whispered.

Kelly's eyes closed again and her head fell back against the chair.

"Kelly," Abbey said again, shaking her arm a little harder.

"My eyes keep slamming shut on me," she slurred, opening her eyes again and lifting her head. "Mom, they shot Daddy!" Her eyes opened wider and she sat a little straighter.

"I know, honey, but he's going to be fine." She patted Kelly's arm. "We just need to make sure we get out of this fine. The drugs are wearing off and once we can get our feet under us, we're going to have to make a run for it."

"Okay," Kelly said, blinking rapidly. "But I hope we have a few minutes, I'm really doped up."

"I think we will. Shhh," Abbey whispered, pulling her hand back as Pearl stepped out of the bathroom dressed in a long, dark, flowing robe, her hair and face covered by the hood. She walked past Abbey and Kelly without a word and stepped through the connecting door. "Where the hell is everyone?" she whispered angrily.

Mike, dressed in a long robe, a hood covering his head,

pulled her back through the doorway by the arm. "These are all the people that showed up and a couple have already left, if we're going, we need to go now."

"We need at least thirteen people!" Pearl snapped.

"Well, we don't have thirteen, we have six. It'll have to do," he insisted.

"Fine." She sighed. "Let's go, we need to get them in the boat."

"Ralph," Mike called into the connected room, "can you give me a hand?" A large man in a matching dark robe stepped into the room. Mike picked up Kelly, while the man named Ralph picked up Abbey and they followed Pearl to the door. "What about the candles?" Mike asked.

"They must be left to go out on their own," she explained. "Is everyone ready?" Pearl called out and three more people stepped into the room, their faces obscured by the hoods of their robes. "Let's go." She opened the door holding an antique lantern aloft and led the way across the metal and concrete balcony and down the stairs.

Abbey peered up into the hood of the man carrying her and

recognized him as the owner of the feed and seed in Locknee, Ralph Adams. Adams Feed and Seed was the same company that delivered supplies to her house in Oak Tree twice a month.

The procession wound through the bottom washed out floor of the building and onto the marshy ground in the rear of the building. It was dark out; the moon had yet to rise and as they approached the frogs singing along the bank suddenly silenced their song. Waiting for them on the water were four metal, flat-bottomed boats. One of the robed men from the rear of the line came forward and held the boat steady as Ralph placed Abbey on the center seat. Finding she could hold herself upright, she held onto the side of the boat and Mike placed Kelly beside her. Kelly's body began to slide onto the floor and Abbey wrapped an arm around her waist, pulling her close.

Pearl stepped in behind them, sitting on a metal bench seat and Mike climbed in beside her. "Before you girls get any funny ideas about taking a swim…" he held up a gun. "It would not be nice to be floating in this water with a bullet hole in your back." He placed the gun on his lap and adjusted the small trolling motor into the water. As they began to move upstream, Mike called out softly to the men piling into the next boat, "Remember, no lights until we're outside of Locknee."

Pearl dimmed the flame in the lantern and they moved, almost silently, through the water on the edge of town, passing under a bridge. Abbey saw cars, heard traffic and radio noise, but no one noticed their dark passage. Once the city had fallen behind them Mike picked up speed, turning on a small spotlight and scanning the top of the water. Pearl dialed her phone and spoke briefly. "Meet us at the edge of the water," she said and slid the phone into a hidden pocket in her robe.

Abbey glanced down at Kelly, trying to see her face in the dark folds of the hood. "Are you okay?" she asked.

Kelly nodded.

"Shut up! The time for talking is over," Pearl barked.

In some areas the trees hung low over the water and they had to duck to keep from being knocked out of the boat. "I sure hope a snake doesn't fall in here with us," Abbey said. "Some of these water snakes are mighty poisonous."

"I said, shut up!" Pearl repeated.

Abbey smiled. She was beginning to feel a glimmer of hope as she realized that the event wasn't going as well as Pearl had planned. It's falling apart on her, she thought.

"There they are," Pearl said, pointing to the beam of light shining across the water.

The boat slowed, bumping along the shallow bottom. A man wearing black with a holster at his waist grabbed the front and pulled it onto shore. Headlights from a SUV illuminated the small piece of marshy land and the man tied the boat to a tree. Mike jumped out of the boat, holding his hand for Pearl to step out gracefully and pointing the gun at Abbey. "Get out. You should be able to walk now."

Abbey stood up and sat down again as the boat wobbled.

"Get out," he demanded.

Abbey tried again and stepped onto the marshy soil with her bare feet, her legs felt weak, but steady. She reached back into the boat and helped Kelly step over the side of the boat onto the moist, cool ground.

"In the truck," Mike said, stepping behind the women and placing the gun at the base of Kelly's spine. "Walk."

Abbey held onto Kelly's arm and led her to one of the waiting SUVs. Mike opened the back door and they climbed inside. One of the armed men stepped into the driver's seat and Pearl slid in the front seat beside him, balancing the lantern on her knees. Mike climbed into the back, pushing the pistol firmly in Kelly's side.

"Let's go," Pearl said. The driver started the vehicle, turned around and headed up the hill toward the circle. The other SUV, with the occupants from the second boat, pulled in behind them. The SUVs drove slowly over the rutted road and soon they arrived at the nearly hidden path leading to the circle. "Stop here," Pearl said, opening the door.

"Why don't we drive straight in?" Mike asked, stepping out of the truck and pointing the gun at Abbey and Kelly. "Get out."

"Because, this is already screwed up enough, we're going to do this the right way, we walk from here," Pearl stated, straightening her robe.

Abbey helped Kelly out of the car and they stood on the road, waiting as the other robed figures joined them on the path.

Pearl surveyed the small crowd and held up the lantern in the air. "Okay, boys, this is it. Relax, enjoy, and trust the Master, it's going to be a hell of a night." She turned, the lantern casting a small glow in the thick darkness created by the overhanging branches. "Single file," she said and stepped into the thick and eerily silent tunnel.

"Abbey," Mike motioned with the gun and Abbey fell into step behind Pearl. He pushed the gun into Kelly's back and shoved her into line. "Just remember if you try to run, Abbey, she gets it in the back," he warned and the other men fell in line behind him.

Abbey wasn't sure where the armed men went and she scanned the tree line, thinking she could hear movement in the woods.

*

"They're in," Danny whispered into the phone.

"We're almost in place," Larry responded. "Just keep them in your sight."

"Will do," Danny whispered, watching the procession move down the road as he moved silently through the woods.

Think! Abbey demanded to herself as the tunnel gave way to the recently widened trail. She stepped on a sharp rock jutting through dried grass in the center of the road. "Ow!" she cried out, hopping on one foot, while rubbing the bruise with her hands. The procession behind her slowed to a stop.

"Shut up and walk!" Pearl said, turning and pulling Abbey's hands away from her bruised foot. "Walk."

Abbey sighed, feigning helpless frustration, and started walking again, the procession falling back into step behind her. "Damnit!" she cried, going down onto one knee and when Kelly bumped into her from behind, she grabbed her hand.

"What in the hell! How hard is it to walk?" Pearl burst out in frustration as the group stopped again.

"I'm freaking barefooted here!" Abbey lashed back, squeezing Kelly's hand.

"Jesus Christ!" Pearl bellowed, turning to face the procession. "I am up to my eyeteeth with y'alls damned bullshit! Grow a fucking back bone!" She turned around, lifting the lantern back into the air and took a deep, calming breath.

Abbey squeezed Kelly's hand tightly and then let go, slowly getting back to her feet. Pearl glanced over her shoulder to assure that Abbey was up and the procession resumed. As they began moving forward again Abbey heard movement in the woods, she pulled back the hood a bit and looked into the dark forest. Taking several more steps, the top of her head began tingling and she felt dizzy. Shit, she thought, it's stronger!

"Feel that boys?" Pearl called back to the rear of the procession. "It's going to be an amazing night." She began chanting in Latin.

The energy seemed to increase with Pearl's chant and the hair on Abbey's neck and arms stood on end. The field that contained the path to the circle came into view, the rising moon illuminating the tall yellow grass. The hammering headache slammed into Abbey's brain and she groaned, grasping her head with both hands. Behind her Kelly groaned in pain and stumbled hard, falling into Abbey with all her weight.

As Kelly fell into Abbey, a white streak rushed out of the woods hitting Mike full force in the ribcage. With the sound of a cracking branch, Mike hit the ground and a gunshot rang out into the air. The force of Kelly falling into Abbey caused her to tumble into Pearl. Pearl fell onto her knees and the lantern hurled out of her hand. The lantern hit the ground with the sound of shattering glass and exploded in a small burst of oil and flame, igniting the dried grass.

"What the fuck?" Pearl raged, struggling to get to her feet. The white streak rushed back out of the tree line and butted Pearl solidly in the head. The sound of a pumpkin splitting rang out and she collapsed on the road. Silly reared up on his hind legs, clucking victoriously, and ran back into the forest.

"Run." Abbey bit out against the brutal pain in her head and grabbed Kelly's arm, dragging her to the edge of the road. Mike's gun exploded again as they jumped over the newly cut debris separating the woods from the road. They ran into the forest and the pain in her head subsided, only to be replaced with the pain in her feet, as broken branches, rocks, and briars tore into soft flesh.

They had only gotten a few yards into the woods when gunfire erupted, seemingly surrounding them. Abbey threw Kelly down onto the ground beside a thick tree and covered her daughter's body with her own.

"Who's shooting all those guns?" Kelly yelled.

"I don't know, but we're getting out of here!" Abbey responded and when the gunfire slowed, she jumped to her feet. Pulling Kelly along, she ran again.

"Where are we going?" Kelly gasped, keeping up with her as they ran through the branches, briars, and undergrowth.

"This way!" Abbey said, following an inner compass.

Chapter Twenty-Seven

They burst out of the forest into a garden; the scents of tomato blossoms and ripe strawberries were almost overwhelming to Abbey's senses as she inhaled great gasps of air. She saw the house just ahead and the ground began to vibrate underneath their feet. "What the …" she gasped and a huge explosion reverberated through the woods, the force knocking them both onto the soft ground.

"What the crap was that?" Kelly yelled, as the sky turned orange and a large cloud shot up above the trees.

"I don't know," Abbey said, pulling Kelly to her feet and dragging her through the soft dirt. They ran across the dewy grass and up the concrete stairs, pounding on the door. "Mr. Jackson, Mrs. Jackson!"

"Git on in here!" Mr. Jackson demanded. He carried a shotgun in one hand and grabbed Abbey by the shoulder with the other, pulling them both inside. He slammed the door behind them and peered through the glass, watching the cloud in the sky. "Jimmy!" he called.

Jimmy stepped out of the living room with a pistol in his hand. "Got it, Papa," he said, backing into the corner and peering into the yard. "I sure don't know what just blew up."

Abbey and Kelly stumbled into the kitchen to find Mrs. Jackson, a kerchief over her hair, setting a pie on the kitchen table. "Come in, girls," she said, her voice shaking. "I ain't believin' I'm doing this agin at my age."

"They're after us!" Abbey exhaled, pulling Kelly close.

"That's what I knowed," Mrs. Jackson nodded. "But yous a'safe now, look in the living room."

"What?" Abbey asked, confused.

"Look in the living room," she repeated with a smile.

Abbey and Kelly glanced at each other and with their arms entwined, they moved toward the next room and peeked inside. There were four heavily armed men peering out through the windows, two in the uniform of the sheriff's office, two were local farmers.

Mr. Jackson sat at the kitchen table, the shotgun across his lap, watching his wife slice a strawberry pie. "Set down, girls, yous gonna be okay."

Mrs. Jackson laughed nervously. "Smaller pieces tonight, we gots more folks to feed."

Abbey turned to Kelly. "Are you okay?"

Kelly smiled. "It's not been your average week."

"You're telling me!" Abbey agreed. "But you're okay? Nobody did…" she paused and looked at the Jacksons sitting at the table.

Kelly glanced at the Jacksons and back at her mother.

"Nobody did anything except shoot my dad, dope me up, and mess up my vacation. I never did get to see Old Faithful!"

Abbey pulled her into her arms, hugging her tightly. "I'm sorry, baby."

"I'm fine, Mom," Kelly whispered in her ear.

"We got men!" Jimmy announced from his position by the back door.

"Git down, ladies," Mr. Jackson said, rising and peering through the kitchen window.

Mrs. Jackson joined Kelly and Abbey beside the refrigerator and they wrapped their arms around each other, trying to make themselves as small a target as possible.

"Mr. Jackson?" A voice rang out. "It's Rex Andrews! Are you in there? Are Abbey and Kelly here?"

Mr. Jackson laughed. "It's your uncle, Miss Abbey." He walked to the door and opened it. "Come on in, Mr. Andrews, they's here. You want a piece of pie?"

Rex stepped into the kitchen, followed by Larry and another man. Rex nodded at the Jacksons and swept Abbey and Kelly into his arms. "Thank you, God!" he said over and again. "Thank God, you're all right." He let them go and wiped a tear away. "That was too close."

"We're okay, Uncle Rex," Kelly said, wiping her eyes.

Rex pulled out his phone, dialed and said, "They're okay, Summer, we've got them." He handed the phone to Abbey; she spoke to her mother for a moment and then handed the phone to Kelly.

Abbey turned to Larry. "I'm glad you're okay, I was worried."

"I was worried about you, too." He smiled. "Oh yeah, this is Danny Downs."

"Nice to meet you." Abbey said.

Kelly hung up the phone and handed it to her uncle. "What was all that shooting going on down there? And that explosion? It sounded like we were in the middle of a war zone."

"Set down, set down," Mr. Jackson said, settling the shotgun in a corner and taking his place at the kitchen table. "All I knowed is the state police flew down that road a piece ago, going faster than a scalded dog, and the next thing I knowed it sounded like world war three down there." He took a bite of pie.

"It was already tense with the state police and local law challenging the private security hired to block the road. Once the shooting started in the woods, it went downhill fast," Rex said and more police cars zoomed down the dirt road, followed by a fire truck.

"We've pulled our men back, there's a heck of a fire burning down there, hopefully they'll get it under control. I have no idea what exploded, but it was big, whatever it was." He sighed. "Abbey, you and Kelly are going to have to give your statements to the police, but we need to figure which police, I'm not going to have you all giving your statements a hundred times to every branch of the law. It's a jurisdictional nightmare down there."

"I think Pearl is dead, Silly butted her in the head," Abbey said, cringing as she remembered the sound of Pearl's skull splitting. "Did the police get the rest of them?" she asked.

"What's a Silly?" Danny asked. "All I saw was a white streak."

"Silly's our goat," Abbey explained.

"He's a cocky bastard." Mr. Jackson laughed.

Rex laughed. "So it was the goat that broke up the party?"

"Who would have ever believed that that psychotic goat would end up saving our lives?" Kelly asked, shaking her head slowly and smiling. "His timing was perfect."

"I guess I have to keep him now." Abbey sighed.

"As much as I hate to say it, Mom, I agree," Kelly said.

"As far of who will be arrested, Abbey, I don't know. We're out of that part of it, we'll just have to see what the police do," Rex said. "The sheriff will stop by in a little while."

Mrs. Jackson got to her feet, pulled down a serving tray from the cabinet and set plates of pie and silverware on top. She carried the tray into the living room, placing it on the coffee table. "If'n y'all got a minute to eat, here's some pie." She returned to the kitchen, handing Abbey a jar of cold cream and a box of tissues. "Yous all painted up."

"I forgot," Abbey said, opening the jar and dabbing the cream on her face. She wiped her face, staining the tissue with blues and reds. Kelly grabbed a tissue and helped her remove the rest of the gaudy make-up. As she stared at the soiled tissues, she remembered the conversation with Pearl. "Uncle Rex, Pearl said she is my mother and her father is also my father. She said she sold me when I was a baby because they needed the cash. Caroline really was my sister and the plan was to kill us both back in Colorado, she said our existence was a weight holding her back." Tears slid slowly down her face as she looked across the table at her uncle.

"Oh, Momma," Kelly said, wrapping her arms around Abbey's neck.

Rex sighed. "Well, shit." He turned to Larry. "We need a DNA sample."

Larry nodded. "Might be a little tricky to get one, but we'll get it."

"Where did they take you after pulling you off the road, Abbey?" Rex asked.

"To that old falling down motel on the bank of the Red Fork in Locknee," Abbey said, taking a deep breath and rubbing Kelly's back.

Larry stood up and pulled his phone out of his pocket. "I'm sending some guys to go look around before the big guys get there." He stepped out of the kitchen.

"Does anyone know what happened to my Jeep?" Abbey

asked.

"If it's a white Jeep, scraped up down the side, it's down there by the cemetery. A guy pulled it in a couple hours ago," Danny said.

"Well, I hope it's not getting burned up in the fire," Abbey groaned.

Kelly giggled. "You sure are tough on cars, Mom."

Rex pulled his phone out of his pocket and placing it to his ear, he stood up. "Jack! Good to hear your voice." He listened for a minute and smiled. "Yes, they're both fine, here she is." He handed the phone to Kelly.

"Daddy?" She started crying. "I was so afraid that you were dead."

"Boy howdy!" Mr. Jackson exclaimed, slapping his leg with a laugh as an ambulance raced down the road. "I ain't never seen so much traffic on that road."

Mrs. Jackson started stacking the dishes in the sink and Abbey helped her wash them. Kelly hung up the phone, wiped the tears from her eyes and smiled. "He's okay," she said.

"The sheriff is here," Larry said, stepping back in the

kitchen.

"Come on in and set a spell," Mr. Jackson called out.

Sheriff Davis and Captain Wellington stepped into the crowded kitchen and removing their hats, they sat down at the table. The men looked at Abbey and Kelly and with a sigh, Sheriff Davis spoke first, "Abbey, Kelly, are you all right? Do you need medical attention?"

"Our feet are pretty messed up." Abbey pulled up the long gown, showing her dirty, scratched, and bloody feet.

"Oh lord," Mrs. Jackson said. "Let's git your feets fixed up." She folded a dishtowel, placing it on the side of the sink, and left the kitchen.

"But other than that, I think we're fine." She glanced at her daughter and Kelly nodded in agreement.

The sheriff nodded. "Can you tell me what happened down there tonight?"

"They were taking us into the woods to kill us or in Pearl's words, offer a sacrifice to their god, Lucifer," she said and the two men in uniforms glanced at each other. They pulled matching black pads from their pockets and began scribbling.

"Mrs. Brown, when is the last time you saw your husband?" Captain Wellington asked.

"Sunday night, he stormed out of the house and I haven't seen him since."

Mrs. Jackson called Jimmy from the room to help her in the bathroom.

"A man fitting the description of your husband, carrying your husband's ID, washed up on the shore of Lake Lanier a few hours ago," he said, watching her reaction.

Abbey slowly nodded her head and Kelly's eyes grew wide. "I had a feeling they killed him."

"Who is they?" the captain asked, as Jimmy stepped into the room with a big bowl of foamy and fragrant water.

Jimmy set the bowl on the floor gently, making sure not to spill any of the liquid, and pulled a chair up to it. "Grandma said to soak your feet in this," he said, leaving the room to retrieve the second bowl.

Abbey pushed Kelly toward the chair. "Soak your feet, honey," she said and turned back to the officer. "I assume part of the same they that just tried to kill us. My husband was part of that group, I just found out a few days ago that he'd been drugging me."

"Can you prove he was drugging you?" he asked.

"Yes," Rex spoke up. "We can prove it, we have the capsules that he prescribed, with a unhealthy mix of medicines in some of them and I'm pretty sure we'll find his fingerprints on the altered ones."

The captain nodded and made a note on the pad. "Abbey, where were you Sunday night and Monday?" The captain held up his hand to Rex. "I have to ask and you know I do," he defended.

"I was home Sunday night and yesterday morning I left," she said, sitting down and sliding her feet into the bowl of warm water Jimmy had placed on the floor. "I went to my mother's in Windslow and then drove up to Helen where I spent the night."

"Were you alone?" he asked.

"No," she said. "I was with Larry." She pointed at him standing in the doorway.

"We've been following Richard since Sunday." Larry said. "He spent the night with Pearl Sunday night and Monday morning they drove into Atlanta in Richard's car. They went to the offices of Winston Chambers, Pearl left soon after, returning to Locknee and my men never saw Richard again. They watched his car until Monday evening and then I pulled them back. Some time today his car was moved to an auto body place, I can get you the address." Larry pulled out his phone.

"That would be helpful," the captain said.

"I can verify that I had dinner with Abbey and Larry Sunday evening," Sheriff Davis stated. "And Abbey filed a report Sunday afternoon with me because someone shot her dog. She also filed a police report in Locknee Sunday morning because somebody tried to run her off the road when she was taking her dog to the vet."

Larry hung up the phone and handed the captain a piece of paper. "The car was last seen at this address."

The captain read the scrap of paper, nodded and slid it into his pocket as an ambulance passed the house headed to the highway, sirens blaring. He sighed. "I've got at least two dead bodies down there, one injured and we really won't know much else until we can get some dogs out there to search the woods. And, of course, there is the fire and something mighty big blew up down there." He shook his head.

Mrs. Jackson stepped back into the kitchen. "How's your

feets?" she asked, patting Kelly on the shoulder.

"Feels heavenly." Kelly smiled.

"Good. Now who wants coffee?" she asked and stepped between Abbey and Kelly to reach the counter.

"Coffee sounds good," Rex agreed.

"Please forgive me for being a little dense, but can you tell me how you came to be with those people, dressed like that, and in the middle of the woods?" the captain asked.

Abbey told him about being pulled over by Locknee police in Windslow, how they tased Larry and took her away. She explained how Kelly had been abducted from Montana, while her father was shot trying to protect her. And then she gave him the details of the old motel, the syringe, the bath, the makeup and the boats on the creek. "Our clothes and stuff should still be there and Pearl left the candles burning," she concluded.

"Speaking of the woman, Pearl, do you know what happened to her?" he asked. "She wasn't shot, but she is definitely dead."

"My goat, that's been lost in the woods for a couple days, butted her in the head," she explained. "He pretty much saved our lives."

"All right," the captain said, standing. "I need to know where you'll be staying, I'll be back in touch. Get some rest," he said after writing down her information. "We'll be in touch tomorrow." He stepped out of the room, lifting his radio and dispatching a couple cars to the old hotel in Locknee.

"Coffee, Sheriff?" Mrs. Jackson asked, holding the metal coffee pot with an oven mitt.

"Yes, ma'am. That would be nice. It's going to be a long night."

*

Hours later, just as the sun was rising, Abbey stood in her mother's driveway, wearing soft pajamas, a bathrobe, and forgiving slippers. Larry leaned against his truck, watching her.

"It's probably going to be a little crazy for a while and I'm sure Kelly and I will have to testify," she explained nervously.

He nodded his head.

"I've got a lot to do, find us a place to live, get Kelly back in school, I don't know when I'll see you again." She looked at the ground.

"Are you breaking up with me, Abbey?" Larry asked with a slight smile.

"I just have a lot to think about. Evidently, I have a problem with being a little impulsive. My impulsiveness nearly got my daughter killed and I have to find a way to forgive myself for putting her in harm's way. I'm not ready to be in a relationship." She glanced up at him; he wasn't smiling.

"I'm not looking to hurt you, Abbey," he said, reaching out for her waist and pulling her toward him.

She placed her hands on his chest, preventing him from fully embracing her. "I'm not ready and I don't know if I'll ever be ready for a relationship again." She shook her head. "You just never know what kind of secrets people are carrying and I've got to concentrate on raising Kelly." She pulled out of his arms, crossing her arms over her chest. "I didn't mean to lead you on, hell, by my own actions you can see I have impulsiveness issues."

He sighed and slid his hands in his pockets. "Okay." He pulled out a card with his phones numbers printed on it and pushed it into her hand. "I'll wait to hear from you." He climbed into his truck, gave a wave, and pulled out of the driveway.

Abbey watched him go and dropped the card into the pocket of her robe, wiping a tear off her face as his truck disappeared behind the stand of trees. She turned to walk back into the house and saw Rex standing on the front porch. "He's a good man, Abbey."

"I know," she said, stepping gingerly up the steps. "And the last thing he needs is a mess like me in his life." She wiped her cheeks with the sleeve of her bathrobe and sniffed.

He pulled her into his arms. "Baby girl, you may be a bit of a mess, but I'd take a hundred of you."

"That's because you love me." She laughed softly, sniffing.

"You got that right." He kissed the top of her head.

Chapter Twenty-Eight

Abbey stared at the morning paper and took a sip of coffee. She glanced up at her mother, busy making breakfast, and sighed. "It just seems it will never end." The headline read 'Locknee Scandal' in bold letters across the front page and then the subtitle announced that several Locknee police officers had been arrested on charges of conspiracy to commit murder. A picture of Abbey and Kelly dressed in black and looking harassed at Richard's funeral was centered prominently.

The last weeks had been a media circus with reporters from the national networks and local stations camped in town and outside of Summer's house. Rex had to call the security team back just to keep ambitious photographers out of the yard. Everyday it seemed Abbey and Kelly's lives were national news as the world grieved for the young widow and her daughter caught in a strange multi-state conspiracy.

The headlines proclaimed that Pearl Hollister, Dr. Mike Almond, and Pastor Wayne Munis had been killed in a gunfight with police after the three killed Dr. Richard Brown and were attempting to kill his wife and step-daughter. The daily articles continued to explain that several prominent business people in Locknee had also participated in the plan, which extended all the way to Montana. It was scintillating news, but the satanic part of the story had been completely left out of the articles.

"People like gossip," Summer said, sliding toast on three plates.

"But they aren't telling what really happened," Kelly said, taking a sip of juice and returning her attention to the driver's manual she was studying.

"You remember what Rex said, people wouldn't believe it even if they did report it. It's just too far fetched for most to believe and people are scared to face the truth." She set the plates on the table. "It'll die down soon enough and someone else will be the center of this media chaos. God help 'em."

"It sure seems like it's taking forever. I'm not a big fan of being followed and photographed everywhere I go," Abbey said, adding a little salt and pepper to the eggs.

Summer sat down at the table and nodded her head. She sighed, took a bite of food, and changed the subject. "How's Silly? Kelly said Mr. Williams called last night."

Silly had turned up in the Jackson's yard the morning after the shooting and fire. He was sooty and ornery, but otherwise unharmed. Jesse Williams, a farmer from Farmdale and one of the armed men in the Jackson's living room that night, offered to take him until she could get a place. "It seems Silly butted a fence post a couple days ago, his horns finally came through his skin and he's a little calmer now." Abbey laughed.

"Woo hoo!" Kelly pumped her arm in the air. "Thank God for that."

"He also said that he and Mr. Jackson drove down to look at the circle and it's not there anymore. He said the fire burned everything flat; the gravestones are still standing, but black. He said you can see the foundation of the old Starnes place up on the hill, the fire on that side stopped at the creek. The weirdest thing though, he was pretty certain that the unexplained explosion we all heard and felt that night was the big rock in the middle of the circle."

"How can a rock explode?" Summer asked.

"I don't know, but Mr. Williams said it was gone, like it just shattered or something, leaving behind a big hole in the ground." Abbey shook her head.

"Weird," Kelly said, her eyes wide. "Maybe the gate or the doorway shut. From what I've been reading, Mom, there's all kinds of weird places on the earth. Now when you try to figure out the whys, you go in like a million different directions." She laughed and then grew serious. "Some folks see the earth as a living creature, capable making its own decisions, when to explode a volcano or cause a tidal wave. Other folks think that there are people, or perhaps otherworldly beings, at the top making those decisions and actually have the power to create tidal waves and stuff. You know, the power to be gods. Of course, others say it has to do with our interactions with space, the pull of gravity, the magnetic fields wavering and a hundred other things."

She took a sip of juice, closing the driver's manual. "And then some believe it's a good and evil thing that has been going on under the surface since the beginning of time. A spiritual battle occurring right under our noses and we are just too blind to see it. I don't know what happened to that rock, but I'm choosing to believe the gate was shut."

"Well, that would be nice," Summer said.

"It would. Mr. Williams said that the fire took out more than a hundred acres, but no one lost anything. Except for my Jeep, that is." Abbey sighed.

"Yeah, Mom, you sure are rough on cars. How long did that one last you? Three or four days?" Kelly laughed.

"Smarty pants." Abbey reached across the table and messed her hair.

"It's just a car." Summer smiled, sipping her coffee. "You have a new one."

"Yeah, it would be nice to drive it without a hoard of news people following me." She ate quietly for a moment. "Okay, enough of my whining, they'll be gone soon enough and someone I know is taking the test to get a driver's permit today." She smiled at Kelly and added, "Which will probably be on the front page of the paper tomorrow."

"That's because I'm special," Kelly joked.

"Summer!" Rex called from the front door.

"In the kitchen, Rex." Summer stood with her plate in hand as he entered the room. "Morning. Do you want some breakfast?" she asked.

"Good morning, all," he said, sitting at the table. "No, thanks, but I'd love some coffee."

"Coming right up." She patted his shoulder.

"How are you girls today?" he asked.

"I'm taking my written test today so I can get my learner's permit," Kelly said. "Silly's horns finally broke through his skin, and that rock altar blew up."

"Yeah, I heard about the rock. The guys on the ground down there said it felt like an earthquake. Damnest thing." He shook his head. "Sheriff Davis said there's just a hole there. He said it's still creepy, though, everything's flat and black and those two angels from the cemetery are kind of overseeing everything. He said the foundation of the Starnes' house looks like some kind of ruins from Rome or something. He's pretty freaked out about it." He chuckled. "He said he finally understood why his grandpa liked *The X-files* so much."

Changing the subject, he said, "Well, thank goodness,

Silly's horns finally broke free, I figured that goat would give himself brain damage before they finally came out."

"Mr. Williams says he's calmer now." Abbey smiled. "Any word on Chambers? Has anyone seen him?"

Rex accepted the cup of coffee from Summer. "No. He took off in a helicopter the evening of April 30th and no one has seen or heard from him since. It seems ole Pearl kept pretty detailed notes and videos; half the town of Locknee is going down. Captain Wellington is also interested in David Hollister; he's pretty sure David was driving the day Kelly was hit. He thinks David got his friend drunk later and arranged the accident that killed him. I don't know if that will be proven, but they got David on a couple other things thanks to his mother's videos. They also found the truck that tried to run you off the road in Ralph Adams garage." He sighed.

"Most of this won't come out in the press, they will do their fluff job, concentrate on the pretty victims and ignore most of the story. I'm not sure who all you and Kelly will have to testify against, most of the people you actually saw are dead, besides the deputy and Ralph Adams. Of course, there is the mess in Montana also. This could go on for years. Good news is I talked to Jack and

Holly's boss hired her back. Once he found out she was involved in all this, another victim in this mess, he gave her a call." He sipped his coffee. "Abbey, I've talked to the attorneys handling the trust since Chambers disappeared, they have agreed to either give you back your investment in the house, or you can have the house itself, but you'll have to move it off of their land."

"How can there even still be a trust?" Abbey asked, taking her plate to the dishwasher.

"The tangle of lawyers that trust has around it would take more years than I have to unwind," he explained. "I finally found out what BLZ stands for, Beelzebub. Can you believe it?" He shook his head. "You still get all of Richard's holdings, everything after his debts are paid, except the house on that land. So what do you want to do?"

"I wonder how much it would cost to move a house." Abbey leaned on the island and looked at Rex.

"I don't know, but it shouldn't be hard to figure out."

"Abbey, would you want to live in that house again?" Summer asked, sitting back down at the table.

"No, I don't think so. Although, Mom, you designed most

of it." She laughed. "No, I was thinking about the Jacksons. I know their grandson and his family are living there now, all of them in that little house. Jimmy's clearing the land across the road, saving up to build a house or buy a trailer. I was thinking I'd give it to them. Wouldn't be far to move it, either."

"That's a good idea, Mom," Kelly said, setting her plate in the dishwasher. "Just in case there are more strays coming out of the woods. Very cool idea, Mom."

"I like it," Summer agreed with a smile.

Rex grew serious. "Abbey, come sit down for a minute, I've got some news."

Abbey felt fear slither down her spine and slipped around the island, sitting at the table beside her mother.

Kelly joined them. "What's going on?" she asked.

"The DNA results are back, baby girl. Pearl was your mother." He spit it out quickly. "It's hard to get real information about the birth houses, if records are kept I never saw them. I called my contact back; she used to be a nurse in the one in Chicago. She remembered Pearl from her pictures, said she was just a teenager when she sold the first baby back in 1974, she also remembers the same girl delivering another baby a couple years later." He picked up his coffee.

Abbey sat back in her chair and sighed, as different expressions flittered across her face. "I won't say I'm surprised. Why else would she follow me across the country like that?" She looked around the table; all eyes were focused on her. "I'm okay, guys, I know who my family is and they're sitting right here." She smiled. "It'll take me a bit, but I'll accept it somehow, I hear God moves in a mysterious ways and if I ever doubted his sense of humor before, I don't now."

Summer rubbed her shoulders. "Honey, I don't know what to say."

"Yeah, me either, Mom." Kelly put her hand on Abbey's arm.

"I'm okay," Abbey said again and got up from the table. "I've got to get ready to take Kelly for her driving test." She left the room and felt her family's concerned eyes boring into her back.

She went upstairs and gathering some clothes, she locked herself in the bathroom. She stepped to the mirror, staring into her eyes. "What about that?" she whispered. "I'm the daughter of the psycho satanic family."

This is no big surprise, Abbey. The unwelcome voice spoke. *Why do you think you've never even wondered about your real family?*

"I've been busy," she explained to her reflection.

Yes, you've been busy, trying to avoid what you knew all along. You also were smart enough to know there are just some places you don't go; some paths aren't even worth looking down. You are who you are because of God and miracles, not a group of Satanists. How often do you think a goat kills the bad guy just in the nick of time?

Abbey stared into the mirror for a moment longer, but found the voice had nothing else to say. She washed her face, pulled on her clothes and as she was hanging her robe on the hook on the bathroom door Larry's card fluttered out of the pocket. She picked it up off the floor, studied it with a sad smile, and returned it to the pocket of her robe.

*

"Make a left at the next road," Summer said, looking at the map.

"Yes, ma'am," Kelly said, turning smoothly onto the gravel road.

"I told you, Mom, she's great driver," Abbey said.

"She is," Summer agreed. "Go slow," she cautioned. "It's up here on the right."

Abbey looked at the tree-lined road and liked what she saw. "It's nice out here, Mom."

"This road circles around the lake, the county maintains it and it gets a fair amount of traffic, I figure they'll pave it one day," she explained. "Just wait until you see the house. I lucked out; it's not even on the market yet. This would be your closest neighbor." She pointed to a small white house set back from the road, almost hidden by trees.

"Do we know who lives there?" Abbey asked.

"A single man, Rex checked him out, he's okay. He works out of town a lot." Summer said quickly. "Turn into the next driveway."

Kelly turned onto the dirt driveway nearly hidden by trees. The heavy growth, separating the property from the road, cleared and a large lot filled with azalea bushes, dogwood, and magnolia trees came into view. A moderately sized white farm house, with a broad porch wrapping around three sides, sat in the center of the lot and was surrounded by well placed ornamental and flowering growth. "Wow!" Kelly said, stopping the Jeep.

"It beautiful," Abbey agreed, opening the door of the vehicle and stepping out onto the sandy lane. She walked into the yard and listened to the birds sing. She looked at the house, admiring the low shrubs lining a rock walkway that led to the porch. To the right of the house, the land extended about fifty yards and the view stopped at a thick wall of wild growth, to the left was pasture and fertile farmland. She walked around the side of the house and found several outbuildings for equipment, a chicken house, and a large barn. "Wow."

"Now some of the buildings might need work and some of the fences may need mending," Summer said.

"It's amazing, Mom."

"We could get a horse!" Kelly bounced on her feet,

clapping her hands.

"The land butts up to Cherokee Lake. If you go down that lane, there." She pointed to the road on the property dividing the pasture and farm areas. "It opens up on a private, sandy beach so you could swim or get a boat."

Kelly laughed and gave Abbey a wink. "I don't think we want a boat."

"Okay, maybe not a boat," she laughed. "But a jet ski or one of those things."

"Now that sounds fun! Yea!" Kelly bounced.

"This house still has most of the furniture, the man who owns it moved in with his kids up north a little over a year ago and I don't think he wants to go through the hassle of coming back here and getting rid of everything. I've heard there's some nice things in there and since we have the keys, lets go look." Summer turned to the house.

"How did you hear of this house, Mom?" Abbey asked.

"A woman I took a pottery class with knew the wife. The wife died a couple years ago and the man was never really the same." She sighed. "I hear they were a lovely couple. He's in his

90s now, though, and there is too much work out here for a man his age."

Summer unlocked the door and they stepped into a large mudroom. One wall was lined with hooks ready for coats and jackets, while underneath a built in bench had plenty of room for muddy boots. On the opposite wall was a deep sink with enough counter space to clean odds and ends. "There's room for a washer, dryer and even a freezer in here," she said and stepped into the kitchen. "And the kitchen is sunny and roomy."

Abbey walked into the kitchen and smiled, it was perfect. "We'll take it," she said.

"You haven't seen the rest of the house, yet." Summer laughed.

"The kitchen is the most important room, Grandma, and this is a good kitchen," Kelly said, peering through the line of windows behind the sink.

"Well, let's just walk through the rest of the house so we can say we did," Summer said and continued the tour.

Abbey and Kelly grinned at each other, following her. The kitchen opened into a den, which contained a large fireplace. From the den they stepped into a large, wide hall that ran shotgun style from the front of the house to the back. A staircase took up most of the hall and the rails were carved delicately. The formal living room was furnished with antiques and velvet upholstery covered the couches and chairs. "There's a bedroom and bath downstairs and two baths upstairs, as well as three more bedrooms. Plenty of room and the house has been updated and kept up."

"We'll take it!" Abbey and Kelly said in unison.

Summer continued to show off closets and specialized built in nooks. "It even has a laundry chute." She started up the stairs. "Kelly will still be in Windslow school district, but it will be a long drive on the bus, guess she'll be due a car by the time school starts."

"Woo hoo! We're definitely taking it!" Kelly laughed.

"The bedrooms are large and sunny and you even have an attic," Summer said.

Abbey walked through the large, airy bedrooms and looked down into the yard in which she was already in love. "Mom," she said, "we'll take it. What do I have to do?"

Summer laughed, pulling out her phone. "We need to make an offer."

*

Abbey shut the gate of the pasture. Mr. Williams had been right, Silly was much calmer. He occasionally gave halfhearted attempts to butt her, although he still pressed his head into her hip seeking a scratch on the head. Of course, with the addition of four does he had enough to keep him busy.

She wandered over to the chicken house, a professional crew had recently repaired the fencing, and she stepped into the enclosed yard. She peeked into the empty building, ready and waiting for chickens and shook her head. Why do I keep putting off ordering the birds?

She ambled over to a bench placed in the shade under a tree and sat down. She was tired, she realized, deep bone tired and not the kind of tired that could be resolved with a good night of sleep. The last few months had been a flurry of chaos, first with the constant media attention and police interviews. Then, moving her things out of the old house while photographers followed her and the headlines screamed of how the poor widow had also lost her home.

Moving the house onto the Jackson's property had been full of tiny details she never would have considered and then ensuring they were in the new house in time for Kelly to start school, it all seemed so rushed. And then Kelly turned sixteen, got a car and her driver's license and suddenly, for the first time in years or maybe in her whole life, Abbey had free time on her hands and was too tired to do anything productive.

Maybe it's time for some rest, Abbey. The unwelcome voice spoke. *You've been running since you were a kid, running from your past, maybe it's time to take a break and think about it for a while. There is a season for everything, after all.*

"What am I supposed to do?" she whispered as Tom and Jerry ran to her, returning from the lake wet and happy. "Lay in bed and feel sorry for myself?"

You're very good at taking care of others, why don't you concentrate on yourself for a while? Why don't you spend some time thinking about all the things you've been avoiding thinking about for years?

"And how will that help?" she asked softly as the dogs settled at her feet.

You may be surprised. You are not meant to stay constantly busy like a machine. Remember, ebb and flow, movement and repose.

Abbey sat on the bench a while longer, but the voice had had its say. She pulled herself up and walked slowly into the kitchen. She stared at the dishes left in the sink and then looked out the window at the yard. She tried to remember the last time she had cut grass and couldn't pull up the memory. Had she even cut it once since they moved in?

She picked up the phone book and sat down at the table. Half an hour later she had made arrangements for a housekeeper, a lawn care crew, and a gazebo to be placed by the water. She made a glass of tea and settled into a rocking chair on the front porch. She observed the way the high grass moved in the wind, listened to the birds in the trees and rocked. She was still rocking when Kelly pulled into the driveway, home from school. She jumped out of the Volvo, a gift from Abbey, Rex and Summer for her sixteenth birthday, and walked through the thick grass, stepping onto the porch.

"Hey, honey," Abbey said, rocking. "How was school?"

"It was good," Kelly said, dropping her backpack on the porch and sending up a puff of dust. "Mom? Are you okay?"

Abbey smiled, but even the small bit of energy felt like effort. "It seems I'm tired, Kelly, and I've decided I need to take a break for a little bit."

"Okay?" she said nervously, turning a rocker to face Abbey and sitting down. "What does that mean?"

Abbey sat up a little straighter. "It means I've hired a housekeeper and a crew to take care of the lawn. I'm having a gazebo built down by the lake and I'm going to spend some time thinking about things." She smiled again, it came easier. "It means you're going to learn a lot about ordering take out or maybe you should think about becoming a chef so we can eat. It means I'm going to be lazy and reflective for awhile."

Kelly smiled and slid out of her chair to wrap her arms around Abbey's neck. She pulled away with tears in her eyes, but a bright smile. "That's the best idea I've heard in a long time, Mom. I know the last couple years have been really weird, but before all that my life was peachy keen." She grinned, tickled that she had used a word her Grandma used on occasion. "But when I think of what you experienced as a kid, I can't imagine. Maybe Grandpa Martin was right when he said sometimes you have to look back before you can move forward."

Abbey kissed her cheek. "Thanks, honey, I'm glad you understand. So what are we having for dinner? And remember, in this journey into the world of take-out, we can't live off pizza." Abbey chuckled and it felt good.

Chapter Twenty-Nine

In the next weeks, Abbey would rise with Kelly in the mornings, tend to the goats and spend the day rocking on the porch. The lawn crew took care of the yard and the maid saw to the house. Once the gazebo was finally constructed her days changed a bit and she'd sit by the water with a notebook and jot down her memories.

Some of the memories from the first seven years of her life were vague, unclear snippets, but others were full of recognizable faces, scents, and locations, and those memories she emailed to Rex.

The newly prescribed sleeping pills from her old doctor in Windslow fell to the back of the medicine cabinet as she began taking the notebook to bed and jotting down her dreams. Some of the dreams seemed important so she began sending copies to Rex, just in case he may find the information useful in helping someone escape a horrible situation.

Soon the weather called for a jacket and she sat bundled up watching the leaves flutter down onto the water and wrote down her thoughts. She wrote about Richard's deception and Pearl being both her mother and the woman who sold her into the sex slave trade. She wrote about her sister, Caroline, the little wise sage who loved her and who she missed. She wrote about her father and all he had done for her and how even from the grave he'd protected her. She wrote about the love she felt toward her mother and Rex, who truly were her family despite the lack of a shared blood. She wrote about Kelly and the pride and joy she felt at seeing her daughter turn into a beautiful, compassionate, and well-rounded woman.

And then her thoughts shifted to Larry and she set the notebook down. She pulled his card from her pocket and stared at the small piece of cardstock. She thought about the trip to Helen and how they shared the happy memories of their childhoods. She thought of how he defended her against Richard and then she let her mind drift to making love with him. She'd never felt that kind of connection with a man before, sex had always felt empty to her, but with Larry it was different. She hadn't seen him since that morning in Summer's driveway when he asked if she was breaking up with him and she remembered the pain in his eyes when she pushed him away. She was sure Rex was in regular contact with him, but he never mentioned Larry's name to her. She sighed, staring at the card for another moment and slid it back into her pocket.

There is a season for everything, Abbey. The unwelcome voice spoke. *You've condemned yourself for your impulsiveness, but your impulsiveness is part of who you are. If you weren't impulsive, you wouldn't have lived past seven years of age. If you weren't impulsive, you wouldn't have had Kelly.*

"That's not what you were saying at the time," Abbey stated.

It wasn't the season, Abbey. The voice responded simply.

Abbey gathered her things and walked back to the house. She smiled as she passed the pasture and saw Silly lying in the sun surrounded by his harem of females. She stepped into the kitchen and glanced at the calendar, realizing it was almost December. Wow, she thought, I've done nothing for three months except rock and gaze at the water. She stepped over to the refrigerator and pulled a check out from under a magnet. The check was made out to her and issued on the account of Songbird Security. The memo line read: Consulting, and it was signed by Larry Sanders.

She had called Rex the day she received it in the mail. "Why do I have a check from Songbird Security?" she'd demanded.

"The tips you've been sending me have been very helpful," Rex stated simply.

"So I work for Songbird now?" she asked, placing the check on the counter and staring at it.

"As long as you're sending me information, you do," Rex said. "You're helping people, Abbey."

She glanced at the amount on the check again. "I sure never made that kind of money as a file clerk."

"What you're doing now is a little more important than

paperwork." He laughed. "I'm really proud of you, baby girl."

She glanced at the calendar again, looking at the check from Songbird in her hand, and picked up the phone. "Mom. I want to throw a party."

"Wonderful!" Summer exclaimed. "What's the occasion?"

"I'm thinking Christmas Eve," Abbey said. "I think I have a lot to be grateful for and I want to say thanks to some folks."

"Where are we having this party?" Summer asked to the background of singing birds.

"My house," Abbey said and stepped over to the sink, gazing through the window.

"I think it's a good idea, Abbey, but it's a lot of work. I can help, but I don't want you to wear yourself out."

"Mom, I've discovered the joy of ordering things by phone and internet. I won't knock myself out, I promise," Abbey said, smiling at the chicken house and imagining the spring and a house full of birds.

"Okay. Who are we inviting to this party?" Summer asked.

"Everyone," Abbey said. "Everyone. The Jacksons, the Williams, Jack, Holly and the kids, and I think since I'm now working for Songbird, we should invite those folks too so I can say thank you."

"All right." Summer giggled. "Stop by tomorrow and we'll start making plans."

"Thanks, Mom," Abbey said, hanging up the phone and sitting down at the table. She opened her notebook to a blank page and started making lists.

Soon Kelly stepped into the house. "Mom?" she called.

"In the kitchen," Abbey called back, lifting her head and taking in the various lists littering the table.

"I was worried when I didn't see you on the porch," Kelly said, setting her backpack on the counter and looking at the papers on the table. "What are you doing?" she asked.

"Planning a party," Abbey smiled.

"A party? Really?" Kelly bounced, clapping her hands. "Yea! When? Can I invite some people?"

"Yes, really. Christmas Eve and you can invite whomever you'd like. Now, grab a snack and let's go get a Christmas tree."

"Woo hoo!" She opened the cabinet, pulling down a can of nuts. "I've got a snack, let's go!"

*

Abbey pinned the loose bun on her head, fine tendrils tickling her neck, and looked into the mirror. The sheath dress she wore was red, long sleeved and looked quite demure from the front, but the back was bare down to her waist, exposing quite a bit of skin and making a bra impossible. Her legs were covered in fine, black, silk hose and on her feet she wore red pumps. It's too much, she thought, way too much.

Kelly knocked on the door, opening it. "Wow! Mom, you look hot." She walked around Abbey to get a view of the front of the dress. "I mean really hot, like classy hot." She grinned. "Who would have thunk it?"

"It's not too much?" Abbey asked self-consciously.

"No, Mom, not too much. We're celebrating. It's Christmas. We've had a hell of a year and you look beautiful." Kelly wrapped her arm around Abbey's waist and gazed into the mirror. "I think we both look pretty hot."

"You do look beautiful." She smiled, admiring Kelly's slim-fitting green dress in the mirror. "Are we ready?"

"The caterers are busy in the kitchen, we both look great, the goat is put away, and the house is clean. I'd say we're ready." Kelly laughed.

They walked downstairs, admiring the decorations that had been provided by a professional decorator. The lights, the tinsel, everything had been done by someone else, all except the tree. On the tree was a mishmash of ornaments they had collected through the years, both store bought and home made. They stood by the tree for a moment, Kelly pointing out a paper snowflake she made in kindergarten. "I can't believe you saved all this stuff."

"Of course I saved it. You can't throw stuff like that away." Abbey turned toward the kitchen to check on the caterers.

"Mom, I forgot to tell you something," Kelly said, following her through the den and into the kitchen.

"What's that?"

"Do you know our neighbor?"

"I know we have a neighbor, honey, but I haven't met him yet," Abbey said, sliding a stuffed mushroom in her mouth. "Hmm. That's nice." She smiled at the woman leading the show in the kitchen.

"Well, I invited him over to just say hello before the party. I thought it would be nice, you know, the neighborly thing to do," Kelly said, nervously.

"That's fine, honey," Abbey said, mixing a bit of wine and soda together in a glass.

"The bartender should be here shortly, Mrs. Brown," the caterer stated.

"It's no problem, y'all are doing a great job," Abbey said and the doorbell rang.

"I'll get it, I bet it's our neighbor." Kelly skipped through the den on clunky heels. "She's in the kitchen, it's through there," Kelly said. "I'll be right back."

Abbey stepped into the den to meet her neighbor and froze in place when she saw Larry entering the room carrying a bottle of wine. He stopped when he saw her. "Wow," he said and smiled, his eyes taking in her dress. "You look like candy."

Abbey was stunned and that damned tingle worked through her body as soon as she saw the skin beside his eyes wrinkle with his smile. She knew he was going to be at the party, but later when there were more people around as a handy distraction, not now.

"You didn't know I was coming." The smile left his face. "I should have known when Kelly ran out like she did." He set the wine on a convenient table. "I'll go." He turned toward the door.

"No, wait," she said, following him into the foyer. "I knew you were coming, but I expected you later, I thought I was coming in to meet my new neighbor."

"I am your neighbor, Abbey," he said. "I guess you didn't know that either? That would explain why Summer was sitting in the driveway with her engine idling."

"Are you serious?" Abbey moved past him, looking through the glass of the front door to see taillights pulling onto the road. "Well, damn." She turned to face him. "So you're my neighbor?"

"Yes, but if it's any consolation, I didn't know for awhile myself, but once I saw the company you keep I figured it out."

"I've never seen your truck over there," she said.

"Got myself a new one."

The doorbell rang; Abbey opened the door to find the bartender and pointed him into the kitchen.

"Is there somewhere we can talk for a minute?" Larry asked.

"Sure," she said, taking his hand and leading him into living room to find white-coated caterers putting out bowls of treats. "This way," she said, stepping into the hall to find more caterers. "Okay." She laughed and opened the door to the guest room, peering inside. "This looks safe." She pulled him inside and shut the door. "It probably won't last long."

Larry took the glass from her hand, set it on the dresser, and pulled her into his arms, kissing her.

That tingle worked through Abbey, becoming a shudder and she groaned in her throat, wrapping her arms around his neck.

He pulled his mouth away, breathing hard and rested his forehead against hers. "I've missed you," he said. "And knowing you were just right next door has been hell." He kissed her again.

"How long have you known?" she whispered, lightly running her fingers over the wrinkles beside his eyes.

"Since around the time the gazebo was built."

"And you never thought of dropping by?"

"Every damned day, but I said I'd wait to hear from you." He put his hands on her waist, pushing her back a bit so he could look her. "You're killing me in this dress."

"The plan wasn't to kill you, just to get your attention." She laughed.

"Mission accomplished," he said and looked into her eyes, growing serious. "I was wondering, I know you're not ready for a full-blown relationship, but what about a little courting? You know, the old fashion way, sitting on the front porch and drinking tea, maybe a movie or dinner now and again?"

"Aren't you my boss now? I'm not sure that would be the right thing to do."

"I'm not your boss, you are an independent contractor. You are your own boss."

"I have missed you," she said. "I'm still not ready to jump into anything too serious, but I may have some free time on the weekends now that Kelly has started to date."

"I promise, I won't ask you to marry me until after Kelly graduates college." He grinned.

"I think that's the nicest thing anyone's ever said to me." She laughed. "I'm sorry I dumped you in Mom's driveway like I did."

"You needed time," he said. "I understood that, but the

waiting has been hell."

"Mrs. Brown!" the caterer called, knocking on the door. "Your daughter's on the phone."

"I bet she is." Abbey chuckled, glancing in the mirror to check her hair and lipstick. She opened the door and took the phone. "Hello?"

"Hey, Mom. Are you mad?" Kelly asked.

"No, I'm not mad." Abbey smiled at Larry.

"Is Larry still there?"

"Yes."

"Can I come home now?"

Abbey laughed. "Where are you?"

"Sitting in the car just down the road, listening to Christmas songs on the radio with Grandma."

"You're just sitting in the car on the side of the road?" Abbey asked, wiping some lipstick from Larry's lips.

"Yes, ma'am. We thought y'all could use a few minutes alone together."

"Well it turns out you were right. Thanks. Now, you ladies get home, we're having a party."

"Woo hoo!" Kelly laughed. "We'll be there in a few minutes."

Abbey hung up the phone and smiled at Larry. "Seems I have some matchmakers in my family."

"Well, I'm not complaining," he said, pulling her into his arms.

"Me, either," she smiled and rested her head on his chest. She turned her eyes skyward and for the first time in her life she truly believed that a normal life was possible.

Manufactured by Amazon.ca
Acheson, AB